Missouri Folklore

Society Journal

Special Issue:

Hell's Holler

by

Ruth Ann Musick

Volumes 38 and 39
2016-2017

Missouri Folklore Society Journal

Volumes 38 and 39
2016-2017

Special Issue:

Hell's Holler:
a Novel
Based on the Folklore
of the
Missouri Chariton Hill Country

by
Ruth Ann Musick

Sketches by Archie Musick and Pat Musick
Preface by Adam Brooke Davis
Preface by Pat Musick
Afterword by Judy Prozzillo Byers

General Editors
Dr. Jim Vandergriff (Ret.)
Dr. Donna Jurich
Dr. Adam Davis

Missouri Folklore Society
P. O. Box 1757
Columbia, MO 65205

This issue of the *Missouri Folklore Society Journal* was published by Naciketas Press, 715 E. McPherson, Kirksville, Missouri, 63501

ISSN: 0731-2946; ISBN: 978-1-936135-96-7 (1-936135-96-5)

The *Missouri Folklore Society Journal* is indexed in:

The *Hathi Trust Digital Library*: Vols. 4-24, 26; 1982-2002, 2004. This library essentially acts as an online keyword indexing tool; only allows users to search by keyword and only within one year of the journal at a time. The result is a list of page numbers where the search words appear. No abstracts or full-text incl. (Available free at http://catalog.hathitrust.org/Search/Advanced).

The *MLA International Bibliography*: Vols. 1-26, 1979-2004. Searchable by keyword, author, and journal title. The result is a list of article citations; it does not include abstracts or full-text.

RILM Abstracts of Music Literature: Vols. 13-14, 20; 1991-92, 1998. Searchable by keyword, author, and journal title. Indexes only selected articles about music that appear in these volumes only. Most of the entries have an abstract. There is no full-text.

A list of major articles in every issue of the journal also appears on the Society's web page. Go to *http://missourifolkloresociety.truman.edu/MFSJ-cnts.html.*

Notice to library subscribers and catalogers:
Though the cover date on this volume is 2016-17, the volume was actually published in 2020.

The Society's board is working to produce enough issues to catch up with the journal's publishing schedule as quickly as possible.

Hell's Holler

Acknowledgements

The *Missouri Folklore Society Journal* wishes to give special thanks to the Colorado artist, Pat Musick. Niece of folklorist Ruth Ann Musick and daughter of artist Archie Musick, Pat has generously and enthusiastically shared family materials from the Archie Musick Estate, including drafts and synopses of her aunt's works and dozens of "Missouri sketches" done by her father at about the time Ruth Ann Musick was writing *Hell's Holler*. We are especially grateful for the three illustrations (pp. 14, 80, and 124) which Pat herself did for this book—in what she gleefully calls a "posthumous collaboration" with her father and her aunt. We're sure that both Archie and Ruth Ann Musick would love her renditions of George and Mary Moore.

The *Missouri Folklore Society Journal* also wishes to thank Judy Prozzillo Byers, once protege, then friend and colleague, to Ruth Ann Musick, and finally Executrix and Archivist of the Ruth Ann Musick Folklore Estate. Dr. Byers has generously encouraged us to undertake this project and been eloquent in explaining some of the deep impulses which led Ruth Ann Musick to become West Virginia's premiere folklorist. Dr. Byers' biography of her mentor was the spark which first led Dr. Adam Davis to Musick's 1943 dissertation, *Hell's Holler: A Novel Based on the Folklore of Missouri Chariton Hill Country*. And the rest is (folklore) history.

Contents

Preface by Adam Davis

Synopsis

The manuscript announces itself as a novel rooted in the folklore of Adair County, Missouri, completed in 1943. The dissertation has been checked out with due-dates of 24 November 1944 (probably very shortly after binding); 27 Feb., 28 March, 1945; 18 Feb., 31 May, 1946; Jan 29 (year?); Feb. 19, 1951, June 11 1979 and Sept. 2, 2003. The last date is when I first read it; the one before, probably her biographer, Judy Prozillo Byers. The folklore, strictly considered, consists of some weather and wildlife lore, sundry superstitions and an anecdote or two, as well as a few snatches of song, deployed in the regionalist technique then in vogue.

The novel is set in the present of its writing – after Prohibition, but without any notice of WWII or of technology beyond the Model T (which is nonetheless regarded as less than up-to-date). George Moore, age 38, and his longsuffering wife Mary (26), married ten years, live on a twenty-five acre parcel of Chariton River land (Adair County, MO) with their children: the dutiful and cruelly overworked Lawrence, age eight, along with a number of younger siblings (Mark, Hubert, Vida and perhaps some others). The farm is more than necessarily decrepit, since George is unable to work, due to a shiftlessness that is never definitively attributed to either mental disease or character flaw.

Nearby live George's parents, Sarah and Lige, and somewhat further away (in Sullivan County, which is indeed adjacent to the realworld Adair), Mary's father, the loud, frequently repentant and relapsed alcoholic Jonathan "Happy John" Praytor, with his wife, recently crippled by a stroke.

Also in the neighborhood is the responsible — and single — Ben Bragg, a former suitor of Mary's.

Keatsville refers to Kirksville, and the sinister "rub-doctors" are the osteopaths of the Kirksville College of Osteopathic Medicine, whose medical practice was originally indistinguishable from the earliest forms of chiropractic (and originated in the traditional art of bonesetting). The town of La Plata, a dozen miles from Kirksville, becomes *La Fever*. The "rub doctors" are engaged in buying up the hill country land, with an eye to building a reservoir (reflecting historical events, though in reality the intent was philanthropic rather than predatory).

The unhappinesses of Dr. Musick's own life appear in some form: the brutality of the slaughtering of Lawrence's pet pig Sampson clearly recalls the horror which turned her to vegetarianism, and there is the institutionalization of her alcoholic husband, echoed in George's stay at the asylum in St. Joseph.

Mary stoically endures George's almost incredible selfishness and laziness. There are hints of a Freudian diagnosis for George's trouble. (Mary at a certain point blames George's condition on his overdependence on a too-helpful mother, and the word "hysteria" is tossed-out.) But the outward signs look like a closely-observed case of psychotic depression, certainly with serious character disorders as well. The main plot concerns George's one genuinely good deed: he had secretly sold his body (to be delivered after death of course) to the medical school in order to pay for an operation which would save Mary's life; and his subsequent worries about his bodily resurrection drive the main action. Sub-plots include the machinations of the rub-doctors to acquire the hill-folks' land, the possibility of rekindled romance between Mary and Ben Bragg, and the feud between George's parents and a pair of neighboring brothers, the Tittles. The novel reaches its climax in an outbreak of cholera.

The novel bounces uncertainly back and forth between pity and contempt for George – is he the victim of forces beyond his control and a condition he didn't bring on himself, or is he indeed to blame for the suffering his indolence and self-centeredness bring on his family? Perhaps its most interesting feature is its ambiguity about whether George or Mary is to be the reader's sympathetic focus. As a novel, it is an apprentice-piece, gathering confidence and subtlety as it goes.

Preface

Ruth Ann Musick completed *Hell's Holler* in 1943 as the culmination of her doctoral studies. The University of Iowa was beginning to make a name for itself with its then-new writing program, and its unusual openness to accepting creative productions as theses and dissertations. In our own time the region remains associated (in popular imagination) more with corn and hogs than with the kind of cutting edge innovation which is, in fact, the school's core identity. That juxtaposition of the old-and-vanishing with the new-and-emerging was much more striking a lifetime ago. It is a dynamic that shaped the book's creation in a number of ways.

Musick headed her manuscript with an oddly tentative statement of its meaning:

POSSIBLE THEME

The old, established community, with its folk code, its superstitions, its prejudices, imaginations, etc., in direct opposition to the new or modern world of reality and progress, can hardly survive. A man from this community sells his body to some fairly modern doctors, and from then on lives in fear and cowardice – continually weighing his fate after death, including the idea of resurrection, against the moral obligation of his bargain – and after his death becomes the community hero.

Why "possible"? One would think the writer herself ought to be able to say what the theme is, unless she was not particularly engaged with the idea of *theme* as she wrote it. Committees routinely require such capsule descriptions, and perhaps this was offered after-the-fact. It suggests that a conscious awareness of theme is not necessarily part of the creative writer's working process, at least not in the same way it guides expository, scholarly work. The paragraph itself calls for interpretation – the insistent polarity of "old," "established," "folk" on the one hand, and on the other, "new," "modern," "reality," "progress." And the country between those? "Fear," "weighing fate." That is where the novel does its work – in that middle ground of tension.

The writer herself was the product of a series of similar opposed gravitational fields.

Kirksville (Keatsville)

Ruth Ann Musick was born outside the little market town. A five-acre farm could be sustainable and sustaining, but it took energy and ingenuity – which apparently the Musick family had in abundance. They modeled the mythic trajectory of pioneers whose hard work had made more genteel careers possible for their progeny. Her elder brother became a success in the printing business, her younger brother Archie a prominent artist who would illustrate several of her volumes. She of course, entered the life of letters and scholarship. But she was rooted in a community that had been taken by force from the Indians within the memory of those alive at her birth. Adair County, sparsely populated, was perhaps not entirely un-wild, but neither was it in a pristine state. Was its relation to "Nature" and origins best understood as innocence and purity lost, something to be mourned? Or something stuck, maybe even sickly and ingrown, a failure to fully achieve civilization? Both views of the folk and their lore have always been in play. To Musick, the more remote settlers of "Hell's Holler" are perhaps seen as feral rather than as romantic *Naturvolk*. That was the contested ground of folklore then, and it remains so now: in a music education program, the student who wants to turn her violin to fiddling may find herself dismissed as crude beyond redemption (students have told me such stories) or welcomed, as the kind of renewal-from-the-source that Bartok sought and celebrated.

Kirksville, in the day, was something of an island. Musick's childhood was witness to the explosive growth of technology and commerce in the early twentieth century. She would have talked with not-yet-elderly citizens who had seen the Civil War battle fought around the town square in August of 1862, since which days the thousand or so inhabitants had quintupled. The town was Union-sympathizing in a southern-leaning county. She likely heard of the atrocities that seldom made it into official narratives, dreadful things I'd learn at only second-hand in the 1990s (that is, from those who'd talked to witnesses and participants in bushwackings, murders and massacres). The deep past and the old ways were fully present, and could present themselves as barbaric horror. Musick was traumatized into (then) highly countercultural vegetarianism by witnessing the use of hammers to dispatch hogs for slaughter, an event that appears in the novel. But it was also a world passing away, and thus full of pathos. At all times, there were sharply, clearly divergent ways to understand the place, as a world a-borning or one a-dying.

Also in her day, her quintessential prairie town–gathering-point and loading-dock for the corn and hogs of a good-sized county–was being transformed by the anomalous presence of two institutions of higher learning, however modest. A Normal School (dedicated to the "norms" of curriculum and pedagogy) had been established with the rather novel idea that educators had to be educated in the methods of education, and that these could be articulated, studied and improved in the same way as farming methods. A student sending a postcard home in 1910 characterized it as "the schoolmarm factory." Before Musick was ten, her town would boast a famous "model rural school," a laboratory where future masters and mistresses of the country's one-room schoolhouses would put their work on a scientific basis, and go forth to teach the nation. It is perhaps a challenge for us, in our days of consolidated high schools, to see the little red schoolhouse for the modern innovation it was, and not an object of nostalgia. But that is what understanding the novel in the context of its time requires. It is folkloristic, in that it examines the dynamic interaction of tradition and innovation, but it is not itself primarily a vehicle for folklore.

Ruth Ann Musick would attend the local high school. Her photo in the 1916 Tigris yearbook is tagged "Nature hath formed strange things in her time. A cynic." That is a basketball uniform.

At the very same time, a reputed quack doctor who had claimed he could cure ailments from whooping cough to alcoholism by manipulation of bones and integuments, established a school where he proposed to teach his art to others. At this stage, the American School of Osteopathy (like most medical schools) was an unapologetically commercial enterprise, turning profit and promising its graduates they would do likewise. But what its descendant, AT Still University, professes today – training physicians to bring healthcare to the underserved – was already implicit in its mission, and in its isolated, even desolate location, at that time. Andrew Taylor Still claimed to be founding a new science, of his own discovering, though somewhat earlier in what he himself admitted was a rocky career, he had called himself the "lightning bone-setter" – an acknowledgment of the folk-medicine roots of his new practice.

Again, the old, the traditional, the folkish and the new, the modern, the scientific eyed each other from opposite sides of a canyon.

Lines of Influence: Hamilton, Belden and Field Folklore

Musick attended the teacher's college in Kirksville from 1916 to 1919, taking a bachelor of science degree in education. She narrowly missed studying with Goldy Hamilton (1881-1955), who must nonetheless have continued to be a presence in the small school. Hamilton had taught there from 1911-14. It seems likely they met, virtually certain they had mutual acquaintances, and beyond doubt they experienced the same cultural forces.

The elder was also a scholar, in a time not much welcoming of women, and would also be resolutely single and astonishingly peripatetic. At the University of Missouri, Hamilton had studied under Henry Marvin Belden, who'd come from Nebraska (where he had worked with folklore-energized writers Louise Pound and Willa Cather). He helped to organize the English Club. "The *M.S.U. Independent,* the campus newspaper, reported on March 6, 1903, that the Writer's Club had met in the office of the English Department" and that there was "interesting and informal discussion upon 'folk' songs and 'literary material' to be found in Missouri." (Pentlin)

The club would become one of the most popular organizations on campus, and would eventually provide the nucleus for the Missouri Folklore

Society. In December 1906 the group declared as their aim "to encourage the collection, preservation and study of Folk-Lore in the widest sense of the term, including customs, institutions, superstitions, signs, legends, language and literature of all races, so far as they are found in the State of Missouri."

Between her days at Mizzou and her time in Kirksville, Hamilton taught in a number of places, and deliberately emulated Belden's method of using students as fieldworkers to collect the local lore; this was powerful pedagogy and wise use of confederates with exclusive access to the informants and tradition-bearers. Musick would do the same, and for decades. It was in a way a forerunner of the *Foxfire* and *Bittersweet* projects of the 1970s. In the preface to his monumental 1941 collection, *Ballads and Songs Collected by the Missouri Folklore Society* (re-issue in press), Belden writes of the volume's single most prolific contributor: "Miss Goldy Hamilton – at first from her pupils at the West Plains High School, Howell County, then from her students at the Kirksville Normal School (now Teachers' College), and last from her students at Palmer College in Albany, Gentry County– has made the largest contribution to this collection."

At one of the meetings of the club, Belden heard a song–possibly sung by Maude Williams, an almost exact contemporary of Hamilton, who would also go on to make important contributions to folklore fieldwork–which he recognized as a Child Ballad.* Susan Pentlin and Rebecca Schroeder explain the flashbulb moment:

> Child's belief that traditional balladry and song had *not* survived into the late 19th century was shared by many of his contemporaries and adopted by many of the scholars who followed him. Belden recognized the significance of his discovery that "many such songs were known and sung by the country folk in Missouri," and his students soon became aware of the importance of their mission. The May 20, 1904, article points out that the idea of collecting Missouri ballads is one which the Club could claim as its own, "as very little has ever been done in this direction before." The Club planned to publish the ballads as soon as a sufficient number had been collected, and it was believed that a very interesting collection could be put out the following year.

Pentlin and Schroeder further cite an article in the *St. Louis Globe-Democrat,* February 5, 1905 in which Belden spoke of his work to the

Modern Language Society:

> Professor Henry M. Belden of the Missouri State University in
> a paper on "Folk-Songs in Missouri," read before a meeting of
> the Modem Language Association in Chicago last month, made
> a surprising and interesting statement that ancient English bal-
> lads were sung in rural sections of the state. An organization
> of students at the state university known as the English Club
> has been carrying on an investigation, and thus far has found
> at least 11 of the old songs in Missouri.

–(Pentlin & Schroeder)

Further Education and Development

Although Musick can hardly have been unaware of either Hamilton or
Belden, or have escaped their influence, her protégé and literary executor,
Judy Prozillo Byers, ascribes the more immediate inspiration to Musick's
doctoral advisor, Edwin Ford Piper–but that encounter lay beyond long
years of preparation.

Musick's career cannot be interpreted according to clichés about family opposition to women working or pursuing the scholar's life. But her preparation does seem to have been male-governed, and by men who steered her in directions they thought represented her strengths, or at least promised employability. It was a hard eight years to the MA. As Byers says: "In 1920 she continued her education at the State University of Iowa in Iowa City. Even though her natural forte was English and literature, her father influenced her to earn a Master of Science Degree in 1928 with a major in mathematics and a minor in English." (The two halves of her brain were indeed on speaking terms.) It would be another 16 years to the English PhD in her mid-40s. Her doctoral enrollment dated only from 1938; time along the way was spent in wandering teaching gigs, all the way to Phoenix.

It is an error, both intellectual and ethical, to turn artistic production into mere autobiography. That said, writers pillage and process their own and others' experience. Judy Prozillo Byers gives a terse account, which we may take as all that Musick wished to read into the public record, of a brief and unhappy marriage to an artist who became an alcoholic and was committed to an institution. The marriage ended in 1941. Dr. Musick remained private about this period in her life. George is clearly an object alternately of contempt and pity, with occasional hints of wistful affection. For me, the most moving moment in the entire book is his recollection of the sanitarium, the sunlit peace he briefly found there, and Mary's remarkable reaction, free of the resentment to which she had earned every right. It is another field of dynamic tension in Musick's characteristically humane but unsentimental, unromaticizing thought. The novel never resolves its central question, which is how to understand George's behavior – in traditional, moralistic terms, or modern, no-fault psychology?

While engaged in her doctoral studies, Musick began college teaching: in 1942-1943, for example, she taught algebra and trigonometry in V-12 programs that provided liberal arts education to future Naval and Marine officers. She could not have been more thoroughly embedded in the modern world. And somehow, with all this, she still found time to do her doctoral coursework and to draft and revise a three-hundred page novel. In this process, she learned to dig into her own past, to bring it forward into the light of the present. Her friend, biographer, and literary executor Dr. Judy Byers, summarizes her relationship to folklore studies at the time:

It was not until her doctoral studies that an affinity for folk-lore began to blossom. Her dissertation director and doctoral committee encouraged her to use folklore as they guided her writing of a creative dissertation, a novel entitled *Hell's Holler*, which incorporated folklore from the Chariton Hills of Mis-souri. As part of her doctoral work, she also collected the folk songs of her family in Missouri. Professor Edwin Ford Piper, folklore professor at the State University of Iowa, first interested Musick in folklore and encouraged her to remember and set down songs she had heard during her childhood. As a member of Professor Piper's last folklore class, Ruth Ann Musick collected her family's songs, many of which had been brought over from Scotland and England and preserved orally. Professor Piper had hoped originally to use her family songs in his extensive Midwest collection. Unfortunately, however, he died before the [fall 1939] semester was over. Later, when it became evident, after a fire had destroyed much of his material, that no one would use the recordings and texts Ruth Ann had given him, Dr. Musick revised and enlarged this collection into a book-length manuscript, "Folk Songs From Missouri and the Ozarks." It was selected for the 1947 Memoir of the American Folklore Society, and co-edited for publication by J. W. Ashton of Indiana University, but due to lack of funds, it was not published.

Later, in 1950, after Dr. Musick had moved to West Virginia, she reorganized and re-edited the manuscript, adding a rather large number of other Missouri folk songs she had collected or acquired, many of them given to her by Vance Randolph, eminent American regional folk scholar. Randolph had already completed his four volume work, *Ozark Folksongs*, and planned no further publication in this field. Dr. Musick dedicated her completed manuscript to Vance Randolph, and to the memory of her mother and Professor Edwin Ford Piper.

Relation to "Local Color"

Musick was stepping away from a treasure-hunting paradigm of schol-arly activity that saw lore as a thing to be collected, and the folk as a sort of geological matrix for these cultural fossils, to a newer understanding of folk and lore as engaged in an ongoing and mutual shaping and reshaping. The book has relatively little actual folklore, that is, discrete objects or practices – superstitions, sayings, stories, songs, foodways. It is more concerned with what eventually came to be known as *folklife*, the complex of interacting traditional social patterns, and its collision with non-traditional ways. The distinction has been and will continue to be the subject of many books. Folklore emerges in the Industrial Revolution in an awareness that something is passing, and something is coming to be, a sorting of the gains and losses, an attempt to archive what was writ in water.

In a way the novel is also a late representative of a robust tradition of American Literary Regionalism, which shares some originary impulses with folklore – the Brothers Grimm had set out to put a foundation under the idea of a unified Germanicity that would unite the nearly two hundred petty sovereignties with more or less similar languages; the young United States was anxious as to whether it had a culture at all (with snooty critics across the water, asking "who reads an American book?")

The supreme exponent of this "local color" movement was Mark Twain, but think also of Flannery O'Connor: "Anything that comes out of the South is going to be called grotesque by the northern reader, unless it is grotesque, in which case it is going to be called realistic." *Hell's Holler* could almost be considered a forerunner of the "Missouri Noir" represented by films like *Winter's Bone* and *Gone Girl*, the Netflix series *Ozark* or the novels of Laura McHugh. One of the first multiform folk narratives I identified as distinct to the area on my arrival in the early 90s was a reminiscence of a family member who had to sit on a grave until the deceased was unfit for use as a dissection specimen (lore accelerated by early scandals concerning cadavers irregularly purchased, but not stolen, in distant cities). Interestingly, this item of genuine lore enters Musick's narrative as plot-element, to be taken at the level of sober fact (I was unable to identify a single instance of grave-disturbance in any public record).

Additional Folk Materials

Regional speech is the common territory of folklorists and sociolinguists. In terms of dialectology and historical analysis, the talk here does seem to carry far more Southern markers than one would expect in the present day. This should not surprise: folklore is as readily linked to anthropology, linguistics and social sciences as to arts, letters and humanities, and this latter cluster was Musick's intellectual home. She was not trying to practice field linguistics. Additionally, she is writing primarily of the hinterland, not the (comparatively) cosmopolitan Keatesville, and archaic features might well be expected. And finally, Adair County's settlers came from Kentucky and Tennessee (a generation out of Virginia and the Carolinas), and those speechways are indeed detectable into the present. Reading the "eye dialect," the use of nonstandard spellings to represent distinctive pronunciation, is one of the challenges in reading the novel. It was not in the least uncommon in published writing at the time, and its careful use in Twain and in Joel Chandler Harris is of enormous documentary value for historical linguistics, but it was often tainted with racism and classism, and for that reason, no modern editor looks favorably on it. Needless to say, it carries no such contempt in Musick's work.

The human concerns are inextricably involved with larger environmental ones, and that too is a modern feature of the book. The memory of how-the-land-was is also part of the shaping of the folk. People exist in cultural and physical spaces, Musick insists. In fact, the plans that would result in Forest Lake (more commonly known here as "1000 Hills," after the state park), were unfolding as Musick wrote her novel. The "rub doctors" (osteopathic physicians, specialists in manipulative medicine) were indeed behind it, but without a profit motive: the area needed a more reliable water supply and these civic boosters relished the economic opportunities of enhanced recreation. The descendants of Dr. George Laughlin, son-in-law of Old Doctor Still, master of the medical college and its hospitals, donated his magnificent cattle ranch for the purpose. Again, one should not turn a novel into a coded essay – this is not a screed against this particular project, but a reflection on the kind of disruptions such engineering introduces. In the preface to *Coffin Hollow*, published posthumously in 1977, Musick inveighs against stripmining, clearcutting and the "slaughter" of wildlife.

Musick no doubt regarded the inundation of Big Creek's valleys with a sense of loss. But *Hell's Holler* is not a work of grief. The novel was written before righteous rage at deep structural sin was recognized as a reason to write, and maybe that was never in Musick's character. One does suspect there's a lot of unprocessed fury here; Mary is subjected to such emotional abuse and physical injury and suffering it is hard to watch. George is equally difficult to contemplate, both when he shucks responsibility and when he draws painfully near to self-understanding. Throughout the novel it is hinted, and made quite clear by the end, that much of George's incapacity results from his mother's over-indulgence of him (and generally overbearing approach to everyone else). It is not hard to connect Mary's excruciating processes of discernment to what Ruth Ann Musick had gone through with her husband, in an era when the "disease theory" of alcoholism was just emerging, and Freudianism bid strongly to explain choices previously attributed strictly to ethical failure. But the older explanations were by no means out of consideration. This is perhaps the most interesting dynamic of the novel, the way in which it is most of its time, and even a correlative of the way it treats folklife, resolutely refusing both to romanticize it and or to hold it up for the contempt of the self-consciously modern reader. The book is a long internal argument about how to understand things. It represents a very contemporary kind of folkloristics, not incorporating and preserving objects, but exploring the interplay of traditional and modern. The book is about people in relationship, and they live in a context of traditions; the people do not serve merely as vehicles for the lore.

*Documenting a rural greybeard singing a medieval ditty was the brass ring of folklore fieldwork in the era. Francis James Child published 300 English and Scottish ballads with their American variants between 1882 and 1898, often referencing the yet older *Reliques of Ancient English Poesy* of Thomas Percy [1765]) This line of folkloristics, largely transcended but still dominant in the popular understandings of the field, is known as the "popular antiquities" approach – the idea that geographically, socially, culturally isolated folk groups preserve ancient ways lost in the larger, "modern" society. While it is true that in the Ozarks the word "reckon" still means what Shakespeare meant by it, isolation is as likely to foster rapid change as fossilization – that is, both things happen. The approach is still regarded as important under the heading of "salvage ethnography," the recognition that cultural materials, unless recorded, pass out of existence as the tradition bearers die, or as the social conditions that supported folk transmission change: as the African proverb has it, "When an old person dies, a library burns down."

Works Cited

The reader is directed to *The Missouri Folklore Society Journal, Special Double Issue, Dedicated to Missouri Collectors.* Ed. Donald Lance. Volume 8-9, 1986-1987. Of special interest here are three essays:

Byers, Judy Prozillo. "Ruth Ann Musick—The Show-Me Mountaineer: A Missourian Adopts West Virginia";

Pentlin, Susan L. and Rebecca B. Schroeder, "H. M. Belden, The English Club, and The Missouri Folklore Society";

Pentlin, Susan L. "Maude Williams Martin: Early Ballad Collector in Missouri."

About the Author

Adam Brooke Davis is Professor of English at Truman State University. He is permanent secretary and webmaster, and past president of the Missouri Folklore Society, unofficial editor of the *Missouri Folklore Society Journal,* and Managing Editor of the *Green Hills Literary Lantern.* His areas of publishing, research and teaching include folklore, historical linguistics, sociolinguistics, medieval studies, mythology, comparative oral tradition, creative writing, rhetoric, German language, the history of medicine and medical education. He's been known to don the costumes and personas of Mark Twain and of Dr. A.T. Still, Kirksville's founder of Osteopathic Medicine–the original "rub doctor."

Preface by Ruth Ann Musick's Niece, Pat Musick, Artist

Ruth Ann Musick's Missouri Family, Childhood

"Well, Archie, Ace is Mamma's favorite, and I'm Daddy's favorite, so you can be my favorite."
—Ruth Ann Musick as a child, to her younger brother, Archie. (Ace was their older brother.)

Ruth Ann Musick and her younger brother, my father Archie Musick, were very close throughout their lives. They shared a spirit of curiosity, adventure, and creative explorations. All their lives, both retained a love of music, stories, and writing, and both taught. Ace, a printer and musician, started his family when quite young; Archie didn't settle down to family life until his late forties. Ace's daughters grew up near Kirksville when Ruth was still mostly in the region, well before she settled in West Virginia. She brought two of them, Pat and Ginny, to visit Archie in Colorado long before I was born. Pat (for whom I'm named) settled in Quincy, IL; she corresponded and traveled with Ruth throughout her life. I'm indebted to Pat's daughter, Rainy Horvath, for sharing family papers and correspondence.

Archie found his calling in painting, studying mainly in Colorado, beginning in 1927, but traveling back to Missouri to visit his mother several times a year until her death in 1949. Though the Archie Musick illustrations in this publication were not done specifically for *Hell's Holler*, they are almost entirely taken from Missouri sketches he made in the course of those visits.

Ruth was Archie's lifelong supporter. She commissioned him to illustrate the three books of West Virginia ghost stories and folktales (*The Telltale Lilac Bush, Green Hills of Magic,* and *Coffin Hollow*) which she compiled during her lifetime. I remember him working on those scratchboard drawings throughout my childhood. Both siblings retained a sense of wonder, mystery and the ineffable. Even apart from those illustrations, many of Archie's paintings embody a sense of fantasy, whimsy, or a mysterious atmosphere.

All three siblings—Archie, Ruth, and the oldest, Asa (Ace)—grew up in a family that valued literature, song, story, the exercise of imagination, learning, and culture—as well as hard work. Their father, Levi, had the only personal library of anyone they knew as children. As Ace's daughter, the *other* Pat Musick, puts it, he was:

> a great storyteller, an agnostic realist, highly moral, shrewd man with a keen sense of humor.... He saw through foibles and chicanery and had strong values. He was frugal and all three kids had to work on the five acres to get money for clothes, etc, but he was quite willing to invest in their education, and tickets to plays, concerts, or lectures that came to Kirksville.... Ruth adored her father and practically worshiped him. [Their mother, Zada] was a docile, religious, music loving woman who became progressively deaf. She was fiercely maternal and her three children could do no wrong.

Zada sang ballads, broadsides and popular songs of the era to her children. Ace became a musician as an adult; Ruth compiled a book of Missouri folk songs that drew strongly on the songs she had heard from her mother as a child. My father sang these songs to us children. Zada, Ace, and Archie played various instruments: piano, organ, banjo, ukulele, ocarina.

According to Ace's daughter Pat, Ruth "loved to play basketball and frequently stubbed the ends of her fingers, catching the ball, which may have accounted for their later appearance of being bent." The children swam, ice-skated, and hiked. In his unpublished memoir, *The Door Step*, Archie wrote of his childhood:

> After a hard day of playing in the woods a reaction sometimes set in. Swinging on grapevines hidden in bowers of dense foliage, sometimes thirty feet off the ground; wading along a particular bend in the stream where moss drooped over a concave bank; climbing willows that would bend with our weight, depositing us on the opposite side of the stream: these pastimes brought me to such a high pitch of happiness during the day that twilight settled down like the end of creation. It was not terror, nor even gloom. It was a beautiful sadness that put me to crying as though my mother had been taken from me. Such was my shame at this display of weakness that I'd have to make up a lie and say my foot hurt.

Ruth was at least equally sensitive, and likely had the same experiences playing in the woods as Archie describes. In *The Door Step*, Archie recalls an event that impacted her life:

> One time my sister and I caught some fish with our hands and took them home to clean them. She held one fair-sized catfish on a board with one hand while the butcher knife in her other hand sawed the head off. The futile wiggle of his tail as he struggled for survival incited me almost to hysterics. The fact that he was denied the power to cry out struck me harder than if he had actually screamed his pain. I put up such a din of grief that my sister caught the spirit and began crying too. Then the enormity of the deed really took hold of her and she made a vow. Never again would she kill a living thing, nor eat the flesh of fish, animal, or fowl. That vow was made when she was seven; she lived another seventy years and never broke it.

Besides this sensitivity, Ruth and Archie shared a spirit of curiosity and adventure–a spirit embodied further back in the family line in Old Bill Williams, mountain man, and Captain Meriwether Lewis.

Archie Musick, Artist

In Archie, that spirit of exploration manifested quite literally. He was intrigued by sights of far-away places seen in the pages of *National Geographic*. On a trip through Colorado, he encountered a place he had seen in a stereoscope viewer while sitting on his mother's lap in 1907: "Many of the scenes [had] fired my five-year-old imagination, but none more than the Garden of the Gods...." Hopping a freight train during an interlude in his college career, he headed West and found himself there.

> One after another of those precious childhood images from the stereoscope loomed up big as life right out of the wilderness. It was like dreaming of an ancient ruin you never heard of—one of those vivid, lasting dreams—then suddenly finding it after you'd all but forgotten about it. (——*Door Step*)

His formal art studies began in his mid-twenties, in the summers of 1927 and 1928, at the Broadmoor Art Academy in Colorado Springs. However, two of his first commissions were in Missouri: a mural at South Church in Moberly (1927); and a painting of the recently burnt-out Old Baldwin Hall at Northeast Missouri State Teachers' College (now Truman State University) in Kirksville (1928). His sister had received her B.Sc. in Education there a few years before the 1924 fire; Archie followed with the same degree, in 1928.

Thereafter, his focus was art; he studied with Thomas Hart Benton at the New York Art Students League, 1929-30, and with Stanton Macdonald-Wright at the Los Angeles Art Students' League, 1930-32. The mountains and red rocks of Colorado continued to call him, and he returned there as a "perpetual student" until WWII. He and Benton remained good friends all their lives, Archie visiting the Bentons as well as his mother when back in Missouri. In 1937, Archie and four other student-friends of Benton who worked with him in New York collaborated on folio editions containing one lithograph from each. The other artists were Joseph Meert, Guy Maccoy, Bernard Steffen, and Jackson Pollock.

In Colorado, his mentor was Boardman Robinson, the director of the Fine Arts Center school and the regional director for New Deal public art programs in Colorado and neighboring states. Archie was on a visit to Kirksville when he received a telegram from Robinson in early 1933, telling him to return: he had been chosen to paint a mural in Colorado Springs, funded by the first New Deal public art program.

He later painted two New Deal post office murals, in Red Cloud, Nebraska (1941) and Manitou Springs, Colorado (1942). For the Manitou mural, with Benton's help, he developed a special made-from-scratch egg-tempera painting technique that remained his signature medium throughout the rest of his life.

After civil service during World War II, he began building his "dream house" in Colorado, and in 1946 began teaching art in universities in Columbia, Missouri, where he met and married my mother, Irene Kolodziej, head of the ceramics department at the University of Missouri. They spent summer vacations in Colorado working on the house, and moved there permanently in 1951. The "dream house," built by hand around several massive sandstone boulders, was inspired by Frank Lloyd Wright's ideas of fitting architecture to the natural surroundings.

Like his sister, Archie wrote articles and stories throughout his life, including an unpublished memoir, *The Door Step*. He wrote and illustrated three children's books, publishing one, *Jigger Flies First*. His informal recollections of the Colorado Springs art world from the late 1920s -1950s, *Musick Medley*, became a standard reference on that era. His work was exhibited widely in Colorado throughout his life, as well as in the 1939 New York World's Fair; 1941 Carnegie International, Pittsburgh, and a major retrospective solo show in Colorado Springs in 1978, the year he died. His paintings are in the collections of the Missouri Historical Society and National Museum of American Art, and others. I have recently created a website to display some of his works: *< https://musickstudio.webnode.com/archie-musick/ >*.

Underlying all those art studies and odd jobs was Archie's love of the outdoors–ice skating on ponds and streams, hiking, and exploring, summer jobs in national parks. He sketched assiduously: landscapes, rock, gnarled trees; Missouri farmlands and family members. Many of his paintings have an air of mystery, melancholy, or whimsy; many emphasize the grandeur of nature and humanity's small place in it, as in Oriental painting. Craftsmanship, composition, visual rhythmic flow, and skilled technique in the service of communicating feelings and ideas are applied in all his work, including his illustrations to his sister's collections of ghost stories and folktales. Their sensibilities, very much in harmony, were doubtless rooted in their shared childhood and flowered in each of their own fields as adults.

Ruth Ann Musick's Creative Writing

Ruth left her folklore archives to Fairmont State College (now University), where she taught for so many years, and they are now housed at the Frank and Jane Gabor West Virginia Folklife Center there. Judy Prozzillo Byers, Dr. Musick's protegee, created the Center to carry on her mentor's work, and her folklore collections are archived there. (Judy also succeeded in having the University's library named for Ruth Ann Musick.)

Yet Ruth Ann was also a prolific writer of fiction: short stories, plays, poems, novels, and children's books, as well as songs. She left her fiction to her brother, Archie, and it currently remains in the care of the family. (Much of this Preface depends upon the family trove now in my possession.) Ruth loved writing fiction and—as her brother did in his paintings—made numerous variations on favorite material, themes, and characters. Her work draws strongly on folklore, her childhood surroundings and experiences; it's marked by her passionate advocacy for animals, the underdog, and environmental causes, and for compassion and good sense. One of her novels is told entirely in the voice of a white cat.

Many of her writings were likely begun during her graduate creative-writing work in Iowa that culminated in *Hell's Holler*; others were probably written in workshops she attended in New York during breaks from teaching in Fairmont; rewriting and re-working she may have done at other times, between her teaching and folklore work. The examples mentioned here are only a small sampling from the archive of her unpublished creative writing work. There are no dates on her fiction manuscripts, but most carry her address at Fairmont State College in West Virginia. Many of the stories embellish and elaborate on local lore from Missouri; some are from West Virginia, such as her play, *The Snake-Witch*. A few of her songs were published in Arizona, where she lived and taught for a few years before commencing her creative writing work in Iowa.

In a 1962 query letter to a Bantam Books editor, Ruth writes, "This is the type of story I like to do best, I think—a combination of fact, folklore, fantasy, and exaggeration...." (The story, "Jesse James and the Mortgage Holders," was published in *Colorado Quarterly* in 1963.)

The elder Pat Musick wrote, "...Ruth Ann told me that in her writing class with the famous Mari Sandoz, she tried to tell her about the plot of the story she was writing, and Mari said, 'Dammit, Ruth Ann, stories

AREN'T plot, they're PEOPLE.'"

Her novel, *The Boy Who Wanted Warts*, is dedicated to Archie; its narrator is a sister looking out for her younger brother (who wants warts in order to be seen as tough); there is an older brother in the family as well. As with most if not all her fiction, she weaves in beliefs, signs, superstitions, and other forms of lore. In proposing *Be Prepared*, a novel whose main characters are boy scouts, she explains her intention to incorporate ghost stories from her collection in each chapter. Of the protagonist, she says, "I thought I'd base him on my younger brother, Archie, when he was a little boy, say 10 or 12....[The protagonist] loves 'scary' stories, and since he wants to... have the courage to face danger in spite of fear, he thinks he will be braver through hearing these stories...."

In a 1958 letter to an editor who provided feedback on (but did not publish) one of her novels, she proposes a biography of or biographical novel about A. T. Still, the founder of osteopathy: "I probably have more material about Dr. Still than most people, since I am from Kirksville, Missouri, and his life has always fascinated me. I have set down all the stories I've ever heard about him, and have talked and corresponded with his granddaughter, who is my friend...." Her story, "Miracle Man Steele," published in *Prairie Schooner*, was suggested by tales of Dr. Still's cures, "only... I let myself go completely wild in exaggeration.... Parts of it [were compared] to Mark Twain, which pleased me no end, of course."

Works Developing Themes Encountered In Or Derived From *Hell's Holler*

Ruth championed her characters, and her dissertation novel provided rich material from which she drew for later projects. For example, she crafted the play, *An Ear for an Ear OR Jim Tittle's Ear*, from an episode in *Hell's Holler*, copyrighting it in 1954. She experimented with at least one other chapter as a stand-alone story.

"The Rub-Doctor," a story she also wrote as a play, focuses on a particular *Hell's Holler* theme: the conflict between superstition and a crippled girl's genuine desire to be healed. The townsfolks' conviction that "if the Lord didn't want her to be crippled, He wouldn't have made her that way" conflicts with the rub-doctor's certainty that he can heal her. She must confront her own beliefs and find independence in the face of the widespread conviction that the doctor is in league with, or is, the devil. The insertion of a dramatic hint of the supernatural is just enough to increase ambiguity and dramatic tension.

Ruth gives all her characters dignity and full humanity even when shining a light on how they are often held back and limited by ignorance and fearful superstition. She respects their lore and beliefs, and the strengths they derive from them, while also lamenting the self-limitations and even harm that some of those beliefs impose. Yet, in her proposal for her novel,*A Little Learning*, she makes clear that education, in and of itself, does not guarantee common sense or right behavior:

> 'A *little* learning is a dangerous thing.'
>
> There are fools in all walks of life—educated or otherwise— and sometimes it's a toss-up as to which is the worst. But it's the ones who have a *little* learning… that are dangerous—that want to boss everything and everybody, although they are obviously incapable of running even their own business halfway sensibly…. And such people are represented in all walks of life. And whoever dreams or even thinks that such cases do not exist in more "educated" groups or communities, is doomed to disillusionment….
>
> Ignorance (or absolute or near-illiteracy or superstition) is *not* the root of all evil, as some people may believe. So-called "educated" people, (or people who overestimate their knowledge) without any common sense whatsoever,… who insist upon being leaders in a community or town, although they are utterly unfit for leadership, may do more harm than the totally uninformed person—or even the complete ignoramus or idiot…

Ruth so believed in her *Hell's Holler* characters and story that she later expanded on the original dissertation text that is published here. That expanded version, which she called *George: His Body and Soul*, is largely the same except for the transformation of a minor character (mentioned a few times in passing in *Hell's Holler*) into a major figure who brings additional conflict and complexity. Her synopsis of this later version articulates how she saw George and the novel's symbolic theme:

> George Moore, dreamer, idealist, and hill musician, has been

brought up in an atmosphere of superstition and non-progression. Although he tries to please everyone as well as he can (even humoring his mother's conviction that he is "poorly" until he becomes more or less of a hypochondriac), he is always unlucky in all that he does, just as his mother warned him he would be, except on two occasions... ironically enough: when he (voluntarily, partly) goes to the insane asylum; and after his death, when he becomes a hero and idol to them all.

Among other things, he is amorously pursued, in spite of the fact that he is entirely true to his wife, by the young, attractive, not-too-bright Elvira Jimpson, who has no scruples whatsoever about anything. ... George is really religious and worries a great deal over the possible destiny of his soul—since, by selling his body to pay for Mary's operation, he is afraid he has sacrificed all hopes of salvation. However, in spite of (or maybe because of) his complete honesty, his ability to always see the other fellow's side, his loyalty to his wife, his high moral character, his really religious nature, his kind heart, his natural common sense, his love for music... he is a complete and utter failure in his own locality until after his death. In his own hills, nobody understands him or gives him credit for any good qualities besides fiddle-playing... outside of his own relatives, with the exception of the beautiful, amorous young half-wit, who unintentionally brings about his death. In a way, Elvira Jimpson symbolizes the web of superstition and ignorance that finally enmeshes and kills him, after ruining his life.

Some Sources of Characters, Episodes, and Lore in *Hell's Holler*

While, like all authors, Ruth was undoubtedly–and inescapably–working through events in her own life as she wrote (to whatever extent that may have been conscious or subconscious), there are identifiable sources for some of the episodes and personalities in the novel. She drew on experiences, places, people, and lore from her childhood for *Hell's Holler*, as for her other Missouri fiction. These were, of course, starting points; a framework on which to build and develop her own ideas, themes, and narrative

No written identification has been found for the fictional "Hell's Holler" as a place name, but it is clearly a settlement not far from Keatsville (Kirksville). A clue for its location may be found in the opening to her story, "The Man Who Could Ride Lightning" (*Colorado Quarterly*, 1957):

> They tell more strange tales of witchery and bedevilment in the Chariton Hills than in any other part of Missouri.... The good folk... are one and all under the firm conviction that the whole place was once under the complete sway of the devil, and may be again unless they all carry out the omens and beliefs that have been handed down for years. It seems the older folk still believe that a loud clap of thunder is a kind of handwriting-on-the-wall for somebody....

Chariton Creek ran behind the Musick farm. The area is not far from Thousand Hills State Park, site of the reservoir whose proposal, in the novel, is felt as a threat by the people of the community. (Ruth Ann would be delighted—and would find it fitting–to know that part of the Chariton Hills Conservation Bank in Adair County is now a protection site for endangered bats.)

According to Rainy Horvath, Ruth's great-niece, "Ruth's first editor, idea person, and workshopper was her mother.... Ruth was gathering background for her characters, so she typed a list of questions about the characters and stories her mother had told her, and her mom wrote back on the [same sheet]." In the following series of questions, Ruth asks about Fred and Marie–clearly models for some aspects of George and Mary in the novel. (Fred's mother, like George's, was named Sarah.). Responses provided by Zada, Ruth's mother, are in italics:

> When Marie left for Iowa, to what part did she go? *–I don't know.*
>
> Did she take all five children with her, at first, or leave them with Sarah until she could get work? *–She worked and sent money for her children.*
>
> Oh yes, about Fred's and Marie's courting—how long after Sarah said, "Fred, I seen my girl today," was it before Fred met Marie? *–Very shortly.*
>
> How did Sarah come to meet Marie in the first place? *--Some kind of a bee—quilting or rag tacking*

> Was Fred practically the laziest thing in the world, even at that time? *–I don't know*
>
> Didn't Marie know it? *––No*
>
> How did Sarah come to meet Marie in the first place? *––Some kind of a bee—quilting or rag tacking*
>
> He liked Marie from the first time he saw her—especially since Sarah so thoroughly approved, didn't he? *–Yes*
>
> How long after Fred first saw Marie—before they were engaged? *––Not long*
>
> How long before they were married? *–Shortly*
>
> Did Sarah engineer the engagement? *– No.*
>
> The marriage? (By supervising their courtship or coaching Fred ahead of time what to say, etc?). *–I think not. Fred was very ignorant, but was no fool.*

The real-world situation of Fred and Marie seems to have provided an outer shell or framework within which Ruth's fictional characters' lives, challenges, personalities, and characters developed within her own narrative.

Some aspects of Ruth's father seem to appear in the characters of Andrew—avid reader, something of an intellectual, straightforward, and kind, patient consultant to George, as well as in Lige's pragmatism and agnosticism. But there is no written evidence from Ruth about this. The boy, Lawrence, and some of his experiences are inspired to a large extent by Archie; some of the scenes, such as the schoolyard bullying episode, are similar in *The Boy Who Wanted Warts*, suggesting something that happened in real life.

Many of the descriptions of events on the Moore farm in the novel, not to mention the colorful similes referring to farm life, are clearly drawn from Ruth's vivid childhood memories.

An insight into Sarah's insistence that George take pills practically from infancy (intending proactively to ward off illness) is found in Ruth's proposal for the biographical novel about A. T. Still:

> It was the age of change, of course, and he [Still] was part of the change. The trouble was, people didn't want to be changed.

They particularly didn't want to stop taking pills. Most of them had practically been brought up on pills, and their folks had before them, so naturally they thought that was the only way to ward off illness. When Dr. Still told a patient… to go home and drink plenty of water, he just looked at him, as if wondering if he'd lost his mind.

The hog-butchering scene is one that must have been witnessed in their childhood by both Ruth and Archie, and made an indelible impression on both. Archie's unpublished memoir, *The Door Step*, recounts a hog-killing that is almost identical to the one in *Hell's Holler*, along with a description of the man who sounds just like Old Man Jimpson:

Old Man Fleck was a hard-times farmer whose alphabet consisted of the letter X and who prayed so audibly at night the neighbors across the road were sometimes awakened by it. His greatest boast was that he did not swear. He had a long beard and a spavined mare named Elizabeth whose bones were assiduously working their way toward daylight. Elizabeth and her master did not see eye to eye on the time element involved between home and town. She had long since become indifferent to the lash of a whip. But now, with the old man jabbing a pitchfork into her jaded rump all the way to town and reining her head high as a camel's, she cut a more dashing figure than her less hungry cousins…

But Old Man Fleck was unique in his butchering technique. He made it a sporting proposition. He was a matador at heart. Armed with his axe he would open the chase by lopping off an ear or a tail. The hog was given an even break. It was given the chance to run for its life—within the confines of the pen. With the old man's beard waving as he sprinted after his victim, axe performing weird convolutions, he cut as dashing a figure as Elizabeth. At full speed the axe would descend, now in the middle of the hog's back, now it would glance off the hip taking a slice of ham with it, till the victim was spurting blood in all directions.

Witnessing this cruelty was likely a factor in Ruth's lifelong commitment to vegetarianism, along with the incident with the catfish.

The numerous ballads and snatches of songs and poetry sung or recited by characters throughout *Hell's Holler* are ones with which Ruth grew up, sung to her by her mother or commonly sung and played in the community. A quick perusal of just a few reveals excerpts from two Child ballads, "Lord Bateman" (Child #53) and "Barbara Allen" (Child #84). A few lines from "Sixteen Come Sunday," a traditional British Isles song, show up mixed into the square dance call. The novel includes a few lines from "The Butcher Boy," a broadside ballad, and "Sweet William" ("Sweet Sailor Boy"), another traditional song from Ireland and Britain and one my father often sang. The humorous song "There was an old woman, in London she did dwell…" is a variant of a British/Irish song sometimes known as "Marrowbones"; in various versions, "London" is replaced by "our town," "Wexford," "Yorkshire," and so on. On one of George's visits to Andrew, the quatrain Andrew is reading is from *The Rubaiyyat of Omar Khayyam*—another family favorite.

Ruth included many signs and superstitions familiar to the community in the novel, not least being "born with a veil" (caul) giving the ability to see the future; bad luck to change a shirt to right-side out if it was put on wrong-side out; breaking a needle brings a year of bad luck; death foretold by a hen crowing; rattlesnake rattles put inside a fiddle to prevent cobwebs, and others. Much later, writing her West Virginia folklore column "The Old Folks Say," Ruth listed twelve Missouri superstitions collected around Kirksville, in hopes of inspiring readers to send her unusual West Virginia superstitions. Four of those she listed in that column are found in Hell's Holler, including that of killing the first snake seen in spring to prevent bad luck. In her column, Ruth appends, characteristically, "Please, don't anybody try this out. My sympathies are entirely with the snake."

Some folk beliefs and signs were taken seriously by the Musick family; in particular, that of a bird fluttering against a window at night as portent of death. Even the skeptical Archie noted, in a pair of diary entries in Colorado in 1942: "March 13: beautiful delicate bluebird fluttered against window at midnight…. March 14: found the bluebird dead outside my window." The war was on everyone's mind; some artist friends had been drafted, and Archie's Japanese-American artist friends in California were being evacuated from their homes, some sent to internment camps. (No deaths are recorded in the diary around that time, but his noting it reveals the lasting impact of "signs" as a constant in his childhood.)

Aunt Ruth: Some Family Memories

Ruth Ann was beloved by all, and she was a wonderful aunt. Pat Musick the elder wrote:

> Ruth was a part of my life from early childhood, and was so good and so much fun that we loved her. She taught me to swim, tutored me in Algebra, let my sister and I badger her into hiking up Pike's Peak with us, and on our trips to Kirksville every summer, we swam, hiked, made fudge, confided, and mostly talked for Ruth was good company. She was the same age as my mother but seemed more like a sister for she was young at heart and had so many interests.... I think one of the things I most admired about Ruth was that when I introduced her to friends, she looked so ordinary and inconspicuous, until she started talking, and then she lit up, and was so interesting, and vital and had so many anecdotes, stories and ideas that everyone was charmed.

Pat's sister, Ginny (Virginia) commented in a letter, "As we know, Ruth was very high-strung… and she was always so damned kind-hearted…."

Both my brother Dan and I recall her taking long walks by herself (as well as with us) in the Garden of the Gods when she visited, her energetic striding up and down mountains, and her boundless enthusiasm, curiosity, vivacity, and passion for her work, causes, ghosts, the underdog, culture, family, animals, nature, people. The fact that she had ever been married was never disclosed to us as kids, and reflects how private and "best forgotten" was that chapter in her life.

Ruth was very interested in Dan's taking up the Highland bagpipes and always asked him to play for her. She took great interest in both of us; her gifts (usually books) were perfect, tailored to our own interests: fantasy books for him, such as *The Hobbit* (when he was five years old, long before its mass popularity). I was sent books featuring animals, and later my very own complete Shakespeare. Ruth sent treasuries of American folklore, the Opie book of children's folklore, *Aesop's Fables*, Vance Randolph's collections of Ozark folktales, and many other books to the family.

Besides her love of hiking in the hills and mountains, Ruth loved swimming all her life, and for many years—almost until her death—she spent part of Christmas vacation snorkeling in the Virgin Islands. (Swimming may have been for her what ice skating was for Archie: he was still doing figure-eights on frozen streams in the Colorado mountains practically until he died in 1978.) Ruth was a lifelong champion for animals and co-founded the Humane Society chapter where she lived in West Virginia. She was an environmental activist, speaking and writing about the horrors of acid rain and strip mining as well as habitat loss through excessive development—as foreshadowed by the community's concerns in *Hell's Holler*. She spoke out against racism (one of her short stories, in particular, is centered on this issue), regarding both African-Americans and Native Americans; she was conscious, and vocal, as few non-Natives are, of present society having dispossessed those who were already here.

And of course, her work with West Virginia folklore and ghost stories: I remember my father working on the scratchboard drawings for each collection. Sometimes Ruth indicated a particular aspect of the story she envisioned for an illustration; in other cases, she left it to my father's imagination. She was invariably delighted with his visual representations of the tales; I now appreciate, more than ever, how it was not only a paid commission but a joy for them to collaborate.

When I stayed with Aunt Ruth in her final weeks of life, in 1974, she looked back with pride on her achievements in the world of folklore, and hoped it could be continued—a task to which Judy Byers devoted her life. I met Judy at that time, and she invited me to carry on the family tradition of illustrating the remaining folklore collections. (The first of these to be published was *Mountain Mother Goose: Child Lore of West Virginia*, 2013.) She also always believed in and loved her fiction writing. Ruth's great-niece Rainy writes,

> I remember that trying to publish her dissertation was really important to her and she was so disappointed every time it was turned down.... My mom, and Aunt Ginny, sat around the kitchen table with Ruth discussing this more than once. Ruth really believed in this manuscript and was crushed when it was rejected repeatedly.

It's hard not to think that her ghost or spirit has been involved in publishing *Hell's Holler* at last: so many things have come together, transforming the project from simply a published dissertation to an illustrated book.

Collaborations

When I was first told of the plan to publish *Hell's Holler*, it occurred to me that perhaps some of my father's illustrations from his Missouri sketchbooks might fit in to lend some visual aspects to the story, though I wasn't sure to what extent this might be the case. Thanks to the publishers, Archie's images have been matched wonderfully to the text, with the exception of the main illustrations for George and Mary: none of the images seemed to be quite right. Although almost all the images are from the Missouri sketchbooks, a few are not: the skeleton and some of the child pictures are from Archie's lithograph illustrations to his unpublished children's book, *Cities in the Rainbow*; two other child images are from *Jigger Flies First*.

Months after I had sent the images, I came across a drawing of a little boy in a big hat that I recognized as drawn from a photograph of Archie as a small boy. I sent it on, thinking it was a perfect illustration for Lawrence. Not long after, I was rereading a letter from my aunt to my father, written in early 1940 when she was apparently going through a very tough time. I had never read the letter all the way through, but this time I discovered, on the last page, a complete change of subject. Ruth writes:

> Your idea of illustrating my book is a marvelous one....I thought for the illustrations:
>
> I. George, fiddle under chin, mouth agape
> II. Mary, his wife, drawing water by hand to water mules
> III. A skeleton...in the Osteopath hospital
> IV. Lawrence, the little 8 yr-old boy... mostly from that child picture of yours with big hat and no teeth...
> V. Lige cuts off Jim Tittle's ear...

If that isn't a message from the Beyond...!

Because it seemed that none of the existing images would quite work for George and Mary, and the first two on this list seemed essential, I drew them myself (p. 124, p. 14), using these descriptions of what Ruth envisioned. A skeleton image (from *Cities in the Rainbow*) had already been chosen for this book. Archie had indeed made the drawing of the little boy from the photograph—so we had Lawrence (p. 111). (Perhaps the scene of Lige cutting off Jim's ear is best left to the reader's own imagination; I hope Ruth's spirit agrees.) For another illustration of George, lying down and depressed (p. 80), I added hair, shirt, and overalls to my copy of my father's life-drawing class sketch—in a sort of virtual collaboration.

Ruth Ann Musick cared deeply about the people, animals, places, and issues in her life, and that includes in her creative writing. Her fictions, rooted primarily and deeply in Missouri soil, were vehicles through which she explored and expressed her heritage, values, questions, dismay, and delight in this world. I'll go out on an unscholarly limb and say that—unless anyone involved with this project is struck by one of those Chariton Hills thunderclaps—wherever she is in spirit, she is thrilled that *Hell's Holler* is published at last. And she must be tickled to be collaborating, albeit posthumously, with her brother once more.

Sources

Hovarth, Rainy. Letters to Pat Musick. 2019-2020. Personal Collection of Pat Musick.

Geoghegan, Zada. Letter to Ruth Ann Musick. 1942. Personal Collection of Pat Musick.

Musick, Archie. *Musick Medley: Intimate Memories of a Rocky Mountain Art Colony*, Creative Press, 1972.

Musick, Archie. *The Door Step*. Unpublished Memoir. Archie Musick Family Archive.

Musick, Archie. Unpublished Personal Diary, 1942. Archie Musick Family Archive.

Musick, Daniel. "Aunt Ruth." *Traditions: A Journal of West Virginia Folk Culture and Educational Awareness* 6 (2000-2001): 35.

Musick, Pat (daughter of Asa). Letters to Pat Musick (daughter of Archie). Personal Collection of Pat Musick.

Musick, Ruth Ann. Letter to Zada Geoghegan. 1942. Personal Collection of Pat Musick (daughter of Asa).

Musick, Ruth Ann. Letter to Archie Musick. 1940. Personal Collection of Pat Musick (author).

Musick, Ruth Ann. Many letters, book proposals, synopses and drafts of stories, plays, and novels. Archie Musick Family Archives

Colorado Springs Fine Arts Center, Stanley L. Cuba, et al. *Pikes Peak Vision: The Broadmoor Art Academy, 1919-1945.* University of Nebrasks Press, 1990.

About the Author

Pat Ruth Musick's work encompasses illustration, calligraphy, teaching, research on early manuscripts, making murals of glass fused to metal, and artist residencies in national parks. A Colorado-based artist, writer, and educator, she is the niece of Dr. Ruth Ann Musick and shares the affection and admiration her aunt felt for West Virginia's people, lore, creatures, and land.

Publisher's Note

Typesetting the roughly 200,000 words in *Hell's Holler* raised a fair number of editorial questions.

First, Musick uses dialect spelling, both in dialogues and in the internal monologues of multiple characters. Some critics object to using dialect, considering it a demeaning sort of stereotyping. However, we believe that Musick is attempting to let readers hear the spoken English of her characters, so we have left the ear-spelling and dialect as they were. We don't change "younguns" to "young ones," or "I know wheres you can git it" to "I know where you can get it," or "You cain't have no idy," to "You can't have any idea."

Second, Dr. Musick employs 1940s punctuation and spelling conventions. She underlines where we would italicize for emphasis. She hyphenates "to-day" and "news-papers" and makes simple compounds of "coaloil" and "churchdoor." She's inconsistent with dashes and capitalization, sometimes using "a-going" and other times "a going," sometimes "Ma" and other times "ma." She uses three versions of one useful contraction: "ain't" and "aint'" and "aint." She spells her own name "Music," without the "k" which she used before and after her time in the University of Iowa's creative writing program. Except for the underlinings becoming italics and the "Music" spelling, we have kept those features. We don't change occasionally debatable grammar/spelling/punctuation choices–e.g. "affect" instead of "effect," or "our'n" instead of "ourn." We even let water occasionally spill over a "damn" instead of a "dam." And we allow commas or periods to remain inside or outside of end-quotation marks, wherever she put them.

However, the third issue, genuine typos, gave us pause. Yes, *Hell's*

Holler is a historical document, and its dialect and 1940s features should be retained. But it is also a doctoral dissertation. As a dissertation, it would have been hand typed on a machine which had no revision capacities, so that correcting a single typo would have required retyping a whole page. It would have been read by a committee skilled at judging the sound of dialect and the quality of writing, but less stringent about simple typos than today's computer-ready committees would be. Judged by its success in what was becoming one of the best creative writing programs in the country, *Hell's Holler* met a high standard as a piece of historical fiction. Still, 21st century readers are trained to judge novels harshly if they notice more than one or two typos, and *Hell's Holler* averages almost one per page. What should we do about them? They're just typos, things computer programs today routinely catch and quickly fix.

After weeks of worrying, we've decided to silently corrected the genuine typos in *Hell's Holler*. When Musick types "sign" instead of "sing," or "sand" instead of "sang," we've fixed the glitch. When she drops a letter, word, or punctuation mark, we've inserted the dropped item, so that people drink "sassafras tea," not "sassafras ta." And readers now watch young Lawrence "going to the door" rather than "going the door." We did this somewhat reluctantly, recognizing that we're not staying fully historical, and that we're not fully modernizing either. So, as a sort of compromise, we're leaving the typos in one sample chapter. Chapter 26 (aka Chapter XXVI) has the usual dialect spelling and 1940s freedoms, but it also comes to you with a dozen genuine typographical errors. How many do you notice, dear reader? How much does it matter to you?

Musick's Summary of Her Dissertation

A dissertation submitted in partial fulfillment of the requirements for the degree of Doctor of Philosophy, in the Department of English, in the Graduate College of the State University of Iowa [in Iowa City]

December, 1943

POSSIBLE THEME

The old, established community, with its folk code, its superstitions, its prejudices, imaginations, etc., in direct opposition to the new or modern world of reality and pro- gress, can hardly survive. A man from this community sells his body to some fairly modern doctors, and from then on lives in fear and cowardice – continually weighing his fate after death, including the idea of resurrection, against the moral obligation of his bargain – and after his death becomes the community hero.

OUTLINE OF CHAPTERS

Chapter 1: Dinner at Mary's

The last strains of "Turkey in the Straw" diminished and died away. George Moore raised his chin from the fiddle and gazed out over the Missouri farmland. Beyond the patches of scrub oak and hickory, the Chariton Hills hovered along the blue haze of the river. The ruggedness of the hills, weaving up and down like a split rail fence, on and on, fascinated George, but their worthlessness, with the nearest market fifteen miles away, reminded him of his own misfortunes. For George, with his bulk of body and broken-down health, was no good as a farmer, and he knew it. He was "marked" by a sick cow.

The red-headed woman peeling potatoes looked as if she would never finish her task. Her blue-dyed sugar-sack dress, limp over sagging shoulders, gave her a kind of wilted sweet-Williams look, and her voice sounded dragged out, even when she sputtered. She glanced at the old wooden clock and turned to the bulk on the bed.

"George, how can you set there, with your ma and pa coming and so much to do?"

"What is there to do?" His open mouth widened.

"For Heaven's sake, George! Put up that squawking fiddle and git me some wood!"

"Why, Mary, if I'd a-had any notion you wanted something done –"

"Something done! I wisht I'd a-never left Ioway. You never git nothing done! I told you, and your pa told you to fix that lower bridge two months ago, before the rains set in and the crick gits up, and you ain't touched it yet. Some of the younguns'll be drownded shore, that is, if they ever git out of bed from that summer complaint. Me nor Lawrence cain't do that. We do everything else, might near."

George raised the eyes of a whipped dog.

"'Tain't rained all summer, till last night, and the younguns's been down in bed –"

"Well, it's a-going to rain now."

"I cain't help it, Mary, I ain't got no health – marked like I am. I take medicine all the time, but don't seem to git no better – worse if anything. And taxes a-coming on and all. As a feller says, 'I don't know what in the name of the Lord'll become of us!'"

She poured water on the potatoes and started cutting them in little chunks. "Well, marked or not, if you'd a-went to them rub-doctors, like Andrew said and I always wanted, like as not they'd a-rubbed some of it out of you, so's we could a-got along. Or, if we'd a-sold out to the *government* –. Well, git me the wood now."

"Where's little Lawrence?"

"He took some corn to mill to be ground. He ort to be back before long."

"It ain't right. Him only eight and a-doing a man's work. And me not able to do a thing! And the place needing fixing and my tools wore out, and the mules old. Sometimes, I just want to bust out and bawl."

"Well, don't think about it."

"I cain't help it. I want to git my mind off my troubles, but I cain't seem to git it off. I want to do the right thing, and I ain't able to do nothin', and as a feller says –"

"George, *please* git me the wood. The fire'll be out!"

Helpless against misfortunes, George plumped the violin in the wooden box under the bed, and solemnly picked up the axe by the door. "I wish to the Lord I was strong." He paused in the doorway. "Here comes Lawrence now, and old Whitey's a-limping worse than ever. It just looks like things git worse and worse every day. I don't know what in the name of God –"

"George, for the Lord's sake git the wood!"

She looked up from the steaming iron kettle as the steady plod-plod of the mule drew nearer and stopped.

"Mommy!"

A bang of the door, and she untied the red and blue lettered cotton bag, as Lawrence slid down and tried to lift it to his back. His father's oversized straw hat gave a kind of umbrella look to his spindly frame.

"Lawrence, you cain't carry so much. It's too heavy for you!"

He ran ahead to open the door. Inside he helped himself to a raw potato, and mumbled with crisp bites.

"I'm strong, Mommy. I ain't sick like Pappy."

"No."

"I wisht he'd git better. Maybe I wouldn't have to sell Sampson then.

"Well, he thinks he's sick, and his ma does, and I reckon he is. They been a-doctoring him for over thirty year now – Looks to me like, though, if he was marked by ten sick cows, he could do more than he does."

"Well, Mommy, he's always a-thinking of us."

"Yes, but work'd do so much more good."

There was a clatter of plates as Mary set around the dishes from a stack in her arms. The boy watched, his head on one side.

"Mommy, why didn't Grandma and the rest of 'em want the government to take over the old mill and dam and build a reservoir and all?"

"Taxes mostly, I reckon. They cain't hardly pay 'em the way things air. And then too, some of 'em would a-had to sell, and they don't want no outsiders a-coming in, and they don't want to move out – none of 'em. They've lived in these hills so long, they cain't see things no other way."

He braced himself against the rough hickory rocker.

"Looks like they'd want a reservoir – for swimming and such. Sampson would, I bet. Reckon I better feed Sampson now?"

"If you don't shut up about that pig, every breath, I'll give him back to your grandma! Drag up some more wood before it rains."

The boy's jaw dropped half way to his chest, and his eyes, half hidden in tangled red hair, had the look of a ringed pig caught in a fence. His mother stared up from cups and saucers.

"I didn't mean it about Sampson, Lawrence. He's yourn. But we git along so poorly – I wisht to the Lord we <u>had</u> a-sold to the government, and could git away from these hills, some'ers where there's a law to keep younguns in school–"

"Mommy, I don't keer nothing about school, honest."

The long wooden spoon scraped noisily in the iron kettle, where the beans simmered.

"I used to love these hills, when I first married your pa and come to live here, but now I hate 'em!"

"Why, Mommy?"

"Because – there's no gitting away, seems like, once you're here. You're shut out from the rest of the world, and have to work like a dog all your life to keep from starving to death."

"Mommy, would we eat Sampson – to keep from starving?"

"I reckon we would, but we ain't starving, yet."

"No, Mommy. I better drag up that wood now."

"See if your grandma's a-coming, won't you?"

His small red head darted to the front door.

"She's a-coming way yander," he yelled, as he disappeared around the house.

Mary took down part of an old brick, and scraped scouring dust into a saucer with a butcher knife. She did not hear the door open or George come in, until he interrupted the noise by dropping three small pieces of wood, one at a time, to the floor. Then he stretched himself unhappily on the bed. Mary looked up, wiping her hands on her apron.

"Why, George, that ain't half enough!"

He sighed motionless.

"I couldn't cut no more, Mary. I tried to, but I got to thinking about how things used to be and the way the Lord knows they're a-going to be, and I just couldn't stand it."

"Never mind. I'll git the wood."

She laid the sticks on the dull coals, and slammed the screen door as she left. George turned over on his face. The beans began to bubble over.

"Anybody home?"

The front door opened and a tall, thin, somewhat stooped woman pushed her way in, loaded like a pack mule. Setting down her bundles, she marched to the cookstove, and jerked the iron kettle away from the fire. She took off her starched blue polkadot sunbonnet, displaying a neat brown and gray twist that rose up from the crown of her head, and spoke in a flat, nasal voice.

"George, I brung you some beet pickles like you like, and some fried chicken and peach pie and pound cake. We almost didn't come, looked so much like rain."

George did not answer.

"Why, George, what's the matter? The younguns ain't no worse, air they?"

He turned over on his side and shook his head.

"No. They're about all right, only the doctor said to keep 'em in bed a day or two longer. They're still in yander."

She tiptoed to the bedroom door and looked in.

"Asleep," she whispered, "bless their little hearts." On tiptoe she eased back to George. "Well, now, what *is* the matter?"

"Oh, Ma, I don't see how we're a-going to make it! I was a-cutting wood, and I got to thinking about things, and I just couldn't stand it. Mary had to finish gitting the wood."

"You poor boy! Sometimes, I just wonder what I ever done, that the Almighty should visit *you* with this awful health."

A little man stuck his head in the door. He was almost all hair from his neck up, with a small clearing near the top, where two wistful eyes peeped out. He was muttering through his beard as he came in.

"There you go, Sary, babying him as usual! 'Tain't no wonder he don't amount to nothing, laying around and letting his wife do all the work!"

Sarah sat up like a hatching hen.

"Now, Lige Moore, you just tend to your own business. It won't do for George to git upset. The doctor said so. If you're so uncommon sorry for Mary, go out and git the wood yourself!"

"I knowed it! I knowed you'd begin hollering for me to work the minute we got here. Why in the name of the Lord, don't you make that strapping youngun do somethin' – stead of jawing me? Looks like –"

His voice died away in the whiskers. Sarah stood firm.

"Now, Lige, just shut up, and git that wood. I know what I'm a-doing."

There was a disturbance in the beard as Lige left, but nobody heard a word of it. Sarah turned soothingly to George.

"Now tell your mommy all about it. *She* understands."

He sat up and rubbed his big hands helplessly.

"It's just – I don't see what'll become of us. We aint got no cow that's any account now. Baldy's might near dry, and my tools 's all wore out, and the mule's old, and the place's all run down – "

"Well, George, tools do wear out, and mules git old. There's nothing alarming in that."

George looked out at the hills, considering.

"Yes, but Mary's unsatisfied, all the time. Wanting to sell out and go to Ioway, where she come from, and a body cain't blame her, the shape I'm in. Ma, I been a-thinking – maybe we ort to go to them *rub-doctors*, like Andrew said. They claim there's a new one here now, that can might near work miracles. Had something about it in the paper tother day."

"Why, George, if anybody could do anything for you, old Doc Ceburn could. He's been a-doctoring you all this time, and if he don't know what ails you, nobody would. I don't believe in gitting mixed up with outsiders. Anyhow, some say the rub-doctors is hitched up with the devil."

"Well, Ma, maybe they air, and maybe they ain't. Ben Bragg don't seem to think so, nor Andrew, and considerable others. Seems like this new feller's more on the Lord order. Don't charge a cent to find out what ails you, and cures might near everybody he touches."

"Maybe he does, but, George, – somehow I feel like you'd be better off to stay away from him."

"Yeah, but, Ma, many as he's cured that other doctors 's give up – don't seem right to me nor Mary airy one not to give him a chance. Might make a new person out of me."

"Well – I'll think about it, George, and look at that paper agin. The Lord knows I want your ailments cured, if there's any way of doing it, and the Almighty's willing – and I know Andrew's turrible smart about some things – but I hate to see you git mixed up with uptowners – let alone rub-doctors. Did you say Mary was still a-wanting to sell out?"

"Yeah, she's had it in her head a long time – ever since her pa took to living on hard liquor, so to speak – and now, after that government offer, and Ben Bragg and his folks a-wanting to go, she's worse than ever. Says nobody gits ahead in these hills. Says she hates 'em for keeping little Lawrence and the rest of 'em from a education and easier living –"

"Well, don't you sell! Let Braggs go to Ioway, if they want to – just so they don't sell to outsiders. Mary'll git over that tomfoolery. I felt the same way when I married your pa. Thought maybe I was belittlin' myself, living here, me plum through the fourth reader, and most of 'em not able to write their own name. Sometimes, I don't know if education is right or not, unless you got money to go on. Turns you agin your own home and folks, and makes you want to be better'n what you air."

"Mary ain't so turrible educated, Ma."

"She's got a fine education. Been clean through the eighth grade! And got a di-ploma too. That's more'n anybody else around here can say. And maybe she'd be better off with- out it. I don't know."

Mary opened the door and Lige staggered in under the wood.

"Thank you, Pa Moore. You folks's shore good to us. I don't know what we'd do without you. I'll have dinner ready now, soon as I can."

She went back to the old cupboard for the rest of the things. "Why, Ma Moore, you shouldn't a-brung all this. I shore do thank you, but it's too much for you. It looks awful good though, all of it."

"I reckon it's eatable," said Sarah with modest pride.

There was a wail in the next room.

"George, see what ails the younguns, will you?"

"I'll do it if you say so, Mary, but the sight of four of 'em a-laying there all this time with that-air eummer complaint just takes the heart out of me —"

Sarah jumped up like a Jack-in-the-box. "Don't you go if it upsets you, George. Your mommy'll look after 'em."

She swept out, her long, gingham skirt swishing about her bony ankles. Lige filled his corncob pipe, and twisting up a piece of newspaper, lit it at the stove.

"That woman ain't got good sense."

George got up and sauntered out to the porch steps. There was a gurgle of water as Mary filled the few glasses.

"'Tain't no wonder George don't amount to nothin'," Lige went on, "the way Sary acts. He's gitting so he don't lift a hand, does he?"

There were little clicks of knife and fork as Mary paired them off on the red and white table cloth.

"He don't do much."

"Anybody but him could a-made a good living on this place."

"That's just what I thought, Pa Moore. I thought with twenty-five acres to start with, we'd just do fine. Thought maybe George could cut ties for the railroad like Ben Bragg. Ben says he thinks George could do a-plenty if he was a-mind to."

"Pity you didn't marry somebody like Ben Bragg. I never seed such a worker. And when it's raining, or so's he cain't work, he's up and down the river, hunting and fishing with his dog."

"I was a-most too young to marry anybody when I married –sixteen, and George *was* awful good-acting and stout-looking then. And I don't know as I'm sick of my bargain – leastways, I wouldn't feel right to go off and take the children, helpless as he is and all, even if the Bible said different. But I do wish he'd work. If him and his ma could just git it out of their heads he was sick and cow-marked and all, he might do as much as anybody – but I don't reckon he ever will. I'd better git that milk and butter from the cave now – what there is."

Sarah tiptoed back from the sick room.

"Lige, couldn't we give old Blackie to George? His cow's might near dry, and they have such a time anyhow. He has to have a cow with five younguns and four of 'em sick!"

Lige puffed placidly into far away space.

"I don't care if he does, He didn't have to have so many younguns. "

Sarah threw up her hands and opened her mouth.

"Why, Lige Moore, such talk! You know it says in the Bible to multiply and replenish the earth!"

Lige looked up, still smoking.

"Well, it don't say – for *George* – to do it *all* – does it?"

"Now, Lige, shut up a-talking that way and give him that cow."

"I ain't a-going to do it! I give him half of all I had, might near, when he got married, and if he'd a-done right, he'd have something now. I'm gitting old, and I need what I got."

"You ain't a natural father, Lige Moore, refusing your own blood like that. Well, Mary's unsatisfied agin, a- wanting to go back to Ioway. She's a-going to leave him yet, them gitting along so poorly. You just see if she don't."

Lige puffed profoundly, and little wisps of smoke pushed out at intervals like a cookstove with the damper up.

"If she'd a-had any sense, she'd a-left him long ago, before there *was* so many younguns. What she ever married him for in the first place's more than I can figure out."

"Ain't you shamed, a-talking like that about your own boy, and him sick? Why there ain't a better boy than George nowheres. He ain't got one bad habit. He'd no more think of putting a filthy pipe in his mouth than anything. And he used to play the fiddle right well – but Mary's *so* unsatisfied, now – . Well, if she does leave him, you and me 'll have to take the younguns."

"Good Lord Almighty!" Lige exploded, "we cain't do that!"

"We'd have to. You know we would."

"Why, they'd drive me crazy – five of 'em, at my age."

"Well, you'd better give 'em old Blackie – "

"I won't do it, I tell you!" he declared, but as a child whimpered in the next room, added thoughtfully. "Well, maybe I will. I don't know. But, what'll become of us, the Lord only knows!"

The milk sloshed in the tin pail as Mary backed in with her arms full. A fog arose as she took up the steaming food from the stove.

"It's ready now, I reckon. George!"

The big man responded with the alacrity of a pig trotting toward the feeding trough. Mary pushed back a sugar-sack patched screen.

"Lawrence! Oh, Lawrence! You folks set down and help yourselves. I'll be in soon as I take the younguns some gruel."

They pulled up chairs and sat down. The platter of chicken, the plate of biscuit, the bowls of beans and potatoes passed from hand to hand. When Lige had some of everything, he was ready to talk.

"George, you ever git that lower bridge fixed?" he asked.

"Not yit," replied George, from a drumstick. "Mary was saying something about it a while ago."

"I'm durned! Had all summer to fix it, and ain't touched it yit?"

"Now, Lige," interrupted Sarah, "he's had other things to do, I reckon."

"Yes. Might near worked himself to death! Just the same, young feller, you better git that bridge fixed, soon as you can. Somebody's a-going to git drownded. I told you and Mary, way last spring."

"Well," said George, blowing into his saucer, maybe I could do it tomorrow, if it dries off – "

"Why in the name of the Lord didn't you fix it when it *was* dry? You had all summer. When the rains set in, it rains steady, and that river's all over this bottom-land, and you know it! And you know, too, you cain't git nowheres on this place hardly, without'n you cross that bridge."

George reached for more potatoes and gravy.

"Well, I reckon I cain't do it – right now," he said helplessly.

"Of course not," Sarah defended. "Lige, cain't you let the poor boy eat in peace?"

"Well, remember what I said! There's been more than one drownded here in my time. That river's mean when she's up!

"Lige, do shut up! Have some chicken, George."

Lige commented upon the breast of the chicken.

"Well, George, your appetite don't seem to be affected none by your ailment."

"Naw. That's a funny thing, No matter how sick I am, I can always eat – usually more than most people. I got all the doctors puzzled. None of 'em cain't find out what ails me. One doctor said maybe the well part of my stomick craved victuals, but the sick part couldn't digest 'em proper."

"Now, Lige," put in Sarah, "lots of sick people have big appetites."

"Could I have some of them beans and salt pork?" said George.

Mary came in with the children's dishes rattling in the empty pan.

"Mary," Sarah beamed, "maybe I'm a-doing wrong, but I been a-mulling it over, and I concluded to do like Andrew said."

Everybody looked up expectantly.

"The first time we kin git to town this week – maybe we'll find out what ails George?"

"What do you mean?"

"I see by the paper there's a fine doctor came to Keatsville now, some-body from way off. He's a-going to be with the rub-doctors from now on, and examine folks free. I never took no stock in rubbin', my self, but it says *he* can find out what ails might near anybody, and cure 'em too, generally. Maybe George can be well like other folks."

There was a clap of thunder, as Lawrence burst in the door, big-eyed.

"It's all black outside. Looks like it's going to storm turrible. Reckon I better bring Sampson inside, Mommy?"

He speared a chicken wing and bit into it, his eyes on his mother.

"No. He'll be all right. I better git in my chickens in, though."

Sarah jumped to her feet.

"I'm a-going to git mine in too. Lige, hitch up that team as fast as you can. We're a-going home right away, before the rain!"

"Why, good Lord A'mighty, woman! We just come!"

"That don't make no difference. I ain't a-going to let my chickens drown. I aim for half of them chickens to be George's, Mary's and hisn, and they need all they can get. Come on, now, I'll help you. Anyways, I'll hurry you up."

He pushed up his coat collar as he plodded after her.

"It's a-starting to rain already. I'll catch my death of cold, but that don't make no difference to her. I tried to git her to stay at home in the first place – but nothin' would do her –"

"Come on, Lige!"

At the door, Sarah turned for a final word.

"George, take care of yourself now, and don't git your feet wet, whatever you do. I'll be by to take you to that doctor the first day I can git through the roads. Maybe everything's going to be all right!"

Chapter 2: After the Storm Mary Draws Water...

For three days the black mud oozed and thickened, and farmers, who tried to get through, stuck like flies in molasses. But gradually the persistent sun, like an old lady sucking on a clogged pipestem, drew up the water and left the road dry and caked in splotches.

An immense figure in faded overalls hunched forward in a screaking rocking chair by the window, as if making a special study of Missouri soil. At times he stood up like a small boy on stilts, as if to see farther. He rubbed his right hip gently and breathed out soft groans. Either by accident or because sounds seemed to relieve his pain, a louder, more pitiful groan escaped. The dishpan echoed an answer.

"Oh, George, don't take on like that!"

"I cain't help it, Mary. Seems like everything in the world goes contrary with me. No telling when Ma'll come and now with this-here rheumatism running through me like a knife, on top of everything else, I don't see how I can stand it."

A faded face, fringed in soft red, lifted from behind the milk pail.

"I think maybe she can git through this morning, the way it's a-drying up. I hope so. I want to see that doctor too."

The dishwater splashed into a bucket of potato peelings. There were little zings of milk pail and strainer and dull clicks of dishes. She turned a rough oak chair on one side, set an old wooden tub on top and emptied a kettle of steaming water over a large tan and brown slab of lye soap. A pan tinkled with water that dripped from the dry staves. She took the drinking pail from its shelf and tipped it toward the suds until she could jab her hand up and down without scalding. Then she scurried into the bedroom and backed back with a bundle of soiled clothing. She set in a greenish washboard and scrubbed and rubbed as if somebody stood over her with a whip. George, with the helpless look of a chicken carried head down, limped to the bed and stooped for the wooden box. She paused in wringing out a child's dress.

"For the Lord's sake, George, don't play that fiddle this mornin'. I'm just about crazy anyhow, with so much to do, and my side like it is. Slop the pigs, won't you? So's to have that done if your ma comes."

A cat that has been deprived of a mouse would have shown no more surprise.

"Why Lawrence always takes keer of the pigs."

"I know it, but you do it for a change."

His helpless hands hung like spading forks.

"Mary, you're the best wife a man ever had, and I love you fer it. I cain't bear to see you work like you do, or Lawrence either, but somebody has to do it, and I cain't. Seems like I'm always ailing one way or tother. Sometimes, I don't know what in the name of the *Lord'll* become of us, when I git to thinking about things – "

"Well, stop thinking and slop the pigs."

Scrub – scrub – scrub. The door opened and a red-haired boy backed in with a hill of sticks higher than his head. A small pair of soiled overalls tripped him and toppled him over head first. Something sudsy and wet reached out.

"Lawrence, you'll break your back if you keep on."

"Oh, that didn't hurt none, Mommy. Can I feed Sampson, now?"

She looked at the unhappy figure that had folded up by the window.

"Yes, I reckon you better. Feed all of 'em, won't you? Take 'em that bucket of sour milk now, and the slop after dinner."

A small arm raised to balance the one that tugged at the heavy bucket. At the door he rested and changed arms.

"Pig! Pig! Pig! Pig! Sampson!"

The soiled clothing changed into neat, wet, clean-smelling little bundles that filled the dishpan. The woman glanced toward bulky overalls, dried her hands, and dragged the tub to the door. The cistern pump rattled and clanked as the tub filled with cold water. She dragged it back and bundles from the dishpan splashed into it. A small red head appeared at the door.

"Pappy, the mules's down at the barn well, and there ain't a speck of water nowheres, nothin' but mud."

The man at the window looked as if he had swallowed a bullet. The wash-woman became a sputtering fire-cracker.

"George, you water them mules right now. I ain't able to draw water this morning."

"Well, Mary, I know they ort to be watered. They need water, but I reckon the shape the barnyard's in, I'd git my feet plum muddy and damp, if I went out there now. Maybe Lawrence could do it."

"No he cain't. He ain't strong enough, and you know it."

She doused a blue chambray shirt up and down and squeezed it dry. Lawrence gnawed slippery elm bark as he eyed his father.

"What'll you give me if I kin, Pappy?" he asked.

"Something nice, one of these days, soon as I kin."

"Pappy, would you learn me to play the fiddle – like you?"

His father's face lit up like a lamp in darkness.

"Why, Lawrence, course I will. Anytime you say. I didn't know you was so much like your pa."

Lawrence ran out in the wind, his hair flying.

The woman squeezed water from a small nightgown and threw it into the dishpan.

"George, you surely ain't a-going to set there and let little Lawrence draw that water, air you?"

"Why, Mary, he said he'd do it. I just didn't want to get my feet damp, and hisn air already. 'Twon't hurt him, I reckon –"

"If the pump was fixed, 'twouldn't make no difference, but drawing all that water by hand is a man's job. I've heard of younguns being made cripples for life for such as that. I reckon after something like that happens to him, you'll be satisfied."

"Why, Mary, you know I wouldn't have Lawrence hurt for nothin' in the world. I'll git the water right now if you say so, but you know what the doctor said about wet feet, him and ma both – "

"Then I'll get the water myself, but Lawrence ain't a-going to."

The door slammed and George, using chairs and table for crutches, hobbled over to where he could look after her. She marched to the well and pushed Lawrence aside. Hand over hand the rough rope went down and the wooden bucket came up, brimming and splashing, as she turned it into the trough. The mules put back their ears, stretched down their heads, and the water rippled down their long, white throats. When the water was almost gone, they washed out their mouths and waited for more. Once or twice she seemed to grab at her side, as if to hold it together, but she kept on drawing bucketful after bucketful. Then all of a sudden, she gave a little yell and toppled over backwards like a chopped tree. The full bucket fell back with a loud spank and splashed high. The puzzled mules shied off. Shaking their heads and making a funny little noise, they looked on from a distance. She lay where she had fallen –

"Pappy! Pappy!"

The stillness was broken by the high voice. George hobbled to the door and poked his head out.

"Pappy! Come here, quick!"

He looked as if he were being torn limb from limb. Where on earth were his gum boots? The boy's troubled eyes zigzagged from woman to man.

"Pappy! Mommy's busted her head wide open!"

George broke into a clumsy run, his hand on his lame hip, and then stood helplessly looking down, much as the mules were doing.

"You reckon she's dead, Pappy?"

"Oh, surely not, Lawrence, I don't know what in the name of the Lord'd become of us, if she was. Pull on her arms a little, cain't you? I've heard tell that helps sometimes."

The boy tugged frantically at limp hands.

"You reckon that's enough, Pappy?"

"I don't know, Lawrence. I'm so worried and nervous, I ain't got good sense, hardly. Maybe you ort to wet her face a little."

There was no water at hand but what remained in the trough for the mules. Little wisps of dry grass, bits of seed, and yellow corn floated through it, but it was wet. He dragged over the trough and sloshed most of it into his mother's face. The sediment settled on face and hair, and water soaked the sugar-sack dress, but she moaned a little and opened her eyes. George and the mules looked on.

"Mary, speak to me! For the love of God, open your eyes and say something!

Her eyes fluttered and focused upon the spading forks.

"George, I don't believe you'd lift a hand if I was dying."

His face glowed like a fresh-lit corncob pipe.

"Thank the Lord you're all right, Mary," he breathed.

"Your head's all bloody, Mommy."

Her hand stretched to the back of the red hair.

"That's nothing; just a scratch. But my side does hurt a heap. Has your ma come yet, George?"

"Not yit. I reckon she couldn't git through the mud. Somebody's a-coming yonder. 'Tain't Ma, though."

"It's Ben Bragg and Brownie," squealed Lawrence, relieved at his mother's revival. "Hi, Ben!"

A man who seemed to have eyes, hair and disposition much like the shaggy dog that wagged its tail behind him, sauntered up, smoking a pipe.

"Anything the matter?" he asked. "I heard Lawrence a-yelling."

"Mary just keeled over like a stuck hog. Like to scared us all to death," explained George.

Lawrence and the dog promptly entered into a swift game of tag, knocking each other continually, and climbing up again as if they had never been off their feet. Mary looked something like a last year's calico dress.

"I was a-drawing water, and everything went black all of a sudden. I'm all right now, I guess, all but my side."

"You oughtn't to be a-drawing water here nohow. It's a man's job," said Ben. "What's wrong with your side?"

"I got caught out in that rain Sunday, and there's been a stitch in it ever since. Reckon it's just cold."

"Hmmm. Maybe you ought to see a doctor."

"We're a-going to the doctor to-day," put in George, "if Ma ever gits here with the spring wagon."

"I don't know if Mary ought to ride over these roads in a spring wagon, with her side ailing so she's liable to keel over any minute, or your ma either, for that matter, old as she is. I'm a-going to town in the Ford with the cream in a little while now. One of 'em could ride with me, well as not."

Mary pried herself to her feet and squeezed water from wet splotches. Ben stood ready to catch her if she should fall again.

"Thank you, Ben. Whatever Ma Moore says about the ride. I'd like it, and I know she would, but we'll wait and see. She's a-coming now, ain't she George?"

George shaded dull eyes with an awning of a hand. Down the road a piece, a team clopped along – a mule and a spotted horse.

"That's her," he said.

"I'll hang out the children's things and get into something dry again she gets here."

She wabbled toward the house like a lame goose in a strong wind. Ben tapped ashes into his hand and onto the ground, and reached for the hip pocket of his overalls.

"George," he said, "I wisht you'd see to drawing the water for the stock, till you're able to get a pump. A woman ain't able to do that kind of work."

George's mouth grew to an open cave.

"I know it, Ben. I know Mary ortn't to do the work she does, and sometimes I just want to bust out and bawl, me not able to lift a hand. Nobody knows, hardly, what I go through. I reckon most folks think I'm plum lazy."

The dishpan pushed open the screen and little dresses and shirts and underwear dangled from the line. Ben pocketed his hands and pawed the ground with one foot.

"Don't make no difference what folks think, but a woman cain't do a man's work. They ain't built strong enough for it."

"I know it, Ben, but what can I do?"

"Well, if something was to happen to Mary or Lawrence, what'd you do then?"

"The Lord only knows, Ben. I don't."

Ben looked as if he'd just got the worst of a horse trade.

"Well, reckon I'd better be getting my cream and stuff ready. Have one of the women-folk come down when they're ready."

He gave a low whistle and the dog bounded after him. Lawrence looked after them and darted to the clothes line.

"Mommy, you reckon I could let Sampson out, and play with him for a while?"

She dried her hands and straightened his twisted suspenders and shirt and smoothed the flying red hair.

"No, I reckon he's getting most too big. Anyhow, he might get into something while we're gone."

The door slammed on woman and dishpan. A spring wagon rattled up, shrieking and grating, and the team stopped and stared. Lawrence climbed the hub of the front wheel.

"Grandma, who's a-going to ride up with Ben Bragg–you or Mommy? Maybe Mommy ort, seeing as she might near killed herself –"

"What?"

"Oh, she's all right now. Who's that a-coming yonder? Looks like old man Jimpson – but tain't Bill – "

Over the hill two heads appeared that stretched into shoulders and legs. As they came up, one of them yelled.

"Is Lige here?"

Old man Jimpson was a little dried-up cucumber of a man, but as lively as a spring chicken. His cotton beak of a beard twitched at every other word he said, like a cat's tail before a spring. Behind him stumbled a gangly boy of fifteen or sixteen, whose boot-top of a mouth stretched in continual grin. Sarah swung around in the wagon seat.

"No, he didn't come. Say, ain't that boy of yourn the one they sent off to the crazy house, long about three or four year ago?"

Old man Jimpson jiggled his beard.

"Yeah, that's him. J. P., his name is. J. P. Morgan Jimpson. J. P. ain't crazy though, or foolish neither. Some ways he's smarter'n most. Seemed like God teched him a little before he was borned, so he's always been sort of odd-like, but he can hear uncommon good, and smell too. I never seed such ears and nose. Always finds the best eatables in the woods before anybody, and he's a regular rustler for news. – finds out everything, maybe too much. Wouldn't a-had to a-gone off in the first place, if it hadn't a-been for Chipwood's cow, over here about five or six mile east. She got into their corn patch and et it plum off to the roots, so's 'twouldn't make no crop, and 'twas too late to replant, and they was so plum put out, they said they wisht she was dead. Well, J. P. heerd 'em say it, and just took 'em at their word. Slipped a dose of rat poison in her shorts, and she didn't last no time. Suffered turrible, they said, seeing as she was half foundered already. He never meant no harm–aimed to please – but somehow or other they found out who done it, and the law got him and put him in that insane asylum about a hundred mile west of here. Claimed he was clean crazy. But seemed like they wasnt doing no help for him, and him so out and out dissatisfied all this time, we concluded to take him out. They said 'twas all right, that is, if somebody'd watch over him, so's he wouldn't git in no more trouble. I don't know why he never liked it. Seemed like they was good enough to him, to hear him tell it."

Everybody was impressed, George seemed to be listening with his mouth. Lawrence walked around J. P. three times, studying his ears and nose.

"I wisht the Almighty'd a-made me like J. P.," he said.

J. P. grinned. Old man Jimpson looked first at one, and then another for further commendation, but Sarah kept her eyes focused on J. P.

"Well, Mr. Jimpson, whether they was good to him, or wasn't, they had no business a-taking him off in the first place, the way I look at it. Born right here like he was, and teched by the Almighty, this was the *place* fer him, and his folks the ones to look after him."

The white beard ticked off each word.

"Yes, but seems like everybody's always wanting to run other folks's business – just like the government wanted run ourn. They *did* offer us a good price, but if a body cain't live here what *good'd* it do?"

"Yes, and mark my words, if you'd agreed to sell and we had, Webb-stringers and Braggs'd both a-sold, the way they talk now. Said it's a-been better for them that sold and them that stayed. Said the government had money to fix up things the way they ort to be – build a reservoir and save the old mill and dam and I don't know what all. Said, some ways we was a hundred years behind the times. What if we air? People got along then, same as now. Besides, who wants to straddle a hundred years at one jump, with government people and uptown know-it-alls crawling in and out the hills like so many ants?"

Old man Jimpson's beard made a complete circle of everybody there.

"That's what I say, Sary! That's *jest* what I say! These hills air for *hill* people, and outsiders ain't got no call *a-nosing around* – a-sending our younguns off to crazy houses, jest cause they been teched by the Lord, one way or another – much less a-trying to *buy* out the land we was borned on. But I might near forgot what I come fer. You reckon you could tell Lige somethin'?"

Her broomstick back seemed glued up from the wagon seat.

"Well, I reckon I can, if I don't forgit it, and it 's something he ort to know. What is it?"

"Well, the woman claims Elviry – that's that oldest girl of ourn – was born with a veil over her face, so's can see things way ahead. Time and again she's seed this or that warning, and it always come true. Just before Brother Bill died she seed a light in their winder, long about noon, and when she got there – 'twas gone. So she figgered it was a warning, and sure enough, not long after that he dropped dead a-plowing. Well, tother night, she seed a light in that line hickory tree betwixt you and Jim Tittle – half on your side and half on hisn, and when she got up to it – 'twasn't there. Her and her ma claims it's some kind of a warning for one of you, though they don't know which – maybe both."

Sarah turned completely around.

"*I do know*! You bet I'll tell Lige. I felt all along there was going to be trouble betwixt Tittles and us, and now I know it. Thank you for telling us, and thank that woman and girl of yourn, too."

Old man Jimpson and J. P. started down the hill. Sarah turned fondly to the big man, who stared down at muddy feet like a child caught at a cookie jar.

"Why, George, what *air* you a-doing out here without your gum boots on? I never noticed before. I'll bet your feet's soaking wet."

"I reckon they air," he admitted morosely, "but when Mary keeled over, seemed like I *had* to do something fer her."

"You could a-done just as much with your gum boots on, I reckon. Now your rheumatism'll be worse'n ever. What's the matter with Mary?"

"Oh, the Lord only knows. Cold more'n likely. Been bothered with a stitch in her side ever since that rain Sunday."

"I reckon a little medicine'll fix her up, and a physic maybe. 'Tain't as if she'd been sick all her life. Air you all ready to go?"

"I am, and I reckon Mary'll be, agin she changes her dress. Lawrence slushed water all over her other one a-bringing her to. Ben Bragg said something about her or you one a-riding up with him in the Ford."

"He did? That's mighty thoughtful of him, and I reckon it'd be nice for her, her side a-ailing and all, but I don't low the wagon ride'll hurt her none. Anyhow, maybe it'd better hurt a little. I know Mary's a nice girl, but Ben's been so good, and him a single man – there's liable to be talk. I know folks. I'd like to ride with him myself but I expect I'd better drive, me being used to the team. *You're* the one to go, George, bad off as you air, and long as you been ailing. Whatever ailments Mary's got, or me, from some little cold or other, ain't a drop in the bucket compared to yourn. You go, George. That'll be best, I reckon."

Ben was about as talkative as a case of eggs that morning. For one thing, if he took his eyes off the road, the Ford slid into ruts half-way to the hubs. So George rambled on, uninterrupted, of rheumatism, indigestion, headaches, and sizes and shapes of pills he had taken until Ben spoke.

"George, how'd you come to marry Mary in the first place? She ain't from these parts. I thought she come from Iowa."

"She did. Her folks moved down east of here, about ten year ago, I reckon. Ma picked her out for me. Met up with her at some sewing something or other. Liked her the first time she set eyes on her."

"Hmmm."

"I reckon I never will forgit her a-telling me about her. 'George,' says she, 'I seed my girl to-day.' I was long about twenty-seven or eight year old then, and she'd always raised the devil if I so much as looked cross-eyed at a woman, so I figured there was a ketch to it. 'Ma,' says I, 'is she red-headed?' 'Why, yes,' says she, 'how'd you know?' 'Freckled?' says I. 'Yes,' says she, 'but, George, she's awful good.' 'So's a sack of potaters,' says I. Well, she kept on till she had me a-thinking Mary was one of these-here homely, stoop-shouldered, squint-eyed old school-ma'ams, like they generally have at Hog Crick School, and when I first laid eyes on her, sixteen year old, and the purtiest woman or girl ever I seed, you could a-knocked me down with a feather."

"Yeah, but you a-ailing like you air, and all – don't look like you'd a-married."

"Oh, I could do a right smart then, and I played for dances might near every Saturday night. And Pa, he deeded me this-here twenty-five acres – Ma made him do it, I reckon – and helped me build the two room house, and give me a span of mules and a cow, and hogs, and chickens and tools, and I don't know what all, and Ma raised a garden for us that first year, so's we'd have it after we was married. And, we'd a-got along first rate, I reckon, if I'd a-had any health."

The model-T jumped over road and ruts like a good sized jack rabbit, and George arrived at the red brick building long before the others. The doctor was a solemn little man with a dab of hair on lip and chin about the size of a pullet's tail, and spectacled eyes that set so far back that he seemed to have to look harder and longer than most people to make up for it. He opened a little black toolbox, took off his coat and got into a kind of white nightshirt, such as butchers wear. He thumped and pounded the big chest until a voice protested.

"My God, Doc! I cain't stand that – I – "

Strong arms whisked him over on his face. More thumps, and careful listening. Then continued pinching up and down the spine. The dab of hair wagged and a little gully opened down the center of the forehead. George shifted his bulk and babbled on.

"I hain't been no account for years, Doc. Seems like I git worse all the time. As a feller says – "

A cold little glass thing jabbed into his tonsils and stood there to warm up. More tests. More examinations, and the gully in the forehead deepened. George's jaw dropped as his face whitened. His lips moved, but it was no use with the glass thing in his throat. A big tin wish-bone looking thing hooked up his heart to the doctor's ears. One ear was pinched numb and a needle jabbed through it. My God! Would he have to wear medicine ear-rings in his ears the rest of his life?

"Doc, I might as well know the worst now. Ain't there no hope for me?"

The doctor looked at him as if he were trying to focus upon his insides.

"Well, I doubt if we can do anything for you, or that you'll ever be much better, though to tell the truth, I don't think there's much the matter with you but bad teeth and too much medicine. I don't honestly think our treatments would help much, as long as you keep that up."

"Oh, Doc, I couldn't *live* without medicine, I reckon. I've took it ever since I was a baby. Not that I was ailing then, exactly, but marked by a sick cow, like I was, Ma 'lowed she'd be a jump ahead of things and fix it so's I never would be. I reckon I've took a wagon load of medicine in my time."

"Hmmm. Well, there's nothing we can do for a chronic pill-taker. Not that there's much the matter, as I said, but medicine just doesn't work out with treatments. We don't believe in it here, and would feel we were wasting our time – and yours. I expect you might as well go on taking it, though, the way you feel about it. Exercise should help, but I suppose you get plenty of that in your farm work."

"Well, Doc, what I kin stand to do."

"Hmmm."

Mary arrived almost in the screaming stage. Ruts and caked mud had jolted more than they had expected. She held her side as Sarah helped her along, and sucked in little gasps of breath. The doctor took her in for examination as soon as possible and came back with the look of a crawfish about to be used for bait.

"Your wife will have to have an operation right away."

The big man began to moan like a camp meeting.

"What in the name of the Lord'll I do? I cain't set here and let her die!"

"She won't die, if we operate."

"Oh, Lord, she cain't die. But how in God's name can I pay for an operation? I don't know how we'll make it as it is, everything a-going wrong, and me not able to lift a hand, seems like – "

Sarah laid a comforting hand on his shaking shoulder.

"Never mind, George. Hit don't pay to count chickens before the eggs's sot. Let's go in and see what's what, before you take on any more. Maybe 'tain't as bad as you think, and if it is – I reckon the Lord'll send a way."

Chapter 3: George Sells His Body

George was as bewildered as a chicken at a sun eclipse. He stumbled after the brown-dyed sugar sack dress and heavy shoes, that clumped into the side room where the soft voice moaned. It was hard to believe – Mary worse off than he was, long as he'd been ailing. Sarah's lank, brown arm tightened around the crouching figure as if to shut off the sound that bubbled out like vinegar.

"Don't, Mary. Hit might make you worse. You've got to think of George and the children."

Her long red hair had tumbled down, and curtained off her colorless face like a parlor window.

"That's what I am a-thinking about, and there's no hope nohow. The doctor says George won't never be no better. Says they cain't do nothing fer him."

"Well, – there's *other* doctors, I reckon."

"And this operation, Ma Moore, hit's out of the question. We cain't pay for it no way, but – if I don't get well – what'll become of the children – and George? If we'd *only* sold out to the government – maybe I wouldn't a-tore myself to pieces a-drawing water for the mules."

George backed out, eyes blurred and blinking, through the hall to the first open door. In ten years, it was the first time Mary had gone all to pieces. Without her – they would be left like a wagon and no horse. The thought was too much. He braced himself against the wall, head pillowed on big, blue sleeves, and wracking sounds, like the howl of a frightened dog, rippled out. Gradually sounds mixed with words, something like a prayer.

"Oh, Lord, don't let her die! What on earth'd become of us? Five little childern, the shape I'm in – and Lawrence not able to do another stroke. Surely there must be some way."

He hunched over lower and lower, shoulders shaking and head bobbing, until bulking hips bumped into something light and rattly, like a dead snag. Red eyes peered through strings of straw-colored hair, like a small boy who has been spanked and is expecting more. Jaws gaped as he backed away from the hollow-eyed thing that clutched his hind parts.

He was in a long room, a kind of three-ring circus, with skeletons everywhere – and behind and around them, stuffed birds, stuffed bears, stuffed heads with horns that stuck out from the walls! But more skeletons than anything – a whole graveyard, looked like, risen from the dead!

What was it Ben Bragg had said about grave-robbing and body-snatching? Surely these doctors wouldn't –. But it stood to reason they got them somehow. Ben Bragg knew of a fellow that *sold* his body to doctors. They'd given him six months to live – claimed he'd drink himself to death in that time – but he turned teetotaler, and lived twenty or thirty years. (Pity Mary's pappy didn't try it.) Anyhow, if body snatchers got busy the minute a person was laid away, seemed a pity not to get something out of it ahead of time, especially with your woman's life on a see-saw, so to speak. A man's body ought to be worth as much as a good-sized hog, surely – twenty-five or thirty dollars, anyway – according to size maybe. Of course, it would be a sorry funeral, when the time came – no grave, no coffin, no burial – not even a sermon, maybe. But it looked like it might be one way, anyhow, to save Mary.

He turned back to the circus room and the skeleton he had shied away from. There was *something* about the shape of that head, reminded him of a fellow that used to accompany him on the guitar. Same finger missing too, near as he could remember. To think of somebody you knew, maybe – being hacked to pieces. – But to sign an agreement yourself – He felt he had to get out in the air. His forehead felt like grass in the morning before the dew has dried, only hot as a scalded tomato.

He stumped to the steps outside the rambling red building. Across the street Spot whinnied and Dolly gave a sudden snort, as the spring wagon screeched. George looked as if he were about to bray, as his eyes bulged at the over-stuffed bundle that weaved from the back of a mud-colored mule. Like a hen that has just laid an egg, the bundle rose from its nest, poking out wings of arms, and stretching a lump of a neck that swelled as it cackled.

"My name is Jonathon Praytor! I Live in Sullivan County!"

Clump! Down he went, over to the right, almost head first, and the dun-colored heels barely missed him. George's long legs stretched across the macadam road.

"Whoa, Theodore!"

The mule walked on a ways and stopped.

"What you a-doing here, Happy John?"

The bundle stirred and turned over.

"Want to see Mary, George. Want to talk to her."

"Why, Happy John, how'd you know Mary was up here, sick?"

"Sick?"

"Liable to die, the doctor says – "

"Lord, George, it's the hand of God guided me up here to-day. I aimed to go straight to your house, but I had Mathildy's butter and eggs, and I figured I might git a better price up here –"

"Well, Happy John, you'd a-saved ten or fifteen mile, a-coming straight over, but you wouldn't a-seed Mary. Maybe never would. Doctor says she cain't git well, 'thout she's operated on."

Happy Jonn shivered and turned over.

"Damn the doctors! All alike! Ain't satisfied less they're a-cuttin' on somethin' or somebody. I thought these-here was rub-doctors!"

George blinked at the red building.

"They air, but they say Mary's beyond rubbing. Want to go in and see her, now, Happy John? I'll help you, if you say so – "

His face seemed about to turn inside out.

"No, for God's sake! Damn doctors's liable to start right in cutting me, the shape I'm in. I'm drunk – see?"

"I reckon might near anybody can see you're drunk. Hit's a wonder to me you didn't kill yourself, the way you dove under Theodore's hoofs, and if you had, I reckon Mary'd just a-flickered out."

Happy John's mouth sagged to a half circle.

"I know it, George. She always thought a heap of me and I ain't never been the right kind of pappy to her, or none of 'em fur as that goes – drunk, no-count son-of-a-gun –"

George eyed the big building like a truant school boy.

"You ortn't to drink the way you do, Happy John, hard up as you air, and it a worrying Mary and all."

Above the round stomach the right hand raised like a flag on a mail box.

"That's all passed now, I'm a-going to git me a steady job, soon as I sober up, and make up for the way I've done. And I'll never touch another drop, so help me!"

"You reckon you kin stick to that, Happy John? 'Pears to me like Mary says you've promised it before."

Solemnly the right hand raised.

"I mean it this time. Tother was talk – nothin' but talk. But I'm a changed man, now. I'm through drinkin' – long as I live – so help me!"

"Well, Happy John, it'll please Mary a heap, that is if we can figure out how to pay for this operation somehow and she lives to see it."

The lolling head lifted unsteadily.

"Listen, George, – *I'll* pay fer it. Tell 'em to go ahead and operate, and

I'll foot the bill, soon as I git a job. I don't take much stock in cuttin' or cuttin' doctors – but if Mary has to be cut to live – cut her by all means!"

George's thick sole kicked the edge of the pavement.

"I don't 'low they'll do nothing, Happy John, – without *down* money. I've got to get back and figure things out myself."

Happy John had the hopeless look of a pig bogged down in mire.

"No, don't go, George! Don't leave me like this, with a houseful o' doctors ready to pounce on me –"

George turned from building to bundle, like a bird watching two cats.

"I've got to, Happy John. I tell you, Mary's in bad shape, though I reckon you're worse off yourself than common. Never seed a feller before, so drunk he was plum down on doctors."

"Always *been* down on 'em! Never had a doctor in my life, excepting for the woman, when her childern was born, or my old pappy before me!"

George's mouth opened wider and wider.

"I reckon Ma couldn't last no time, 'thout doctors. Leastways, she 'lows I couldn't –"

Happy's round face reddened as it reared from his stomach.

"I know your ma thinks a heap o' doctors, and they're all right in their place, but their place ain't around me.

"'Twas a doctor hisself set me agin 'em in the first place, telling of grave-robbing, – draggin corpses home under his coat, their hands tied around his neck, and this, that and t'other."

George squatted, neck outstretched like a huge grasshopper, about to jump.

"You sure that ain't one of Ben Bragg's tales?"

"No, this come straight from Illinois – first hand. Doctor told Pap when I was a boy. I heerd him myself. Said he was a-whittlin' on a corpse one night – young woman he'd dug up – buried that day – and all of a sudden she let out a sigh, and hollered for help. Said he never was skeered so bad in his life. But he worked with her, and brung her to, and she lived and afterwards married and raised a family. He claimed she'd been buried alive, but I claim, – her not cold yit, and being chopped to sausage meat – she was simply *skeered* to resurrection! Anyhow, just goes to show what a itch they're in to be eternally cuttin'."

George was getting more and more wiggly, as his bulk expanded upward.

"Yes, but, Happy John, Ben Bragg says there's a law now –"

"Shucks! Law or no law, doctors have to practice cutting now, same as always, don't they? Listen, you recollect Lem Webbstringer – used to play the guitar with one finger gone? Well, after he was laid to rest, I dreamed I seed doctors hacking him all to pieces. Time and agin, I dreamed that same dream. Many a time, I've thought to dig into his grave myself, out of curiosity, but I never did. Anyhow, I'm dead sure his coffin's empty. They've dragged him out and cleaned his bones long ago, sure as I'm a-settin' here. I've always wondered how skeletons come to be so white. Reckon they *boil* the meat off?"

George looked as if his mouth were fixing to rip.

"Oh, Lord, I don't know, Happy John, but listen! If you believed way down inside you, that a woman was busted loose some'ers, so's she couldn't get well, 'thout being cut and sewed up, wouldn't you let the doctors do it – even if you was agin cuttin', and it meant a turrible hardship fer you?"

The split in the red face became a triangle upside down.

"You mean *Mary's* busted inside. Oh, good God, George, don't let her die! Tell 'em to do all they can!"

A lump that he could not swallow joggled up and down George's throat like a bubble in a bottle. To think of being cut up warm, like a chicken – not even dead, maybe –But Mary in there moaning and groaning, maybe dying –. He just had to do something.

"Happy John, do you reckon it's got to the point where doctors ransack a body's grave, soon as they're laid to rest – whether they're bargained for, or not?"

"Well, I wouldn't want to say yes, and I wouldn't want to say no. But I do know every time I go through the cemetery here lately – seems like there's more and more graves sort of scooped-out lookin' in the middle, and a body cain't help putting two and two together."

George kept fidgeting as he stared at the red building.

"I've got to git back, Happy John. Mary's turrible sick. If you think you're sober enough to stay on old Theodore, I'll help you on before I go. Air you?"

"Well, George, I don't know whether I am or not, but I'd a-heap sight ruther take my chance with Theodore than to wait out here, for God knows what. Doctors with knives is devils. Grave-robbing and cutting up dead people is bad enough, but I cain't bear to think of 'em jabbing out my poor insides, and me too drunk to know anything about it –"

Fluid oozed from his eyes and nose and his face puckered like a paper sack. George hoisted his bulk from pavement to saddle, and turned to the big red building. Half a block away, the wavering voice punctuated each near-fall with a rise in pitch.

"My name is Jonathon Praytor!"

He almost went over, but pulled himself up and over to the other side, as the mule clumped westward, around the corner toward home.

As his heavy shoes dragged across the street, George felt as if his insides were squeezed dry. For years he had dreamed of doing something for Mary – Lawrence, too, maybe, – something big, to show how much he cared. Something maybe they would never know, nobody but him, but *now* – could he go through with it? At the head of the steps, the little man with the black funnel beard, and eyes half way back in his head, grabbed him.

"Where've you been? Your wife asking for you and your mother looking everywhere – Don't you realize –?"

"Well, I reckon I realize, Doc, but I don't know what in the Lord's name to do –"

The beard jerked out like an accusing finger.

"Do? There's only one thing *to* do!"

"Air you dead sure about that, Doc? Sure she cain't git well, 'thout you operate?"

"Positive. Nobody could live long, the condition she's in. We don't operate here, except as a last resort."

"You mean that, Doc?"

"It's her *life*, man, her only chance. Understand?"

It was as if the moon had come out bright and clear, all of a sudden, from behind a cloud. If Mary could stand being cut up alive, surely he could stand it, dead. What would it matter? Cutting sow-belly in chunks didn't make a hog squeal.

"Listen, Doc, I've got to talk to you first. Do they buy bodies here?"

"What?"

"Bodies – dead bodies –"

The black beard jerked like a chicken with its head off.

"*She's not dead*! We want to *save* her!"

"I know it, Doc. That's what I'm a-gittin' at. Don't doctors have to have bodies to cut on, here, for new skeletons and such? And couldn't a feller sell his'n, before he dies, if his wife's on the pint o' death, and he ain't got a nickel to his name?"

"You – you mean – you want to sell *your* body?"

"Well, Doc, I figured, sizable as it is, it ort to bring top-notch price –"

"Look here, this isn't a *body* market. We don't make a *practice* of buying dead bodies –"

"Well, Doc, I don't know as it makes any difference to me, whether you do or don't, long as you buy mine. I ain't got no busted bones nor nothing, and I don't reckon you'd have so long to wait for it, neither, – would you?"

"Mmmm. I couldn't say. It might be forty or fifty years, or such a matter. Barring bad teeth and eyes, there's not much wrong with you, except you've been medicined to death. We don't go in for medicine much here, but it's not out and out poison. I *don't* think whoever sold you pills and tonics by the cartload did right, to you or your children after you."

"Well, Doc, I expect Ma had considerable to do with it. She's a powerful believer in medicine – always was. But, 'bout this body business, will you buy it?"

"Why – uh – I don't know – I suppose it *would* contribute to science, but –"

"Listen, Doc. You said yourself Mary couldn't get well 'thout a operation. I've got to save her, Doc, somehow or other, and selling my body's the only way I know."

"You *honestly* think you *want* to do this?"

"Oh, Lord, Doc, – I don't *want* to. I cain't hardly bear the thought of being cut up like a pig, soon as I'm dead, and if Ma was to find out, I reckon it'd kill her. But I got to save Mary. All I ask is – be *sure* I'm dead. I want that in writing. And cain't we fix it somehow, so's nobody'll know – Ma nor Mary nor none of 'em?"

The eyes seemed to sink deeper, as the hand stroked chin and beard.

"I think – possibly we could. Your mother thought maybe she could pay something, Under the circumstances, I doubt if we could allow more than fifty dollars for your body."

"Fifty dollars? Oh, Doc, that'll save her, *surely*."

"Well, I think so, with what your mother can furnish. You see your wife has to stay here in the hospital a while to heal. We'll go in and talk to the old doctor."

They filed across the hall and down the circus room. Shiny eyes stared, tangled horns pointed, and skeletons along the way, grinned a welcome. Beyond the menagerie was a cubby-hole, where a little old man with a handful of cotton waving from his chin, looked up from colored pictures of human insides. The black beard ducked and mumbled something in his ear, as sharp eyes stared over spectacle rims. Little scared shivers trickled up and down George's backbone. More talk. More mumbling.

The old doctor was writing something on a paper, and pushed it to

George to sign. Blurred eyes made out most of it – something about a body going to such and such doctors at such and such a party's certified death – and a wabbly hand scribbled a signature. The bunch of cotton bent back over stomachs and hearts and the others wound back through skeletons to the little room where Mary lay.

"Oh, George, where've you been?"

It was like the wail of an animal, trapped and wounded.

"Well, Happy John come by for one thing. Fell off his mule –"

Sarah pushed up sagging shoulders.

"Drunk, I'll bet!"

"Yeah, he was. And after I talked to him a little, I helped him on his mule."

"George, Happy John's too heavy for you to lift. You'll be in the same wagon with Mary, if you keep on."

George's big hands fingered his muscles.

"Well, Ma, I didn't seem to feel the strain much. After that I was a-talking to the doctors about Mary's operation –"

Above the brown shirt waist, sharp eyes softened.

"Don't you worry no more, George. It'll upset your stomick. I can pay for Mary's operation myself – twenty-five or thirty dollars. I had it laid by for a coal-oil stove. Mommy give it to me, but I guess the stove can wait."

The crouched figure on the narrow bench moaned and turned.

"The only thing is, Ma Moore, that'll barely cover the operation. If we cain't pay for hospital care and move me right afterwards, the stitches'll bust out, more'n likely, and the money'll be gone for nothing. And what good'll that do?"

Troubled eyes stared from a nest of lines.

"Is it true, Doc? Do we have to have *more* money for hospital keer?"

Fingers smoothed black bristles as bushy eyebrows twitched.

"Well, ma'am, – I've been talking it over with the old doctor, and we've decided –everything considered – we can arrange to keep her here until she's able to ride home. You see – this case is not exactly ordinary, – and all things taken into account, – the benefits we may derive from all developments, – *should*, in years to come, I think – take care of – hospital expenses."

Sarah beamed from the doctor to George's baggy overalls.

"That's mighty kind of you, Doc, George, did you hear? You've got nothing to worry about now. With Mary a-getting well and all, and nothing a-hanging over you from now on, so to speak, – I just believe your nervousness'll get a heap better – don't you?"

George had a kind of hooked catfish look as he stared toward the hall door.

"Well, Ma, – somehow – I cain't say I feel very hopeful."

Chapter 4 : Mary's Homecoming

In the front yard of a two-room house, an eight-year-old farmer plowed corn. His red hair and ragged blue shirt sleeves kept trying to fly away, and the wind whipped up his patched overall legs, and puffed them out like sausages.

"Git up, Sampson! Whoa, Sampson!" he shouted.

A knotted twine string thrown over his shoulder hitched horse and driver, and hands stretched out to guide a fine new plow. The temperamental horse divided his interests between a natural curiosity of everything and the sudden galloping instincts of derby winners.

"Sampson, if you break this harness agin, I'll skin you. Leather costs money. I 'low I could buy a wagon load of medicine for the harness you broke a'ready!"

He paused to wipe away perspiration.

"Old woman, you got that washing done yit?"

Two little housekeepers brushed up rooms and rebuilt walls, which fluttered away with each gust of wind. Dyed blue sugar-sack dresses blew over their heads like umbrellas turned wrong side out, and they kept modestly smoothing them down and wiping moist noses with the backs of their hands. The older one turned to the plowman.

"No, 'cause the stove pipe keeps falling down, and gitting soot all over.

Takes me and grandma all the time a-cleaning!"

"Why don't you git grandpa to fix it?"

Grandpa's short legs wabbled under a leaky pan of water that trickled over his bare toes. He needed a handkerchief.

"Cause I'm a-gidding wader and thigs. That's why!" he managed between sniffles.

The plowman turned back to the woman.

"Well, fix it, somehows! You cain't let washing pile up with a houseful of sick younguns. Why don't you keep 'em in bed?"

"They won't stay."

A baby just able to walk balanced himself with waving hands as he toddled through the leaves. He appeared to have streamed molasses from his chin down, and tried to wipe it off on bare ground. Some of his undergarments had fallen to his ankles and dragged black. Every two steps he toppled over, but pushed himself up and started again. Finally he rebelled against his shackles.

"Waa!" he yelled, kicking where he lay.

A mother who could barely lift him carried him into the little house and covered him up with blankets.

"Now, stay in bed, childern, all of you. You're that sick, you might die. Besides your mommy's got to wash. Grandpa, did you git the wood?"

A small freckled hand indicated a neat pile of sticks, as a snub nose sniffled.

"That ain't half enough. Git a plenty. There's a storm coming."

A pungent smell pushed from the door of the two-room house.

"Oh, Lord!" wailed the plowman. "I forgot all about grandma's 'taters, and I reckon she'll skin me!"

He galloped into the house and the horse promptly began rooting up peonies. A sudden cyclone blew the little house into the air and the blankets with it. Grandpa threw his sticks to the wind, and catching one of the blankets, tied it to part of Sampson's harness. The pig raced about the yard with the white square sailing behind him. Another flopped from Grandpa's fists.

"Whee!" he yelled,

Two housekeeper-plasterers took up an old stub broom and a broken rake, and waited for calm. A kind of train sound chugged into the yard and stopped. They all raised their heads like puzzled sheep, as Sampson scuttled around the house with a snort. Then they plowed through the leaves and climbed on the fender, the baby toddling after.

"Mommy!" they whooped.

She smiled weakly as she kissed and fondled them.

"You ortn't to be outside, children, windy as it is. You'll be down in bed agin. What you doing with Mark's clean diapers, Hubert?"

He sniffed and kicked the fender. A touseled red head popped out from the door.

"Mommy, I burnt the 'taters, but I et all the black part, so I-don't reckon they'll taste much. Do you, Mommy? "

She smiled.

"Maybe not. What's that pig doing in the yard?"

"I'll put him up. The younguns wanted to play farmer, and you might near have to have a horse –"

A bushy haired man climbed from the Ford and opened the door where the children huddled.

"Better get her inside, I reckon. Your ma's in bad shape and she's pretty weak yet. Open the door for me, one of you, will you?"

They all lunged forward and held the door wide open while he carried her in, like she was a baby, or maybe a sack of flour. Lawrence jogged back from the pig pen.

"Ben," he said, "I b'lieve you like Mommy better'n you do Pappy."

"Why?" asked Ben with a grin.

"Pappy's sick a heap, but you never did carry him."

"Your pa's might near too heavy to carry, but most any feller could carry your ma."

"Feller?" asked Georgie, grinning, and then sang out, "Mommy's got a feller!"

"Bobby god feller! Bobby god feller!" echoed Hubert, punctuating with sniffles that failed to clear his nose.

Little Vida put her finger to her mouth and the baby stared.

"*Two* fellers!" corrected Georgie suddenly, on second thought.

Lawrence turned on her with the scorn of a school teacher.

"She's got one feller and no more. And Pappy's it."

"Where is George?" asked the woman.

"Over to Grandma's. His stomick was upset, and he never had no pills, so she took him over to make some sasafras tea. Looks like them a-coming yander."

"Then I might as well be getting along home," said Ben. "There's considerable I ort to be doing."

She nodded. Lawrence followed him to the door.

"Ben, – don't forgit that crow you're a-going to git me, maybe, when spring comes!"

A plod of hoofs and a grating of wheels stopped outside. Spot whinnied as Blackie announced her own arrival. At the door a sunbonnet appeared and Sarah pushed in followed by Lige, with George straggling in the rear.

"Why, Mary, we thought we'd git back before you got here. Took a little longer'n we figured, George being sicker than common, and we brung old Blackie. How air you?"

"Pretty well, Ma Moore, thank you."

The children flattened against the bed.

"You're a-looking first rate, though a mite washed-out like," Lige commented between puffs.

"Yes," put in George, "better'n common. Looks like cuttin' agrees with you. It was real nice of Ben to bring you. I'd a-done it, if I'd a-been able, but I reckon that Ford of his'n was better'n jolting over the ruts with a team. I don't know as I could a-stood it myself."

"What's been the matter?"

"Oh, just about everything. I've had rheumatism all the time, and now my stomick's set in agin, a-giving me Hail Columbia."

"George," Sarah put in, "you'd better set down, the way you been a-feeling."

"Why, I plum forgot my own ailment, I was so glad to see Mary." His bulk weighted down one side of the bed.

"Good Lord Almighty!" Lige choked with smoke. "I never seed such a woman. The way you baby him, I'll never git at that fence."

"Now, Lige, shet up! I know what I'm a-doing. Anyhow, you'd a-better killed that snake last spring like I said. It'd a-saved a heap o' worrying."

"What snake? What in the name of the Lord air you talking about?"

"That snake that wiggled out from under that log by your pa's tombstone, about corn-planting time. 'Twas the first one we seed. That's why I wanted you to kill it, but you said 'twas too little, and first thing I knowed, it'd got away."

A long whiff of smoke.

"Good Lord Almighty, Sary, that wasn't much bigger than a good sized fish worm. A body'd feel plum mean and heartless, a-cutting off its head, no bigger'n what it was. Besides, 'twasn't nothing but a garter snake."

"That don't make a bit of difference! It's the *first snake* you see in the *spring* that counts. If you don't kill it, you won't git the best of your enemies. I've heard that time and agin!"

"Well, a body orn't to have no enemies, nohow."

She punched at the fire, and shoved in part of an old post.

"Well, they do. Everybody does – all that I know of, anyhow. If you hain't got none, you're different from most. A body'd think you had a whole drove of 'em, the way you been a-worrying and stewing over that graveyard fence, here lately –"

"*Hogs* ain't a body's enemies, air they? It's *them* I'm a-worrying about."

"Well, if you had right good sense, you'd be a-worrying about Jim Tittle, the way he's been a-acting – specially after what old man Jimpson said. Mark my words, before you get through with him, he'll do as much damage as airy five hogs."

"Oh, Sary, Jim ain't as bad as you make him out to be. He always done what he ort till this right o' way business come up. I wisht he'd pay fer it, and git the deed signed myself, but I reckon we'll have to wait till he's a mind to do it. You're just riled cause he said we ort to be a-doing our own work, and let George do his'n, him as stout agin as airy one of us, – and I reckon he's right –"

"Now, Lige, shut up a-talking that way. George ain't able to set up half the time – let alone do all this work. I guess I know how stout he is or ain't a heap better than Jim Tittle. The idy! If I'd a-been on the best of terms with him before, I wouldn't be now, him a-talking that away about poor George. Anyhow, I'm worried about my turkeys. I wisht you'd a killed that snake."

"Oh, that's all tomfoolery."

"Well, I don't know as I believe in it myself, but I don't like to take no chances." She swung open the cupboard doors. "Mary, is there anything you can think of, that you can eat, you'd like me to make?"

"No, Ma Moore. I don't reckon I'd better eat to amount to anything for a while."

"How about you, George? You been a-setting there, saying nothing all this time."

George collapsed on the bed, stretched out both legs.

"Oh, Ma, now on top of everything else, I got one of them awful headaches – one of them kind that clamps down on your head, like a big hand a squeezing your brains out. I don't know whether I can eat anything or not, but – I reckon I can."

She turned from the cupboard, her head wagging.

"You poor boy. I reckon the Lord knows what he's a-doing, but it does look like he just tries hisself, a-visiting misery and suffering on you. I just hope you can eat. You better lay down in tother room, and git your strength back. Maybe you can eat."

He made his way to the bedroom door. The children were all shouting at once.

"And what do my little darlin's want?"

"Cake, Grandma! Yellow cake with raisins."

"Cookie! Cookie!"

"Pie. Custard pie!" sniffed Hubert, well pleased that one side of his nose had thawed out, and little Mark made some unintelligible noise.

"Bless their little hearts! Wait'll your mommy can have some."

The tin lid clinked against the side of the meal jar. "Lawrence, don't you reckon you'd better git some corn ground? We're might near out of meal, and your mommy ort to have gruel this first week anyhow."

He was on his hands and knees absorbed in a cricket with one leg.

"Wait till I put Lazurus where nodbody'll step on him. He's the smartest cricket you ever seed, but somethin' got one of his legs, so I kinda look after him. Him and Sampson's all us kids's got."

"Well, hurry. I ain't right sure we got enough for dinner."

"We ain't got no sack, Grandma. I busted out the only one as'd hold meal, tother day."

She turned to the whiskers and smoke.

"Lige, you take him with the team. The mules ortn't to be rid nohow, lame as they air, and you ain't unhitched yet. Anyhow, they ain't got no sack, so stop and get one of our'n."

The smoke thinned as Lige jerked out his pipe.

"Good Lord Almighty! Why cain't George do it? He don't do nothing."

She bridled like a hen with young chicks.

"Now, Lige, I'll tend to this. *You ain't* done a lot of things neither, and you ain't got George's excuse. You ain't fixed that sorghum pan, and you ain't got the corn in, and – you *ain't found out* what's a-going with my turkeys. No telling where they air, the way Jim Tittle's been a-talking and acting, here lately, and us gone all the time, like we air."

"Aw, Sary, Jim hain't a-bothering nothing, just a-driving through like he's a-doing –"

"Well, he's a-going through mighty often. You never did have a lick of sense about knowing who to trust and who not to. Just because Jim and his brother air the homeliest two the Lord ever made, might near, don't mean they make up fer it in goodness. It does look like the Almighty could a-give 'em something or other, but He never done it, fer as I can see. Anyhow, I say and I always did say, Jim Tittle nor his brother, nary one, ain't half as good as you think they air, or they let on to be."

"Well, whether they air or ain't, George ain't helpless. He's got eyes, and he can drive same as me. If I got time to do that, I got time to fix that grave yard fence!"

"Now, Lige, dry up. As sick as George's been, he ain't able to do nothing, not till he feels like it. And Mary, here, just back from the hospital, and you a-talking like you begrudge the little you do fer 'em!"

"I don't begrudge nothing I do for Mary, and you know it, or the youn-guns either. But George's abler to work than me, a heap sight. I'm old. And, Sary, I tell you I got to git that fence fixed before the pigs git in. It's a-worrying me to death."

"Now, Lige, go on and take Lawrence, like I said, and see about them turkeys too. I'm a-aiming to take the money I git fer 'em, and put it with some more I got laid by, and seed George's land fer him, in timothy see, or clover. I might have to build it up with fertilizer. Hit's plum wore out, ain't it, Mary?"

"I rekcon it's wore out, all right, but 'twon't raise nothing nohow, 'thout somebody tends it."

"Well, you'll be a-feeling all right by spring, Mary, and I hope to the Lord George does. Anyhow I want the land built up and George's tools fixed up, if we can. I think it'd sort of put new life in him. He ain't been hisself since Mary's operation. And, Lige, I told you I'd help you with that fence, and fix the graves too, soon as Mary's able for us to leave her. I reckon nothing'll happen till then!"

"Yes, but if the hogs git into the graves and root the carcasses all over creation, it'll be too late then. Come on, Lawrence!"

"Can I drive, Grandpa?"

"Oh, I reckon."

From the top of a hill overlooking Lige's farm, Lawrence, who had confined all previous remarks to Spot and Dolly, pointed to a bug-like thing that crawled through Lige's corn field.

"What's that thing, Grandpa? 'Tain't a worm, is it?"

Lige shaded his eyes with one hand as he stared.

"Well, I'll be – I reckon Sary's right."

"What is it, Grandpa?"

"Hit's – a skunk."

"Skunks catch chickens, don't they? You reckon that's what's gone with Grandma's turkeys?"

"I wouldn't be a dang bit surprised, you're right."

"They kill skunks, don't they – some folks?"

"I'll probably kill this'n, with your grandma egging me on."

"Air they good to eat, Grandpa?"

"No. Ain't good for nothing, 'cepting their hides, maybe, and skunk-oil."

At the house, Lige got out a red and blue lettered sack, and puttered around somewhere, while Lawrence chunked it full of yellow ears from the crib. All the way to the mill and back, the old man chewed, spit and sputtered – about skunks.

When they opened the door of the two-room house, potato soup and a pan of yellow custard steamed out to meet them. Lawrence sniffed, as Lige grunted in under the heavy meal sack.

"Mmmm – something smells good. Mommy, might near everything's happening to-day!"

She shifted her head on the pillow. "What, Lawrence?"

"What, Lawrence?" echoed all the children.

"The dam's about to bust! Ain't it, Grandpa?"

"They're afeard of it. The last rain soaked something loose, some'ers. Anyhow, there's men a-working on it."

"If it busts, Mommy, the mill cain't run, and the river'll be all over everywhere! Won't it Grandpa?"

"Oh, I reckon they can fix it, someway. They're a-aiming to, anyhow, though I don't reckon it'll ever be any account till it's plum built over. Pity they cain't do that."

"And that ain't all," went on Lawrence. "The paddle wheel's might near gone, took, on the old mill. Ain't it, Grandpa?"

"I reckon they can fix it for a while yit, though I don't know for how long. Maybe they ort to a-let the government had it."

The tall woman sprinkled salt into bubbling water, and stirred in meal. Her head wagged over the stove.

"I wouldn't want no outsiders a-coming in, but – 'twouldn't seem like the same place, 'thout no mill and dam, – and where'd a-body get his corn ground? They been there ever since I can remember, both of 'em, and that's a long time."

Lige was pacing back and forth like a caged bear.

"They'll be there a long time yit, more'n likely. I got something to worry about, a heap sight more important than the mill."

"What?" asked Sarah, sipping the gruel for salt.

"It's a skunk," explained Lawrence. "I was saving that for last."

"It's a skunk by the name of Jim Tittle!"

"Where'd you see him, Lige?"

Her voice was low, as if they talked of a corpse.

"Over on the place. Lawrence seed him first, a-cutting cat-a-slaunch-ways through my corn, so's he ruins the whole field. I'll keep him out, if I have to go to law!"

"Did you say anything to him to-day, Lige?"

"Yes, I did. I went down and talked to him whilst Lawrence filled the corn sack. I told him I'd shoot him if he didn't stay out."

"What'd he say?"

"He said, 'Shoot and be damned!' Said he wasn't a-going no three or four miles out of his way to please nobody!"

"See anything of my turkeys, Lige?"

"Nary a one, but the old gobbler. Looked half dead, like somebody'd set the dogs on him."

"They'd better not –"

The iron spoon stirred and scraped as she went on.

"Lige, I expect you'd better sell him a road through. We're a-going to git into trouble, if you don't."

"I'd sell him a road in a minute, and he knows I will, but he wants it cat-a-slaunch-ways, like he's going now! He'll either have to buy it straight, or go by the devil's lane. I'm danged if I keer which, but he ain't a-going through my corn!"

"Lige, you ort to see somebody as knows the law, Andrew Moore, maybe. There might be trouble, real trouble. I reckon that Jimpson girl didn't see them lights for nothing. You might lose all you got!"

"Dang right they'll be trouble! A body don't need flickering lights to see that. He was a-setting there, a resting by the graveyard. What business did he have around Pappy's grave? More'n likely I'll kill him yet, before I'm through with him!"

"Now, Lige, don't talk like that. And don't lift a hand, no matter what happens. I don't want to git mixed up with the law. I'd like to know what become of my turkeys, though –"

"Turkeys, thunderation! Them pigs is a fixing to root up them graves, anytime now. I seed tracks ever which-a-ways, all around, – and nine chances to ten it's Tittle's hogs as well as our'n. I don't care what you say, Sary, I ain't a-coming over here *airy other time* till that fence's fixed – 'thout somebody's a-watching the graveyard. If George won't do his own work, he can at least set, and he can *set* down yander as well as here –."

He slammed the back door. George stared after him, open-mouthed, and turned helplessly to Sarah.

"Well, Ma, God knows I want to do what little I kin, that is, what I can stand to do, and if you say so, and I'm able to git down there, – *I'll* watch the hogs out, through chore time, that is, on nice days, when I ain't ailing no worse'n common –"

Sarah turned to him, tight-lipped.

"Well, George, I don't want your ailments aggravated none, above all things. But the way Jim Tittle's a-acting, no telling what'll happen, so I reckon your pa's right to git at that fence, soon as we kin. And if you *do* feel like setting down there a few mornings, till Lige can git the post holes dug – whilst we do up the chores, that is – I wisht you would. Maybe your pa can carry you down a chair, and a piller, to set on –"

Chapter 5 : George Watches the Hogs

"Buffalo Girls" trickled on and on like a leaky bucket till it sort of ran out and stopped. The fiddle lowered from chin to lap as George smoothed out pillow and quilt, and hitched the old rocker farther into the shade. He pushed his oats shock of a head deeper into the pillow and stared at the unfenced graveyard through half-shut eyes.

It was lonesome enough to have to sit and watch this graveyard day after day, and think of the nine or ten laid to rest here, no telling how long ago, or what shape they were in now. But to always get back to one's own burying, or rather the burying he would never have, was like a pig watching the ones ahead sledged and scalded – knowing it was only a matter of time for him. Ailing like he was, he might go any minute now, and when he thought of how Sarah would take things, he just about went all to pieces. Maybe she'd have the preacher all spoke for, and his Sunday outfit laid out ready to put him away – and here would come the rub-doctors! She would more than likely go out of her mind. And, even if she didn't, come Decoration Day, she would have to drive thirty miles, both ways, unless the roads were good enough for the short cut, and nine chances to ten they wouldn't be – to get to stick a bunch of "pionies" or "flags" in amongst his ribs.

And still, a body couldn't hardly blame the rub-doctors either. They hadn't come to him in the first place. He'd gone to them. But they came now. Came every few days, trying to buy up land in the hills, all they could get a hold of – seemed like. Claimed they wanted to raise angus cattle, and have summer cabins and the Lord knew what all – maybe build a reservoir themselves, and fix up the old mill and dam like the government wanted. But the more George thought things over, the more he concluded it was just an excuse to keep tab on him, so that he couldn't possibly get away – if he got too crazy afraid, and tried to skip the country. Ben Braid [sic] said the doctors never did get that old man that sold his body and then lived so long afterward. Said when time came to die, he disappeared, and nobody knew what became of him – not even relation. And the doctors looked all over and wrote just about everywhere – but had to give up. More than likely that was what made these rub-doctors so leary-like.

Funny the rub-doctors hadn't tried to do anything for him – even before the body business came up. Andrew Moore, or rather Andrew's woman, claimed they'd cured this one and that one time again. Said some girl or woman hadn't walked for fifteen years, that is, without crutches, and one day some of them called in a rub-doctor, when her father wasn't there – he wouldn't allow a rub-doctor on the place – and first thing anybody knew, he'd rubbed her into walking. Told her to throw away her crutches and walk, and she did.

Then there was Andrew's woman's uncle. He was getting along in years, and was chopping down a tree, when it fell on him and broke his neck. First one doctor and then another was called in and they all claimed nobody could do a thing for him. Said a body couldn't live with his neck broke and they might as well save their money. But they finally sent for a rub-doctor and the man got well and lived ten or fifteen years. Had to keep his neck in a potato poultice for a long time, and take no telling how many rub-treatments, but he got so he could sit up and look around, and walk just like anybody, though his neck always was stiff.

But either they couldn't do anything for him – or wouldn't. Didn't even try. Maybe they didn't aim for him to get well. Some said, some of them could sort of look ahead and see things, like Elviry Jimpson. Maybe they did. Maybe they saw this body business coming, and didn't want him any too healthy. No telling.

Or maybe they knew about him being marked like he was, and saw it was no use. Didn't seem to be any mark-doctors, though plenty of people were marked. Not cow-marked, though, like he was. He was about the only one. Somebody'd fed their cow glass – the cow-doctor said – and she afterwards died. And his mother had watched her, and worried about her, and carried her water and all, till it was no wonder he was marked. Seemed as if all his life he'd never felt comfortable unless he were sitting or lying.

Of course there were lots of folks worse marked than he was. Snakes seemed to mark the worst. One woman had a regular fight with a snake, and when her baby was born, it tapered off like a snake's tail from the waist down, and the rest was like a human, only there was a hole in the top of its head, and it died and the woman too. Another woman had twins, with the top halves out and out snakes, and they kept running out their tongues at people and hissing, till the neighbors called a kind of judgement-meeting and smothered them to death with a featherbed.

Six or eight of these graves were children. Maybe some of them had been marked to death, so to speak. Might even be the ones that were smothered, though nobody'd said so. Even so, maybe they were better off than he was. They had a grave, and their bodies were buried.

Funny, all the things that pass through your head when you're sitting by a graveyard. It seemed though, no matter what he thought about, he soon got back to burying, and his own trouble. If he kept on thinking about it, he might go out of his mind, and maybe it would be a good thing if he did. Old man Jimpson knew of a fellow, and Ben Bragg too, that got in some kind of trouble, so he had to deed his property to his brother to save it, and the brother wouldn't deed it back. The fellow had been hurt in the head a short time before, so he got himself sent off to the insane asylum, and when he got back the law struck out the deed. Claimed he wasn't in his right mind when he made it. To hear old man Jimpson and J.P. tell about it, the asylum wasn't such a bad place to stay – sounded real nice for winter, and might work out all around. He hitched his chair closer to a tree and squinted at the weed-grown mounds.

Old Tim might be solid rock now – if he was anything. Seemed like the rock kind. Ben Bragg knew of somebody that had moved some graves once. Said when they opened coffins, some of them had kept like strawberry preserves – as fresh as when they were put away – but after the air got to them a little while, they crumbled into nothing. Said one or two had turned into rock, and took eight or ten men to lift them.

Time and again Lige had talked of moving Old Tim to the Jim Cullop cemetery, or the one at Hell's Holler, where the grave would be kept up and the body safe – after he was gone. But he never did. Said he hated to dig into it – after all these years – with probably nothing left of Old Tim now anyhow.

George became more and more fidgety as he mulled things over. What did Lige mean? Surely he didn't think rub-doctors had got hold of him, nosing around like they were, here lately. They didn't have any bargain with old Tim, surely – though maybe they didn't need bargains. Maybe they just helped themselves, like Happy John said they did with Lem Webbstringer. But Lige didn't know or think or care anything about body-snatching, or put any faith in it, more than likely, if he did. He thought old Tim had just rotted out, and like as not, he had.

"Why, George, what you a-doing down here?"

George had settled himself back in his pillow and closed his eyes, so that he had to blink several times before he could make out who it was, much less say anything.

"Why, Mr. Jimpson, *Pa* wanted me to watch the hogs out of the graveyard till him and Ma could git the fence up. 'Lowed they might git at the carcasses."

Old man Jimpson looked at George as if he thought he didn't have good sense.

"Why, George, – airy one of these graves is ten or twelve year old anyhow, and most of 'em considerable more. And there's nothing' left in 'em in all that time, or any time after the first three or four days, or week or such a matter, – that is, if they're where they ort to be. How long did it take the Lord to resurrect, and why should He want us to do different? You're just a-wasting your time, the way I look at it. Has Lige been down yit?"

George had his mind on resurrection. "No, but they'll come – him and Ma both, agin they git the chores done."

"Well, I'll try to git back, if I kin."

Old man Jimpson straggled off, and George pushed back into pillow and quilt. Old man Jimpson stuck to it that the body rose, the same as the soul, like Christ Himself. Said if Old Tim was saved, there'd been nothin there all this time. Sarah said he wasn't saved. Said there was a regular downpour up to might near the time he died and before he was buried. But the *first twenty-four hours* after he breathed his last, it *didn't rain a drop*. But in any case, if there was even a particle of him left now, he must be as completely crumbled as the bottom of a rotted-out post.

That was odd in a way though, old man Jimpson's notion of resurrection – not like most people's anyway. He claimed the body went right up with the soul – three or four days, or a week or two, after it was laid to rest. Said the grave just opened-up, unbeknownst to anybody but angels and such, and away would sail the body, straight up to the Almighty with the soul a-sitting on top. Said that was why so many graves sunk in, and settled down like, after so long a time. Sounded reasonable, in a way.

Christ rose in three days – body and all. The Bible said so. Went straight to the Almighty, just like [when they] put him away – nailprints and all. Maybe He aimed for the rest of us to do the same, when time came to die. Maybe considerable people half-way thought that. Maybe that's why a body always wanted to be laid away in Sunday outfit, and why they washed the dead all over when they laid them out – so they'd be ready in body and spirit to meet the Lord for all eternity.

George gulped like a chicken with a bug that won't go down. If this were so – how would *he* go to meet his Maker? If the body *was* the wagon, so to speak, that took the soul Up Town to the Doctor – and there was no body – what then? Did that mean he couldn't resurrect? Or, even if what was left of his body – after it was hacked off the bones, that is, or however they got it off – *did* manage somehow to get up there, in chopped-up bloody chunks and the like, so the Lord Himself wouldn't know who he was or which from tother – what good would it do? Even, if the rub-doctors concluded, after they cut into him, that his bones weren't good enough to suit, and just pitched the whole shebang out to the hogs, so to speak, or maybe buried what was left of him in a jumbled mess, with a chunk gone here, and a chunk there – he couldn't go around in this half-cut up shape, through all eternity. Anyway you looked at it, his body stood a pretty poor chance – but the soul was supposed to be different. Of course, old man Jimpson couldn't read or write, but the Bible didn't say reading or writing helped sanctification any, or the understanding of the Word. Had he sold all hopes of salvation for fifty dollars? The thought was too much. He doubled over to save the drip from the fiddle, and tears seeped down and trickled from his chin to the ground.

"Well, I'll swear!"

George jumped and raised blurred eyes.

"Why, Jim, I didn't know you was anywheres about. You like to scared the daylights out of me!"

Jim Tittle propped both hands on his hips, and his lips ruffled like the bottom of an umbrella. His head set so close to his body, that one had the feeling that his neck had been mislaid in the making, or had been smashed to a rim, by blows on the head. His overalls looked as if they had not been changed all summer.

"What in the name of the Almighty air you a-settin' there, fer?"

George settled back in pillow and quilt.

"Well, Jim, to tell the truth, I don't know as I see much sense in it myself, but here lately, Pa's got it in his head the pigs's a-aiming to root up these-here graves – though looks to me like there's a heap of other things they'd ruther be a-rooting on. But anyhow, worried and worked up like Pa was, and little as I'm able to do most of the time, looked like I ort to be willing to watch the hogs out whilst they done the chores – that is, till they could git the fence fixed. Pa 'lowed your pigs might git in, same as his'n."

"Well, they hain't been in yit, fur as I know, – though if I'd a-been right smart, I'd a-turned 'em in, after all the damage your ma's turkeys done. Why don't you finish digging the post holes, whilst you're a-waiting?"

George burrowed deeper into the quilt.

"Oh, Jim, I ain't able to lift a hand, hardly – let alone dig post holes –"

Jim hunched over and braced one foot on a hickory stump.

"George, if anybody'd a-told me they was fellers like you – that is, if I hadn't a-seed you with my own eyes, – I wouldn't a-believed it. I swear you're the no-accountest critter, ever I seed. Whoever heard of the like – you a-weighing betwixt two and three hundred pounds – and a-setting there for your ma and pa to wait on you, long as they live. A body'd think you'd be ashamed!"

"Why, Jim, I do all I kin, that is, what I can stand to do – no stouter'n what I am –"

"Good Lord, George! You're as stout agin as your ma and pa put together, with your woman and little boy throwed in – and you a-setting there, a-letting them do all their work and your'n too. What'd you do if they was to die – or get down sick?"

"The Lord only knows, Jim. I don't."

"Well, you'd better figure it out. They cain't stand it, forever, old as they air – a-doing the work on two places in all kinds of weather. And Mary cain't – or the little boy. From the way Ben Bragg talked, Mary might not a-had to had that operation, if you'd a-lifted a hand to a-done something, so's she wouldn't a-tore her insides to pieces, like she done. A body'd a-thought you'd a-learned something – but you never –"

George's face puckered like a rotten apple.

"Well, Jim, I want to do the right thing, and I aim to, if I ever git any health – but ailing all the time like I am, what in the name of the Lord can I do?"

"*Do*? Do some of this work and quit talking about your ailments eternally – before your ma and pa and the rest of 'em work theirselfs to death. After a-body's laid away, all the bawling in the world won't bring 'em back. You'll *have* to work then – and you'll always have it on your mind, 'twas you that killed 'em – nothin' else!"

"Oh, Jim, for the love of God, don't talk like that – I cain't stand it –"

Jim snorted a little and kept right on.

"Anybody but you, when they marry and children, aim to do *something* about gitting grub and clothes and the like fer 'em, but you don't. And you have them children a-waiting on you, soon as they can walk, might near. No wonder they ain't got no health, none of 'em. I never heard tell of the like. Hit's a plum shame. Everybody says so!"

"Jim, I swear to God I aim to do the right thing – soon as I git able. You ain't no idy how things air –"

"You been a-saying that, I reckon, for the last twenty or thirty year – and you ain't done nothing yit. But, mark my words. If you keep on like you're a-doing now – making dogs of your whole family – something turrible's a-going to happen to the whole shebang, and you're going to might near go out of your mind. I've seed that happen time and agin."

Jim stalked off down the road, as if he'd just got the best of a dog fight. George stared after him, big tears seeping down his chin. Then he shook his head and bridged his eyes with one hand, his mouth working like a fishworm. He did not look up when he heard voices from the woods – not even when his mother spoke.

"Why, George, what on earth ails you?"

She set down the hand sickle and hoe, and patted his big shoulder.

"Oh, Ma, just looks like things get worse and worse. And now, I reckon everybody thinks it's all my fault – Mary's operation and all, the way Jim Tittle was a-talking –"

Lige leaned axe and spade against the tree. A quick spurt and the leaves of a hazel bush turned brown.

"Jim Tittle? I thought I told him to keep his team out of here till that right-o-way was paid fer –"

"He didn't have no team, Pa. He was a-foot."

Sarah's mouth was a tight line.

"Well, he didn't have no business a-going through nohow. What'd he say to you, George?"

"Oh, Ma, – he was just a-saying I ort to be a-doing my own work, 'stead of settin' here – and something turrible'd come of it, and I don't know what all. The way he talked, a-body'd think I was out and out lazy."

"Well, don't pay no 'tention to what he says. Jim Tittle never did have any too much sense, nohow – and 'tain't none of his business, if he did. The idy! You go to the house now, and lay down, and maybe you'll feel better. And don't waste no worry on anything Jim Tittle said!"

Another spurt and Lige wiped his whiskers.

"Sary, you'll keep on a-babying George till we'll have to carry his everywhere he goes. Jim Tittle's right – fur as that's concerned –"

She stooped over and whacked with the handsickle as she talked. "Now Lige, shut up a-talking that away. I don't want to hear it. Anyhow, I know what I'm a-doing."

All this time George had been easing himself up, and boxing his fiddle. Now he straggled off through scrub oak and hickory, hugging the wooden box, and half dragging the chair and all after him – or rather starting to. As he rounded the hill for the two-room house, he turned for a last look at the graveyard, and as he mulled over old man Jimpson's words and Jim Tittle's, he became so nervous and worried, he collapsed in the chair with the pillow and quilt under him. Surely nobody had troubles like he did, and the way it looked, there was no hope nohow.

Chapter 6 : The Quarrel

Sunlight blinked on a roll of new hog-wire fence. Piles of fresh dirt and deep holes about six feet apart outlined a curry-comb shaped plot of ground that jutted out from the fence, separating cornfield and timber. Split posts sprawled at intervals and sent out incense of seasoned hickory. A little man, who seemed to keep time to steady jabs of a rusty spade by perpetual motion beneath his beard, paused to eliminate surplus tobacco juice.

"Might near done, Sary," he commented.

"Well, I ain't."

The tall woman stooped so that the limp, slat sunbonnet almost touched the ground. Long black stocking-legs, with holes cut out for thumbs and fingers, covered neatly patched sleeves of a dyed sugar-sack dress. Jimpson and ragweed, plantain and dogfennel toppled around her as she pulled and whacked with an old hand sickle. As the weeds fell, mounds came into view, some marked with white slabs. The largest slab had fallen flat, and seemed to have been hit with a sledge hammer, but Sarah pieced it together, jig-saw-puzzle wise until it read:

Timothy Moore
b. March 3, 1837
d. December 30, 1912
aged 75 yrs. 9 mos. 27 days
"He is not dead, he's only sleeping
Father, we shall meet again;
Though we are behind left weeping,
We know you're in the Heavenly reign.

It was strange, Lige's loyalty, but did even *he* believe that last line? If Old Tim was in Heaven, nobody need worry. The way he had beaten and pounded Lige as a child, it was a thousand wonders he had as much sense as he did. But, if it had not been for Old Tim, there might have been no George. He had practically made Lige leave Melissy, wife number one, and little Tim, because she walked in her sleep. Melissy had died a short time after that. Her folks had raised young Tim and Lige had never forgiven himself. But if he held any grudge against the dead, he never showed it.

Sarah looked up at the convolution of hair above her. "Lige, whose graves air these-here, without no marks?"

"Children's graves, neighbor children. I don't recollect who, now. We ort to keep 'em clean, though, same as the others. Nobody else will."

He plunked a post into the hole. The woman held it while he hammered with the back of the axe.

Clong! Clong! Clong!

It was as if the weight of the world had been lifted from Lige's shoulders. For weeks he had been worried over his father's bones, and now, he had no outlet but a cracked voice, half lost in the stuff he was chewing, which rose and whined:

> "The was an old woman;
> In London she did dwell;
> She loved her old man dearly,
> But another twice as well.
> And it's lawsy, law, what ails you?
> Dear, oh dear, what ails you?
> Thinkses I, what ails you?
> And what's the matter now?"

The sunbonnet pushed back and Sarah stared much as she had done at Andrew's artist boy's pictures of naked women.

"Why, Lige! I wouldn't sing that rough old song, 'round your pappy's grave."

A stream of brown substance spurted out.

"Oh, I reckon he won't care. I wouldn't be surprised but what he feels like singing hisself, now that he knows the hogs cain't git at him.

> "She went to the doctor,
> To see if she could find
> Some medicine of any kind,
> To make the old man blind.
> And it's lawsy law, what ails you?
> Dear, oh dear –"

"Lige, do shut up. I thought I heard somebody a-coming. What'll the neighbors say, a song like that, at such a time? Besides, you'd be a heap smarter if you'd figure out some way or other to patch up his tombstone, it all broke to pieces and laying flat on his grave!"

Another brown stream.

"Oh well, Pap was never one to take much stock in tombstones nohow. He didn't care for style none.

> "She bought seven bottles,
> And made him take 'em all;
> And then he said 'Oh dear, oh dear,
> I cannot see at all.
> And it's lawsy law –"

"Lige, hush! I tell you, I keep hearing wagon wheels. Somebody's a-coming!"

He looked into the whispering timber and back at the waving corn.

"I don't see nobody, nor hear 'em neither. That's over on tother road."

"Maybe it is, but I don't believe it."

He pounded the last post deep. The shiny roll unwound at the end and bright staples clamped it to a post. The faucet turned on, and off.

"You don't know what a relief it is to git this fence up, Sary. You have to let pigs run, this time of year, with all the acorns down on the ground, that might as well be turned into pork. But I keep a-thinking about 'em gitting in the graves, and three times already, I dreamed of seeing 'em root his skull around, like it was a bucket or somethin'."

"Well, Lige, they won't do it now."

"No, – not unless something happens to the fence."

"Anyhow, there's worse things could happen."

"What?"

"Well, if Mary was to leave George, for one thing."

"Oh, she won't leave him. Not that I'd blame her if she would, but she won't. If she'd a-been going to she'd a-left him long ago."

"Yes, but looks like he gits poorlier all the time, a-worrying about everything, like he does. He's as bad agin as he was before Mary got down, and now, with her poorly too, what in the name of the Lord – ?"

"Oh, she'll be all right, agin she gits over this operation, I reckon, or if she ain't maybe it'll be the making of George!"

"Now, Lige, shut up a-talking that away. I don't want to hear it."

A silent spurt, and they moved on to the next post. The woman tugged at the wire, while he pounded.

Clong! Clong! Clong!

A dull gray shirt sleeve soaked the wet from above eyes that stared over the fields.

"Well, I'll be everlastingly danged!"

"What is it, Lige?"

"That low-down skunk! That good-for-nothin' son-of-a-gun! After all I've said to him too!"

"Who, Lige?"

His eyes blazed like the new fence-roll. His doubled fists rested above his pockets as if eager for duty.

"Jim Tittle, dang him! We had it out tother day. I give him to under-stand, he was to stay off till the road was paid fer, and fenced off!"

The plod of hoofs and the screech of wagon wheels drew nearer. The woman pushed back her bonnet as if for air, and listened, barely breathing. She clutched the soaked chambray sleeve.

"Now, Lige, you be careful. If you git in a fight, and the law's not on your side, you'll lose everything you got."

He shied away from her.

"I ain't a-going to fight. I'm a-going to skeer him off of my place, once and for all!"

He swung the axe to his shoulder, and waited, his eyes blinking fire.

"Jim Tittle!" he shouted, "Git off of my land and stay off! I'm telling you for the last time!"

A man who seemed to be mostly shoulders and baggy overalls, stopped the mule-team and pushed back an immense straw hat. Above a flat nose, that crouched down at the end like a sorry dog, sharp little rat eyes turned from one to the other. Full lips ruffled into something like a smile, as he pulled his corn-cob pipe from his hip pocket, and crunching some home grown smoking tobacco in his palm, filled it.

"What's the matter, here." he asked, showing his teeth a little, and twitching ears that stuck out like funnels, "we got a crazy man?"

Sarah picked up the spade and marched ahead of her husband.

"If anybody's crazy, hit's you, Jim Tittle! I'll handle this, Lige, and there won't be no fuss, neither. Jim Tittle, if you brung fifty dollars to pay for the right o' way, go on through. If you hain't, stay out till you do.

Big shoulders hunched forward, as a match struck on grimy overalls and hands hovered over the pipe.

"Well, I hain't got it with me, Sary, but I got it in the bank. Sold a cow fer it. I thought things over, and concluded Lige was in the right tother day. I brung you a brand-new gate, to kind of square matter, till we can git things fixed up. You never did have none as was any account."

He climbed from the spring wagon and lifted out a heavy boarded thing, new and bracketed together. Above the whiskers, wistful eyes stared like a small boy in a toy shop. Fluted lips puffed, and went on.

"Cost me five dollars – the best I could git. Hain't she a beauty, Lige?"

The head tilted as the whiskers parted, but the woman cut in shrewdly.

"I'll bet my turkeys went to buy that-there gate. Jim Tittle, I want to know what's become of my turkeys?"

Fingernails rasped on a rough chin like a rat gnawing a board.

"Well, Sary, to tell you the truth, I killed most of 'em, or the dog did, and me and my brother et 'em."

The sunbonnet shook as the flat voice twanged.

"What business did you have a-killing my turkeys, I'd like to know? That's neighborliness for you, Mary in the hospital, and us having to be over there most of the time –"

"Well, if it's neighborly to raise turkeys off of tother feller's eats and corn, I don't want none of your neighborliness. I figured I fed them turkeys, so I had a right to eat 'em. I told you, Sary, three or four times, you had to keep 'em out. A turkey eats nigh on to as much as a hog."

"I don't care if they do. I done the best I could. I'd a-paid fer it, I reckon."

"Mmmm, maybe, if George hadn't a-needed something or other, before you spent the money."

"Leave George out of this. It's none of your business, what I do fer him!"

A whiff of smoke curled from the corner of his mouth.

"No – o. Not unless you owe me money. I knowed that was the only way I'd git pay for my feed, by eating the turkeys. Anyhow, I 'lowed I had as good a right to 'em as George, me a-feeding 'em. I'm a-going to say something now, Sary, that you won't like, but hit's the truth. Seems like you got sense enough about everything else, but you're a plum fool about George! Everybody says so. There's nothing the matter with him, but laziness. He's twist as stout as you or Lige, airy one!"

Sarah's hands tightened on the spade handle as her elbows extended like a hen hovering chicks.

"Jim Tittle, you git off of this place and stay off! Don't you ever dare step foot on it agin!"

"I reckon I can go through, like Lige said, if I buy the right o' way, and put up a brand new gate."

"You put up that gate and I'll tear it down, fast as I kin! You ain't got no right o' way yit. The very idy, a-talking about poor George like that. Git off of this place, I say. Lige, git Jim Tittle out of here. Steal my turkeys, will you? And you think you can put up a five-dollar gate, for the right o'way the rest your life! Well you cain't!"

The little man stepped up beside her, waving his axe, something like a flag.

"Jim Tittle, don't you put up that gate!"

Jim's lips curled as his big hand fingered hair that reminded one of a hay field, after harvest.

"S'posing I say I *will*?"

"Just you dare, till the right o' way's paid fer. You've done enough devilment, as it is. Now, git out, like Sary said."

"I reckon I'll finish my pipe first."

The man and woman waited without so much as batting an eye. The big man puffed in solemn contemplation.

"Now, Lige Moore, if you and Sary think you can make me drive three or four mile out of my way every time I want to git to my place, you're wrong! I ain't a-going to do it! I'm aiming to do what you said – "

"You lie, Jim Tittle! You know you do. You want to fix it so's you can cut through like you been a-doing, and ruin everything. That devils' lane's only half a mile down the road. But if it was ten mile, 'twouldn't make no difference. This ain't no public road! It's mine, and whoever goes through hereafter, *buys* his way."

"I said I'd buy –"

"Well, you hain't bought, and I don't b'lieve you *'low* to buy, 'less you can buy *cat-a-slaunch-ways*, through the whole dang eighty acres! You'll buy a road where I say and you'll buy before you start putting up gates –"

"Now, Lige, damn it, we talked this out tother day. I know I had no business cutting through like I done, but didn't look like there was much to hurt, and to tell the truth, I 'lowed you'd never know the difference. I'm a-aiming to buy the right o' way like you said. I wouldn't a-brung this brand-new gate, if I wasn't. I got the money, and we'll git the papers fixed up, first time both of us is in town. There's nothing to fuss about. There wouldn't a-been no trouble if I'd had sense enough to keep my mouth shut about that lazy George!"

"Jim Tittle," Sarah shook the spade, "You watch what you're a-saying about my poor sick boy!"

He threw back his head and laughed until the lump in his neck stuck out like the spout of a pitcher.

"Poor and sick – the devil! If he's poor or sick airy one, I don't know the meaning of them words. Why, he weighs nigh on to two hundred and fifty pounds, and is stout as one of them mules. He lets on he's sick, so you'll do everything for him. Crazy damn fool – but smart enough to git out of work."

"Jim Tittle, git off of this place, I tell you – and stay off!"

"I ain't a-going to do it, Sary Moore. This is betwixt me and Lige. We fixed it up the tother day. I'm a-going to put this gate up, if I have to fight to do it."

"You won't put it up! Lige! A purty one to talk, you air, a-killing all my turkeys. You're a-aiming to git the best of us somehow. You always do. If you put up this gate, you're a-aiming to make us go to law, before you pay for the right o' way. Lige, git this turkey thief out of here!"

The little man waved the axe.

"Sary's right, Jim Tittle. What she says, I say. You pay for the right o' way, before you put up anything, and we'll fence off the road, so's you'll go where you ort. You've done enough devilment here. Now git out and stay out till the road's paid fer!"

Jim Tittle blew out a long line of smoke. Then he knocked the pipe against his palm, and reached for his hip pocket.

"Well, I'm damned! I never seed a man let a woman boss everything before. No wonder George ain't got no back-bone. I'm a-going to hang this gate if I have to kill somebody to do it. And if anybody tries to stop me, I got a clawhammer, and I'll use it."

He dragged the heavy gate to the barb-wire gap. The man and woman closed in and a gray sleeve reached out.

"Jim Tittle, if you don't git out, I'll split your head wide open!"

The clawhammer poked out and pushed the little man to the ground. Sarah's spade bounced from Jim's broad back.

"Keep out of this, woman," Jim snarled, poking with the clawhammer.

Lige pushed himself up like a mad bull.

"Jim Tittle!" he panted, "don't you *dare* touch her agin! Git out, or I'll kill you!"

"Shet up!"

The axe swung up and came down flat as the woman screamed.

"Lige! Lige! You don't know what you're a-doing – They'll hang you –"

The spade shoved in between the descending axe and Jim's solid shoulder, but only turned the blow. The sharp edge swerved upward and cut off most of the fleshy part of Jim Tittle's ear, slashing cross-wise. Blood spurted over the new gate, as he sank to the ground.

"My God!" he kept saying, "my God! You've killed me, Lige Moore. My God!"

Lige backed off like a cornered mink. Sarah untied her apron and threw it to Jim.

"Tie up your ear, Jim Tittle, before you bleed to death!"

The fluted lips twisted into a hard line.

"I don't want none of your rags. I can use something of mine, I reckon. You cain't kill a man, might' near, and then make up to him. I'm a-going to town to see a doctor, soon as I can git there, and so help me, I'll sue for every cent you've got."

The wagon wheels groaned out a solemn warning, as long as they could hear them. The man and woman turned to each other like trapped weasels.

"Oh, Sary, I only meant to keep him out – oh Lord!"

"I tried to stop you Lige, but I couldn't. Not that he didn't deserve all he got, and more too, the way he talked about poor George. But I'm afeard of the law, Lige."

"He'll sue. He's the sueing kind. I reckon I'll have to go to jail –. Oh, Sary!"

"Never mind, Lige. You was in the right. Go up and see Andrew."

"I don't know, Sary. I don't know what to do. Maybe I ort to stay here. If they come to take me to jail, I ort to be ready. Let's go home – ."

The glistening hogwire stood where they left it, half unrolled. The new gate, splotched with blood, sprawled on the ground. Sarah shouldered the spade and marched ahead, silent. A little old man stumbled after her, dragging the axe, his head bent –

From behind a clump of scrub-oak, old man Jimpson's white funnel of a beard pointed after them, as rheumatic knees creaked, and eyes half popped from his head.

Chapter 7 : George's Reaction to Ear-Cutting

Bad news always seems to get around as fast again as good. Sort of tells itself. Jim Tittle was not much more than de-eared than all Hell's Holler knew about it. Old man Jimpson made it known to his family and Bill and J.P. did the rest.

George had seen considerable himself, for that matter, and then gone home and taken to his bed. He had been almost out of his mind anyhow, since that talk with old man Jimpson, and then Jim Tittle, and now with his stomach upside down from the sight of Jim's blood, on top of his other worries, he was worse than common. He and Mary were both flat on their backs when Lawrence brought home the Jimpson version of ear-trouble, but the more he thought about it, in spite of his ailments, he needed no great sight of urging to go over and see how things were.

It was not over three quarters of a mile at the most, from one house to the other, through the woods – even circling eight or ten wagon lengths out of the way to dodge the graveyard – but George, ailing like he was and nervous and worked up anyway, was not downright sure he'd be able to make it. Seemed as if the hills were straight up and down. No wonder outsiders wanted to build a reservoir. If they'd dam up two or three hills in a bunch, they'd have a regular well of a pond, as big as most farms.

He kept thinking about that ear-cutting – and Lige. If they sent him to the pen, it would probably be the last of him. He would never get out. Wouldn't want to, more than likely, but wouldn't live through it, if he did. He'd been used to feather beds and shuck ticks all his life, and they wouldn't have them down there. He would die of pneumonia, nine chances to ten, the first cold spell. And, even if they didn't send him, if Jim sued and got all he had, it would be about the same thing. If they took his land away, he couldn't make a living – there or anywhere else. He would be just like an oak or hickory washed out in a storm, with no dirt on its roots.

And his own land – could Jim Tittle get that, if he sued and got the rest? Lige had made him a regular deed, but would it hold in law? Outsiders seemed determined to root out the hill people, one way or another – anyway him. Weren't satisfied with his body. Now they were after his land, his and Lige's, and if the land went, more than likely Mary would go too. Would just fizz out sooner or later like soured peaches from a leaky can top, and a body couldn't blame her. It did look like a man ought to furnish the land for his woman to work on, even if he wasn't able to lift a hand himself.

He kept mulling over the poor excuse of existence ahead of him. Mary gone, no land, no children, himself as droopy as frost-bitten tomatoes all this life, and worse still in the next – but what could he do? Most people had the satisfaction of watching their children grow up and taking care of them in their old age, but he wouldn't – the way things looked. Like as not he wouldn't have any old age, in the first place, and in the second, Mary and the children might pull out any time, so they wouldn't be anywhere around to take care of him if he did. The more he thought about it, the more be-dwindled the future seemed.

This might be a judgement. Some said the Lord visited his wrath on a whole family sometimes, for the actions of one. Maybe He had them. And, if signing that rub-doctor paper hitched him up with the devil eternally, and robbed the Almighty of his due – a body could hardly blame Him. Still, it did seem a little hard on Lige, be-deviled into cutting off somebody's ear for other people's mis-doings, and then going to the pen, or paying out all he had to keep from it. But, like as not the Lord aimed to deliver Lige out of it, somehow or other, and whatever happened, *his* soul and body were safe. It was George the judgement was aimed at. If it hadn't been for the ear-cutting, and lawsuit and all, he *might* have been able to buy his body back in time – might have wheedled the money out of Sarah – but now he couldn't possibly – ever. It would take all they had to save Lige from the pen and he might go anyhow. And, having signed that paper, there was no other way of getting out of the bargain. His body was gone, and more than likely his soul too.

When he reached his mother's he was as fagged-out as if he'd worked all day in the hayfield. He stopped on the back porch, partly to get hold of himself, more or less, before he went in, and partly to see how they were taking it. In a way, old as they were, they didn't have a great deal to lose, any way you looked at it, but still, the way his health was, they might outlive him ten times over. He braced himself against one end of the window ledge, where he could peep in ever so often.

Nobody was there but Lige, and he looked as if he'd just been laid out for burying. All cleaned up from the hide out, looked like – clean shirt and overalls, anyway, and the hem of underwear that poked out from the bottoms of his shirt sleeves, looked fresh-changed. His eyes were half closed, and might as well have been penny-weighted, for all they saw. Even the kitchen curtains bunched back from the window like the white inside of a burying box.

George kept going over in his mind things he could say to make Lige feel better, but everything seemed to be an out and out lie, or something not worth saying. He couldn't very well say as some did, that everything happened for the best – no matter what – that Lige would be better off in the pen or poorhouse, for as far as he could tell, he wouldn't. He thought of saying if the worst came to the worst in law, and Lige lost his place, he'd deed back the twenty-five acres, that is, if he could hold on to it, himself, which he probably couldn't – but of course Mary would have something to say about that. He couldn't go so far as to say Lige was entirely in the right and Jim wrong – that anybody else would have cut off both ears, or at least all of one – not hardly knowing what the fuss was about, worried and worked up as he was. Like as not there were two sides to it – leastways there generally was, or rather three side, Lige and Jim and the lawyers, and the lawyers would have things their way in the end. Hill people didn't stand a chance against uptowners – always wanting to try out something, and then take it out in taxes. But, about Lige and Jim, – what could he say. He could say that Jim, not being what a body would call even half-way nice looking to start with, it didn't matter much anyhow – that half an ear, more or less, wouldn't make a great deal of difference anyway – but nine chances to ten, Jim wouldn't feel that way about it. And the more he thought about it, there didn't seem to be much of anything to say, so he just of leaned there, and didn't say anything.

The door opened and Sarah panted in with a slab of ham and an apron of eggs, which clinked into an empty milk crook. On the cookstove an iron skillet scraped as a wooden spoon clumped in lumps of lard from a tin bucket. Lige, huddled-up on a chair, half hidden in whiskers, looked as old again as he had that morning.

"I don't know as I want anything, Sary."

He stared past her, though he didn't seem to be seeing anything or wanting to. The butcher knife clipped through ham to breadboard.

"Lige, you've got to eat! You might not get a chance at eatable victuals again, soon –"

Ham and eggs popping and sizzling, the smell of coffee, thick slices of home-made bread, over brown and bulged at the the top. Sarah smoothed up loose hair with side-combs.

"Lige, you've gone and put your shirt on wrong side out, but don't change it now – I wouldn't. They say it's bad luck if you do, and the Lord knows you'll need all the luck you can get. I've dreamt of shoes, I don't know how many times lately, and shoes mean trouble. And that looking-glass tother night. Like as not this ear business comes from that –"

"That's all dang foolishness."

"Now, Lige, you don't know. Maybe it is, and maybe it ain't. I don't know as I believe in it, exactly – but it does seem like everybody that looks in a looking-glass after dark, has bad luck sooner or later. Besides, looks like everything's gone wrong here lately. I broke a needle a-quilting tother day, and that's a year's bad luck right there. And I dreamt of Uncle Jim and Aunt Siny a week or two ago, and aunts and uncles is always bad –."

"Oh, Sary, them signs don't mean nothing, one way or tother. Just something for folks to talk about – that don't know nothing else. They couldn't all of 'em come out right."

"Well, you notice might near all of 'em do. And, Lige, I didn't tell you the worst yet. I was afeard it might worry you. But tother night I dreamt I seed Mary kiss George right smack on his mouth, and when two kiss in a dream, it's a sign they're a-going to fall out. I never knowed it to fail."

By this time, George was half lame from ledge sitting, and looked as if he'd just swallowed three or four green crabapples. He limped into the kitchen and collapsed in the nearest chair.

"Why, George, what on earth? Where did you come from, and what ails you?"

"Oh, Ma, I come over to see if I couldn't do something for Pa. Looked like, old as he is, and worried and all, I could at least *say* something to get his mind off his troubles, even if I couldn't *do* nothing. But seems like I cain't say nothing or even think it – that's got any sense to it, or any git-up or life or anything. Just seems to me like things get worse and worse all the time. I don't know what in the name of the Lord'll become of us."

Lige livened up a little as he turned on George with a snort.

"Good Lord Almighty, George! What on earth air you driving at? You talk like a plum fool. You're a hundred times better off than me, and you know it. You ain't cut off nobody's ear. Ain't got spunk enough."

Sarah's eyes raised from the frying pan.

"Now, Lige, cutting off a body's ear don't take such uncommon spunk, and it's nothing to brag about if it did. I'm glad George ain't spunkful, if that's the way it turns out. One ear-cutter in the family's enough. Now, George, I want you to tell me what's a-worrying you."

"Oh, Ma, you ain't no idy how things air. Doc Ceburn said I ort to have some kind of a change, but where in the name of the Lord would I go? I don't see how we're a-going to make it anyhow, and now if Jim Tittle sues and gits my place along with Pa's –"

A long handled fork flipped over a chunk of ham.

"Oh, surely he cain't git your place – no matter what happens. Can he Lige?"

The blank, blue eyes focused upon the knot on top of her head. "What?"

"Jim Tittle cain't git George's place, even if he was to git everything else, can he?"

"Oh – I don't know. I reckon not, though a body cain't count on law or lawyers, one way or tother. Lawyers 'll more'n likely git the whole shebang, before it's over –"

She studied the rag carpet.

"Maybe they will – George's too, and everybody's. They been at it considerable time now – first one, and then another. Bound and determined to buy our land and put a reservoir In whether we want it or not. We need a reservoir about as much as a pig needs a umberel – much water as they is here. It's them rub-doctors that's at the bottom of the whole thing. I wouldn't be a bit surprised but they'd git that mill and dam anytime now, the shape it's in – and the Lord knows what else. For some reason or other, they're a-aiming to git a hold in these hills, if they ain't already done it. It may be they're mixed up with something or somebody down here now, and want to keep an eye on 'em. Or maybe they just naturally want to boss. But whatever it is, they're a-aiming to git in, and mark my words, they'll git in. And once in, it'll be just like hog fleas in a house – you cain't get 'em out. I wisht we'd a-never took Marry and George to 'em in the first place. "Pears to me like they been a heap noisier, since then."

George's color had faded to strained gooseberry juice, and his teeth started little gallops of chattering. Sarah watched him corner-eyed, as she set around the plates.

"George, as soon as I git your pa's dinner, I'm a-going to make you some sassafras tea, and I want you to lay down. You ain't well."

Lige exploded in a little ripple of coughs.

"Oh, Sary, don't start that eternal babying. There's nothing the matter with him – no more than common, that is. He ain't cut nobody nor been cut on –"

"Yes, but, Pa, you ain't no idy how nervous I am, – a-thinking about it –"

"Nervous, thunderation! I'm might near worried to death. You said you aimed to do something for me, and if your ma don't talk you out of it, I wisht you take me to town in the spring wagon. Not knowing when I'll git back, I ortn't to take the team and wagon by myself. And, besides, I'm so worked up, I'm might near afeard to. Ain't right sure I could hold the team if they was to shy at something, and was a mind to run away. And I thought if you'd take me –"

George looked as if he had half a mind to run away himself.

"Pa, I'd like to, and I know I ort to, but nervous and worried like I am, I don't reckon I could set in the wagon seat – let alone drive. Maybe you'd better go a-horseback."

"Well, I reckon I will – if you won't take me. But thirty mile is a long horseback ride, worried like I am. I wisht you'd take me. It might be the last thing I ever asked you to do."

"Oh, Pa, don't talk like that for the Lord's sake. I cain't stand it."

Sarah turned from her cooking.

"Now, Lige, if George was able, it'd be different. But he ain't. No telling what might happen, him like he is, and a-gitting poorlier all the time, and I don't aim for us to have no regrets. I've seed I don't know how many yaller wooly worms this fall, and that means fever. And if he gits the fever, he'll go – I'm might near sure. You'd better go on a-horseback, as soon as you eat something."

"Oh, Sary, I cain't eat. I keep thinking about the blood from Jim's ear. George'll eat whatever you fixed I reckon."

"Well, Lige, maybe he will and maybe he won't, though I hope he's able, after I git through doctoring him. But there's something terrible the matter now. I b'lieve he's going to have a chill, if I don't git him to bed. I wisht you'd bring in that shuck tick and feather bed from tother room, before you go. I want to make a pallet for him in here on the floor, where I can look after him."

Lige slouched out grumbling, and staggered in under the corn-shuck tick and quilt, and afterwards a featherbed. "It does look like, Sary, me a-going to lose all I got and all I ever will git, and worried half to death like I am, George could carry his own shuck tick."

"Now, Lige, I know what I'm a-doing."

George kept opening and closing his mouth in little fish gasps. "Pa, I'd like to take you like I said, but I ain't able. I expect Ma'll have to bring the victuals to the bed, fer me to eat. You ain't no idy how things air, and how upset I am."

"Oh, George, you don't talk like you had lick of sense. A body'd think you'd had your ear cut off – or somebody was a cutting it off right now. I never seed anybody act so plum foolish. Nothing's happened to you or won't fur as I can see."

But George had flattened on tick and featherbed as starchless as new-washed mosquito-bar, and Sarah covered him up, and then set on two flat irons, and poked at the fire.

"Lige, I expect you'd better go on. George ain't able to go nowhere like he is. I don't know what ails him – but it might be pneumony. I didn't see all them yaller wooly worms for nothing, and we'd better look out fer him a-head. You'd better go on now, like I said."

Lige stared a minute and then went out. A little while afterwards, they heard the clink of bridle and the clump of old Spot's hoofs.

Chapter 8 : A Hen Crows

Red hair flopped over bulging eyes. "Grandma!"

From a wooden biscuit bowl beamed a face as wrinkled as a dried tobacco leaf. "What, Lawrence?"

"Grandma, you got a hen out here as crows like a rooster! And Bill Jimpson says his pa says if a hen crows and you don't git rid of her, one of the family'll die before a year!"

Sarah nodded toward a haze of smoke.

"You hear that, Lige?"

A corncob pipe untangled from bushy whiskers as rheumatic knees straightened.

"I don't put no stock in no such tomfoolery, no-how. Which one was it, Lawrence?"

"That reddish un, Grandpa, that un by the spring wagon."

"Good Lord Almighty, Sary! That's one of your Rhode Island Red pullets!"

"Is?"

She pushed to the window, extending doughy fingers. Lige puffed a series of short, quick puffs, like an engine about to start.

"Now, Sary, you know as well as I do, nothing'd do you, but you had to have Rhode Island Reds, like Andrew's! Now, I ain't a-going to pay a dollar a settin' for eggs, and wring their necks, soon as they're half grown. That's all dang foolishness, anyhow!"

Dough-covered hands, back at the wooden bow, mixed in clabber milk, that bubbled with soda.

"Well, Lige, I don't know as I believe in it myself, but don't look like we ort to take no chances – Mary just over her operation, and George sick all the time, like he is."

A blast of smoke belched from the whiskers.

"Chances, thunderation! Why old man Jimpson cain't read or write airy one. What does he know about it?"

Dough thickened as both hands pinched and squeezed.

"I know, Lige, but – we're a-aiming to have chicken anyway, with George and Mary and the younguns here, and they do say hit's an awful bad sign. You'd better kill her, Lige. Might mean bad luck for your trial, too, fer as we know."

"I ain't a-going to do it. Kill the purtiest pullet in the whole shebang –!"

"Now, Lige, you always said the chickens was my say-so. And, if they air, shut up, and do like I said."

"All right, but understand, I'm through with the whole business! Don't ever mention full-blooded chickens to me no more. You just ain't got good sense, Sary!"

"I don't care whether I have or not. I ain't a going to have my boy's life in danger a whole year – full bloods or none."

Whiskers parted to receive the corncob pipe, and disappeared as the door slammed. Lawrence padded after him but a voice from the biscuit bowl called him back.

"Lawrence, what was Bill Jimpson a-doing here, this morning, anyhow?"

The red head tilted as eyes watched the settling lump in the nest of flour. "Nothing, Grandma. Just talking.:

"I'll bet that's what's been a-going with my big hickorynuts. Lawrence, how'd you like to take the younguns and go after what's left of 'em after dinner – them great big uns, down yander in the holler?"

"All right, Grandma."

The door banged as he bounded out. Sarah turned to Mary.

"We'll divide 'em, of course. But if we don't git 'em to-day, there won't be none to git. Them Jimpson children'll have 'em carried off to sell. They take everything they lay their hands on. I never seed the like. Feel better, George?"

A silent bulk arose from the bed, where it had relaxed like a cow after an all-day's meal.

"I cain't say as I do, Ma, and I cain't say as I don't. Hit's jest one of them nasty headaches, you have to wear off."

"'Pears to me like you've had a heap of headaches, here lately. I thought maybe you could ride old Dolly, George, and go with the youn-guns after hickorynuts – haul back the sacks for 'em. You feel like it?

"I reckon so, Ma. You don't s'pose there's any danger of varmints, do you?"

"Why, George, if I thought there was danger, I wouldn't send the chil-dren and them barefoot."

He fingered big knuckles and stared toward the hills. "You reckon – Dolly'd be apt to pitch me off, being if she was to shy at something."

The biscuit cutter paused in the air.

"Why, George, what ails you? Dolly never did pitch. Ain't moved above a snail's pace hardly, the last ten year. Dolly's twenty-eight year old; too old for skittishness."

"I know it, Ma, but Ben Bragg was telling tother day, 'bout a horse that shied at a pole-cat or something, and broke a feller's neck."

"Well, George, when you hear such things, just figure there's maybe one chanct in a hundred of it happening to you."

"Well, Ma, I dunno as I want to take that one chanct. Somehow or other, I've got it in my head my time may come any minute, and when I think of all the ways a feller might git killed –"

"Well, George, when a body's time comes, there's nothing you can do about it, I reckon, indoors or out. I heard of a feller, died onct, a-setting in a chair. They claimed his heart just balked on him, like a contrary mule."

"I know it, Ma, but you ain't no idy the way things air. Just seems like there's something a-hanging over me, like a club. I don't know how many times, here lately, I've dreamt of being dead and laid out. I wake up all a-sweat."

She clucked as she washed her hands in flour.

"Why, George, I thought you knowed better than that. T dream of a death's a sign of a wedding, though I don't who'd be a-marrying, hard times as it is."

"Jim Tittle's a single man, Ma. Maybe it's him – or Ben Bragg."

Something like a snort burst out as the gray twist tossed.

"I'd like to know who'd have Jim Tittle, ugly, flat-nosed, not even half-way clean-looking, turkey-stealer of a thing –"

Lige pushed in, carrying a headless, half-grown, plymouth rock rooster.

"Sary, I couldn't ketch the one Lawrence said crowed, nohow. I tolled 'em with corn and done everything, but 'twasn't no use. Anyhow, I'm dead sure the one that crowed is a rooster. Two of 'em look might near alike, and whether 'tis or 'tain't, it ort to sell for a dollar before long."

Lawrence trailed after him, solemn-eyed.

"Yes, Grandma, I'm purty sure Bill Jimpson was wrong. Anyhow, looked to me like there was *three* or *four* of 'em a-crowing, and Grandpa said maybe hit was just a scheme to git you to sell your pullets to them for a little of nothing. They ain't got no full-bloods."

Biscuits went into the warming closet, but bony hands still squeezed lard and flour; pie dough.

"Well, Lige, I wisht you'd a-killed it, like I said. Not that I'd put anything past Jimpsons, but now if anything *should* happen, you'll have nobody but yourself to blame fer it."

But the whiskers were hidden in a curtain of smoke. She turned to the bed.

"Anyhow, George, 'twon't hurt none for you to be extry careful from now on. Not that dreaming of death mounts to a hill of beans, but I don't trust crowing hens. I've heard too much about 'em. I don't want you to take no chances in nothing, no matter what happens."

A picnic spirit was in the air. After gooseberry pie was cut and nibbled from corner to crust, little bodies wiggled and bare feet kicked till Sarah passed out buckets of sacks and offered a final counsel.

"Look after the younguns, Lawrence, and George, you watch out for yourself. My mind's none too easy about that hen, much as I've dram about shoes here lately. Lige, maybe you'd better catch old Dolly fer him, won't you, him a feeling like he does and all?

Whiskers broke through the smoke.

"Good Lord Almighty! Cain't do nothing by hisself? This is as purty a day as ever I seed. Looks like –"

"Now, Lige, go on! George is over-nervous, and if something was to happen to the poor boy this next year, I'd never git over blaming myself."

They were not much beyond the barnyard, when George called the mule to a halt and turned back to the children.

"Looks to me like that's old man Jimpson and J.P. a-coming yander, and if you younguns don't mind waiting a mite, I'm a-going to see what he says about that pullet crowing."

He swallowed a time or two as they came up.

"Mr. Jimpson, do you believe, if a hen crows, and you don't kill her or git rid of her – one of the family'll die before a year?"

Old man Jimpson's beard ticked as he talked.

"Well, might not always work out – but I never knowed it to fall. Why?"

"Oh, I was just a-wondering. Seems like some of them signs go contrary, at times. Ma always said if it rains in an open grave, so's they have to scoop the water out, one of the family'll foller in next to no time. But, near as I recollect, they scooped out water by the bucketful form Grandpa's grave – and no near relation of his'n went. His second woman did, but they was already parted, so's I don't reckon that'd count hardly."

The white whiskers wagged.

"Well, George, looks to me like a womarn's a womarn – parted or not. I don't take much stock in this parting and divorce business myself. I claim if God jines a couple together, He aims fer 'em to stay. But about this hen-crowing business – you heard of any a-doing it lately?"

"Yeah. One of our'n."

"You don't say. Well, if 'twas me, I wouldn't waste no time a-gitting rid of her. If you don't you'd better leave these parts yourself – all of you – and I don't even know if that'd help."

George gulped. "How's J.P. a-making it?"

"Oh, first rate, I reckon. I watch over him purty clost, most of the time myself, though the children take him at times, too. He's a great hand to do what a body says – though they don't always mean it. I mind one time, he dreened somebody's cowpond so's it never could be fixed. Somebody'd been a-watering their stock there, unbeknownst to 'em, and leaving gaps down, and I don't know what all – and they said they wisht it was dry, so J.P. dreened it. He didn't mean no harm, but they like to sent him off fer it, jest the same."

"Did he ever say much about the victuals down yander, and the kind of work they done and all?"

"Well, he did and he didn't. He ain't much of a talker, but from what he give out, they had all a body could eat, and 'twas warm too, in cold weather, with no wood to cut and carry and no great sight of work to do, no time. But, seems like, he wants to be out a-rustling – a-finding wild plums, and hickory nuts, and climbing trees – I 'low he could climb any tree in this-here woods. But, seems like, he don't want nobody to sort of keep an eye on him. Wants to be off by hisself."

The children's banging buckets all but drowned out everything else.

George looked down from the mule.

"You children go on. I'll come in might near no time. Be there soon as you air, more'n likely."

"All right, Pappy, but hurry. Mr. Jimpson, we couldn't borry J.P. – could we?"

"Oh, I reckon, but J.P., you come when I call."

They swushed off through dry leaves. George turned back to old man Jimpson.

"Mr. Jimpson, how crazy does a body have to be to git down yander? Do you know?"

"Don't have to be crazy at all. J.P. ain't and never was. Jest teched. He's a heap smarter than some that sent him – some ways. Seems like if some uptowners – doctors and the like – git it in their heads you ort to go, you go, and if they don't, you don't."

George twiddled the halter.

"Say, – did you ever know of a body gitting out of some kind of bargain – 'cause he'd been in this hospital place?"

Old man Jimpson clawed the top half of his beard.

"Yes, come to think of it, seems like I did. I don't recollect who it was now, or what 'twas about – but anyhow, they claimed he wasn't in his right mind when he made the bargain, and it didn't stick."

"It didn't have anything to do with the rub-doctors, did it?"

"No. If it had, I reckon he'd a-been smart to a-sent hisself off. I 'low if they've asked me fifty times. After me a-telling 'em too, we aimed to keep outsiders out. I never seed sech ticks of critters to git shed of, did you?"

"No, Mr. Jimpson, I don't know as I ever did. Well, I reckon if I'm a-aiming to catch up with the younguns, I'd better be a-doing it."

As the mule kicked through hoof-deep leaves, George gaped up at the overhanging oaks – stripped to skeletons now, most of them – much as he would be –. And still – there might be a way out. Sarah always said a way would be sent, no matter what, and if the law would let him out of his bargain – that is, if he could get down to that hospital somehow, for the cold weather, say – it ought to do wonders for him. He kept mulling it over as he jolted down house-high hills and up again, sometimes through as an undergrowth of wild crabs, and then a stretch of willows that hovered over the water. And below him, Turkey Run Creek bubbled and splashed as it pushed on to the outside world, and the last of the frogs croaked "goodbye".

Half-way to the bottom land, his troubles took on new worries. A quarter-grown white pig galloped past him to where the children huddled, and Lawrence plowed through the leaves to meet him, hugging him till he squealed, and then scratching the bristly back and chin. Sampson kept up his soft grunts, twisting and turning to offer new scratching ground, with Lawrence talking to him all the time, like he was somebody. Lawrence would take it hard when they butchered, much as he thought of Sampson, but he would get over it, of course. It wasn't like having a body's own butchering hanging over him, so to speak. George clumped a little nearer.

"What you children a-doing here? I thought you was a-gitting hickorynuts for your grandma."

Lawrence gave Sampson a final pat.

"We was, Pappy, but J.P. was a-showing me how to climb, sort of, and then the other Jimpson kids come along a-looking for a tomcat – Elviry'd seed some kind of a sign – and we was a helping 'em."

"Where air they now?"

"Over at the fur end of the woods."

"Why, Lawrence, looks to me like they picked the place where the big hickorynuts is, to hunt theirselves."

"You reckon they done it o'purpose, Pappy?"

"I ain't no idy."

He galloped over the hill, hardly breathing, the white pig at his heels, the three smaller children toddling behind. George clopped through bushes and underbrush and reached bottom land just as Lawrence panted up. Nobody else was there. Bushes sidled and branches swished as if a dog had

just brushed against them, but no Jimpsons – nothing, not even many hickorynuts. With Sampson at his heels, Lawrence kicked through pile after
pile of leaves, but the nests of big hickorynuts seemed pretty well empty.
Not many in the trees either, except one telephone pole of a thing, with
branches all at the top, like an umbrella. Lawrence hugged the trunk and
boosted himself up a notch at a time. Blistered hands and scratched arms
and legs, but he made it.

"Look, Pappy!"

Hickorynuts rained down immense hail.

"Waa!"

The three children rubbed heads as they wailed. Sampson scuttled to
safety with a snort. George called form the sanctuary of Dolly's back.

"You children run over there under them willows, till Lawrence gits
'em shook down."

Wails subsided as Lawrence crawled through and over limbs, shaking
branch. The girls squatted on a hollow log under an elm that reared up
apart from the willows, but Hubert waded through leaves with the vague
hope of still finding Tom.

"Eeeh! Snake!"

He jumped back, and then stood panic-stricken, watching the rustling
leaves. The man on the mule opened his mouth and leaned forward like
a young bird expecting a worm – or maybe a viper, for he could neither
move nor talk. Finally words came.

"Run, younguns, fast as ever you can! Don't stand there like bumps on
a log till you all git bit. Might be a rattler. Run!"

But they only stared, pointing, as the leaves parted nearer the log,
where the little girl huddled. Lawrence was sliding down the trunk of
a hickory tree fifteen feet away. Suddenly Sampson snorted and leaped
into the leaves. He shook the snake as a dog shakes a rat. Then, grunting,
he swung it around his neck like a string of popcorn, and slowly chewed
it down, all but the end of the tail. Lawrence panted up, well pleased.

"Sampson, you air the best snake killer there is! Look Pappy, there's some of them button things on the end of its tail!"

The mule plodded nearer.

"Git it, Lawrence, if you can. They say it keeps cobwebs out of fiddles."

The boy picked it up as it fell from Sampson's mouth.

"Seven rows! Whew! This ort to keep all kinds of cobwebs out. Here, Pappy."

One by one, he boosted the children up the mule's side, and a big hand pulled them upward where they crouched waiting, while Lawrence, with Sampson at his heels and a stick to whack the leaves, picked up the hickorynuts he had knocked down. Then Dolly plodded over the hills, through the leaves, her back a row of big and little bumps.

For half an hour after they reached home, Sampson was a hero. Then Lige stormed in, his beard heaving.

"Who drunk my buttermilk?"

Nobody seemed to know anything about it.

"I set the bucket out there in the shade of that snow-apple tree, and now it's empty – turned over, but there's no milk there."

"Sounds like some of the pigs, but they're all in the woods."

"Sampson's up here, Grandma. We let him come back with us, seeing as he's a hero."

"Hero, be danged! All my buttermilk –"

"Grandpa, he killed a rattlesnake, that was after the younguns, and et it up!"

"Did? Well, all I got to say is, rattlesnakes and buttermilk ort to make mighty good porkchops!"

Chapter 9 : George, Depressed, Thinks of Asylum

Winter swooped down like a hawk. The Chariton River was like thick glass, and Turkey Run Creek popped loose from the banks, a long, swollen stick. George, huddled behind the heater, stretched out big hands and stared at the stove. He could hardly bear to think of Mary and Lawrence doing all the work, their hands chapped and split open like they were, but with that rub-doctor bargain hanging over him, and snow drifting and wind whimpering all the time, he just couldn't bring himself to step outside hardly – let alone work. It might be a kind of warning to him – all this bluster outside – reminding him of what would happen if he caught his death. And Mary's eternal washing, swinging like boards from the line, always put him in mind of an unmade burying box.

It looked as if they were in for a long cold spell. Sarah always said when corn shucks grew clear over the ear like they had, it meant an uncommonly hard winter, with no let-up hardly till out and out warm weather. If he *could* make some kind of a change, like old Doc Ceburn said, it did look as if this were the time to do it. He kept mulling over what old man Jimpson had said about the insane asylum. Sounded like a first rate place to be in winter, and if the *law* were on his side after he got out – that would help more than anything. Nervous and worried like he was, it *might* be he was out of his mind enough to go. The more he thought things over, even as blizzardly as it was outside, he concluded he ought to see Andrew. Andrew would know about such things. He watched Mary as she went from one thing to another – chunking wood in the heater, filling the coaloil lamp by lantern light, jangling the milk bucket and tipping the teakettle into a pan of bran shorts. It did look as if she could get along as well or better without him to do for too, no better than his health was. He cleared his throat.

"Mary, I been a-thinking, I been so downhearted and discouraged lately, seems like, I thought if you didn't care, I'd try and ketch a ride to town to-day, and maybe see Andrew. A talk with them might do me a heap of good, and I ain't no help to you here, nohow."

She kept her eyes on the bran mixture.

"Go – if you want to."

His head poked out from behind the stove pipe like a crated goose.

"You shore you won't care? Don't seem right, hardly a-going off in dead of winter-like, leaving you to do everything. Still you and the boy do it all anyhow."

"I ain't a-caring, if you wan't to go."

Her voice was a monotone. He tetered from one foot to the other.

"You reckon you could fix me up a snack, just in case Andrew might not be home, or something?"

"I reckon. Lawrence, fix him some bread and side-meat, and some of them doughnuts your grandma sent over. I got to git at my milking."

The door banged and George piled on socks, shirts, coats – all that he had – till he resembled a well-stuffed pillow. He tucked the lunch Lawrence wrapped in Lige's weekly newspaper under one arm, rammed big mittened hands into overall pockets, and tramped out into the snow.

A mile of crunching, and then luck. A team clopped up and the driver shifted a corncob pipe.

"Going to town?"

"Yeah. I was a-aiming to."

"Git in. Right cold, hain't it?"

Long legs stretched from road to wagon bed, and he eased onto the seat.

"Yeah, turrible. I was a-telling the woman, I just wisht there was some place I could go in the winter, weak and nervous like I am, and not able to do nothing, seems like. But them things ain't for such as us, I reckon, sick or well."

"No, I reckon not. 'Pears to me, though, I heard of a feller going some'ers, a year or so ago. Didn't cost him nothing neither. Let's see. Who was that?"

George hunched forward like a dog expecting a meaty bone. "You don't say so!"

"Hit was Sam Flynn's boy, I believe. He got so nervous and run-down, plum discouraged-like, and no 'count generally –"

"He hadn't been to no rub-doctors, had he"

"Naw. Didn't b'lieve in rubbin'. And, as I was saying, the doctor said maybe a few months in Saint Jo, or some sech a place – they got a hospital there for sech folks – might be good fer him. And he went, and he said it was awful nice. Warm all winter, might near like summer, and meat and potaters, and ice cream on Sunday sometimes, and didn't cost him a cent. Said some of 'em there was in purty bad shape, but a lot of 'em was a smart as me or you."

George's ears tilted forward as his lower jaw dropped.

"Well, I swan, I didn't know they had places like that – just for *nervousness* – that is, that didn't cost."

At a red and yellow filling station, the wagon left the highway, but a car picked him up, and let him off at the by-road that led to Andrew Moore's. Another three quarters of a mile's crunching, and he rapped and peered in at the front door. A plump little woman in a blue mother hubbard and a heavy pile of a black hair, bent over a sizzling skillet. A bushy haired, middle-aged man bellowed as he dressed, in his standard tune for all songs:

> "In London lived a noble lord,
> And he had wealth and high degree;
> He sailed away, on board a ship,

The foreign countries for to see."

George knocked again, louder.

"He sailed east and he sailed west,
Until he came to the Turkish shore;
And there he was taken and put in prison,
Where he could never see nor hear."

George banged insistently as the smell of bacon and eggs seeped out.

"Whoop!"

The little woman looked around, and the man motioned to the door, as he tightened his suspenders, and slid into old congress shoes. She padded to the door.

"Why, George, come right in!"

"Come in! Come in!" echoed a heavier voice. Been to breakfast, George?"

He stretched big hands toward the heater.

"Well, yeah, I had a snack on the way, but I might eat a bite or two more, for company."

The woman did not hear, but she set a plate for him. Coat and shirts peeled off like corn shucks, and he blew into red hands and stretched long legs under the table.

"Andrew," he began, splitting open several biscuits and sliding in slabs of butter to melt, "I'm in bad shape."

Two bites, and a biscuit went down with a gulp. The older man, who had suffered from dyspepsia for years, watched with a kind of childish envy as he offered bacon and eggs.

"How so?" he asked mildly.

"God only knows." George scraped half the contents of the platter on to his plate. "I wisht I did."

"You seem to have plenty of appetite." Andrew passed fried potatoes and watched them disappear.

"Yeah, that's a funny thing about me. No matter how sick I am, I can always eat. Many a time the woman's brung victuals to bed fer me."

He helped himself to a seventh biscuit and the remainder of the butter.

"Andrew," there was a kind of pride in his voice, "I've got all the doctors puzzled. Not one of 'em can find out what ails me."

"I wonder if it could be something like hysteria," suggested Andrew.

"Hysteria? What's hysteria?" His eager eyes followed the woman, but she only ladled water into the teakettle. He turned back to the man.

"Well, nerves, and imagination, partly. You think you're worse off than you are."

"Well, this hain't no imagination, Andrew, though I'm as jumpy as a rabbit. You ain't no idy how things air."

There was a sucking sound and a gurgle of coffee.

"How do you feel?"

"Oh, nervous like, and worried and discouraged. Ready to bust out and bawl the minute anybody scolds me, or comes up all of a sudden."

Andrew pushed back his chair.

"We might as well go in the other room. It's chilly away from the fire, and there's no more to eat anyhow."

The grate clanked as he shook down ashes and clumped in coal. He reached for his sack of home grown, and a straw to poke through the pipestem. Then he settled back in his rocking chair and stretched his stockinged feet toward the fire. George hunched his chair closer to the stove and propped his chin on his big palms.

"When we was married," he began, "we didn't have much, but we had *something.* I wasn't in the prime of health, but I was able to do a *little.*"

Andrew toppled a crunched handful of brown dust into the corncob pipe, and struck a match.

"Who does the work now?"

George whiffed out about all the air in his insides.

"The woman and the little boy, what there is done, and it just about *kills* me to see 'em do it. But Andrew, I'm not able to set up half the time, with my health, and a-*worrying* like I do. And when I git to thinking about how things used to be and how they air now, I cain't do a thing but bawl. As a feller says, I don't' see what in the name of the Lord'll become of us!"

"I expect work might help more than thinking."

"But I *cain't* help it! As I was a-saying, when we was married, my tools was new; the mules was young; the place was fixed up; and I was able to do something. Now, the place needs fixing up; the mules is old; the tools and machinery's all wore out; I'm not able to lift a hand, hardly, worried to death like I am; and, as a feller says, I don't know what in *God's* name'll become of us."

Long whiffs of smoke circled up.

"Did you ever think of changing professions, doing something besides farming? Something you could do, and would like to do?"

He huddled closer to the heater.

"I've thought of it, Andrew, though I don't know what Ma'd say – about such. I was a-thinking to-day, I'd like to be the feller in one of them-there oil stations. Just set there in a warm place, and do might near nothing. I'd *like* that."

"Well, it's not all sitting, George. When you had to go out and change oil or grease in this kind of weather, you mightn't like it so well."

"That's so, Andrew. I was just thinking, if I could raise a little money, somehow – though I ort to have an indoor job." He stared hopelessly at the heater.

"Maybe a year or so in the foundry might do you good. It's hard work, but you'd be so busy you'd forget all about your troubles in no time."

"My God, Andrew, I couldn't stand hard work. And besides, my troubles is such a body cain't fergit, hardly."

"Now about clerking in a store – a grocery store, maybe? How'd that strike you?"

"All right, I reckon, but I couldn't do no delivering in the wet, and I ortn't to be on my feet a great sight."

"You wouldn't want to try a job in a factory? The shoe factory must have any amount of work to be done, sitting down."

George's whole frame shuddered.

"I don't think I could stand factory work, Andrew. Sometdays [sic] I'm not able to lift a hand! I'd bust right out and bawl if they begun scolding me, when I was ailing."

"Why don't you go on a regular bumming trip around the world, at least over the United States? Just tramp it for about a year? I'll guarantee you'd forget all about home troubles then."

"I'd like to, Andrew, though gitting shed of my troubles is another matter. I'd ruther travel than anything – 'specially if I could be sure of catching rides. But I cain't stand to be on my feet no time, hardly, if I'd starve to death away off, some'ers, and nobody'd know where – or git a arm or leg cut off, somehow, the way things air – . Oh, you ain't no idy, Andrew!"

Puff– puff – puff.

"You wouldn't want to work for a doctor, would you? I heard of a job the other day, that might just suit you. All you have to do is lie still while they tap your stomach – some kind of tests for cancer cure – at the clinic, where Mary had her operation. I believe you'd like that. Good pay, too, and if one of your bad spells got the best of you, you'd have the whole hospital force to work on you."

But the eager look on George's face had turned to frozen milk.

"You mean – the *rub*-doctors? Oh, my God, Andrew, don't say such a thing! I cain't bear to think of it. You ain't no idy!"

Smoke carried into a background that set of the bushy white hair and deep-set eyes. "Did you ever think of anything you *would* like to do?"

"Well, I don't know that I have, exactly, Andrew. But the doctors says I ort to have some sort of a change. Just git away from it all for a while, though God knows how I'm a-going to do it." He cleared his throat as his chair scraped over the floor. "You know, Andrew, I was a-thinking about this change business – maybe I could come up and stay with you folks for a while. I could bring a hog, maybe a hog and a half, and a sack of meal, I reckon, to pay for my keep, and I might git well just a-staying here, a-talking law and the like with you – stead of worrying all the time like I do."

The puffs had quickened into little popping explosions.

"Oh, good Lord Almighty, George! I couldn't have you here! Nancy's not able to wait on anybody, and we're not fixed for it anyway. And I wouldn't do it if I could! What would Mary and the children do? A man that marries and brings children into the world has some responsibilities for them. Why, my God, George, I can hardly imagine a man that has a spark of manhood about him, going off and leaving his family at all in the dead of winter. Let alone thinking of *staying* away."

Big tears seeped over George's lower lids and dripped from his chin. Andrew went on.

"This is a pretty serious business. You might go home and find them all frozen to death!"

"Oh, there's plenty of wood."

"Enough chopped to last several days?"

"Well, no, it's not chopped, but the woman and the little boy always do that as they use it."

"But there's plenty of it hauled up?"

"Well, it's not exactly hauled up, but there's plenty of it, a-laying loose in the timber. The little boy brings it up when we need it."

"How about food?" Is there plenty of everything to last while you're gone?"

"Well, there's three hogs there, though they ain't butchered yit, and there's plenty of corn. All that needs to be done is take it to mill, at Hell's Holler, and the woman and the little boy generally do that. It don't make much difference, Andrew, whether I'm there or not, the shape I'm in. I'm not much help when I am there. Mary said so herself."

"Hmmm."

"Mary's one of the finest women in the world, and I love her, and always will love her. But if I have to stay there and watch her do all the work that I'm not able to do, I believe I'm a-going to lose my mind."

"Well, George, you and Mary'll have to figure that out. I can't."

George stared at the heater a few minutes, and then dried his eyes and nose on the back of a heavy shirt-sleeve.

"Andrew, is there a place around Saint Jo, where a body can stay for nothing – some hospital, or something?"

"Why, I don't know of none. The *county* usually takes care of such cases. Why?"

"Somebody was a-telling me about a feller going down there for nervousness – to some hospital place. Said it was *real* nice. Warm all winter long, with plenty of grub, and no work to speak of – and didn't cost a cent."

"Well, the state hospital for the insane is down there, and there's no doubt they should know how to treat nervousness. The question is, would you want to go there?"

"Why, I don't know Andrew. Do the patients have to work?"

"Some very light work, I judge."

"And there's plenty to eat?"

"Yes, I'd think so."

"Warm?"

"Oh, I suppose so."

"All free?"

"Yes, I think so, if you're not able to pay for it.

"You reckon I could git in, 'count of my nervousness?"

"You might, that is, if the doctors and county court say you need treat-ment."

"Say, Andrew, if a body was sent to this-here hospital place, and he'd made some kind of a crazy bargain, a month or so before or such a matter, maybe being out of his head when he done it – you reckon there might be a chanct of it's being struck out?"

"There might?"

George blinked about five times before he said anything.

"Good Lord, Andrew! Sounds like this might be the very place for me to go and rest up in. I sure do hope I can go. Stands to reason they'd have better doctors in a big place like that. Maybe I can git cured of my ailment, for all time. I'm a-going home now, like you said. Mary and the younguns ort to have a man with 'em through this cold spell, I reckon. And, anyhow, I want to think more about this thing. But first chance I git, after Pa's trial, I'm a-going to town and see a doctor!"

The little woman was nodding in her chair in front of the stove now, so he did not awaken her. He stretched up, buckled his four-buckle over-shoes, buttoned his coats and shirts, and crunched down the cinder path to the road.

Chapter 10 : The Trial

November came in, cold and crisp as corn fodder covered with frost. The trial was set for the eighth, and Sarah got up at three o'clock, in order to get breakfast and the chores over and into court by nine. Fifteen long, tedious miles. The little courage Lige had seemed chilled and numbed, as he stumbled into the courtroom after Sarah's brown dress, like an ox that has already received one blow, and is waiting for the end.

He had never been to court before, and peered timidly around at the curious faces, like a mouse in a wire trap. They reminded him of a crowd that had assembled for hanging, ten or fifteen years ago. He looked over at Jim Tittle and his brother, John. It occurred to him that god Almighty must have been well nigh out of material when he made the Tittles, expecially Jim – no neck to speak of, a nose that looked as if it had been thrown at him, and a mouth that billowed out like the flounce on a petticoat. It may have been Jim's quarrels from time to time altered divine intentions, but it was evident not much had been intended. Now with one ear half gone, and a jaggily scar that puckered his near eye, he looked like a tomcat, that had got the worst of it. The two brothers stared back, on the order of stalking dogs about ready to spring. Lige turned toward twelve men that settled like mud-pies in two rows of wooden benches. There was not a flicker of expression on a single face, and he knew he could expect as much mercy and understanding from them as a chicken, cooped half a week ahead of time, can expect from a man with an axe on Sunday. He turned to the little old man with the wooden hammer, whose fuzzy forehead reminded one of a green peach, who had just enough nose at the end to keep his spectacles from falling off. He seemed to have turtle eyes – always half shut, so that little more than the whites showed, but maybe he had got up at three o'clock too.

Tap! Tap! Tap!

Lige blinked and sat up, but it was somebody else's trial; somebody stealing corn, or not stealing it. He tried hard to follow what they were saying, but monotonous voices droned like a swarm of bees or rattled as fast as "The Devil's Dream" on the fiddle.

"Do you swear – ta – ta – ta – ta – 's help you God?"

It took him half the morning to figure out that much of what they were saying, and by that time the main question seemed to have changed to something else. One after another hands stuck up like Happy John's in the spirit of renunciation, and words whined on and on, like repentant sinners at camp meeting. Finally the lawyers shouted a while, and the twelve men filed out like cows at milking time. It was three o'clock by the time they got to Lige's trial.

Tap! Tap! Tap!

Lige could feel his heart pounding with the wooden hammer. The little old man seemed unable to prop his eyes open, but he cleared his voice to partial understanding.

"We come to the case of James Obadiah Tittle against Lige Bartholomew Moore — – ta – ta – ta – ta – twelve good and lawful men, chosen and summoned – – ta – ta – ta – ta – – this trial hereof proceeds."

His voice dwindled off in a little squeak, and he sank back as if another word would have been too much. Lige felt as if he were at the bottom of a well, with the walls caving in. By the time he looked up from his old congress shoes, the judge's eyes had re-opened to the half-way point, and the first witness had been called.

"Johnathan Tittle."

John Tittle was a man a little shorter than Jim, but with the same general features. His nose had not been flattened in fight, and seemed to apologize for this shortcoming, by crouching as low as possible. His mouth did not quite reach his ears, but the lips were thick, with the Tittle morning-glory flare. He had some pretense of a neck, and his ears were unclipped. Otherwise, he had the same general appearance of his brother – sunburned till he was half nigger, and shirt and overalls so habitually grimy, that one wondered if he *bought* dirty ones.

"Raise your right hand. Johnathan Tittle, do you swear – – ta – ta – ta – ta – – s' help you God?"

"I swear."

"Where were you at the time of this unfortunate bloodshed?"

"Well, I wasn't there when the fight took place. Was up town, a seeing about the right-o-way, but –"

Johnathan's tale meandered around like a path through the Chariton Hills, in spite of lawyer prompting. Above a tangle of whiskers, Lige's blinking eyes watched every move, and seemed ready to burst out at any moment. Twice he was on the point of jumping up and yelling, "You lie, John Tittle!" but fear of the law kept him down. His time was coming. John Tittle mentioned the turkey trouble and went on.

"After we'd agreed on the right-o-way, we bought a brand-new gate, and my brother started to put it up, and would of, too, if Lige and Sary hadn't a-jumped on him, like a couple of fighting roosters –"

Lige listened half in a daze until his lawyer began to pry himself up for cross-questioning. Lawyer Rankin was more of a balloon than a man. Starting with his chin, he gradually swelled out like a cyclone cave to his belt, and then rounded down to his shoes. It was as if he had been poured into shirts and pants, and had not quite jelled. In bulk he equaled two or three ordinary men. Time and again officers had tried to arrest him for Saturday night drunkenness, but he had stretched out, flat of his back, and the jig was up. It took more than the police force to budge him and he knew it. In the same way he seemed to know law.

"About these turkeys, you say you and your brother ate 'em?"

"Yeah. They'd been a-running into our oats and corn all summer –"

"You knew they belonged to Sarah Moore?"

"Yeah, we knowed it, but we figgered we'd fed 'em –"

"Did you have Sarah Moore's consent, to kill and eat her turkeys?"

"Why, no, but we calculated –"

"Do you realize what name is applied to the confiscation of other's people's property, without their consent?"

"I – I reckon you mean stealing, but 'pears to me like –"

"That is all."

The next witness was old man Jimpson. His little red eyes circled the courtroom.

"Ebenezer Jimpson, do you swear –?"

The white funnel beard jiggled up and down as his right hand raised. His face had a kind of baffled billygoat look – one that has butted into a rock wall, and is still in a half daze.

"Ebenezer Jimpson, where were you a little before noon, on the fateful morning of September 27th. Point it out on this chart, to the jury."

He see-sawed from one foot to the other, as he turned to a chair-bottom looking thing with a handle to it, marked off on thick paper, and then all splotched up with a kind of blackberry juice.

"Well, I ain't a-going to swear jest to the inch, but I was some'ers along here, by the graveyard, behind a clump of scrub oak."

"Tell the jury exactly what you saw – in your own way."

"Well, understand, I didn't see the start of this here ear-cutting, but I seed the end of it. 'Twas two agin one, and Jim not a-lifting a hand. The way Lige was a-whooping and hollering, and Sary too, hit's a wonder he didn't cut Jim clean to smithereens. Anyhow, he's been a-aiming to git at him for a long time. Long about the middle of September, I was over to Lige Moore's to see about something or other, and he said he 'lowed to *kill* Jim Tittle, if he didn't stay off of his land. Lige was riled half-way to Hades. Said Jim had stole turkeys of his'n and Sary's, and druv right through the middle of his whole corn crop, till it wasn't worth shucks. Said if done airy other damage, he'd do a little hisself. I ain't agin Lige, mind you, cause him and Sary's been mighty good to us, more'n Jim ever done, till right lately, but 'pears to me like, Jim that skeered he hadn't teched airy one of 'em, Lige aimed to do more'n he done. 'Pears to me like, Jim was real lucky, losing only *half* a ear!"

Lawyer Rankin reared his rounded bulk upward.

"You say Lige was hollering when you came up? What was he hollering about?:

"Oh, one thing and another. Something about killing Jim, near as I recollect. Said if he teched Sary again, he'd do I don't know what all –"

"Hmmm. Sounds as if Jim *had* touched her, don't it?"

"Yeah, but Lige was that mad he didn't know what he was a-saying. He was a-pushing hisself up from the ground, sort a-rubbing the back of his breeches –"

"Hmmm. I don't suppose Lige just sat down, because he was tired out. Did Jim have anything to knock him down with?"

"Had a claw-hammer, to keep 'em off."

"It seems to me, he'd a-pushed them away, when they came at him – in self defense."

"That's what he done. Pushed Sary off, and then knocked Lige plum off his feet. But he got right up, roaring like a mad bull, and –"

"Hold on, a minute. Didn't you say on oath, a minute ago, that he never touched either one of them?"

"Well, if I did, I lied. He teched 'em, but he done it in *self* defense."

"That is all."

The case was postponed until Monday morning.

The long ride home, waiting over Sunday, pacing up and down, three o'clock Monday morning again, the chilling ride to town, twelve chunks of side-meat, hanging from wooden benches, with only staring eyes and twitching ears to indicate any life whatever, the sleepy little man staring over spectacles with half-shut eyes, the wooden hammer – and the trial went on. Jim Tittle took the stand and droned out his tale: Lige's unreasonable demands, the abuse of the turkeys, how he had even cut through Lige's field and smashed down corn to tell the turkeys where they belonged, the gate and axe episode –. Other witnesses, and finally George.

"Raise your right hand. George Moore, do you swear to tell the truth, the whole truth, and nothing but the truth, s' help you God?"

"Why, yeah, I always *did* tell the truth, fer as I know. Leastways, I always aimed to –"

From her chair, Sarah beamed with modest pride, but the judge only frowned and stared over spectacles. Lawyer Rankin cleared his throat and reared back in his chair.

"Where were you when this affair took place?"

George swallowed three times before he could say anything. He was so worried and worked up from watching Lige, – thinking of how they had both been swooped up by circumstances, and how helpless a body was in the clutch of uptowners – that he hardly knew what he was doing.

"Well, I ain't right sure as I know myself, but I was somewhere on the way home, from watching the hogs out of graveyard. I'd stopped to rest a mite, and got to thinking about first one thing and another, till I stayed longer'n I aimed to, and when I heared 'em a-fussing, I was so nervous and worried, I wouldn't want to say for sure what I seed, and didn't see. My wife was sick, just over a operation, and not able to be out of bed yet, and I'm always a-ailing, seems like, not able to lift a hand hardly, and Ma and Pa over a-doing most of the work, what the little boy didn't do. But I do know Ma had ten or a dozen young turkeys, nigh on to ready to market. She was a-aiming to give a good part of 'em to me and Mary, and they all disappeared, all but the old gobbler and two or three hens, and Jim claims him and his brother et 'em."

Jim's lawyer was as lank as lawyer Rankin was round. He looked as if he'd been lost in the woods, and hadn't had anything to eat for a week, but he seemed stout enough. He slapped the table with a hand on the order of a pancake with the soda left out.

"I object."

"Objection overruled. Go on."

But George had shriveled up like a tobacco worm sprinkled with some of Andrew's bug poison. His mouth was open wider than usual and his eyes stared straight ahead. Lige turned and stared too, but saw only an unimportant looking man with a black beard – some uptowner, evidently, curious about trials – coming into court. But it seemed George had worked himself up to one of his nervous spells, ready to go to pieces at the least thing, for they could get no more out of him, after that. He slunk back to his seat like a stray cat, and Sarah took the stand.

"Sarah Moore, do you swear – – s' help you God?"

"Yes, I do. And I swear that Jim Tittle, besides cutting cat-a-slaunch-ways through our whole eighty acres, all summer, spite of all Lige could do, all the time pretending like he was a-going to buy and doing nothing, is a turkey thief of the worst kind. I had nine or ten young turkeys, not counting three old hens and a gobbler, and Jim Tittle and his brother sic'ed the dog on 'em, and killed and et every last one of 'em, all but the gobbler and hens. He said so hisself!"

"I object," interrupted Jim's lawyer.

Sarah turned on him with the ruffled fury of a strutting gobbler.

"And I object. I didn't raise them turkeys for Jim Tittle, or his brother either. I raised 'em for George. If a feller's cattle gits in another man's corn, tother feller don't have no right to start in a-killing, does he? I worked like a dog to raise them turkeys, but I raised 'em for me and mine. I done the best I could, Mary in the hospital with her operation, and then not able to git out of bed. I'd a-paid for the damage they done, I guess, that is, if Jim'd a-left enough of anything on the place, cutting through the way he done, to pay for anything. I always paid before."

She paused for enough breath to go on.

"Nobody's sorrier than me and Lige, the way things turned out – chopping off Jim's ear. Lige didn't intend it."

"I object."

"Objection overruled."

"Lige wouldn't hurt a fly, less'n it was biting him might near to death. Won't hardly kill a chicken, let alone slicing off a man's ear, a-purpose –"

"I object."

Her full skirt swirled as she turned like a hen with young chicks.

"You can object till the cows come home. I'm a-talking now."

"Order! Order! Objection overruled. Go on, Mrs. Moore."

"We tried to reason with Jim, but he was plum hard-headed. Hadn't paid a cent, mind you, and said he'd put up that gate if he had to kill somebody to do it."

"I object."

"Overruled."

"Lige plum lost patience. Jim'd druv through our corn all summer, cat-a-slaunch-ways, mind you, might near ruined the whole patch; killed all my young turkeys; set the dog on the old uns so's I don't reckon they're any account; and was fighting us off with a-claw-hammer. Lige lost his temper, and raised the axe. I tried to stop him, but the axe turned and slivered off part of Jim's ear. We didn't intend it, nary one of us, I swear –"

"I object."

"Objection overruled. Take the witness."

Lawyer Crookshank chewed each sagging inner cheek, by turns.

"Well, – I don't know as I want her."

Lige hardly knew what he was saying when he took the stand. He tried to tell the truth, the whole truth, and nothing but the truth, and stuck to his story in the cross-questioning, but his voice sounded as far away as the Chariton Hills.

More witnesses. More cross questioning. Andrew Moore, Ben Bragg, the family doctor, or rather George's doctor, a banker with whom Lige had had dealings, when he had anything to have dealing about – all testified to Lige's moral character and previous good record. It was time for the lawyers, and Lawyer Ranking finally pushed himself to his feet. It seemed to Lige that he talked enough to clear fifty people, or condemn them, but he kept on.

"Gentlemen of the jury, before my client can be convicted, it must be proved beyond reasonable doubt that he raised the axe against Jim Tittle with deliberate intent to strike off one of his ears, which has not been done. Furthermore, it must be proved beyond reasonable doubt that Lige Moore was in the wrong to defend his property from the whims and ruthless destruction of Jim Tittle. This has not been done.

"There has been proof of previous good moral character, which is sufficient in and of itself to constitute reasonable doubt of the defendant's intentions against the plaintiff's ear, sufficient to acquit the defendant.

"Gentlemen of the jury, I ask you to consider the good moral character of all our witnesses: hard-working farmers, men with life-long records of truthfulness and honesty, reliable men, men of honor, a doctor, a banker. Gentlemen of the jury, look at the chief witnesses on the other side: plaintive and his brother, and a man whose testimony we know is false – *two thieves and a liar!* – two self-confessed thieves, and a man whose testimony under oath is admitted to be lies! Gentlemen of the jury, according to all evidence submitted, even evidence on the opposing side, most of which has to be disregarded, my client only raised the axe in self defense – of himself, his wife, and his property. I rest my case with you."

It was Jim's lawyers' turn. Lawyer Crookshank seemed to have grown thinner since Saturday. His cheeks caved in like Chariton Hill gullies, and his hands seemed to hang from hoe handles. His mouth puckered to a point when not in use, but his booming voice pushed out the drawstring. He begged and bellowed, on and on, and finally concluded:

"Gentlemen of the jury, I appeal to the kindliness of your hearts. Look at my client!"

The profile of Jim Tittle, with flattened nose, short neck and missing lobe, for some reason reminded Lige of a bull they had had when the was a boy – always bellowing and goring till he tore off one horn and scratched his head half to pieces in barbwire, and they had to sell him. Jim's lawyer went on.

"Look at him, gentlemen of the jury, – a fine, specimen of noble manhood, in the prime of life; a handsome, strong-looking chap, until his ear was cruelly cut off by the unfeeling axe of the defendant – his good looks gone in an instant, spoiled and maimed forever! Gentlemen of the jury, my client is a single man, unmarried, – yet of marriageable age. What chance has he now at that greatest of all blessings – a happy home? What self-respecting woman would not hesitate to link her life to a man with half an ear? Gentlemen of the jury, picture his life from now on – a life of loneliness! No loving wife to welcome him home; no child to carry on that venerable name – those noble, God-given features – all hopes of happiness cut off, by the sharp axe of Lige Moore. Gentlemen of the jury, I ask you, should not Lige Moore pay for the ruin of this promising young life? Should he not pay for the destruction of his very soul? Should he not pay for the blight on succeeding generations? That which God gives – and God gives us ears – is not for man to take away! I say, let the defendant *pay*! I rest my case in confidence of your kindly understanding."

The twelve men filed out, and twelve bags of cement could not have shown less expression and feeling. Lige was shaking like a man with the palsy. He turned for a minute and looked at Jim Tittle. There was a sheep-ish expression on Jim's face, something like a dog that has been caught sucking eggs. Finally after an infinite wait, the twelve men filled back and the verdict was read.

"We, the jury, find for the defendant."

Defendant – that was him, Lige. Had he won, and Jim lost? Sarah squeezed to him, through the crowd.

"Lige! It's over – and we won! All but paying the lawyers. I reckon it'll take our two best cows, and all the money we got in the bank for that – but, oh Lord, how much *would* it a-took, if we'd a-lost?"

Lige was still in a daze.

"How much you reckon it'll cost Jim and John?"

"I ain't no idy. But don't think about that, Lige. You won! I might a-knowed you would. I dreamt of blood not two weeks ago – though It plum slipped my mind till right now – and blood is an *awful* good sign. I reckon them shoes I kept dreaming about was the trouble we was already in."

"I wonder what Jim's a-thinking –. I reckon he'll hold this agin me, long as I live – and maybe after I'm dead."

"Oh, Lige, surely he wouldn't hold hard feelings agin the dead –"

Chapter 11 : Butchering

"It's all white outside!"

Lawrence jabbed a long gray underweared leg into a pair of patched overalls, with the look of a dog after a rabbit. The bedroom door pushed open, and four models of winter underwear, graduating downward like a bumpy hill, toddled to the window, sniffling and wiping noses. The woman turned from the oven door, one hand holding her apron, as if shooing chicks.

"Now, you children git back in bed – every last one of you – till it gits warm up here. You cain't go out to-day nohow, without no wraps. You're all a-going to catch your death, spite of all I can do!"

Four suits of underwear filed out like prisoners whose sentences have just been prolonged. The privileged one snapped overall clip over brass buttons and slid arms into an oversized coat.

"Mommy, air there some planks, or something some'ers – I could have to make a slider, with?"

"I don't know of none, Lawrence, and besides – I want you to go back to school to-day."

Her voice sounded thin and strained, like whey from clabber cheese. Lawrence wiggled two toes that peeped out from a home-knit stocking, and picked at a peeled-off place in his shoe sole.

"School, Mommy? Air you sure you're well enough?"

"I'm a-going to be all right now, Lawrence. The doctor said so. I want you to go."

It was hard to give up the sliding idea, with the white hills outside.

"Mommy, seeing as I been out so long – couldn't I just wait and go next term now? Teacher – always asks 'rithmetic tables and such, and – I don't know nothing about 'em –"

"The teacher'll help you, I reckon."

"Mommy, – I wisht I didn't have to go. Teachers don't like to fool with kids that don't know nothing, and come next to no time, like me and Jimpsons. Couldn't I just stay home and carry in wood, or something – cause it might snow some more, maybe?"

Her eyes had a kind of soft sadness, like a lame dog.

"You go to-day, Lawrence, and ask the teacher to show you what all you missed – and maybe I can help you. I'll fix you a nice dinner, and you can carry it in that red lard pail your grandma brung you."

"What'll you fix me, Mommy?"

"Oh, some of that ham and cake your grandma sent over, and some bread and jam, I reckon."

He liked that red bucket, and he never had carried his first dinner in it yet, but he did love sliding, and this was the first day.

"Mommy, that dollar you're a-going to give me when you sell Sampson, – can I do with it what I want – buy me a sled, maybe?"

"Yes. It'll be your'n when we sell him."

Back of the house toward the backyard, a wisp of smoke whipped up-ward, and little flames licked the bottom of Sarah's big iron kettle. A little old man with a cotton batting beard, and a boy about twelve, held out yarn mittens over it.

"What's old man Jimspon and Bill a-doing out there? Air – you a-going to butcher to-day, Mommy?"

She looked up from the cookstove, where she kept punching at the fire.

"Yes, Lawrence, and seemed like your pa just couldn't bring hisself to do it – leastways, he said he couldn't. And your grandpa didn't feel equal to it. That trial took a heap out of him – and rheumatism, and all. And Ben Bragg's ma down sick in bed – so's we had to git 'em –"

"Then I reckon I will go. Jimpsons ain't got no feeling for hogs and such – no more than if they were chunks of firewood. Tell 'em not to be too mean, Mommy. Sampson wouldn't like to see it."

He crunched through the snow, down the road, swinging his red bucket. Nobody had been through to Hog Creek School yet, from his direction, and the wind had swooped up drifts high as his waist in stretches. He straddled through, holding the bucket high, and kicking the snow from his overalls when he reached barren ground.

It was like wading through flooded fields, when the creek was up, so far as speed goes. He had not turned the corner, where mail boxes roosted on an old wagon wheel, when he heard snorting and bellowing behind him. His eyes widened as his small head turned and dived for the nearest fence. Clang! The bucket rose like a rocket – twice. Then the dented lid flew off, and buried cornbread, ham and cake in a snowdrift – on his side. He shinnied up a hickory tree, just in case the barbed wire gave way, and sat there shivering and sniffling until the animal tired of pawing snow, and marched on down the road, mooing a little and shaking it's head. Then he slid down the trunk and fished out his lunch. Cornbread, he didn't bother about, except a bite out the blackberry jam – but the ham and cake tasted good, even though both were snow-cold and somewhat soaked.

Away in the distance a bell clanged. Late! No recess, and cross eyes staring over spectacles! Besides, what was the use to go on, with no lunch to look forward to? His toes felt like separate chunks of ice. He tried to wiggle them to warmth as he stood trying to decide. Should he go on – or back?

Sudden shrill sounds tore the air. Oh Lord, they were killing the pigs! He stopped his ears with his ragged mittens, but the sounds squealed through – as if all the pigs in the world were being cut pieces, bit by bit. Sampson must be crazy-afraid. How would he know that he was safe – that only the others would be killed? Oh, Lord! Would Jimpsons know Sampson was his? Suppose they killed him with the others? Suppose they were killing him now? It sounded like Sampson! Maybe it *was* Sampson!

He rolled under the fence – the old coat caught, but he let it tear – and stumbled through the snow, up the road, toward the perpetual squeals. The sun melted into a cloud, and the sky turned red at the bottom, like the world was a kettle, with fire all around. Snow weighted his feet down, but he straggled on, screaming, "Sampson!"

With blurred eyes that hardly saw, he panted into the yard and out to the pig pen, stumbling and sobbing. It was worse than he thought. Bill Jimpson, hunched over a hatchet, dogged Sampson at a gallop around the pen, whacking him every time he got near enough – like he was kindling wood, or sticks for the stove. And Sampson, all hacked up and bloody, with one ear gone, and his side wide open – squealed continuously as he dodged. But Lawrence outdid him.

"Sampson!"

He seemed to understand – anyway, he stopped and turned – as the hatchet sank deep, and he fell with a final squeal – kicking.

"Sampson!"

He ran around back of the barn and sank into a snowdrift, high piled and soft as goose feathers, and whiter than Sampson. He couldn't stop crying. He pushed his head into the hard gray boards and tightened his arms around head and shoulders, to squeeze off the sounds and the shaking. Something warm and soft pressed around him.

"Don't take on so, Lawrence. You can have another pig if you want."

"No! No! No!"

"I don't blame you none. I told George we ort to sell him, like we said. I knowed you'd take on terrible, but he said it'd take three pigs to do us – and we couldn't hardly afford to take him to town, or have him took, and buy another'n –"

He tried to stop crying – to squeeze back every tear.

"But, Mommy, look how mean he killed him – Sampson, that I teached to drink milk with my fingers, and was good to as a baby."

"I know. Hit ain't right to kill pigs that away. But we didn't have no gun nor nothing, and they didn't, and your grandpa's out of whack, and him worried to death anyhow, and Ben Bragg's ma so sick they don't know whether she'll live or die."

He hid his face in her skirt.

"Mommy, – he was like a little dog, Sampson was, and us kids didn't have nothing else–"

"I know –"

"I don't never want no 'nother pig – just Sampson –"

Her eyes were like rain barrels, running over, after a storm.

"It ain't right, to pet a pig and then kill it –"

"Mommy, you reckon Sampson thought it was me – a-whacking him with that hatchet?"

"No."

"Mommy, you're a-crying too. Don't cry. 'Tain't no use, now."

He burst into another sobbing spell, and she held him tighter.

"We'd better go in now, Lawrence. You'll take your death."

"I don't care none, Mommy. Sometimes – I wisht I *was* with Sampson."

"He's all right, now."

"Yes, but look how long it'll be before I git to see him again!"

"Well, – he'll be better off, I expect."

"Yes, only – he'll forgit all about me – up there, where they're good to him all the time – I reckon."

The arm tightened.

"Come on. Let's go in the house. I'll heat some milk for you. You'll feel better, bye and bye."

The iron kettle lay between them and the house, but they made a wide circle of it. Once inside, Lawrence watched with the eyes of an owl. One after another, the man and boy chunked carcasses into scalding water and scraped away paths of bristles until three pink lumps stretched clean on the snow. Old man Jimpson tramped to the door, and poked in his head, his white-funnel beard jerking at every other word.

"George, can you give us a *lift*? Me and the boy *cain't* swing 'em up *alone*. He's stout, but he's only twelve. This is his *first* butchering – but I wanted him to learn."

George pushed back from the door, away from the wind.

"Well, I'll do what I can, though I reckon 'twon't be much, that is, soon as I wrap up and git on my gum boots."

The white beard flopped in the wind outside. George sauntered to the other room and came back buttoning old coats, and bulging like a balloon.

"I ain't a well man," he began, "but I'm willing to help when I can, that is, what I can stand to do, though God knows that's little enough –"

The door slammed and shut out further words, but Lawrence watched every move from the window. The old man and boy tugged at the tail-end of the middle sized lump, while George lifted the forefeet and swung it to the scaffold. Lawrence turned to his mother with troubled eyes.

"Mommy, you reckon Pappy'll lift so much he'll hurt his back, and be worse'n ever?"

"Oh, surely not. There's three of 'em."

They struggled with the second lump, the smallest one and George swung it up as easily as if it had been a bag of dried apples. The third lump was a problem. They had estimated it at over two hundred pounds – too much for a sick man, a man over eighty and a boy of twelve. Old man Jimpson and the boy lifted at the hindparts, but they couldn't budge it. They left, to look for something to pry up the weight with less strain. George did not notice they had gone. His mouth was moving, and his unhappy expression indicated that his mind was on his misfortunes. Up went two hundred pounds of pork, with nobody else touching it, as the big man rambled on of his ailments, not realizing what he had done. The white beard stuck out like a thick icicle, and the boy stared open-mouthed. Lawrence turned big eyes to his mother, but she had gone back to dish-washing.

Left on the scaffold, the three carcasses stiffened in the cold, like long underwear on the line. At last, JImpsons were leaving, the old man stumping down the road, and the boy, with a heavy kettle of dark red and white pork, slapping his thigh and stumbling after. All morning in the two room house, machines ground, knives whacked and cracklings sizzled, until the boy was half sick.

George did not lift a hand to help in anything. One look, and he shriveled like a bug in a lantern, and collapsed on the bed. Mary steamed over the skillet and tugged at the sausage mill until the heat got the best of her. She sank to a chair and blotted arms, face and neck with a checkered apron.

"George, cain't you take care of the lard making, whilst I cool off?"

He turned over on his stomach, his chin on his wrists.

"No, Mary, I cain't. I aimed to help with all of it, what I could stand to do, but the way I'm a-feeling, don't look like I can do nothing. Seems like it makes me sick at my stomick to look at it. Oh, Lord, Mary, you ain't no idy!"

"George, you surely ain't a-going to lay there and let me cut up three hogs by myself!"

"I cain't help it, Mary. You ain't no idy how things air, or you wouldn't ask me. The Lord knows I want to help what I can, but seems like I cain't stand to even think about cutting up carcasses, let alone cut. If you ain't able to do it, maybe one the neighbors'll help, or Ma or Pa, but I cain't."

He hugged his head in smothered weeping. The woman went back to grinding and sizzling. A small hand tapped his shoulder.

I know how you feel, Pappy. I feel the same way myself.

"Oh, Lawrence, you ain't no idy. Seems like, I couldn't cut up one of them pigs if it was a matter of life and death. And I cain't bear to even see anybody else do it. I cain't tell you what it is, but when I see all that cutting a-going on, and git to thinking, seems like I might near lose my mind."

"I know, Pappy. I'm the same way. I cain't hardly bear to think of chopping 'em in little chunks – them alive and squealing a little while ago,

Sampson all of 'em. I ain't got no Sampson now –"

The small mouth puckered and the eyes filled and dripped over. George turned over on his side, and stared out at the river haze. His mouth opened and closed several times, but it seemed hard to find words.

"Lawrence, there's a heap worse things than killing pigs – but I'm awful sorry about Sampson. If I'd a had any idy you'd a-took on, like Mary said you done, we'd a-done different. I knowed you thought a heap of Sampson – but seems like a feller has to have meat, and that was the cheapest way of gitting it. I don't like to see things a-suffering and squealing myself. I just wisht the Lord'd a-thought of a different way of doing things, but he never done it, so what you going to do? And I always thought Sampson was one of the humanist pigs, ever I seed, and I knowed you did. I just wisht we could a-et the meat, and had Sampson too, but seems like they don't do things that a-way. I'm turrible sorry, like I said, but – a body *cain't* git along without meat, seems like, and how in the name of God you going to git it, without killing things?"

Lawrence was almost happy.

"You're the best pappy a body ever had, you sick like you air, and a-thinking of me that way, and Sampson and all of 'em. I had no idy you was that sorry for pigs, you couldn't bear to see 'em cut up."

George boarded up his eyes with both hands.

"Oh, Lord, Lawrence, you ain't no idy!"

A team and wagon was clumping up the road. George shaded his eyes with both hands.

"It's Ma and Grandma Nesbit and Tizzie. Lawrence, if I was you, I'd try to git on the good side of your grandma, and Tizzie too. I never could, but again they think enough of a body, they'll do fer 'em. Look at all they do for your Grandma. They ain't much to look at, I reckon – leastways, Grandma ain't, – but they got property, both of 'em, and property counts, these days –"

Sarah turned around at the gate. Had to get back to Lige, she said. Grandma Nesbit didn't come very often. She was a little old woman over eighty, but as spry again as most people her age. She humped over half double, and tested each foot before risking a step, but her regular forceful cane clops reminded one of a dasher churn. Her cotton batting hair was parted in the middle and pulled back tight, as if to force out the lines in her forehead. But she had uncommonly sharp eyes, and stared continually over the rims of her glasses.

Tizzie was a younger edition of Sarah, only more on the smile order. Her gray hair was soft, and fuzzed around her temples. Her black eyes snapped with a kind of good humor that Sarah lacked. Lawrence had never felt any too much at home with them – but he forced himself to a combination of side show entertainer, and did his best, only everything seemed to go wrong.

"Look, Grandma! Look, Aunt Tizzie, look at what I can do! Come out on the porch and watch me! Look, Aunt Tizzie, looky here!"

He shinnied up the Ben Davis apple tree to the lowest limb, cupped his knees over, swung, and dropped to his feet. He skinned a cat. He hung by his toes, and swung by his toes. He hung by his heels, and keyed up by success so far, started to swing, but he edged off, and, plump – down he went, head first. His rubbery neck, which he hoped would break and end his misery, merely doubled and straightened like a fish worm, new dug. He rubbed the back of his head and eyed the two women like a crawfish trying to escape. Aunt Tizzie only smiled, but Grandma Nesbit's gimlet eyes bored into him over her spectacles.

"I knowed a boy that hung by his feet when he was little, and he had the spasms!" she chanted. "Besides, it's a wonder to me you didn't break your neck – not saying what harm you done to the apple tree."

She stumped into the house, her cane clicking out each step. Mary called dinner, but the Lord seemed to be against Lawrence that day. At the table he reached for a slab of fresh meat, and then stared, his fork in the air.

"Mommy, air you *sure* this ain't Sampson?"

"Yes. I had him kept separate, when they brung him in. He ain't cut up yet."

He speared a piece to his plate, but his eyes began to drip.

"Looks like Sampson – *might* be Sampson –"

"I'll fix you an egg," said Mary, getting up.

Sharp eyes stared over spectacles rims.

"When I was little, I was told to eat what was put before me, and say nothing about it."

She was still staring when he raised wet eyes.

"I don't like to see things killed."

She tossed her head with a kind of snort, and each word came out with a separate clump, like gooseberries in an empty pan.

"I don't reckon anybody does, – but how'd you git meat without it? Why, even the Lord done it, and what's good enough for Him's good enough for me!"

"I seed that boy a hacking Sampson with a hatchet, and I don't 'low to never eat no more meat –"

"The idy! Whoever heard of the like? If I was your ma, I'd put a stop to such tomfoolery, if I had to take my foot to you."

He felt a lump rising in his throat, but it stuck like a chicken's craw, and wouldn't go down. He started gulping apple sauce, hoping the lump would go with the sauce, but the sharp eyes were still on him. Half way to his mouth, the spoon turned and the sauce plopped on his clean shirt. His quick tongue stretched down and licked it up, but the eyes saw.

"That boy needs a bib! Tie something around his neck, Mary."

"He's just upset. Take some of them canned strawberries and cream, Lawrence. Your grandma sent 'em over, and I know you like 'em. Don't think about Sampson no more."

He ladled out as much as he dared, without somebody saying something, and then turned to the cream. Generally there was not over two spoons apiece, but to-day there was a whole big pitcher, all everybody wanted, and so thick and rich, it looked as if it were half butter. He poured and poured – they were all talking now – and then opened his mouth for a well heaped spoon. It was like expecting lemonade, and getting vinegar. He ran to the door to spit it out.

"Why, Lawrence, what's the matter?"

He tried to smooth out his face. "Sour."

Mary spooned some cream and smacked her lips. "Why, Lawrence, this cream's all right. Ort to be. I skimmed it from the morning's milk."

"I got mine from the big pitcher."

"Why, Lawrence, you used buttermilk."

If she had told him he had five noses, he could have felt no worse. It was bad enough to eat meat – but strawberries and buttermilk! Evidently the grandmother felt the same as he did.

"I never heard tell of the like! Won't eat meat – and putting buttermilk on strawberries! The idy! I never seed such doings. Strawberries and buttermilk! I declare!"

He slid down from his chair and ran from the room. He had tried so hard –. When he heard the team and wagon come and go, he crept back to the house. His mother's eyes were as soft and shiny as sorghum molasses, and he could see himself right on top, his head on one side, staring.

"Your great grandma's bark is a heap worse than her bite, Lawrence," she said. "She left you a dollar for a slider, and soon as they butcher, she's a-aiming to swap one of their pigs for Sampson, if it'll please you any."

It was not such an unbearable world after all.

"Only, – I hope they don't git Jimpsons to do their butchering fer 'em," he added out loud.

Chapter 12 : An Old Square Dance

Rough-planed planks poked out over the bank of the river, and the moon, peeping over hilltops and trees, left long lines of light on the gurgling black. Over the dam, churning foam and water kept up a continual rumble, but the fiddle shrieked out above the waterfall, and old man Jimpson's rooster-crowing voice outdid them all.

> "Pen the pig three rails high;
> Pig jump out and the hog jump in,
> Three hands around and circle agin;
> Hog jump out and four hands around;
> Ladies docee and gents, you know,
> Swing by the right, and right and left go."

George unhooked chin and fiddle and stared through slits and knotholes at the bubbling black water. He was as jumpy as an old sitting hen. Not a week ago the river had been mostly frozen over, and water over the damn had trickled like cold molasses, but now it pounded like a threshing machine. Seemed as if the noise got louder every minute. Maybe it was fixing to go out, with all the thaw and drizzle, the last few days. The Lord knew he was in no hurry to go, but when his time came, maybe this was as good a way as any, all things considered. If the dam would just sweep out and take everything with it, and everybody, and churn up the whole mess together, so they would never find hair nor hide of anybody again, or at least know who was who, or what was what, it might be the easiest way out for him. Still, there was that insane asylum idea. The more he thought about it, the better the whole thing sounded. One of the pill doctors from uptown had intimated, like Andrew had, that anybody could go if he could get three doctors to say he needed treatment, and Ben Bragg even recollected an uncommonly odd bargain somebody'd got out of, for being sent to the insane asylum for a while. The only thing was, seemed like he could hardly bear to pull out and leave Mary, and maybe be gone all winter. Funny thing, but when you've been married to somebody for ten years or such a matter, you get so used to having them around, it's as hard to part with them as an easy pair of shoes, even though you know it's only for a matter of time, and for your own good in the end, more than likely. Without Mary and the children, it would be like going without potatoes every meal for the Lord knew how long. The more he thought about it, the worse he felt. Even his fiddle-playing could not shake off the gloom that seemed to hover over him, and stick to his skin like a wet shirt.

Old man Jimpson's white funnel beard waggled with each word he uttered. When he raised his blue-veined hands and bellowed above the boom of the dam, "Git your partners for the 'Girl I Left Behind Me'", the beard kept time. He turned to George and the fellow from town, who was accompanying him. George nodded, his right ear hovering over strings that twisted and sawed into harmony. Somehow, that tune reminded him of Mary. The fellow from town put up one finger – the only signs of life he ever showed, besides thumping on the guitar.

There was scuffle of feet and considerable talk and laughing before the formations were ready. George clamped the fiddle under his chin and waited. Would there be dances down yonder, and would he ever be able to play for them? He could hardly take his fiddle along. Some of them might be so out of their heads they'd break it to smithereens. Anyhow, surely somebody down there would have one, one that he could use sometimes. But to be gone so long from Mary. The fiddle sang out as old man Jimpson's booming voice teetered up and down:

> "First couple sashaway the center,
> With the lady to the left and gent to the right;
> Then swing, oh swing, and promenade a ring
> With the girl you left behind you.
> On to the left and the left eleman,
> With the big foot up and the little foot down,
> With the once and a half as you come around
> To the girl you left behind you.

"'How old are you, my pretty little miss?
How old are you, my honey?'
She answered me with a tee-hee-hee,
'I'll be sixteen next Sunday.'
'Will you marry me, my pretty little miss?
Will you marry me, my honey?'
She answered me with a tee-hee-hee,
'I'll marry you next Sunday.'"

The fiddle sang on and on, and so did old man Jimpson.

"Hogs in the corn and chickens in the wheat,
With your honey in your arms, and promenade eight."

A whiff of cold air swished in and kept on swishing, as a rounded bulk bowed in the doorway. "My name is Johnathon Prayter!"

Somebody went to steady him as music and dancing stopped and George stared from the fiddle.

"I know I'm drunk, and I hain't no business a-being here, but I heard about this-here dance to-night, and George a-playing, and I felt like, him being my son-in-law, and first time he's played in the Lord knows when, and maybe the last, with the rub-doctors liable to take things over any minute now – I ort to come, drunk or sober, so I come."

George tucked his fiddle into the wooden box and stumbled to the door.

"Why, Happy John, I thought you wasn't a-going to drink no more."

The weaving figure pushed up a right hand.

"This is the last time, George. I swear it, so help me. I didn't 'low to git drunk this time – just figured on a swaller or two to sort of quiet me down, being as I was so up in the air over a trade I made. I 'lowed you and Mary'd never know the difference nohow, and you *wouldn't*, if it hadn't a-been for this-here dance."

George shivered a little and backed from the cold air.

"Well, Happy John, now that you're here, why don't you come in and shut the door, before the rest of us all freeze to death?"

Happy stretched out one hand to strengthen his words, and all but went over backwards.

"You're right, George. You're always right. George, here's, my son-in-law. He married my daughter, Mary. Fine feller. Don't touch a drop."

He stumbled in and the door slammed behind him, as he rambled on.

"Well, George, how air you and the rub-doctors a-coming?"

The pained look on George's face did not dam the continuous flow of words.

"By thunder, I was in there onct, and I never seed so many skeletons in my life. Thick as bristles on a hog's back might near, and by the Eternal, I never went back. I claim, onct in a doctor's clutches, you never git out, dead or alive, more'n likely. But with a whole crop of skeletons meeting you at the door – dead patients, that's gone ahead of you – looks to me like any body'd know 'twas the handwriting on the wall, anybody but George that is."

George, his eyes on the swaying bulk, was as shaky as a treed rabbit.

"Happy John, hadn't you ort to set down, before you fall down?"

"You're right, George, but don't hurry me. I'll set when I git through, but I hain't through yit. As I was a-saying, I never took no stock in doctors nohow, but George, here, more or less living off of pills and tonics and rubbing and one thing and another's, liable to be with the skeletons any minute. I hate to say it, him my son-in-law, and no bad habits and all, but every time I look at him here lately, big-boned like he is, and built to last so to speak, I keep thinking what a rattling, fine skeleton he'd make!"

His arms waved out, and his round bulk toppled, but somebody caught him and eased him to a chair. George had about as much color as a window-glass on wash day, and was as fidgety as if he had a beetle up his breeches leg. He turned helplessly to Ben Bragg.

"Ben, would you mind going after Mary? She's the only living soul, I reckon, that can do a thing with him when he's that fur gone, and she cain't do much. *Onct,* I got him to go home, but I'm so worried and nervous-like now, a-thinking about things, I don't feel like I could talk to him, or it'd do any good if I did. And I'm afeard he'll go to sleep here, and freeze to

death, after the fire goes out, or catch his death, anyhow. Hit's might near
out of the question, waking him, onct he gits to sleep, and a right smart
job a-lifting him too. I was a-thinking maybe Lawrence could watch after
the younguns, and Mary could stay a while. She don't git to go nowhere,
hardly, and she might like it, again she gits here, and her pa's took care of.
She hain't danced a great sight since we was first married, but you could
dance a mite with her, couldn't you, Ben?"

Ben grinned as he pocketed his hands and kicked at the floor. "Why,
yes, I reckon I could."

Dancing and music might as well have been postponed until Ben got
back with Mary. They tried a tune or two but Happy John kept floating
around, one leg kicking in front, and arms flapping like a crowing rooster,
bumping into everybody that got in his way, until he had been floored and
hoisted to his feet so many times, that nobody knew what was what.

> "Lady round lady, and gent solo;
> Lady round gent, and gent don't go;
> Four hands half, and a half a whirl,
> And doceedo the lady; she's a pretty little girl,"

boomed old man Jimpson, and Happy John, as if it were a game of "Bull
in the Pen", broke through the couples, head down, and sprawled on the
floor, smiling foolishly.

Mary bustled in, fixed up uncommonly pretty, and when they heaved
him to his feet, bundled him up as well as she could. But nobody could
coax him on to old Theodore. Only the prospects of a ride home in the
Ford, with old Theodore hitched on behind, got him to go at all.

When Mary came back with Ben from the cold ride, she was as red as
a ripe tomato, and her eyes as big as a cat's at night. Old man Jimpson
nudge George, as he leaned over a little between dances and mumbled
with a snicker.

"If you're as sharp as you think you air, you're a-going to think twict
before you send Ben Bragg out with your woman again. S'posing she'd up
and leave you? Ben's a right nice looking feller, and they look right well
together – best looking couple on the floor, fur as I can see. Must a-had a
right nice time a-taking Happy John home. Look as pleased and sweet-like

as a gallon of sorghum. Put me in mind of a pair of nest-building pigeons.
I declare, George, they *do* make a nice looking couple."

George stared past the white whiskers to Mary and Ben and the rest
of the crowd. Mary had a kind of little girl look she hadn't had in years.
Didn't look a day older than she did when he married her – with her red
hair sort of loose-bunched and fuzzed out, and that blue stuff setting off

the shine of her eyes. That made-over worsted dress of Grandma Nesbit's seemed to liven her up like rain on tobacco plants – or maybe it was Ben Bragg. Whatever it was, seemed as if everybody kept looking at her, and one uptown fellow even went so far as to ask her to dance, but she just laughed a little and huddled all the closer to Ben. George felt as if he had swallowed a biscuit whole and it wouldn't go down, but he had to say something.

"Well, I don't know but what you're right, and with my health and all, maybe she'd be better off. They *air* a right nice looking couple, all right – best on the floor, I reckon. Your woman and Jim Tittle look pleased enough, fur as that's concerned, but Mary being twenty or thirty year younger, or such a matter, I 'low she *is* a mite better looking, and I reckon might near anybody's better looking than Jim."

Mary only stayed a little while, though she seemed to be having an uncommonly good time. After the second formation, she tiptoed to George.

"I'm a-going to have Ben take me home. I'm worried about the children. They ortn't to be by theirselves, little as they air, and late as it is. I used to be terrible scared at night, with no grown folks around, and I reckon all younguns air alike, that way. Ben says you can ride home with him when the dance is over, but I reckon that'll be considerable time yet."

"I reckon. Whatever you say."

He stared after them even after the door closed. Old man Jimpson was only talking to hear his teeth click, but, what if there was something to it, maybe – Ben in love with Mary, or her with him, or both, and him putting his neck in the noose, so to speak, going off to the insane asylum, for the Lord knew how long? A lot could happen while he was gone. The "Devil's Dream" seesawed up and down at break-neck clip, and zigzagged around like a bumble bee in a closed-up room, and old man Jimpson croaked out calls, with the music, but all George made out of it was a gallop of screams, faster and faster, that said over and over. "Look out for Ben! Look out for Ben!" And still, there were the children. Mary wouldn't leave them, surely. And those confounded rub-doctors, always watching every move he made, was enough to shoo anybody away.

Shortly after Ben got back, George got to noticing the little red-headed girl that was staying at Webbstringer's, the ones that owned the dance hall, and mill and dam. Some said she was the old man's brother's girl. Pretty little devil. Looked something like Mary did eight or ten years ago, before her hair sort of ironed out. About the same shape too, that is, before Mary kind of filled out and got bent over with hard work – though to-night she hadn't shown any of this to speak of. Seemed as if this Webbstringer girl was having a real nice time – maybe because she looked like Mary. Ben Bragg danced with her a time or two, and seemed to have his eye on her a good deal of the evening. But that up-town fellow did most of the talking to her and partnering her in dances – the same one that had talked to Mary. If Ben wanted her, didn't look as if he had much show, but more than likely, he didn't. And whether he did or didn't, he might as well make up his mind to give in to uptowners.

When the next dance was about to start, George looked back at the little red-headed girl. Somebody else was looking at her now, talking to her, smiling and waggling his bump of a black beard. George blinked and stared. My God in Heaven! It was the black-bearded man from up town, the rub-doctor from the rambling red building, the man to whom he had sold his body! And he was coming toward him, walking, walking –

George raised hand and bow to his hot forehead, as if to shut out the sight, and slumped to the floor like a half-dry dishtowel that has been knocked down. Old man Jimpson seesawed on above the noise of the water:

> "Join eight hands and circle to the left,
> And when you git around, remember the call;
> Take a chew tobaccer, and spit on the wall."

But there was no music, after a few thumps. The fiddle had stopped. Everybody looked at George, huddled on the floor like a flattened bat. A few strides and Ben Bragg clutched his shoulder.

"What the devil's the matter?"

George was shaking so much he could hardly talk.

"I cain't play no more, Ben. It's him."

"Him? Who's him?" Ben's slow eyes circled the room as if expecting to see the devil himself.

"The feller with the black beard. He's after me, Ben. I cain't tell you why, but he is. And he ain't got no claim on me, Ben – not yit. I ain't dead yit, and looks like he could wait till I am!"

Slow-like, as if he wasn't right sure whether he wanted it or not, Ben pulled out his pipe.

"George, I don't want to hurt your feelings one, but 'pears to me like you're a mite out of your head."

A gleam of hope flickered in the dull eyes.

"Do you think so, Ben? Do you *really*? How long you reckon I been this-a-way?"

"I don't know. I never noticed it before. Don't amount to much, I reckon. Maybe everybody's that-a-way at times."

The gleam died, like a match going out.

"I cain't play no more, Ben. You reckon you could take me home, and git Pa to finish?"

Ben kicked several splinters from the rough boards.

"Your pa's surely gone to bed, by now, late as it is. I thought fiddling was the one thing you liked doing."

"'Tis, but I cain't go on to-night. I feel just like a platter of lettuce, with sizzling grease poured over it. Pa'll git up. Ma'll see to it. I know you got this dance up mainly for me, Ben, and I sure do thank you, but – I got to git out of here. I reckon somebody can play the pianer, till Pa comes."

People were standing around in bunches, talking in low tones. The man with the black beard and the rest of the uptowners had disappeared somewhere. Ben said a few words to old man Jimpson, who bellowed them on to the crowd, though nobody seemed to understand anything he said. George shivered by the stove, and waited. Maybe he was jumping out of the skillet into the cookstove, but –

"Lord, Ben," he chattered, stretching out big palms as Ben came up, "I been a-thinking things over, and looks to me like the best place in the world for me's the insane asylum. You ain't no idy how things air, Ben. I've *got* to git away, and if they'll let me, I'm a-going to this here hospital, soon as I can."

Most of the crowd were staring after them, in little huddles, as they bundled up to go. Ben cleared his throat and mumbled.

"George, I swear to God you air a-losing your mind, if you hain't already done it. Nobody in their right mind wants to live with crazy people, if they can help it."

George tucked the wooden box under one arm and stared out into the darkness.

"Well, Ben, it's according to how you look at things. It's something to have peace of mind, nothing to worry about, and nothing to do, and nobody a-follering you around, a wishing you was dead. Ben, if I do go, I wisht you'd look after Mary – same as you've always done. Will you?

Ben kicked loose a few splinters and then squinted up.

"Well, George, I'll do the best I can, like I always have, and if I was you, I'd see an uptown doctor – somebody besides Doc Ceburn. It might be you're heap worse off than any of us think."

"I aim to, Ben, first chance I git."

Chapter 13 : George Goes to Keatsville to See Doctors

Old man Rainwater threw out his hitching rock as near the courthouse as he could, and made his way over the near wheel.

"If 'twasn't for taxes, a body could have something," he mumbled.

George straddled the other front wheel, and studied signs around the square, the ones he could see and make out. The newspaper package of bread and sausage seemed to belong nowhere. He tried first one pocket and then the other, but it wouldn't go in. If he chucked it under either arm, it seemed to unbalance things, so he shifted it to his middle, steadying it with both hands.

D. H. Cunningham, M. D.

George clumped up a long ladder of stairs and waited. The doctor, a spectacled young fellow that looked as if he had molasses in his hair, came in from somewhere in the back, sharpening one hand on the other.

"Was there something?"

George's mouth opened and stood, like a frog awaiting a waterfly.

"Well, Doc, I'd like to talk to you, when you hain't too busy."

"Go right ahead."

He blinked twice and wagged his head, with a swipe through his stubble hair, as if trying to flatten it down like the doctor's.

"Well, Doc, – I was just a-wondering. Have you ever been in the insane asylum?"

The doctor stared, bullet-eyed, and then backfired, a word at a time.

"Do *you mean* to *insinuate* – ?"

"Oh, Doc, I didn't mean no harm. I was just a-wondering what 'twas like, and thought maybe you knowed, much as you been around."

Little by little the doctor unbristled, like a goat's back after a dog has gone.

"I've been *through* an asylum or two, if that's what you mean."

"Have you been to this un, some'ers near abouts a hundred mile west of here?"

"Yes."

George clasped and unclasped bulks of hands as if trying to squeeze out words.

"Say, what kind of a contraption is this-here hospital thing, Doc? Is it a sizable place?"

The doctor fingered his forehead a little and patted sticky hair.

"Well, fairly good size, yes. They take care of about eighteen hundred or two thousand patients, there, I believe, maybe more."

"Two thousand patients! Is there grub enough to go around, and is it eatable?"

"Oh, good wholesome food, I suppose. Nothing out of the ordinary, but plenty of it – meat, potatoes and bread, probably, with vegetables and fruit part of the time, and milk, I think, to drink."

"Sounds like a right nice place. How do they keep the thing warm, a stove or fireplace?"

"Oh, they'd have furnace heat of some kind, I'm positive, a plant that heats all the buildings on the grounds. It's a nice, warm, even heat."

"Who cuts the wood fer it? Patients?"

"Oh, they'd undoubtedly burn coal, altogether. Have it hauled."

"And if a body cain't pay – they take him anyhow?"

"Why, yes – if he needs treatment."

George hunched forward with the pleased look of a stray cat that has at last found a home.

"Say, Doc, did you ever hear of a feller, a while back, that went down there from these parts? He'd made some kind of a crazy bargain before they sent him off – sort of worried him into going in the first place, I reckon, and had him so nervous he was half-crazy. And when he got back they let him out of it. Claimed he wasn't in his right mind when he made it. You ever hear anything like that?"

"No. I never did, but I should think it might happen. Why? What in the world are you asking all these questions about the asylum for?"

Twice George swallowed the top half of his throat, but it wouldn't stay down.

"Well, you see, Doc, I was sorta figuring on a change of some kind."

"Change? What do you mean?"

"Just – change. Something different. Looks like a body ortn't to stay one place all his life."

"I don't know what you're talking about."

"Well, Doc, I don't know as I do myself, but the doctor down at Hell's Holler, name o' Ceburn, said I ort to have a change."

"What's that got to do with the asylum?"

"Well, Doc, I ain't got a nickel to my name, nor Ma hain't that she can spare, since that lawsuit, and you said this place didn't cost nothing, so I figured it might be just the ticket."

The doctor's voice jumped up two steps.

"What do you think it *is* – a summer *resort?*

"Why, no, Doc, – 'twasn't summer I was thinking about so much. It's now."

"Well, the insane asylum is for *crazy* people – not just anybody that wants a warm place to stay and plenty to eat. You have to be out of your *mind* to go."

"Well, Doc, I thought, nervous and worried like I am, maybe I *was* a mite out of my head. Seems like –"

"Well, you're not. No crazy person *thinks* he's crazy, though nobody with real good sense wants to go to the asylum."

"Well, Doc, maybe I ain't like most."

"Maybe you're not, but you're not crazy – no more than I am."

George stumped down the steps, and out on the sidewalk, propelling the newspaper package before him. Twice he struggled around the square, studying the signs. A little old woman's hat pin caught in the package and ripped a long slit, but George thumbed it together and turned back to the sign.

T. R. Simpson, M. D.

There was nobody in, upstairs, but the door was not locked, so he sprawled on a soft-looking chair and waited. The slit in the package had torn to a kite shaped gully that threatened to lose cornbread, sausage and all. He had just pinched it together and tucked it into the bib of his overalls, when the doctor puffed up the stairs. He was as old as Doc Ceburn, but he had twice as much stomach, maybe three times. He didn't wear spectacles, but he looked as if he ought to, weak and watery-eyed as he was. He settled himself in the nearest chair, and panted four or five times before he said a word.

"I broke my glasses a little while ago, and can't see very well. What is it?"

George kept fingering the lunch inside his overall bib. It seemed to give him courage.

"Well, Doc, I wanted to talk to you about my ailment, and one thing and another – that is, if it don't cost nothin' to do it. Seems like I'm in misery might near all the time."

The doctor eyed the bump under the bib.

"Are you able to work at all?"

"Well, Doc, I am and I ain't. Some days I cain't hardly lift a hand, and the woman and little boy have to do might near everything. Other times I can do a *little.*"

"How long have you been in this condition?"

"Oh, Doc, long as I can remember, might near. I take medicine all the time fer it – have ever since I was a baby – but don't seem to git no better. Worse, if anything."

"What caused it?"

"I ain't no idy, Doc, though Ma says a cow done it."

Bib-high, the doctor leveled a finger at him.

"Do you mean to say a *cow caused that* – in infancy?"

For the first time, George eyed his bulk of bib.

"Oh, Lord no, doc. That's my dinner. The woman fixed it before I left. 'Twas tore and –"

Pushing himself up, the doctor hooked on somebody's spectacles, and his voice cooled to a thick jell.

"Never mind. Just what *is* your trouble?"

"Well, Doc, that's what I want you to find out."

"I mean, does it seem to be stomach trouble, or kidney trouble, or what?"

"Well, Doc, I have all them troubles, but it's my nerves I was thinking about mostly."

"Nerves?"

"Yes, seems like I'm nervous and worried all the time, might near, not able to do a stroke hardly, and ready to bust out and bawl the minute a body scolds me or comes up all of a sudden. You reckon you could look over them parts that have to do with jumpy nerves, and see if any of 'em 's out of kelter?"

The doctor pinched at his spine a little and poked into his mouth.

"Well, you *are* rather nervous. Maybe you ought to have glasses, but your teeth are the main cause of your trouble. You should have them out just as soon as you can afford it. Your gums seem to be full of pyorrhea."

George raised dull eyes.

"Well, Doc, fur as I know, I cain't afford it now or no time."

"Oh, it wouldn't cost so much. I believe a hundred dollars would cover the whole expense – extractions, plates and all. You might even get it done for fifty. If you could afford it, it might be a good thing to get a room in town while you're having it done, where you could have hot baths and modern conveniences. The change might do you good. Maybe you could work for board and room."

"If I had a hundred dollars, Doc, or even half that, considerable of my worries would be over. But I could no more raise that much, nor Ma couldn't, than I could jump over the courthouse. And no stouter'n what I am, I couldn't stand to work, Doc –"

The doctor eased himself back to his chair.

"Did it ever occur to you that maybe a good deal of this trouble was in your *mind*?"

A flicker of light gleamed in the dull eyes.

"Why, yes, Doc, it did. I told tother doctor that nervous and worried like I am, my mind might be in right bad shape – that maybe a few months down at this here insane asylum would do me considerable good."

"What on earth are you talking about?"

"The insane asylum, Doc. Just looks like them hot baths down yander, and all them big doctors and piles of medicine'd be mighty good for a body's nerves. I just feel like, if I could git down there, I'd be as stout agin as I am, and a heap better off, every which-a-ways. What do *you* think?"

"Why, – I don't think you've got any more business at the insane asylum than I have. What put that in your head?"

"Well, Doc, I don't rightly know. One thing and another led up to it, I reckon. Looked like they could help me if anybody could. You don't think I'm crazy enough to go – or the treatments would help?"

"I don't think you're crazy at all. And, even if the treatments would help, what would your wife do, while you were gone?"

"Oh, Mary'd git along somehow; better'n common, I reckon, without me to do fer too."

"She'd have the responsibility of the whole farm wouldn't she?"

"Well, Doc, she does anyhow, her and the little boy. I don't lift a hand hardly, some days. I ain't able, seems like."

"You mean your wife and boy do all the work on your entire farm?"

"Well, they do a-most of it, that is, what's done. 'Tain't such a turrible big farm, Doc, twenty-five acres, nor so turrible well kept up. But no matter how big it is or how little, I cain't do no more than I do."

"Well, it seems to me, no matter how sick you are, and I don't think there's a great deal wrong with you myself, if you sit around and let your wife do all the work on twenty-five acres, your main trouble is, you're just plain lazy. Did that ever occur to you?"

"Well, Doc, I don't know that it has, but I reckon most everybody else thinks so."

"And I think the best cure in the world would be to go home and do some of that work yourself, and give your wife a little rest. Stop thinking about yourself all the time, and think about her."

A step at a time, like an old, worn-out horse, George made his way down to the courthouse yard and pulled out the newspaper package. Dull-eyed, he crunched and swallowed, washing down great mouthfuls with handfuls of water from the pump. Like as not it was meant for him to shiver along behind a heating stove the rest of his life, without any pleasure, so he could look ahead to what came afterwards with less objection. He had just finished the last bite of sausage, and crumpled the newspaper to a twisted wad, when a black beard bobbed up from somewhere, and white teeth grinned.

"Well, Moore, are you following me, or am I following you? Seems to me we keep pretty good tab on each other here lately. How are you?"

George stared with mouth wide open, and then burst into whinnying sobs.

"Oh, Doc, I'm so nervous and worried here lately, I don't know what I'm a-doing harldy. Seems like I git poorlier all the time."

The rub-doctor's mouth fixed in a kind of meat-cutter's smile, that spread as he talked.

"Well, now, we wouldn't want you to *die* on us, – though, of course, we can make room for that *body* any time."

The smile gurgled into a chuckle, and then turned off, as George's face froze. The rub-doctor went on.

"But seriously, I thought you seemed rather nervous the other night. Why don't you come up and get some treatments at the clinic? The students have to get in so many treatments for practice anyhow, so it wouldn't cost you a cent. I believe they could fix you up in no time – put an end to all this worry and nervousness. Anyway, I'm sure they could help a lot."

George kicked at the sidewalk. Just how did he mean that "fix"?

"Well, Doc, I'll think over what you said, though I don't know as I want to be *practiced* on. Anyhow, it's a right fur piece up here, this kind of weather –"

"It might be we could even come down there to you, if a deal of our's goes through."

"What deal, Doc? What air you talking about?"

Every so often the doctor had a way of showing his teeth.

"Well, we're still hoping to buy land down there, and take over the old mill and dam, and possibly the dance hall too. If we do, we may see you real often. Might even bargain with you on your fiddle playing."

George gulped.

"Well, Doc, – I don't know as I want to sign any more papers."

After the rub-doctor had gone, George shook so much he thought he was going to have a chill in spite of everything. He must make one more desperate try for the insane asylum. It was his only chance.

Dr. A. B. Cutright, M. D.

By the time he had climbed the third stairs, his nerves were as jagged as a bucksaw. There were three or four people ahead of him, so he had to look into the shiny eyes of a stuffed bird that was mostly spotted tail for half an hour. He kept thinking of the skeleton room and when his turn finally came, he was almost all to pieces.

"Doc, I *got* to git to that-there insane asylum. Tother doctors say I ain't crazy enough to go, but they ain't no idy how things air. I'm so nervous, I don't know what I'm a-doing hardly, and I *got* to git away. If I don't my nerves's a-going to smash like a busted lamp globe, so's they never can be fixed."

He lowered his voice, and looked around, big-eyed.

"Doc, if you knowed somebody was a-setting around, a-waiting for you to die, watching every move you made, hoping it'd be your last, not letting you git out of their sight, hardly, and more'n likely a-figuring up ways to hurry you off before your time, *you'd* be a-wanting to git away *too*."

The doctor's eyes squinted to long needles.

"What on earth are you talking about? You mean – your *wife*?"

"No, no, Lord no! There never was a better woman than Mary. I hadn't ort to said nothing nohow. I didn't 'low to, but I'm so nervous-like, I don't know what I'm a-doing, hardly. Hit's that hacking the meat off the bones,

I keep thinking about, Doc. Seems like, anymore, I cain't hardly bear to see the woman cut up a chicken or slice hog meat. You ain't no idy, how turrible it is, always a-worrying and thinking about being chopped to giblets, and having 'em pull you bone from bone. Seems like I jest cain't stand it, Doc, and now, being fullered around and watched, every step I take – I'm might near out of my mind!"

"Who's following you?"

"I cain't tell you no more, Doc. I've said more'n I ort to, now. But I've got to git away."

He collapsed into nervous weeping, and the doctor eyed the bulk of body from overshoes to seeping eyelids.

"Hmmm. Maybe you're worse off than the others think. I'm going to talk to them again. Maybe a month or two down there might do consider-able good."

George opened his mouth wider and steadied his voice.

"Thank you, Doc. I hope you *can* git 'em to let me go. I ain't a well man, nor ain't been for I don't know how long, and this might be my one chance to git to be like other fellers. Anyhow, I'm dead sure I'm a-going clean crazy if I stay on here."

The last doctor's words had such a calming effect upon George, that he had almost forgotten the whole affair, by the time he had caught a ride home, after a day's visit with the old men at the courthouse. Then he began to wonder if perhaps he wasn't crazier than even he realized. Mary sort of floated to him like they were both in a dream, or maybe all dead, and put her hands on his shoulders, soft-like.

"George, honey, if I'd a-had any idy how things was, I'd a-done dif-ferent. I didn't dream you was sick like you air. I really thought 'twas out and out laziness ailed you – nothing else – or I'd a-never said a word. I don't blame you for nothing you done, George, nor hold anything agin you. I hain't been none too well myself, and I reckon I done the best I could, but if I'd a-knowed how you was, or had airy notion, I'd a-done more myself, and I wouldn't a-jawed *you* for nothing you done or didn't do, if I'd a-dropped dead in my tracks."

George's mouth widened as she talked.

"Why, Mary, I ain't no more idy what you're a-talking about, than the man in the moon."

Her eyes looked red, as if she'd been crying.

"Well, George, don't worry none. I reckon you wouldn't be able to understand nohow, now. But you do what they tell you, down there, and maybe everything'll be all right when you git back."

George blinked several times as his open mouth stretched.

"Where'm I going, Mary?"

She shook her head, and bit her lip.

"Don't try to think, George. You're a-heap worse off than the doctors figured. Just set there and rest yourself."

A light began to dawn.

"Mary, them doctors I seed up town ain't been out here, have they, or you hain't been to town to see them?"

"Yes, George. Ben took me. They called out and wanted to talk to me first time I could come in, and Ben brought word, and said he was a-going anyway, so I went with him. I talked to them and the sheriff too. They're all a-aiming to do the right thing by you, so don't worry no more. I blame myself now for every cross word I ever said, but seemed like I had such a hard time, and not knowing how you was –"

He hunched forward like an impatient dog, waiting to bring back a stick.

"Mary air they going to take me to that hospital place?"

"I don't know yet, George, and I reckon they don't. They're a-dickering about it, an I shouldn't be surprised, one way or tother. You'll be better off there, honey."

She kept stroking his hair as if he were a small, purring cat. His face brightened as he looked up.

"Oh yes, Mary. They have it might near like rich folks down there. No work to speak of, just easy-like jobs, and hot baths, and plenty of grub, and a warm place to sleep and set, and no wood to chop – furnace heat, they call it, for the whole shebang. You just have to chunk in a little coal every so often, and I don't reckon the patients even do that, cause they might burn theirselves up. And any medicine you need, or tooth pulling, or spectacles, or new duds – the hospital gits 'em, and you don't have to worry. That's what I heard. Pity we couldn't all go."

Her eyes were puddles of water.

"George, I'm so sorry I ever scolded you. I wouldn't a-done it for nothing, if I'd a-knowed –"

His big hands clasped like Preacher Ray at prayer-meeting.

"Why, Mary, I reckon I needed more'n what you said, fur as that goes. Leastways, I reckon you *thought* I did, me looking away stouter'n what I was, and all. Seems like I been a-ailing most of the time for seven or eight year – well, all my life, for that matter, though I done a *little* that first year or two we was married. 'Twasn't much – but, a little –"

Chapter 14 : The Sheriff Comes

Soft white wisps sifted down from the sky and piled deep on the frozen ground. Behind his mother's heater George huddled by the wall, scrushing his head down into his neck and shoulders, and stretching big hands to the stove. He kept thinking of the way Mary had acted that morning. Kept saying maybe he' better go over and spend the day with his folks, though he'd just been a day or two before. And wanting him to say "goodbye" to the children and then asking if he wasn't going to kiss the little things. And he did, seeing as she was so set on it, though what in the name of the Lord was the sense of it – him just going half a mile or three-quarters at the most, and aiming to be back by sun down at the latest – was more than he could see. And, for that matter, if it had been snowing like it was now when he started out, he wouldn't have come at all, more than likely.

Lige was out puttering around somewhere, snow or no snow, and Sarah was taking off patterns. One after another she laid sugar sacks over em-broidered figures and alternated rubbing a tablespoon into her gray-white scalp and over sugar sacks, until the patterns were outlined in oil. George watched a few minutes and then shivered behind the stove until she folded up sacks and patterns and stared out at the snow.

"Who's that a-coming up the hill, George?"

His head poked out like a puzzled chicken.

"Why I don't know. Somebody from Keatsville, I reckon. Nobody around here's got a car that'll make that hill in bad weather. Say, looks like the sheriff. Wonder what *he* wants?"

Outside the chugging soughed and died away as a man, who seemed to be either over-fed or over-bundled, followed by two gaping stragglers, tramped through drifts and kicked off flakes at the door. George goggled through the window and then turned to his mother.

"Why, Ma, looks to me like there's *three* sheriffs. You reckon somebody's *done* something, and we never heard nothing about it?"

She wagged her head, tight lipped.

"I ain't no idy. All I know is, they ain't go no business here, but now they've come, I reckon they might as well git warm. Come in."

The pillow-shaped man looked at George with the simpering expression of an elderly school teacher to a five-year-old.

"George, do you know me?"

George eyed the tomato face.

"Why, yes, well as I ever did. I voted for you."

The sheriff looked down and kicked his shoes a little, but the man behind him spoke up.

"Who is it?"

"Why, hit's Sheriff Shope, or else his shadder. 'Tain't nobody else."

"Who's this?"

He pointed to a crooked-nosed deputy that had helped the sheriff solicit votes and haul people to the poles, that didn't have any other way to go. Just now he looked as if he'd been caught in somebody's hen-roost.

"Why, hit's deputy somebody or other. I never knowed him to speak of, though I seed him time and again."

"And me?"

"Oh, you're another deputy feller. I forgit your name – oh, yes, Longnecker. Why? Is anything the matter?"

One after another the three sheriffs crowded around him and talked and acted as if they thought he was completely out of his head.

"How did you get over here?"

"Why, I walked."

"Do you remember being in town yesterday?"

"Why, of course I do. I was there might near all day, but I didn't see none of you. What else do you want to know?"

Sarah chewed off a thread.

"I want to know what you fellers air a-doing here, a-asking George all that tomfoolery? He ain't a-hankering after no job, and 'tain't time for election yit. What *air* you up to?"

The sheriff fingered a stubbly chin.

"Well, M's Moore, we don't want to worry you none about it. We'll go along, some of us, or send the constable, and see that he gets there all right, but – we've got a warrant here to get George and take him to the insane asylum."

The sugar sacks fell to the floor as Sarah reared up like the head of a snake.

"Insane asylum! George ain't a-going to no insane asylum! The idy! I'm his ma, and I guess I'd a-knowed it, if he was out of his head. He's as smart as anybody, and a heap smarter'n some. He ain't a-going to go! Who said he ort?"

The sheriff's eyes shifted from one deputy to the other.

"Well, M's Moore, as I understand it, thee doctors said it might help him, and his wife agreed to it."

"His *wife*! Why didn't you come to his *ma*? Mary's got children of her own to see to. I'm the one to look after George."

"Well, M's Moore, as I understand it, George was the one that wanted to go in the first place."

She turned from one to the other, and her shoulders slumped as if all the starch had been washed out in a rain.

"I don't believe it. I cain't! Why, George, if that's so, maybe you*air* crazy. I've knowed of plenty a-going to the insane asylum, but I never heard of anybody a-wanting to go."

George kept his eyes on the rug carpet.

"Well, Ma, you see, I don't exactly thing I'm clean crazy, but I might git that-a-way. Seems like my nerve's all gone to pieces. It's got so – every time I see anybody sullen-like, I just want to bust out and bawl. Git worse all the time. And, looks to me like, if anybody could do anything fer me, surely a big place like that could. Then, too, Doc Ceburn said I ort to have some sort of a change, and there's no place else to go. This may be my one chanct, Ma, and hit's warm, down there, they say, and good victuals, and no work to speak of and all."

The three men kept shifting eyes, from one to the other. Sarah sucked in a deep breath.

"Well, maybe you're right, George, but I never will believe it. If you was out of your head, a-drawing butcher knives on this one and that, or a threatening to kill somebody or other, or a-digging up dead people, a-cutting 'em all to pieces, and the like, I'd say, go ahead – but –"

A look of utter helplessness came into his eyes, almost despair.

"Ma, 'tain't *me* that's a-doing all that, or have airy notion of it, but if I stay here, don't be surprised at anything that happens. You ain't no idy, Ma. Times, I'm might near out of my mind, a-thinking about things, and I feel like I ort to git away as soon as I can – thought, seeing as it was me wanted to go in the first place, don't look like it'd a-took three sheriffs to come and git me."

She kept shriveling and hooching up like half-cooked dandelion greens.

"Maybe you're right, – but, looks to me like that's a mighty hard way to cure nervousness – sending 'em down yander amongst crazy people. Looks to me like a-body'd go crazy if he was all right to start with."

George looked first one way and then another, as if about to take to his heels. Somebody rapped and old man Jimpson and J.P. edged in.

"I seed a car drive up, and looked like three or four a-gitting out –. Anything the matter?"

Sarah was as washed-out looking as fish-worms after a rain.

"Mr. Jimpson, they're a-aiming to take George off to that-there insane asylum – where J.P. was. Claim he ain't right in his head. Do you believe airy sech talk?"

The white beard made a jiggly circle of everybody there.

"Why, no. George always seemed smart enough to me. I don't recollect him ever saying anything – no time – that sounded out and out crazy. Maybe they're jest a-aiming to git him out of the way, so's they can fix up that dance hall with them-there nickel machines and the like – with uptown orchestras maybe at times, and *round* dances – nothing else. All I got to say is, if they *do* take George – somebody might as well set fire to the dance hall, and burn it down. And I for one, hope they do."

J. P. grinned, but Sarah was near choking.

"Well, they're a-going to take him, Mr. Jimpson, and there's nothing none of us can do. Seems like George wants to go hisself."

The beard jerked out as red eyes stared.

"Wants to go hisself? I never heard tell of the like. Maybe he is crazy – but seems like a plum shame, sending him off, so's they'll be nothing but round dances from now on, less'n we git outsiders. There's no sense to round dances nohow. More'n likely I'll forgit how to call. Might as well burn down the dance hall, like I said, fur as I see. Is Lige here? I come mainly to talk about them up-towners a-wanting our land."

"He's somewhere a-puttering around on the place, Mr. Jimpson. If you see him, I wisht you'd send him in. Maybe *he* could do something." She turned to George as the door closed. "George, do as you're a-mind to – but I wisht you wouldn't go."

"Oh, Ma, you'd better let 'em take me, now they're in the notion. You ain't no idy what a time I had a-gitting to go. Two of them doctors held out to the last that I wasn't crazy enough. Said there wasn't nothing the matter with me but bad teeth, hardly, and a hundred dollars'd do everything – tooth pulling, plates and all, right in Keatsville. But, Ma, pulling teeth ain't a-going to nowheres near settle all that ails me, like I told 'em, and that last doctor I went to, stuck up for me, I reckon. Anyhow, I can think of a heap better ways of spending a hundred dollars – or half that – even if we had it."

She nodded, a kind of run-down clock nod.

"Well, George *I* know there's a heap more ailing you than bad teeth, and looks to me like that's a heap of money to put in a body's mouth, if there wasn't. And besides, I couldn't raise a hundred dollars, or nowheres near that, if I had to be hung fer it. That law-suit took all I had, and a right smart I didn't have. But seems like the insane asylum's a might hard cure."

"Ma, I feel like I'll be better off there. And don't you stand in my way. Might change my whole life."

She turned away like a rickity old shack about to collapse.

"All right, George, but I just hate to see you go. You're all I got, seems like, besides your pa, or ever had. And I reckon there's nothing means so much to a woman as her children."

The door opened and Lige pushed in. Sarah turned sagging shoulders toward him."

"Lige, – cain't *you* do something? They're a-going to take George off to that hospital place, where J.P. Jimpson was. Claim he ain't right – three of them uptown doctors –

"Well, Sary, if three doctors say he ort to go, I reckon he ort."

"Why, Lige, what would *they* know about it? Never even seed him before – none of 'em. And they ain't never been around hills or hill folks airy one – no time. Wouldn't even know how to plant potatoes. But, Lige, the worst of it is, George wants to go hisself."

"Does?" He turned to look at George.

"It ain't that I'm plum crazy, Pa, but I might *git* that away – and I just think it'll be for the best."

"Well, Sary, they's nothing we can do, one way or tother, if he *wants* to go, and maybe it'll be better for him, like he says.

"Well, Lige, I feel like he's no business a-going, nohow. Air you a-aiming to go, now, George?"

He looked from one to another. The sheriff jerked his head up and down and pawed with one foot like a horse at a pasture gap. George turned back to Sarah.

"I reckon we air, Ma, soon as I button my coats and all, anyhow. I ort to tell Mary. She won't know what's become of me, and don't seem right hardly, a-letting her worry that-a-way. You wouldn't want to go by, would you, Sheriff?"

The sheriff eyed the other two.

"Well, I don't trust these up and down hills too much, with this snow and all. Anyhow, your wife knows all about things. 'Twas *her* sent us over here."

"*Did* she? Hit's a wonder she didn't come along. Not that I *have* to see her, mind you. Ma could tell her anything I wanted her to know, but seems like I ort, me a-going to be gone all winter more'n likely. But I reckon you're right to keep off of the hills."

He buttoned up one worn coat after another, and pulled on yarn mittens. At the door he nudged the sheriff.

"Say, if a feller was to die down yander, would they ship him back here to be laid away, or what?"

The sheriff looked first at one deputy and then the other, and then stammered.

"I don't know. But I'd think they'd bury 'em down there, unless relative sent money for them to be shipped home, or something."

"Well, I 'low my folks couldn't send nothing. Wonder what it'd cost to ship a feller's body back? Twouldn't it be nowhere's near fifty dollars, would it?"

"Oh, I don't think so."

A flicker of light, like a fleeting lightening-bug had risen in his eyes for a moment, but died as he turned to his mother.

"Ma, if anything *was* to happen to me down yander, like I was to die or something, maybe you ort to let the rub-doctors know. Seems like they've took a right smart of interest in me and all. Still, if nothing happens, don't bother. I reckon I can tell 'em myself, when I git back."

She picked up sugar sacks and patters and rolled them all in a little bundle.

"Why, George, 'tain't none of their business what happens to you."

His mouth dropped like a half-open jack knife.

"Now, Ma, you don't know how things air. If I *do* die, looks like they ort to know, the interest they took and all, and obleeging as they been, and I want you to tell 'em!

"I ain't a-going to do it, George. 'Tain't none of their business, I tell you. Like as not, they'd be a-going down there, a-digging you up, and cutting you to pieces, to find out what ailed you. I ain't a-going to tell them nor nobody else. Let 'em find out for theirselves."

Lige hunched forward from his chair behind the stove.

"Oh, Sary, why don't you say you'll tell 'em? What do you want to worry him to death for? Nine chances to ten, big and stout as he is, nothing'll happen no-how, so you won't *have* to tell. But if he does pass away down yander – 'tain't a-going to hurt nothing to tell them doctors. I never seed anybody so out and out contrary."

Sarah's head kept up a succession of little jiggles.

"Now, Lige Moore, I know what I'm a-doing, and I don't 'low to have no more to do with them rub-doctors, now or no time. Don't aim to go about 'em, no matter what, and I hope they don't come about me. We're mixed up enough with rub-doctors as it is, and looks to me like George ort to have sense enough to know it."

George's face looked half hopeful, and half drawn and puckered, like a partly rotten apple.

"I know it, Ma, but you ain't no idy how things air. Well – goodbye, both of you."

"Goodbye, George. Take care of yourself."

"Goodbye."

As long as he could see the house, he kept looking backward. What should he do? Not but what he'd give anything in the world to get out of the clutches of the rub-doctors, but he'd given his word, and signed a contract. He kept mulling it over as they see-sawed up and down the hills. If he had only seen Mary. Mary would have told them. Naturally, he didn't want them to know, if he didn't die, but if he did, it was their due, only *he* couldn't tell them then. Mary was the one. He must see her. By the time he reached his decision, they was almost in town.

"Sheriff, you reckon I could see the woman before I go? I feel like I ort to."

Sheriff Shope was about as friendly as a bulldog after a tramp.

"I thought we settled that down at your mother's; that you didn't *have* to see her."

"I know it, Sheriff, but I just got to thinking. This *might* be my last chanct a-ever seeing her, if I took sick and died down yander, and 'twouldn't seem right, a-going off for all the time, 'thout having said her goodbye beforehand."

The gully in the sheriff's forehead deepened.

"It's a pity you didn't do a little thinking before. You seemed satisfied to come on. I just don't feel equal to going over those icy hills again. It's not safe. Maybe somebody could bring her up with a team – or Ford."

George popped mittened palms together.

"Well, Sheriff, I don't keer how I git to see her, just so I do."

"Well, we'll see. I'll call down and see what's to be done."

Mary had been washing, as usual, and had had to stop in the middle. Her chapped hands were dull red, and her shoulders had more slump than common. She turned dull eyes to George.

"George, I've been half sick all day, about you having to go off, but a body has to do their work. And busy as I was, and hard as it is to heat water and all this kind of weather, looks like you could a-*writ* whatever you wanted to tell me."

He kept shaking his head as he stared.

"No, Mary, I couldn't. I just got to thinking. Like as not I might die down yander – I've heard of such things – and never git to see you again. And I aimed to tell you goodbye before I went. Then too, if I *should* die, I heard they cain't ship a feller's body back, less'n their folks pay fer it, and mine cain't. And I was a-wondering, Mary, if I *do* die, that is, would you tell them rub-doctors soon as you hear? They always seemed so interested like in my ailments and all, I reckon they ort to know – that is, if I *was* to die, understand."

She stared at him as if he were a screen wire, and not a particularly good piece at that, and then tears came into her eyes.

"George, if you've brung me fifteen miles for such foolishness, 'pears to me like you're a heap worse off than what any of us think. You know what all I got to do, down yander, and it dark at sundown. Such foolishness don't come before a body's work, I reckon."

George seemed to be washing his hands without water.

"Well, Mary, if you had any idy how things air, you might think different. I feel like they ort to know. 'Tain't right if they don't, hardly. Anyhow, *will* you tell 'em, Mary, that is, when you hear I'm dead – not before?"

"I reckon I will, if you're so set on it, though you ain't apt to die –"

His worried face relaxed into the calm of Missouri clay.

"You're the best wife a man ever had, Mary. And I love you, and always will love you, and I just hope I can git my health back so's I can help you the way I ort. I cain't hardly bear to see you work like you do, Mary, but I cain't help it, seems like. And it's the worrying about it – that and other things – that's got me in the shape I'm in, I reckon. But I 'lowed I'd let 'em do all they can for me this winter, and when spring comes, and it gits tolerable warm weather again, I'm a-aiming to come home, and you can count on it – cured or not. And I aim to do considerable work next year, that is, what I can stand to do, and I hope that'll be a right smart. Anyhow, I 'low things *might* work out all right, in the long run. And now, goodbye, Mary. Take good care of yourself and the younguns too, and I'll be back, soon as they say I'm able – no matter what – and do the best I can."

"Goodbye."

Chapter 15 : Trip to the Asylum by Train

Over wheels and rails that clanked out a steady tune of "The Girl I left Behind Me", the cornsheller of a passenger train chugged on toward the hospital. George's bulk sank into soft-looking red stuff, that hardened with sitting, as his eyes stared out at a stretch of blackness and occasional whir of lights. A hundred miles is a long way – that is, when you've never been more than ten or fifteen miles from home before in your life. The engine sounded as if it were making for the ends of the earth, but the screech of brakes and wham of cars ever so often, reminded him that there were towns and watering stations along the way.

It was sort of company to have the constable along. Not that he said much or paid much attention to anything anybody else said. Just sat hunched over a paper-backed book with some slit-eyed somebody or other on the front of it. Didn't even pay much attention to lights or anything that whizzed by, until the brakeman yelled out the name of some town three or four times. Then he straightened up as if somebody'd just called him to breakfast, and with one hand shading his eyes, stared at the big letters on the station, – to make sure of finding his way back, more than likely. But as soon as they moved on, he doubled lower than ever over the dull print without pictures, as if to make up for lost time. Once George interrupted him.

"Constable, I don't like to bother you, but I was just a-wandering what you was a-reading, you seemed so wrapped up in. I'd read myself, but I hain't got nothing to read in the first place, and I cain't read to amount to a great deal if I had. Though, for that matter, I don't' know as I'd read on this-here train if I could, cause it sort of jiggles my eyes."

It was like trying to make friends with a dog at meal time. For a split second the constable showed his teeth, and then snapped, "Detective stories."

"Oh. What's that?"

The constable looked as if instinct told him to bite, but common sense urged toleration.

"Oh, – stories about murders and solving crimes of one kind and another. In this one, there's three or four that died suddenly and mysteriously, and when they go to dig into their graves to find out what killed them, there's nobody there. Somebody's robbed the grave. That's as far as I've got. They're trying to find out now, who's done it and what for. The way I've got it figured, it's a bunch of young doctors.

"*Rub*-doctors?"

"Oh, no, not that I know of. Not much of anything, I guess – just some kind of quacks."

George stared at book and constable and then spoke.

"Do you reckon it's got to the point where everybody's snatched from their graves, the minute they're laid to rest, whether they're bargained for – or not?"

"No, of course not. This is just a story."

"Well, all I got to say is, I don't want no such stories. Maybe I'm wrong, but 'pears to me like hit's plum foolish and a out and out waste of time, a-reading the like. The way I look at it, a body has plenty to worry about, just thinking over his own troubles, let alone a-digging up everybody else's."

But the constable had doubled up over his magazine again. It was away past bedtime, four or five hours, but with all that rumbling and bumping and lights blurring, a body couldn't sleep. Still it wasn't much pleasure to just sit there and look at the seats.

They seemed to be shooting straight south, with the hills over to the west. George stared out every so often, but there wasn't a thing to see.

Maybe he ought to try to get some sleep. He hadn't slept any too much lately, worrying like he had, and in jail and all. He leaned back and closed his eyes, but sleep would not come. It was just like trying to finish a nap in the morning, with somebody shaking down ashes and getting out clinkers to start a fire, the way Andrew's did – a continual rumble.

He put his head against the pane and blinked his eyes. Away off over haystacks of hills was a flicker of light. Didn't seem to amount to much at first – just little cat-tongue flames and smoke, and then it flared up like somebody'd doused it with coaloil. Maybe somebody's flue burning out, or maybe a lantern kicked over somewhere, though it seemed uncommonly late for somebody to be up even – let alone out doors. Maybe some sparks from the train had blown over west and set some out-building afire. Didn't amount to much more than likely.

He tried to sleep again, but he couldn't. The constable had stopped reading and had backed back in his seat and stretched out his legs. His mouth half opened as his eyes closed, and sucked in long, rambling snores, with an occasional sharp snort. As they rumbled on, a misty snow gathered in the air and blurred lights could be seen here and there, but not much else. Just as the wind started blowing a regular gale, swooping snow in all directions, the train jerked to a stop and they had to get off and wait for another one. An hour and a half's waiting in some uncommonly hard seats, railed off in two foot pens, so that even the constable gave up all idea of sleep, and the train clanged in to take them on.

More towns. More stops. George fidgeted and looked around while the constable snored. Across the aisle, one seat back, a man with the plump, genial look of a hog a week or two before butchering time, hovered as he beamed. Several times he had eyed George with the friendly look of a candidate before election, but George was no hand to take up with strangers – never was. Finally, however, he decided, with the county constable sitting right there beside him, there couldn't a lot happen anyway, especially when the man smiled and said, "Long, tiresome trip, isn't it?"

George blinked as he eyed the man's softish bulk.

"I reckon you're right. Air you a-going to Saint Jo, too?"

"Yes, I guess almost everybody is, now."

"Where'd you git on at?"

"Keatsville. Same as you did."

George swallowed three times before he could get the next words out.

"Say, – you ain't a-going to a hospital down there, air you?"

"Oh, no. I'm associated with the Keatsville Clinics, on Johnson Street."

George's mouth dropped three inches.

"You mean – the *rub*-doctors? You ain't a-going down there for *them*, air you?"

"Well, yes, in a way. There's a little business matter I have to take care of."

"It – don't have nothing to do with bodies – does it?"

"What?"

"Bodies – *dead* bodies. Is that-there clinic hitched up anyway with the insane asylum at St. Jo, – a-gitting skeletons from 'em and such?"

"Good Heavens, no! Whatever gave you such an idea?

"Oh, nothing in particular, I reckon. I was just a-wondering. You see – I'm on my way to the insane asylum now myself, and I thought maybe I ort to find out before I got there."

The beaming smiled puckered to the look of a mouth filled with vinegar, and no place to get rid of it, as piggish eyes zigzagged from George to the constable's star.

"You – don't smoke – do you?"

George jiggled his head.

"No. Don't smoke nor chew nor nothing. Never did."

"I think I'll go into the smoker for a while."

He never did come back. It looked odd, him leaving the minute they started talking about skeletons. It stood to reason there would be some skeletons down there, not claimed, and somebody got them. Maybe they just didn't want it to get out, but, like as not, this man was going after a load now, and the rub-doctors had sent him.

It didn't seem right, though – that resurrection idea, if old man Jimpson was right. Somebody dying down there out of his head, maybe from a tumor on the brain, or a kick from a horse – and his folks all dead, and nobody to claim him –. Some doctor or other would get him, and that would be the end eternally – and *he* hadn't even got fifty dollars. It was all a sorry business. Maybe the preachers would save more souls in the end to look after the dead, and let the living go.

It was almost getting up time, but the lights were off, and the train whizzed faster and faster, as if it had no notion of stopping for hours. And it didn't look as if there was much of any place to stop, if it did. He hadn't slept all night, but maybe he could snatch a wink or two's rest yet. He leaned back in the seat and stretched out his legs. He kept thinking of the time in jail – all one night and day and half the next night. Like as not he was the only person that ever went to jail on his own say-so, and for that matter, he hadn't exactly bargained for it. Jail hadn't entered his head. Just the asylum.

And that kind of trial the first night, with a judge and sheriff and doctors and all, to find out whether he was crazy enough to go or not – a little bit on the order of Lige's trial, only not so much of it. And all those questions, with somebody writing down all they asked and all he said. And the odd part of it was they knew all the answers before they asked. Somebody'd asked him all of them before – some of them two or three times – and they'd all been written down then. And what they had to do with a body's being out of his head or not was more than he could understand. Asked such questions as how many children he had, and their ages, and the size of the farm, and what kind of crops they raised, and what work he did, and the woman and little boy, and the like, and concluded with three quick questions.

"Hmm. Is your farm ever weedy?"

"Oh, yes. It most generally is."

"Fences run down?"

"Why, yes, might near all of 'em air –"

"Did anybody ever accuse you of being lazy?"

"Why, yes. Just about everybody has, I reckon."

What all that had to do with his being out of his head or not, was more than he could figure out. It was a thousand wonder he got to go. The judge was half a mind to send him back home. Claimed to the last he was no more crazy than he was – just nervous, and lazy. But that doctor, the last one he'd talked to that day in town spoke up and said something about a persecution complex, or something like that. About somebody following him around, waiting to hack the meat off his bones – and he'd just gone all to pieces, and the judge gave in. Funny kind of trial – with no jury and no lawyers to pay –.

And those little two by four beds in jail, about the size of a couple of these train seats, tacked together end for end, and just as hard. You'd have to be worn out to sleep on the like.

There were snakes all around him, and he couldn't move. They all started crawling over him, but he wasn't able to lift a hand. And then the hogs come. One after another they shook the snakes senseless and chewed them down, and then one of them started shaking him. He sat up and blinked his eyes, but the constable kept on shaking.

"Wake up. We're almost there. I heard some Hell's Holler news last night, or maybe this morning. Anyhow I forgot to tell you."

"What?"

"The dance hall burnt down last night."

"Did?"

"Yes. Burnt clear to the ground, I heard."

Funny the dance hall had burnt down the very night he left. Old man Jimpson had said they might as well burn it down. That rub-doctor coming down at that last dance – and that one on the train last night. They'd wanted to take it over – and everything else, just about, in Hell's Holler. Could *they* have had anything to do with its burning down?

Chapter 16 : George's Reaction to the Asylum

Days dribbled into nights and dawn to dusk like apple pulp to juice in cider making time. Up at five and to bed by seven, with nothing much to do and nobody to tell you to do it. But a warm room to dress in, and plenty to eat – things could be worse. As time went on, George liked it better and better.

Back in Hell's Holler, some of them had sort of made light of insane asylums and the like, but what more could a body want? In three or four weeks, he'd been over more country and got to know more people than he had all the rest of his life put together, and it hadn't cost him a cent – none of it. And he'd seen three moving pictures, and he never had seen any before. And Saturday night dances, with seven or eight or nine music-making pieces, some he'd never even heard of before, were things to remember the rest of his life. Even Sunday sermons had a kind of skinned-peach smoothness and mellow that made him look ahead with hope for his soul, if not his body. If he could have just had Mary and the children with him, and maybe his mother and father and a hill or two, he would just as leave stayed on there, the rest of his days.

Some of the patients kicked about the meals. For that matter most of them did – the ones that were able to talk at all. Said the victuals they had, wouldn't fatten a hog. Maybe they wouldn't but seemed as if most of the patients gained considerably. Like as not, not one of them had half as good at home. George hadn't, and he knew it. Never had had half as many different things at once, ever, unless at harvest time maybe, and even then, no such jump in the kinds of victuals as here. It was something like going into a side-show, when that kind of alarm clock buzzed. You never knew what you'd have put before you, or what to expect. Things you might not get on the farm, like rice or raisins or prunes and the like, maybe once in two or three years. And all a body wanted of everything – great big bowls, up and down the tables.

And in all his life, he had never been treated any better or with more respect anywhere. Seemed as if all the doctors and nurses and keepers wanted him to help out, just acted as if it were all a great big blackberry patch, with him needed to look after the pickers. They couldn't have hardly given him more things to look after, or trusted him to do them right, if he'd been the mayor of Keatsville. Even had him catch run-a-way patients, oversee bed-making, and milking, and the like. Seemed to, think more and more of him as time went on, and give him more privileges. Once the superintendent even had him play the fiddle all afternoon for patients, with a nurse-girl seconding on the guitar. And the sense of responsibility of overseeing so many people, and in a way being the cause of the accomplishment of so much, even though he didn't lift a hand himself, hardly, and the knowledge that he was more or less the smartest one there, and the most reliable, when he'd always been so helpless at home – urged him on to the utmost, something like a conscientious assistant in college, or supervisor of a mill, no doubt, till he practically forgot his troubles in this new feeling of superiority and importance.

He hadn't been any too well satisfied at first, though. He was already bawling lonesome for the folks at home, and the superintendent – he found out afterwards who he was, though he thought it was some big doctor at the time – asked all those questions again, the very identical ones they'd asked him at night court, and some of the doctors had asked two or three times before. And the odd part of it was, they had all the answers right down before them on paper, just like he'd given them in Keatsville, but seemed as if they just wanted to hear him talk, or maybe make him worse homesick, or something. Or maybe they aimed to catch him in a lie. Anyhow, seemed as if the superintendent got out and out mad when all the answers tallied. Said George wasn't crazy or nowhere near it, and hadn't a bit of business down there. But the constable talked and he did, and they finally agreed, that now that he was down there, he might as well stay till the cold weather was over anyway.

At first, too, the guards acted as if they were downright afraid of him. That was odd, in a way, for they all looked like uptown cattle killers, and not one of them weighed less than two hundred pounds or over, – but they shied away from him. Acted as if they thought he was so far out of his head, he was liable to start in killing most anybody, or maybe pulling down the building and throwing the bricks as far as he could. Seemed to get over it, though, after they'd talked to him a little.

He hadn't eaten at the tables at first, either. Two of them had given him a bath, like some doctor said, and wrapped him in a blanket and put him in bed for two days, though he'd wanted to get up and eat with the rest of them right from the start. When they'd brought in his breakfast that first morning, on a kind of tin tray, he thought, from the looks of it, he was going to starve to death. Didn't look like enough to feed a good sized guinea hen – let alone him – but when he'd eaten it, it seemed enough.

And all that screaming bothered him at first. There was one boy, about like J.P. Jimpson, that ever so often would get to yelling, and strip off every stitch he had on, and start turning summersaults, till they'd have to sort of whip the devil out of him, or whatever it was, before he'd stop. It seemed sort of heartless and downright mean in a way, though it seemed to work. He got so when he'd feel those spells coming on, he'd go to a keeper that he liked and say, "Mister, I feel like I'm going to have to take my clothes off, so you'd better start in whipping me." And after the keeper whipped a while, he'd say, "I'm sore on that side. Whip me on the other side, won't you?"

And even though the keeper didn't whip uncommonly hard, just enough to keep the devil on the jump, maybe, George could hardly stand it. And one day when the keeper wasn't around and somebody had to do something, he just went up and clamped that boy's arms and legs in a vice of a grip, and talked to him soft-like, till he quieted down and seemed to have the yelling and clothes-taking-off notion scared or talked clear out of him. And nobody whipped him after that – just let George look after him. And he got so he liked George better than anybody, and would do just what he said, without him even touching him. And finally he'd gone home, pretty well cured, and everybody thought George had done the most of it.

At first, if occurred to George that they might start in whipping him – maybe whip the cow-mark out – though he didn't seem to have any such notion. Didn't seem to be aiming to do anything for him, as far as he could see, except giving him a few hot baths, and taking out his teeth, two or three or four at a time. Finally he decided to ask somebody about it and went to the superintendent.

"Doc, there's something I'd like to say to you or somebody, though I'm afeard to say it, afeard I'll be punished for it. But long as I been a-thinking about it, I'm a-going to say it anyhow."

And the superintendent had said, "Why, feel perfectly free to say anything you like."

"Well, Doc, here's the idy. I been here might near a month now – considerable over three weeks anyhow – and not a drop of medicine nor nothing. Don't look like you're a-trying to do me no good. All this time, and not a single pill, or airy tonic of any kind. Not even any rubbing to speak of or cutting – nothing! And how in the name of the Lord air you a-aiming to cure me if you don't do nothing? So far, nobody ain't lifted a hand, except yanking part of my teeth out. Why is that, Doc?"

And the superintendent hadn't even offered to whip him or have him whipped. What he said didn't seem to have a great deal of sense to it – that is, about curing a body's ailment, though it sounded reasonable enough – but it was clear *he* thought they'd done something. Said they *had* helped him considerable, and had all along, whether he realized it or not. That they'd kept sad and worrisome stories away from him, and not let him talk about his troubles. That they'd tried to build up confidence in himself, by giving him certain responsibilities, a step at a time, though maybe at first it hadn't been more than having him hand a dish or two to somebody else to wipe. And the superintendent was so mild-like and agreeable-acting, and out and out anxious to make him understand, that George said he did, though he could not help feeling medicine would have helped considerable too.

And tooth trouble. Tooth pulling may be a remedy for many an ailment, but all out at once, that is, in four or five or six days, is not to be sneezed at. Seemed as if he spent the better part of a week with his head back and mouth wipe open, sputtering through forceps and fingers, while the dentist pried and pulled, squirting water over sore gums, as unconcerned as if it were bug poison on potato vines. And that last day, he hadn't seemed to want to stop. Kept punching and gouging and tearing out chunks of jawbone as if he were cutting weeds with a handsickle and wanted to finish the patch before dark.

They had agreed on one thing. His old teeth had been so crooked and long he couldn't hardly get his mouth more than half shut at the closest, but the new ones were to be more or less straight. The dentist said he *could* duplicate the old ones, and they would look more natural to his folks and all, but it would take more time, and George figured it was considerable like a woman getting a new dress. She wouldn't want brand new goods made just like something she'd had thirty or forty years, and he felt the same. Sort of wanted to see how he'd look in some half way straight ones.

And there had been other things to worry him, though not for long – like that poor old man, the day he'd had the last of his teeth pulled, moaning and groaning in the next red building, till it reminded him more of a hog wringing than anything else. He had been so nervous and worried about it, the girl of a nurse had taken him over there, and it was about the oddest sight he ever saw.

Somebody was stretched out on a kind of cot or table thing, covered with a sheet. At one end two feet stuck out, bony and bulged out, and half mortified, looked like – sort of dried and curled up at the toes, like a dead bird. The doctor didn't look a bit more concerned than a woman who had just singed a chicken and is ready to cut it up. At one ankle, he ripped back the skin, took a cut or two with a kind of butcher knife thing, and sawed a little, till the nurse could unhinge the foot and throw it over on the table. First one foot and then the other – snipped, cut, sewed, and unhinged, like potatoes dug and tossed into a bushel basket. George's eyes bulged as he kept thinking and swallowing. Did everybody go home without feet, when they did go? And *was* this place, after all, a kind of boneyard for the rub-doctors, in spite of what the man on the train had said, and was his carcass to be shipped back to them, chunk by chunk? All this time the moaning had gone on, rising and swelling at times like congregation hymns on Sunday, and then easing off to the unintelligible sounds of the blessing at dinner. George felt he had to get out in the air.

Outside, he asked the girl about it, but she hadn't seemed to want to say much, except that the old man was half insane anyway, almost violent part of the time, and was always running off. That every few days, guards or no guards, he'd get away somehow, and start for town. Said they weren't allowed to talk to one patient about another – it was against the rules, and she might lose her job if she did. But George was so upset and worried about it – and it did look like cutting off a body's feet was a might hard way of keeping him where he belonged – that she concluded to tell the whole story. Said George was considerably better off than most of them down there anyhow, and since he'd seen it and it worried him, she might as well. That the old man had got out and run off one night about a week ago, and had frozen both feet and bruised them so bad, gangrene had set in – so he *had* to have them taken off to live at all. But that, as far as their being connected with the rub-doctors at Keatsville or *any* doctors, they just *weren't*. That they had their own specialists.

And that letter from Sarah. About the rub-doctors coming down to the place, asking about him – three of them in a long, black car like a burying box on wheels – after them burning down the dance hall at Hell's Holler, nine chances to ten, the very night he left, too. The black bearded one had done the talking. Said they hadn't seen George around for some time, and was just wondering where he was and what shape he was in and all. And she'd just given them a piece of her mind. Told them it was none of their business. That nine chances to ten it was their fault for all that happened, – them not lifting a hand to doctor him when he went up there, after pretending to be able to cure just about anything too, and then worrying him to death, telling he'd had too much medicine and the like. And she'd told them if it was just the same to them she'd rather not see them again or have anything more to do with them. That she blamed them for the whole thing, and when she was through with a body she was through. And then they'd trailed Lige and Lawrence down to where they were digging buried apples, and they like to never got rid of them. They'd just stood there and looked at that bulge of ground, where it whooped up for a stretch six or seven or eight feet, like it *belonged* to them, and wouldn't budge an inch – that is, not till they found out what it was, and then, oddly enough, they went off.

George had been so nervous and worried by all this that the superintendent said he thought his mother had better not write to him any more. Said it seemed to upset him too much – that his wife could tell him how things were. And it did take a week or such a matter for him to get over worrying, but after that everybody was so out and out nice, and friendly-like and agreeable, and one thing and another happened, uncommonly nice things – with the superintendent and doctors and all acting like he was about the best patient they'd ever had and the best hand with the others, – and with dances and moving pictures and restful-like sermons to look forward to every week, George wasn't right sure he would want to go home when the time came. And the more he thought about it, the more he wished he could just stay on there year in and year out, till he about half hated to see spring come.

Chapter 17 : [Title Omitted]

Lawrence was starting to Hog Creek School. Aimed to go every day now. It was odd in a way, him wanting to go all of a sudden, much as he'd always hated even the thoughts of it before.

He kept mulling over that trip to Keatsville the day before. They had gone after shingles, that is, Sarah and Lige had, and he'd gone along, just to be doing something. With the trial taking every cent they could scrape together, and Lige so poorly and all ever since, they'd put off roof-fixing, until the sitting room floor was about half buckets and tubs every time it rained or snowed. Finally Sarah could stand it no longer. They had butter and eggs enough to pay for a bundle of shingles or two and a few nails, and they could do without other things.

And then that girl. Nobody they'd ever seen before, or would again, more than likely. Just somebody they'd given a ride to school in the spring wagon, her and her brother. She'd seemed to take to Lawrence from the start. Talked about school all the time, just about, when she found out he hadn't ever gone hardly. Showed him the pictures in her red and tan reader and told about games at recess, till he'd decided school might not be such a bad place after all, though he'd said [it was] in a kind of self defense.

"Shucks, I don't keer for school none. I'd ruther stay home and help Mommy. What I like is cutting wood, plowing, and feeding mules and cows and the like."

She had turned to him in mild surprise.

"I didn't know anybody liked them things. If you do all that, what does your pa do?"

"Pappy's sick, so me and Mommy have to do all the work. My pappy's in the insane asylum. Is your'n?"

He could still see her – yellow hair rippling down her back like corn silk a little before roasting ear time, and cut off straight in front, sort of blocking off her dark eyes that seemed to half melt as they looked at him. She'd said her pa wasn't in the insane asylum, but she seemed greatly impressed that his was, and kept talking more and more of school. Said he'd be more of a help to his pa, if he went to school, and talked on till he about decided he wanted a reader more than anything else in the world. Finally she appealed to Sarah.

"Say, lady, why don't you do without something you was a aiming to git, when you sell your butter and eggs and such, and git this little boy a reader? He ort to be in school."

And Sarah had said, "Well, maybe he ort and maybe he ortn't. There's a heap of things a body needs worse'n readers, little girl, and right now we need to fix a leaky roof. If we don't, somebody's liable to git pneumony. And I reckon a body's health comes before books and the like."

"Yes, but, lady, the teacher claims what you git *out* of books, helps health. Helps fight germs and ailments and such, looks like it ort."

"Well, it don't. leastways, fur as I ever knowed, folks with book learning died same as others. Anyhow, I don't put no stock in them new fangled books. Seems like they don't learn a body nothing." But she had reached back and added, "Let me see that-there reader, Lawrence."

He had kept thinking about that girl all the way to town, and even then he had followed Lige and Sarah around in a half daze all morning, as he mulled over school games and readers and yellow haired girls. Finally he had tired out, and waited for them at the courthouse. When they got back to the spring wagon, Sarah had handed him two paper wrapped packages. He could not help thinking that was mighty little shingles for all the eggs and butter they'd taken, and stood staring until Sarah had said, "It's for you, Lawrence. Both of 'em air, and your grandpa's got something fer you too. Unwrap 'em, and see what they air." And when he'd pushed back the paper, one was a red and tan reader – just like that girl's – and he'd screamed out, right on the square, as he'd hugged it.

"Oh, Grandma, I never 'lowed you'd *git* it fer me, though I wanted it uncommon bad. Didn't you git – *no* shingles?"

"No, Lawrence. That other'n's overalls fer you. We concluded the roof could wait."

And now, it was the next morning, and he was on his way to school – almost there. He kept fingering the new pocket knife his grandpa had given him to keep his pencil sharp. All his life he'd wanted a pocket knife – though he'd never had one.

He was away early, and waited in the hall, trying to study out words in his reader till school time. It was cold to middling warm, but the teacher was doubled up over her desk, with her spectacled eyes fixed on some kind of papers, and he didn't want to bother her, as he stood and shivered. One by one, pupils came in, and stared as they tromped by without a word. When the bell clanged, he edged inside and sat down in the seat nearest the door.

Reading was not what he had expected it to be. If he waited a minute, the teacher clipped in and pronounced the word, until he was so mixed up and bothered he didn't know what was what, and everybody got to snickering. But he was as good as anybody in geography. It was capitals and all he had to do was think of an old song his grandpa chanted at times, and there were the answers.

> "New York, Albany, on the Hudson River.
> Pennsylvania, Harrisburg, on the Susquehanna.
> Massachusetts, Boston, on the Boston Harbor.
> Vermont, Montpelier, on the Onion River."

Recess time found him slinking out after the others, like a lost puppy. He peeped around one corner of the school house. It was like a circus, in a way, with everybody yelling at once, and doing different things – only everybody was in the circus ring but him. Two lines of girls of all sizes marched to meet each other, tossing their hair like young colts, and singing by turns another of his grandpa's songs:

> We come, three knights a riding,
> With a rants, and a tantz,
> And a tit-a-mi-tay."

But what he wanted to do most was play "Old Sow" with the larger boys, only nobody said anything to him about it, and there didn't seem to be any hole for him or any stick. Maybe at noon he could cut him a stick and grub out a hole next to the others and nobody would notice. Anyhow, he could keep his stick in the hole and yell "Fire in my hole!" if anybody knocked it out. All this time he had been carrying wood and corn, and didn't even know there *was* a game like "Old Sow."

But by noon, after dinner pails were emptied, the game had changed to blackman. Bimpy Ryan monkied them out to see who was "it".

> "One-ery, ore - y, ickory Ann;
> Philoson, Pholoson, Nicholos John;
> Queevy, quavy, English Navy,
> Stinktum, stanktum buck!"

A little boy no bigger than Lawrence was "it."

"What you gonna do when you see a blackman coming?"

"Run right through!"

And they *did* run right through, that is, most of them did. When they were all caught but the biggest boys, who never *were* caught, they decided to start a new game with the first one caught as "it," another small boy, of course. All this time nobody had paid the slightest attention to Lawrence, who had stood peeping out from the corner of the schoolhouse, like a young chick watching ducks swim. It had occurred to him to run out where they were playing and yell, "I can play blackman!" but neither his legs nor his voice seemed to encourage him.

At the afternoon recess, he took his post at the schoolhouse corner, and when it was about half over, he noticed to his unbounded delight that some of the bigger boys were coming to him.

"What you doing here?"

"Nothing. Just a watching."

"Well, we don't want you watching us. You go and play with the girls. You might git hurt around us, or git your hair mussed, seeing as your ma curled it. We don't want no sissies around here."

"I ain't no sissy. I got a pocket knife. My grandpa give it to me."

"No? Let's see it."

Proudly he displayed it.

"Girls and sissies don't need knives. You might hurt yourself, or cut off one of your curls. We'll keep it fer you."

"You won't! Hit's mine!"

"Hit's mine now!" and big Tom Rainwater galloped around the school-yard, with Lawrence trailing him, fighting mad, and hardly seeing. One of the other boys tripped him, and over he went, sprawling in mud and slush, new overalls and all. He grubbed at his eyes.

"I'll tell the teacher, and I hope she skins you, every last one of you. And I'll tell Mommy and Grandpa and Grandma, and Ben Bragg and Andrew. And I'll tell *Pappy*, soon as he gits back from the insane asylum!"

"Haw! Haw! Haw! *Insane* asylum! His pap's crazy and I reckon he ain't fur from it hisself. If my pa was crazy, I wouldn't tell it."

"My pappy's as good as your'n, any day, and a heap sight better. And don't you make no fun of him neither, him sick like he is."

"Sick! Haw! Haw! We've heard of him, and there's just two things wrong with him – *lazy* and crazy – so he's your pa, that old crazy George!"

"Don't you dare say nothing else agin my pappy. He's the best pappy a body ever had!"

"Haw! Haw! Some pa! Lazy and crazy – that old crazy George."

Stung to crazed rage, Lawrence ran to the boy and kicked his shins as hard as he could. The boy's laugh twisted to a sneer.

"Oh, so you want to fight, do you?"

He tripped him over backwards, and then straddled him, holding him with one hand, and "ductch rubbing" with the other. The other boys watched, runging their companion on. An unexpected ally appeared in Bill Jimpson.

"What you doing here?"

"Nothing."

"Why don't you pick on somebody your size?"

"None of your business."

"I 'low I'll make it my business. Git off that kid."

Sulkily, the boy unstraddled his victim.

"I've a mind to give you what's coming to you," Bill went on, "but I reckon I'll let it go this time. What'd he do to you kid?

"He was making fun of Pappy, and he's got my brand new knife Grandpa give me."

"Give him that knife."

"Try and git it."

But he handed it over. Bill opened it and looked at it, and handed it to Lawrence.

"And don't let me ever hear nothing more out of you about his pa again. He cain't help it."

Just then the bell rang, and they all crowded inside. But after that, Lawrence couldn't keep his mind on lessons. He did so want to be one of the gang and play games, and do as they did. Ever so often he peeped around wistfully. Just before singing time, he noticed Tom Rainwater thumbing the tip of his nose and wiggling his fingers at him. That was something he could do. Maybe that was the gang sign, and as soon as you learned it, you could play with all the rest of them, and not just look on. Besides, it was a nice pleasant motion, swishing the air with your fingers. He kept practicing it after school, as he got books, dinner pail and coat to leave. Lawrence thumbed his nose and wiggled his fingers, as the big boy stared, frog-eyed. Pleased with himself, Lawrence repeated the performance.

Bimpy turned on him with a bellowing roar.

"Take that back, you little –"

But Lawrence was half way around the school house. He knew by the tone of Bimpy's voice something was wrong, but he had no idea what. Twice and a half, he circled the school house and then stopped.

"I ain't a going to run no more," he said. "Do whatever you're a mind to."

"Take that back."

"I ain't a going to take nothing back."

Bimpy's big hand gripped his shoulder, but Lawrence jerked away.

"You don't need to hold me. I'll fight, and I won't run, like I said."

"Come on over here off the school grounds, then."

Bimpy was considerably bigger and soon peppered him with blows until both his nostrils spouted.

"Take it back?"

"No."

More pounding. Bill Jimpson and Johnathan Ryan came up. "What's the matter here?" asked Bill.

In awed monotone Bimpy explained the gravity of the situation and both boys begged Lawrence to take it back, for that matter all three – but his mind was set.

"Do you know what it means?" asked Bill.

Lawrence's face was all blood and tears, but he shook his head.

"I ain't no idy what it means, but whatever it does, I meant it."

More pounding, but the bloodier Lawrence got, the more stubborn he was.

"Take it back?"

"No. and what's more, I never 'low to take it back."

"Aw, Bimpy," Bill urged, "you're twict as big as he is. There's no use beating him to a jell, just cause he's got spunk. A red headed feller never gives up. I 'low he'll make an uncommon good old sow player for his size, and there's no use crippling him, so's he cain't play."

John Ryan backed Bill up and finally Bimpy was persuaded to let it go at that. The feud was over and Bill and Lawrence walked home together.

"I don't 'low you'll have a heap more trouble at school, after this," Bill said, "though you might. They always try to sort of break in a new feller, but I reckon you're more or less broken, now. If you hain't, that is, if they pitch on to you again, just let me know. And if I ain't there, tell Ryans, and if they ain't – cut yourself a big hickory stick. That'll fix 'em. And if I was you, I wouldn't say nothing again, about my pap being in the insane asylum. Kids'll just laugh, and 'twon't do no good."

"Poor Pappy," mused Lawrence. They was great ones to be a-making fun of him. I hope he don't never find out about it. It'd just worry him, and he's got troubles enough as it is."

But he *did* find out. Somebody told Sarah, and she relayed the whole thing to George, and put it in with one of Mary's letters. And it upset him so much – that and some of old man Jimpson's *soul* talk – the superintendent had to send word to Sarah not to write any more, not even in somebody else's letter; that it seemed to make George too nervous.

Chapter 18 : Homecoming

All the way home George kept staring at his new outfit, and thinking of the nice things this one and that one had said and done. Less than a week ago, the superintendent had given him a brand-new dollar tie, for being the best old time fiddler in the hospital, though when the six or eight had played, he'd said he couldn't decide which was best. And he'd been uncommonly nice, when he left that morning. Talked to him like a brother, and gripped his hand longer and harder than anyone he had ever known. Said he just hated to see him go. That he wished there was some way he could stay on always.

And the nurses had been nicer than common too. Two of them had told him good-bye that morning and seemed out and out sorry to see him go. Had said some tolerably praiseful things, took, both of them. Said that in the two years they'd been there, they'd never seen a patient given as much liberty and trusted as much as he was, and said he was the best help with patients they'd ever had.

In a way, it seemed out and out foolish to leave – them acting like he was yonder better and smarter than the whole lot anyhow, and then offering him that job, with the chance to earn forty dollars a month and room and board the rest of his life! If he only could have stayed on a month or two anyway – till he earned fifty dollars at least, say –. But with the woman and children and his father waiting at home, seemed as if there was no other way out, and as the train chugged eastward, old memories of the hospital were shoved behind him with the present excitement of seeing them all again. Even the rails seemed to realize his up-in-the-air feeling, for they clicked over and over, "You're on the way home! You're on the way home!"

Trees and telephone posts and railroad station signs kept whistling and puffing by, and then the train stopped and he almost swallowed his new teeth. He was at La Fever, four miles from the two room house. Rolling up his breeches legs a little to keep them from the mud, and shouldering his bundle, he seesawed over the hills. Sometimes, along the creek, under oak and hickory ceiling, the banks were a solid splurge of green and blue and white – soft piled moss and long stemmed ferns, with patches of Dutchman's breeches and Johnny-jump-ups and sweet Williams. Once he sprawled down under a whistling willow and listened to the frogs in Turkey Run Creek. Seemed as if they were just welcoming him back. It occurred to him that the world was considerably the same, all over. Down at the insane asylum, about twenty or twenty-five hundred people that didn't know him had grinned and seemed glad to see him, and now these frogs were doing more or less the same thing, though before he'd left they'd jumped every time a body came near.

He started to pick a blue and white bouquet to take home, but so much stooping and straightening is hard on a body, when he's not used to it, and besides he was dead anxious to see the woman and children.

He stopped to rub the small of his back. A little worm of a garter snake wriggled into a bush and then stuck its tongue out at him. If Sarah and old man Jimpson were right, he had to kill it, that is, if he wanted to get the best of his enemies, and the Lord knew he did. He picked up a stick and cornering it, battered its head to a soft ooze of blood and brains. And then he got to thinking about that paper he'd signed, and the rub-doctors, and him and the snake, till, if he could have brought it back to life again, he would. And having picked next to no flowers anyway, he gave up the idea and went on, cooning a log across the creek and straddling up the hill.

The children were out in the yard, the three middle ones racing around after each other in the wind, and out-hooting hoot-owls, with the baby stumbling behind. When they saw him, they quieted down like mice when a cat comes and mouthed their fingers. George stumped on up the hill.

"Why, children, don't you know your own pappy?"

Somewhere around the house, Lawrence jumped up and galloped to his father, the smaller ones following like sheep.

"Oh, Pappy! You come back!"

George grinned down at the small brood that hugged his legs and stared.

"Yes, Lawrence, I come. I believe the little un's might near forgot me. Have you, Georgia?"

The small tow-head wagged, and two short pig tails flopped. "No, Pappy, but seems like, you're different."

"Well, I reckon brand new clothes and teeth ort to make a difference, fur as that goes."

Mary pulled back the plank door and they all stomped inside. George could hardly take his eyes off her. She looked so sort of, like she used to – more hopeful-like somehow, and less tired out, with more lift to her shoulders. And she eyed him considerably too. Said he looked as stout again as when he left. He *had* put on some twenty or thirty pounds or such a matter, but more than likely it was his new teeth and worsted suit that made the main difference. He helped himself to a chunk of cornbread from the warming closet and stared out toward the road. Somewhere in the distance there was a team and wagon sound.

"That's Ma and Pa a-coming now," he said.

The creak of wheels drew nearer and stopped, as Sarah brushed in, loaded chin-deep as usual. Her packages dropped with a rattle of paper, as her eyes centered on George, and her blue-veined hands squeezed his big palm.

"George, you're back, and I thank the Lord fer it! I felt it in my bones you'd be here to-day or to-morrow, so I brung a heap of things I knowed you liked. Lige'll be in soon as he unhitches. How air you?"

George gulped a mouthful of cornbread.

"Why, Ma, I hain't felt better for I don't know how long. Seemed like I was *somebody* down there. Many's the time they sent me to catch run-away patients, some of 'em pretty bad off in their heads."

Sarah's eyes squinted to sharp lines.

"Why, George, you might a-been killed. The idy! Letting you do the like of that! They didn't care nothing about you, or what happened to you. Wouldn't a-lifted a finger, no matter what'd a-happened. Strangers ain't like a body's own folks."

George's grin grew to a puzzled gape.

"Why, Ma, they seemed to think a heap of me, all of 'em. Even offered me a job there the rest of my life, if I'd a-been a mind to took it."

"What kind of a job?" put in Mary from the cookstove.

"Oh, something they was afeard to do theirselves," snapped Sarah, "something he was liable to be killed a-doing, you might know."

"Why, no, Ma, 'twas overseeing the milking. I didn't have to turn a hand hardly, myself. Just see that the patients done it. I'd a-had eight under me– I done it onct for two days – and I'd a-got forty dollars a month and room and board and washing throwed in. That sounds like mighty big wages to me, but I promised Mary before I left, I'd be home soon as I was able, so I come. But if there'd a-been any way to a-worked things, I'd a-sure liked to done it for a month or two or three, anyhow. But they said down yander, the woman and children couldn't git along on that, with a house and grub and duds to pay fer, and they said there wasn't no work there Mary could do without she had a high school education. Said it was agin the rules. So there wasn't nothing for me to do but come. I couldn't a-sent fer 'em, and I couldn't a-just stayed on by myself, after promising I'd be right home. That ain't no way to act nohow, you one place and your woman and children some'ers else, but if we could a made a go of things and Mary a-working too –"

There were circles of light in Mary's eyes, but Sarah snapped.

"You done right to come home, George. I ain't got no use for that hospital place, nor none of the outfit. The idy of them not letting me write to you – a pretending like your own ma made you nervous! It's my opinion the furder you git away from sech people, the better off you air. Anyhow, how could me and your pa a-looked after you, away off down there, a hundred mile from nowhere? 'Pears to me like they had mighty little to do, a-trying to git you away from your own folks. We might a-never seed you again. S'posing you'd *a-died* down yander – or got killed? I cain't bear to think about it, George."

George's bulk seemed to shrink smaller.

"Well, Ma, I cain't neither. Cain't hardly bear to think of dying nowhere, fur as that goes. That's one thing I liked about it down yander. I don't recollect a-ever hearing anybody talk about dying or burying or skeletons and the like, no time. Seemed like I plum got over my nervousness, whilst I was there, for some reason or other, and when I think back on it, I reckon I never had better treatment in my life. Ever since I left this morning, when I git to thinking about things, them a-keeping my mind off of my troubles like they done down yander all the time, and offering me that easy-like job, I keep thinking maybe I ortn't to come. And, now, me a-starting in to worrying the minute I git back, looks like, and gitting nervouser and nervouser when I think what all I could a-done with the money I'd a made down there – I feel like I'm liable to bust and bawl."

Sarah's slumped shoulders pushed back as she talked.

"Now, George, I don't want to hear you talk that-a-way. I wouldn't be satisfied – you some'ers else, without there was might good cause for it. And if you died away off, the Lord knows how fur, I reckon I'd might near go out of my mind. Why, I wouldn't feel nowhere *near* right, without me and your pa looked after your burying and knowed where you was, and what was done to you and all. I just hope the Lord'll let me live long enough to be here when your time comes, so's I can look after you. I cain't hardly bear to think of you not being buried proper, with a preaching service and all – and no telling *what* they'd do down yander. Besides, if you was to die and I couldn't go to the graveyard on Sundays and sort of talk to you, and put fresh flowers on your grave, spring and summers, when I had any, I don't know as I'd want to live myself."

George seemed to be all crumping up.

"Ma, for the love of God, don't talk of dying and the like no more. It always gits me so nervous and worried, I don't know what I'm a-doing, hardly. Say, have the rub-doctors been down this-a-way again, or have you seen any of 'em since you writ?"

She snorted as the twister doughnut gave a sudden jerk.

"Yes, I have. They was out here not much over a week ago, *still* a-wanting to buy property and a-asking about you and the like. Wanted to know when you was a-coming home. What ails 'em? I've told 'em time and again 'twasn't none of their business."

His dull eyes searched the room as if looking for help.

"Yes, but, Ma, in a way *it* is their business. All them they've doctored is, looks like."

She wheeled around like a circular saw.

"That's just it, George. What did they *do* for you when they was pretending to doctor you? Didn't do nothing. I don't feel they got no more claim on you than if they'd never laid eyes on you. Why should they care where you air, or how you're gitting along? And why should I tell 'em? If they'd a-asked about Mary, I'd a-told free enough, for they done a little something for her, and I feel like they got a right to know. But they never. 'Twas *you* they asked about, though what fer, I cain't figure out, and I feel like 'tain't none of their business."

George had a kind of dead fish look.

"Well, Ma, I feel like they got a *right* to ask whatever they want about me – much as they done for Mary and all – and if they ever ask again, I wisht you'd tell 'em. You ain't no idy how things air, Ma."

"I expect I've got a heap better idy than you give me credit fer. Remember I'm a right smart older than you air, and it stands to reason a old horse'd have better sense than a young'un. I know what's best fer you, and I say the smartest thing you can do, the way they been a-acting here lately, is to stay clear from the rub-doctors for good and all. I'm plum put out with 'em. They didn't do nothing when they ort, and now, they can at least stay away and not worry you to death."

"Well, Ma, God knows I don't aim to have no more to do with 'em than I have to. Might be, I won't have to go to *no* doctors from now on. I'm a heap stouter'n what I was."

"You don't look none too stout to me, George. You're a mite fleshier than what you was, but the chances air it ain't good flesh. No telling what them doctors done to you down yander, to make you put on weight, so's you'd look stouter'n what you air. They only had you less than three months, remember, and I had you over thirty-eight year. And I reckon I ort to know a mite more about my own boy then somebody that's been a-doctoring two or three hundred crazy people till he ain't got good sense hisself."

"There was more than any two or three hundred. I heard somebody say they had twenty-five hundred down there at times, Ma."

She tossed her head with a snort as her lips curled back.

"Twenty-five hundred! You know they couldn't do nothing for none of 'em, packed together like bees in a hive, with only a handful of doctors for the whole lot, and leaving you to look after the wild ones. I wouldn't put nothing a-past such people. Hit's a wonder to me you ever got back alive, and like as not they didn't intend it, but now you done it, I want you to take care of yourself."

There was a look of puzzled loyalty on George's face.

"Oh, Ma, I wisht you wouldn't talk that-a-way, not having seed 'em or anything. Seemed to me like they was the best folks down yander, ever I knowed anywhere. I know you always held out for hills and hill people, like they was sort of singled out by the Lord, but it stands to reason there ort to be *some* folks, some'ers, as good or better, and I felt like this hospital place was it. I just wisht you could a-been there and seed for yourself.

Lige inched in a little faster than a measuring worm. The whiskers seemed to have taken over more his face than ever.

"Well, George, why don't you tell us about it, if you're a mind to. I'll never git to see for myself, more'n likely, nor none of 'em here, and you have, and I'd like to know."

"Well, Pa, that's what I thought. You don't git to go nowhere hardly, none of you, and seeing as I seed some of the finest sights down yander ever I seed anywhere, I felt like I ort to pass it on."

Everybody seemed to like the idea, children and all. Even Sarah wiped her hands on the roller towel as they gathered around him.

"Well," she said, "maybe it's best for him to talk about it, and maybe it ain't, but to tell the truth I'd like mighty well to know myself, and I reckon now's as good a time as any to find out. Knowing things never hurt anybody, I reckon, and maybe he ort to git off his mind anyhow. Go on, George, tell us all about what you seed and done down there. We're a-waiting to hear."

Chapter 19 : George's Wonderful Tale

"Well, Ma, I just don't know what to tell and what not to, hardly. Seemed like there was more a-going on down yander, and friendlier people to talk to, and tooth-somer victuals on the table, and better laying and setting beds and chairs and the like, and more to learn every way, than any place ever I been. You ain't no idy, how nice they had things fixed. Every one of them buildings was brick, red brick, and right new, seemed to me like. And I don't know how many of 'em there was, and all of 'em as big again as airy one of them buildings around the square at Keatsville, with the Normal School and rub-doctor place throwed in. And you ort to seed the grounds – acre after acre, as smooth-laying and well-sodded as the best kept up cemetery ever you laid your eyes on, with trees enough, scattered around, so it was plum shady everywhere, all the time. And all around the whole shebang was the highest and prettiest and solidest-built hogwire fence ever I seed or heard of anywhere.

"And seemed like everybody down there just went out of their way to be pleasant to a body; patients and all grinned might near all the time, and some of 'em pretty bad off, too. And the superintendent and doctors and nurses and all was as agreeable and friendly again as half the folks I've knowed all my life – leastways, they was to me. Many as there was down there, seemed like every day or so, some of 'em found something or other to say to me – sometimes, something a-body'd never dream of 'em saying. And the thing I liked the best about the whole shebang was a way they had a making a body feel out and out important and helpful, even though he hadn't been much account all his life. Seemed like down yander, no matter what I done, everybody thought I was as good a hand as any of 'em, or maybe a little better. And I reckon I was, though I generally didn't do a great myself – just overseed the rest. Like bedmaking.

"They had me a-overseeing the bed-making the last six or eight or ten weeks I was down there, and said they never had had a better hand. I never had no trouble with none of 'em, no time.

"The barber's woman sort of started me out. Had me a-helping her make up beds and smooth out wrinkles till I got the hang of it. First she'd take off a cover and then I would, and so on, and she'd leave the wrinkles on purpose and have me smooth 'em out. She was a kind of bony, thin thing, about like Ma and Tizzie only more so – but a right good woman and pleasant. Said she could show anybody how to make beds in next to no time, and I reckon she could. Leastways she did me.

"She was not a well woman, seemed like anyhow, though, and about a week or such a matter after I started in a-helping, she didn't feel like going at all. Told me to take charge in her place. I had to unlock six or eight doors to get the ones that was supposed to work. Course I'd gone the rounds with the woman enough times to know what was what, but when I got to the last ward, one of them two that had the patients in charge there, looked at me as if he thought I was plum out of my head.

"'Moore, who let you in here?' says he.

"'I let *myself* in,' I says, grinning a little. The barber's woman ain't able to come to-day, and told me to take charge.'

"I had a paper she'd writ fer me, a pass she called it, but offish as he was a-acting, I concluded not to show it.

"'Well, they should let me know, when they put new ones on,' he says, 'but I guess it's all right. You wouldn't hardly have the keys if it wasn't. You know which ones to take?'

"I told him I did.

"'Well,' says he, 'maybe I ort to tell you something about taking 'em around, anyhow. When you go to go from one room to another, always turn sideways, with your back to the door, so that none of the ones ahead can hit you, and none of the ones behind can slip out. Understand?'

"I said I did, and managed all right, fur as I know. Anyhow, I took charge of that set of bed-makers from then on. The barber's woman was none too stout anyway, and never did come back – leastways not while I was there.

"One of them eight I had under me was a woman name o' Hattie. She was a extry good bed-maker – hardly ever left a wrinkle – one of the best workers they had. Seemed as if she just *liked* to do most work. But she had a stubborn streak, like most everybody does. She wouldn't dust and nobody could git her to. They'd beat her and punished her and I don't know what all, but it didn't do a particle of good. She wouldn't dust no matter what – that is, not till after they put me in charge.

"I didn't punish her, fur as that goes – didn't even talk a great sight, but I did tell her to dust, not knowing how she felt about it, and told her to smooth out a wrinkle she'd left one day. Well, she just went all to pieces and said might near everything. And some of the things she said made me so nervous and worried and worked up, I just busted out in a big bawl. I couldn't help it. And Hattie, well, she done what I told her. Said all her life she couldn't bear to see a man cry, and when they did, she knowed there was considerable the matter. And said to make up for whatever she'd done, she'd dust long as I was there, and she did.

"Well the superintendent like to went up when he found that out. Said I was the best hand with patients they'd ever had, and he wisht I didn't have to go home, ever. And if I do say it myself, I was as good as any of 'em a-heading off run-a-ways, and maybe a little better. It might be, it was because I was so long-legged and one *of* 'em, but anyhow, seemed like I could always overtake 'em and talk 'em out of it or toll 'em back – better than the guards, even.

"Well, 'twasn't long after that when that overseeing the milking job came up, the one they offered me for all time. There was two young fellers had charge of the dairy – the Roberts brothers, one about twenty-four, and tother'n som'ers around nineteen. They had all day off form morning milking till night, but the younger one was dissatisfied. He wanted to go out nights and be with young people. He couldn't git a substitute, though, without sixty days notice. About this time, the boys' mother died, and they asked if I wouldn't take the younger one's place for two days, as one of them would like to go to the funeral. The superintendent seemed willing enough, but I didn't know what to say, nervous and worried like I was. I told 'em I knowed quite a bit about cows and milking, though I hadn't milked a great sight lately, and didn't know whether I'd be able to manage or not. They all said they knowed I could, so the younger boy got off for two days.

"There was two divisions in the barn, with forty cows on each side, and shifts of eight patients to milk each forty. One of these shifts was under me, whilst that youngest boy was gone, that is. The oldest one told me that first morning, if I noticed any cows not milked dry, to tell the patients about it, and have them milk them over, and if they didn't do it, to take their names. Sure enough, two patients didn't milk their cows dry, so I spoke to 'em, nice as I knowed how.

"Well, they acted awful ugly-like at first – like a couple of snapping turtles. Said I wasn't their boss and I don't know what all. But when I started toward 'em to take their names like young Roberts said, I reckon they thought I was a-aiming to punish 'em, for they changed their minds right off and milked both cows dry. Got about a gallon and a half from both. Them cows give considerable milk – enough for most of the patients, leastways them that worked hard or needed it. The milking crew had to git up at long about four, so's they could milk in time for breakfast – about six or six-thirty. It was early hours, but I didn't seem to mind a great deal. Seemed sort of important to be the head of eight people and have them do like I said. And after that first time, every cow was milked dry.

"The nineteen-year old boy come back after two days but all the time he was wantin to leave. Seemed like too, the superintendent sort of wanted me to have that job. That was might near the last thing he said to me, I reckon.

"'Moore,' says he, 'I wisht you could take that younger boy's job for all time. It pays forty dollars a month and expenses. Would you want to?'

"Well, for a minute I got to thinking about what all I could do with the money and all, till I plum forgot my promise to Mary, and might near told him I'd take it. But when I thought things over, and talked to him – even though I *could* a-used the money uncommon handy, and fur as I was concerned, would just as leave a-stayed on there the rest of my life, that is, if Mary and the children, and maybe you and Pa could a-been there – I knowed there was no way to work it, and he knowed it too. Though he said to the end he wisht I'd take it. Said maybe I could send money back to the woman and all. But somehow, I couldn't see how that'd be much help, the way things air, or was the right thing anyhow, but I was real proud he wanted me to stay. Seemed like that superintendent was one of the friendliest fellers ever I seed, and I will say, I never was treated better or with more respect nowhere, in all my life.

"But I wouldn't want to tell about the goings-on at that hospital place, hardly, without saying something about my fiddle playing, and how they took to it down yander. I wouldn't a believed it if I hadn't a-seed it with my own eyes. Seemed like I had the whole capoodle of 'em under the spell of my fiddling, sort of. And I reckon that was the biggest feeling I ever had in my whole life, or ever will more'n likely, so I was saving it for last, to sort of wind up on, so to speak. That's one reason I like that superintendent so well. Seemed like he thought fiddling was might near as important as shoveling dirt and the like.

"I recollect one Sunday, I believe it was, I was out walking around, me and one or two of the keepers and about seventy or seventy-five patients, and up come the superintendent.

"'Moore,' says he, 'I hear you play the fiddle.'

"Well, that was long about the time I had all my teeth out, and I wasn't feeling none too spry nohow, and I'd been to two or three or four of them Saturday night dances, and I knowed I couldn't hold a candle to that up-town fiddler feller – I never seed fingers move so fast as his'n in my life – and still I was sort of itching to git my hands on a fiddle again too, though I didn't aim to act out and out anxious.

"'Well,' says I, 'I do and I don't. I wouldn't want to play before anybody down here hardly, no better'n what I do, and them all used to that feller from the city.'

"The superintendent didn't seem to give much thought one way or tother to what I said. Just stood there like a horst at a gap about feeding time. Wouldn't go away till he got what he wanted, though why he was so uncommonly set on me a-fiddling I couldn't make out. But he was. Said he just wanted to hear me play, and that he could borrow a fiddle from one of the doctors there. I *told* him I only knowed a few tunes the old donkey died on, and them by ear, and that I was afeard they'd just laugh at me, them being used to so much better stuff, but he just turned around to them that was there and asked how many could play the fiddle, even one note. And when none of 'em could he said, 'Now see? You're the only one here that can play fiddle at all – the other seventy-four cain't even strike a note. We have to find out what folks can do and what they like to do, so's to figure out what ails 'em and what to do for 'em.'

"Well, they brung me a fiddle, though they had considerable trouble a-doing it. That doctor didn't want to loan his'n, seemed like. Said it belonged to his wife, and he was afeard I might bust it to smithereens, but the superintendent got real mad-like and said to either loan it or turn in his white suit, so he did.

"I sawed off 'Turkey in the Straw' and 'The Girl I Left Behind Me' and I don't know what all, and some nurse or other got a guitar and seconded – seconded right well.

"And some of them seventy-five got a notion they wanted to do the Virginia Reel, and they started in, and more fullered, till finally might near all of 'em was lined up, a-clapping their hands and a-bowing and swinging, till the superintendent said it was a sight to see. And he had me a-playing might near all afternoon, first to one bunch and then another'n, till I'd played about all the tunes I knowed to about everybody there. And he said my fiddling was the best medicine them patients had had for he didn't know how long, and told somebody or other that had charge of the state's fiddle, to let me have it anytime I was a mind to play.

"Well, long about a week ago or such a matter, the superintendent called me in and said I was able to go home now, anytime, and they'd fixed me for me to leave first thing in the morning, and I was so excited like and glad and proud in a way, and still sorry to leave 'em all, I was a-going around a-telling 'em all good-bye – and first thing I knowed there was a regular hullabaloo started. First one and then another'n said they wanted to go too, and they all huddled together, a-acting awful ugly-like, and a-saying they was going to leave if they had to kill somebody to do it, and one of the keepers struck one or two of 'em, and they fought back, till it looked like they'd have to call out the whole uptown police force to quiet 'em down. And I recollected how still-like they always got when I played a tune Lem Webbstringer learnt me, a kind of sad-like serenade thing some Dutchman writ, and I went and got that fiddle, and started in, and first one and then another'n sort of crampled up and started to bawl, and said they wisht I wouldn't leave, ever. And some of 'em wanted me to play the Virginia Reel again, for the last time, and I done it, and when the superintendent come up, thinking to see a whopping big fist fight, they was all a-dancing, and he said he never seed anything like it. And said, if there was anyway in the world so's I'd be satisfied and Mary would, and we could pay bills and all, and stay there for all time – he wanted me to do it. And said he wisht I'd stay a few days longer, anyhow, and then slip off unbeknownst to the rest. And I said I would, and told him I'd ruther stay there than any place in the world, if 'twas so I could, and I hadn't promised Mary – but I couldn't."

Chapter 20 : Prayer Meeting at Jimpsons

After George had gone, Lawrence was as lonesome as a hoot-owl, like the last pig, when the rest have been marketed or killed for winter. It was not that he had more work to do or less to eat. It stood to reason their meat and corn and potatoes would go as far again without George to feed too, though the neighbors didn't seem to see it. Seemed as if they just tried themselves, helping with work and bringing in things to eat – things George would have liked uncommonly well – though Sarah shut down on her bringing considerably. But victuals wasn't George, and Lawrence could hardly look at his empty chair, without five or six swallows.

His chief comfort was J.P. Jimpson. Not that J.P. said a word, hardly ever, or did anything, but he'd been in the asylum too, and there was a feeling of closeness to George, just in being around him. Then too, J.P.'s knowing so much about woods and trees and the like, sort of put him all by himself – away ahead of everybody else from the start – something like George. And old man Jimpson's saying he had been touched by God added to Lawrence's feeling of awe and almost reverence.

Even after George got back, this feeling kept on, and grew till at times, it even included old man Jimpson and Bill, though he never forgot Sampson and butchering. Half way back from the mill, one day, he heard a clop of hoofs and a scrape of wheels.

"Whoa, Nig! Want a ride?"

Old man Jimpson's Nig always reminded Lawrence more of a good sized bat than anything. All ribs and hide, and not much else. Then too, he rarely moved above a snail's pace, and since J.P. was not along, and you had to stand up in the wagon bed, there didn't seem to be much call to ride.

"No, I'm in a kind of hurry. Mommy told me to bring back this-here little dab of meal soon as I could."

Old man Jimpson there his head back and laughed till the white beard spangled like Dutchman's breeches.

"Git in. We'll git you there soon as you could walk. Git up, Nig!"

He picked up the pitchfork from the side of the wagon bed, and jabbed it into the mule's hindparts. Old Nig plunged forward with a sudden leap and then slowed back to his regular pace, as Lawrence screamed out.

"Oh, Mister Jimpson, *please* don't ever do that no more. Look, it's all bloody!"

Old man Jimpson guffawed a little, but Bill explained quietly, "Tain't nothing but a mule. A mule's tough. Takes a heap to move 'em."

"Oh no, Bill. We got mules. They'll move just as quick and just as long with a spat of the lines. This un's slowed down already."

Old man Jimpson re-raised the pitchfork and rejabbed old Nig. Blood oozed out as tears trickled down Lawrence's cheeks.

"Pap," urged Bill, "don't jab him no more. Lawrence is a-taking on like you was sticking that fork in somebody."

A brown spurt curved from old man Jimpson's mouth.

"Well, let him git a move on him then and keep it up. I promised to git this boy to his ma's soon as he could walk, didn't I?" He turned sharp little eyes on Lawrence. "Say, there's going to be a prayer meeting at our house tonight, partly to thank the Lord for your pa coming home. Preacher Ray and me got it up. Tell your folks to come over – all of 'em. Be good fer 'em."

Lawrence eyed the red spots on the mule's raw hip.

"Be good for everybody, I reckon," he said.

Old man Jimpson chewed and spat.

"Pity we couldn't have church every day, stid of all the tomfoolery they do have – especially them uptown people. Such things as books and moving pictures and riding around in cars ain't a-going to help a body's soul none. My ma and pa wouldn't a-dreamt of the like, and I don't aim to – not that my salvation's a-bothering *me* any. But Sally's been a-worrying a little ever since that dance, where your pa went out of his head, and they had to send him off. Figured maybe 'twas the will of the Lord – that maybe he'd done something the Almighty didn't like. And them uptown doctors a-nosing around – thought maybe praying and church going'd git 'em out. She's a-talking of jining the church, seeing as she never did, and might hitch up with the Lord to-night. I jined sixty-odd year ago, and I ain't never fell from grace. Whoa, Nig."

They had reached the Jimpson bottom-land, now, and in one corner of the pig pen, a hen was hemmed in by the hogwire fence. Old man Jimpson nudged Bill.

"Ain't that that hen that was a-crowing, this morning?"

"Looks a heap like her to me."

"Well, you'd better kill her to make sure, and now's as easy a time to catch her as any, looks to me like. Lawrence, here, 'll help you."

They climbed over the wagon wheel and jumped to the ground.

"What you going to kill her with, Bill? You ain't got no axe nor nothing."

"My foot, I reckon, same as I generally do."

They closed in on the luckless hen and Bill grabbed her feet. He held her down and stepped on her neck, pulling the feet with both hands. The eyes kept fixed on Lawrence, as he backed off, screaming. And then the head popped off, but the eyes still stared.

"Don't forgit to come to prayer-meeting to-night," yelled old man Jimpson, as Lawrence cut through the timber toward home, blurry-eyed, "and tell your folks to come, 'specially your pa."

About prayer meeting time, Happy John happened in, in his usual state, and Mary had given up going, but Sarah said to take him along. Said maybe it would do him good, so they did. For a long time he sat huddled, half asleep, in a rocking chair at the back of the room, hardly knowing what was going on, but as time went on, he livened up considerably.

The meeting opened with a lusty rendition of "When the Roll is Called Up Yonder" and then a prayer by Preacher Ray. Preacher Ray's prayers were generally so long that a body got to thinking about so many other things, and wishing he could look up and rest his knees, that he didn't remember a thing he said, but to-night some of it stuck.

"– And, Lord, let your light keep a-shining on this-here good and Godly family, a-letting the work of the Lord be carried on right here in their house. Make us each and everyone of us as good as they air, ready to open our hearts and our houses to the work of the Lord. Let us uns that air young model our lives after this-here good old man, that has lived a life of Godliness, the way the Lord aimed all of us to do, ever since he was borned."

Lawrence squirmed from knee to knee. He could not help thinking of Sampson, and old Nig's bloody rump, and the chicken whose head was pulled off. If that was the Lord's idea of sanctity, he didn't want any in his. He kept twisting around as the prayer went on and on. His shifty eyes glanced up at the smug, self-satisfied expression of old man Jimpson, and then at some of the other bowed figures, who seemed to be getting a bit restless too. George bent over in a kind of open-mouthed stupor, but above Lige's whiskers, the wistful eyes batted steadily as old man Jimspon's spotless life continued to be exploited. At last, when Lawrence thought his knees could stand it no longer, the prayer came to an end, and Preacher Ray suggested singing, "Lord I'm Coming Home".

"I just have a feeling there's somebody in this-here congregation to-night that's a-wanting to give hisself or herself to the Lord – maybe two or three of 'em. And if any of you air a-feeling that-a-way, now is your chanct, whilst we sing this song of invitation. If any of you feel you want to lead a better life, now is the time to step up and tell the Lord about it. The Lord is a-waiting to hug you in his arms. No matter what you've done or how deep in the mire you've sunk, the Lord's a-waiting to pull you out, so to speak, and no matter how much you've done agin Him, He'll forgive you. Don't put off giving yourself to the Almighty, and go to eternal damnation, and spend all here-after in the boiling pit of Hell. Do it now! Now is the time to say to yourself and the Lord, 'From now on, I aim to lead a better life.' Come on, now – everybody that ain't saved already, that is, – as we sing this-here song:

"I've wandered far from out the fold'

Now, I'm coming home –"

Everybody felt a little wabbly from too long kneeling, but they sang out with considerable vigor, nevertheless, especially Lige and old man Jimspon, who seemed to be trying to outdo each other. Mrs. Jimpson, a little on the weepy order, got to her feet and shuffled up to Preacher Ray, hugging her arms, and swaying a little, but she steadied up considerably when he took hold of the knob on top of her head.

"The Lord bless you, sister. You'll never regret giving your soul to the Lord's keeping. And you'll never forgit this day neither, or rather this night. You'll remember it long as you live, and the Lord will. He's up yander now, a-looking down a-seeing them that come to him and them that don't –"

No telling how long he would have gone on, but he was interrupted by a sniffling from the rocking chair in the back of the room, that nobody had expected. Happy John, swishing like a horse's tail in fly time, tottered to Preacher Ray and collapsed at his feet. Mrs. Jimpson was practically forgotten. Everybody looked at Happy John, who was making a clean job of it.

"I know I hain't done the way I ort. All my life, I been a drunk, no-count son-of-a-gun, but I aim to do different from now on. I'm drunk to-night, and I know it, and the Lord does, but I hope He believes me and helps me when I say it's the last time. I'll never touch another drop, long as I live, so help me. Oh, Lord, I want to do the right thing by my woman and children, and lay off liquor and make a good living fer 'em. I know, and You know, Lord, I been the triflinest, no-count sinner you ever raised, I reckon, but from now on I'm a changed man. I aim to live a Godly life same as this-here Jimpson's done, and, Lord, I want You to help me. And, Lord, won't you put it in the hearts of everybody here to pray fer me? I aim to do right, so help me, but seems like I ain't stout enough to stick to it, without more help from You, Lord, and everybody. It's the hand of God guided me here tonight, I reckon, and I'm a-asking the prayers of everybody at this meeting to guide me away from liquor and the path of sin, hereafter. Amen."

Old man Jimpson jackknifed to his feet.

"Never do you be guilty of telling of your meanness again. The Lord knows all you do, and there's no need reminding him. And everybody here knows. If you keep out of devilment, you won't have so much to talk about. I couldn't tell no such tales if I had to be hung fer it, for I been a God-fearing man all my life, and I lived a Godly life. Come next birthday, I'll be turning eighty-four, and I've give my whole life to the teachings of the Lord. Let me tell you younguns hit's a pleasure, when you git old and about to die, to look back on a long life chuck full of Godliness, and church-going and praying and the like. Oh, younguns, jine up with the Lord, like I did, when I was a sprout of a boy, and stay hitched up with him, all your life. Let this poor drunken sinner's life be an example to you, and give your whole life to be the Lord's, like I done."

Preacher Ray must have felt mighty proud of his sanctimonious congregation, with only one out and out sinner in the crowd, and determined to do what he could to save him. He put his hand on the bald spot of Happy John's head and muttered some kind of prayer to himself, and then went on out loud.

"Lord, God, we thank Thee for leading Thy lost sheep back to the Fold, and Lord, we aim to stand by You and them too, and we're a-going to start in with this un. We're a-going to try to save the soul of a sinner that's plum sunk to damnation. Help us to keep temptation away from him, Lord. Maybe if he don't see it or smell it or git a taste of it, he'll be all right. Maybe if we one and all went to this-here feller that's got a houseboat down the river and sells liquor, and asked him not to sell no more to this unhappy soul with us to-night – maybe he wouldn't sell neither, if we went to 'em, though a body cain't trust uptowners any too fur. I believe this poor sinner aims to lead a better life from now on, or he wouldn't a-come to the Lord with his troubles, and looks to me like it's up to us to help him, some way or somehow. How many of you Christians here to-night are willing to stretch out a hand to pull a poor sinner out of the mud and slime – into the life-boat of the Lord?"

"I will! I will! We all will!"

Old man Jimpson's voice was the loudest, but it was Lige who suggested singing "Let Me in the Life Boat", in which he and old man Jimpson tried to out-shout each other with Happy John getting in a phrase or two now and then, about half a measure behind everybody else. After the song,

Preacher Ray took up his prayer where he had left off.

"And, now, Lord, I aim to go on, cause I ain't quite finished with this-here sinner of our'n. To think that right here amongst us, there's a sinner of the worst kind, that maybe a little praying on our part 'd turn to a sanctified man. He's so drunk to-night, Lord, 'twas all he could do to set on a chair, and now he just sets here, a-lolling on the floor, a-grunting like a pig. Lord, You know that ain't no way for something created in your image to act. If he's going to act like a pig, let him be a pig! But, if he's the shape of You, Lord – let him act according. Surely, Lord, there's something You can do fer him, now that You've created him, and if there is, won't You do all in Your power to do it? Lord, Lord, You ain't no idy the joy and pleasure and all it'd bring to his poor paralyzed wife and children. But when they're that fur gone, I reckon even You cain't do a heap – leastways, You generally don't. But I wisht you'd make an exception in his case, for he's called for Your help, Lord, and seeing as we're all trying to lead Godly lives, here in this Godly man's house, looks to me like now's the time to turn him to the path of God, eternally. Amen. Now, you reckon there's anybody else we ort to pray fer?"

"Maybe you ort to pray for Andrew Moore," suggested Sarah. "He's a mighty good man, and right smart, but he ain't hitched up with the Lord, so I reckon he cain't be saved."

Lige wagged his whiskers with a chuckle.

"Dogged if I b'lieve Andrew'd turn his hand over for the difference betwixt Heaven and tother place, long as he had his books. I've seed him a-setting around that red hot heating stove of his'n, his shoe soles might near burnt up, and him so wrapped up in a book, he never knowed it."

Sarah motioned to Preacher Ray, and he nodded and bowed his head.

"And now let us pray for one of our members that's been away off, and just got back. That's one of the reasons we called this meeting, but we thought we'd save it for last. Lord, we thank Thee for bringing back our children, the outsiders ship off to the crazy house. We knowed You'd look after Your own, and bring back the marked same as the teched but we didn't know how soon You'd do it. Keep on a-watching over 'em, Lord. Keep 'em in the hills where they was borned and where You aimed for 'em to stay – them and all the rest of the hill folks. And keep outsiders out, especially them rub-doctors. Maybe You could put it in their heads to go some'ers else – clean away – where we'd never see or hear of 'em again. Use Your own judgment as to how to git 'em out, Lord – we've tried everything, might near – but git 'em out, and keep 'em out eternally. Them and all the rest of the outsiders, and leave these hills for hill folks. Amen. And, now, before we go, I wonder if we couldn't sing that old song, "The Prints of the Nails in His Hand"? Somehow, seems like, I always feel uncommon close to the Lord, when I sing that song, and to-night, with all the Lord's done fer us, I believe I feel the clostest I ever have."

And even Happy John joined in here and there as they sang:

> "I shall know Him, I shall know Him,
> As redeemed by His side, I shall stand;
> I shall know Him, I shall know Him,
> By the *prints of the nails in His hand.*"

George squirmed a little and hitched his chair forward.

"Preacher Ray, I'd like to ask you something awful well, if you hain't no objections, and got time to answer it. Like that song we was just a-singing – does that mean the Lord's got them nail prints in His hands *yit* – after all this time?"

"Why, yes, I reckon it does. That's what it says, anyhow. Why?"

"Oh – I was just a-wondering. Would you say the body resurrects same as the Lord's done – or just the soul?"

"Why, yes, I reckon whatever the Lord done, He aimed for us to do the same. Sounds *reasonable* to me for the body to resurrect along with the soul – sort of buggy-ride it up. Anyhow, I always figured the soul was a kind of egg-shaped, flimsy something or other that wouldn't look right by itself – something like going a round all eternity without no clothes on – and you *know* the Lord wouldn't like that. I reckon there's no way of being out and out *certain* – but I claim and always did claim the body resurrects same as the soul, just like the Lord's done. I got my Sunday Scripture reading here, some'ers, and near as I recollect, *it* says something about that. Oh, here it is. 'For if we have been planted together in the likeness of His death, we shall be also in the likeness of His resurrection.' There!"

George kept getting more and more nervous.

"Yes, but Preacher Ray, what about them that *hain't* been *planted*? Sometimes, I reckon it's so's a body *cain't* be laid to rest. Does that mean they won't' resurrect?"

"Well, it sounds mighty like it to me. Anyhow, looks to me like anybody that is anybody'd *be* put away proper – and if they hain't, stands to reason they've been up to some devilment, and wouldn't resurrect nohow."

"Yes, but, Preacher Ray, s'posing they couldn't *help* theirselves?"

Sarah decided it was time to interrupt.

"George, I don't' want you to talk like that no more. Remember, you've been down there three months with crazy people, and folks'll think you're a mite queer yourself. Anyhow, it's time we was a-gitting home and to bed letting Jimpsons do the same."

"Yes," put in Preacher Ray, "only let's dismiss the meeting by singing 'At the Cross, at the Cross, where I first seed the light, and the burden of my soul washed away.'"

Lustily they all sang, and then got their things to go. J.P., who had grinned through the whole thing, kept on grinning. Bill nudged Lawrence.

"Ma looks like *something* was washed away – plum peaked, like she hadn't got her money's worth. I reckon she was aiming to be the whole show to-night, but after Happy John a-saying *he* wanted to join, nobody paid much attention to her. I heard her a-telling somebody that maybe it was one of the Lord's miracles, Happy John's sanctification, and if it was, she was glad He done it in her house, though I reckon she'd just as leave He'd a-picked some other ngiht to a-done it. How long you reckon he'll stick to it?"

"I ain't no idy, Bill."

"Shucks! I don't 'low he'll remember a thing about it, come to-morrow morning."

But Lawrence was thinking of George. He had never seen him so wadded-up looking – like wrung out clothes, before they're hung up. And he seemed to get worse and worse, as Happy John revived just enough to chant:

"She ran and she wrang her lily white hands,
Just like a lady in great despair;
Saying, 'I'm ruined, I'm ruined, I'm undone forever,
Alas, alas, what shall I do?"

Chapter 21 :George Tries to Get Released from Bargain

Winter shrunk wagon wheels rattled and shrieked over hills of mud and thaw as if they too were contesting a bad bargain. Old man Rainwater, blissfully post-deaf, hunched over a wheezing pipe, and George, his arms doubled and wedged between knees and chin, kept wondering what he would say when he walked into the rambling, red building. What could a body say? Suppose he *was* out of his head when he signed that paper, what else could he have done? In a way, if they gave up claim to his body, it looked as if they had a right to slit Mary open and fix her back like she was, and the Lord knew he didn't want that. But if the law was on his side, there must be some way of getting out of it, somehow or other – something he could do or say. The black bearded doctor was in conference when he first got there, so he kept wandering around, trying to figure things out.

Alone in the skeleton room, he stalked from animals to bird and bones, as if expecting some of them to supply him with words for the black-bearded doctor. The skeleton with the missing arm seemed to stare right back, eye for eye, in a kind of "Where have I seen you before?" look. *Was* it Lem Webbstringer or somebody else? His eyes circled the long room. Where would they put him, when the time came? They would have to make room, somehow, but would they take down one they already had, or just crowd him in somewhere amongst the others. Suppose too, when they'd hacked the meat off, and looked at his insides, his bones wouldn't suit – and his salvation be gone for nothing –. That is, of course, if the insane asylum idea didn't work. He must figure out what he was going to say.

He *had* been to the insane asylum. That was easily proved, if it would make any difference in things, and like as not, worried and nervous like he was, he *was* a mite out of his head when he signed the bargain. It looked as if any lawyer that *was* a lawyer would have a clear case, that is, if they went to law and a body's signature didn't count when he was out of his head. Still law and lawyers were out of the question. They cost two hundred dollars, even when you win. If he had fifty dollars, or any way of getting it, he wouldn't need a lawyer. It was just a question of whether these rub-doctors would give in or not, when they found out how things were – that is, if the law was on his side. The only thing was, what could he say? Paying back the fifty dollars was out of the question, and in a way, it didn't seem honest-like to beg off, so to speak, when they'd kept their part of the bargain. Somebody was coming. It was the man with the black beard. His mouth-line widened as he came up, but it seemed to George a kind of butcher's smile.

"Well, Moore, what's on your mind to-day?"

George kept swallowing as he looked up and rammed his fists deeper. Now was his chance, if he had a chance.

"Why, Doc, I ain't right sure I got a mind. Anyways, some of 'em seemed to think I hadn't. I reckon you heard about me a-going to the insane asylum, here a while back, didn't you?"

The black beard pecked the air a little.

"Yes, now that you mention it, we *did* hear something about it, though not until a short time ago. How did you like it down there?"

George, glad to get way from the ticklish question till he'd made up his mind what to say, anyhow, warmed to praise of the hospital like a cock calling hens to corn.

"First rate. Seemed like I felt the best I had for I don't know how long, that is, after the first week or two or such a matter. And I got new teeth, and a suit of clothes, and tie and I don't' know what all. I gained twenty odd pounds whilst I was down there, too. Weigh over two hundred and twenty, now. It's an awful nice place, 'pears to me like. You ever been down there, Doc?"

The black beard zigzagged a little.

"Well, yes and no. I've been through there, but you can't tell much about things just driving by a place, that way. You still feeling better?"

George whiffed out a long sigh. Now was the time to switch back to the question, and he had no idea in the world how to go about it. He'd just have to trust to the Lord.

"Well, Doc, I am and I ain't. 'Pears to me like I *could* be, if I had nothing to worry about. Seemed like I was might near cured down yander, but the minute I got back, they begun telling me this that and tother, – about you a-coming down in the hills a-asking about me, and dickering about property down there – till I'm might near as nervous as ever. I keep thinking about that body business, and just seems like, a-worrying the way I do, I'm a-going to be right back in the same wagon I was before long. If I had the money, Doc, I'd buy myself out of the bargain, but I hain't, so what you going to do?"

Below needles of eyes, the beard jiggled as if to warm up for words.

"Well, you'll just about have to take the consequences. Not that I can see what difference it'll make, after you're dead, as far as that goes. For that matter, I'd be almost willing to wager, unless some sudden sickness gets you, such as pneumonia or some general epidemic, you'll live to a surprising old age, maybe over a hundred. And in all that time, surely you can buy your body back ten times over, if you make your mind up to it."

Hope died in George's eyes, and his head tetered as if with palsy.

"No, Doc. There ain't no possible way, fer me, now – in the hills. I wouldn't want to undo Mary's operation, – but, I wisht they'd a-been some way without signing that paper."

"Well, your body *may* be some great help to science, but remember, it was not our idea in the first place."

"I know it, Doc. I know you ain't in no way to blame for what I done, but seemed like it was the only way, and I reckon I'd do it again, fer as that goes, with Mary about to die, and no way else to save her. But, Doc, here's the idy. Seems like there ain't no chance of me a-ever gitting well, with that a-hanging over me, so to speak. I was just a-wondering, that is, somebody was saying, that if a body made some kind of a odd bargain, and then got sent to the insane asylum, nine chances to ten, he could win out by law. Said he could claim he wasn't in his right mind when he made the agreement, and tother feller couldn't hold him."

Above the beard, black slits blinked.

"You may be right. Probably are, if you take it to law. I don't know.
I do know you signed a written contract, and I'm just bull-headed enough
to say you'll have to *take* it to law, as far as I'm concerned to get free of
it. Remember, you received fifty dollars in treatment for your wife, clinic
prices. We probably saved her life. Any other doctor would have charged
two or three times as much – probably more, and you couldn't have paid it.
But, it was through your urging and yours alone, that we entered into this
unusual contract. Naturally, we were somewhat skeptical of the outcome.
But now, with the thing done and value received, it seems to me it should
be a matter of honor with you to see that we get value received as well,
or our money back. Doesn't it look that way to you?"

George slumped a little as he stared.

"Well, Doc, in a way, I reckon it does. It ain't that I want to bet you
or anybody else out of what's his'n, or ever did. I just thought if there *was*
such a law, to look out, so to speak, for crazy people, I –"

The doctor squinted one eye a little.

"What did they say about your mental condition down at the hospital?"

"What?"

"Did they say you were actually insane when you arrived there for
treatment?"

"Oh, no. Said there wasn't a great sight of anything wrong with me,
fur as they could see, only nerves and bad teeth. Said I really didn't have
no business there, but seeing as I was already down there, and so hard up,
and nervous and all, I might as well stay, till warm weather."

"Hmmm. I'm not at all sure you could win out even by law. But – there
is a way, that wouldn't hurt you at all. Would help you out financially
more than you realize, if you're willing to do it."

"Is there, Doc? How?"

"Why don't you sell us *your* property – or at least part of it? We'll allow you three times whatever it's assessed at. We know a good thing when we see it, and we want to take advantage of that government offer. And, anyhow, surely you people don't want the old mill to collapse in the river, and that's just what it's going to do if it isn't repaired before long. Webbstringers have finally agreed to let us take things over, *provided* somebody else from down there agrees to sell first. That would be an easy way out for *you,* and we're offering you a good price – more than you'll ever get again."

The light in George's face died out.

"I know it, Doc, and the Lord knows I'd like to, – but I *cain't.* Ma'd never forgive me, and I don't reckon anybody else would. You ain't no idy how *agin* outsiders, hill folks air. 'Twould be might near like selling the Lord for thirty pieces of silver all over again – and I reckon I'd be better off to go through with my bargain – ten times over than that."

"Well, if you change your mind, let me know. My offer still holds until this land question is settled. From the way you talked, I thought you wanted to buy yourself out."

"Well, Doc, I want to, God knows, but I don't reckon I ever can."

As he slumped past the circus room, he paused for a last look at the nine fingered skeleton. If it was who he thought it was, they had been together many an evening, a few years before. Perhaps they would be together again.

He clumped down the steps and stared off toward the hills. It was all over, all hopes. It was only a question of time till he would be mincemeat, and one of the skeletons. If he could only have taken that job down at the insane asylum! Two or three months at the most, would have set him free from the yoke that spanned both life and death, and maybe nobody would have ever known. But a promise is a promise, and besides, six months without seeing any of them, when he'd never been away before in his life, seemed an eternity, when he was free to go home. It might be the job was not filled yet, but nine chances to ten it was, or would be by the time he could get back, and anyway, it didn't seem right – going off and leaving them again for two or three months, even though he wasn't much help when he was there. besides, what would they think, and what could he say? If he sent the money home, there was no use to go, and if he didn't, they would think he was completely piggish. Mary probably did already.

No, he would just have to let things go, as the contract read, for so far as raising money any other way went, it was utterly out of the question. There might have been a time when he could have wheedled it out of his mother, but now, with the lawyers sucking up even her egg money, it was as easy to think of raising ten thousand dollars as fifty. Even if she'd had anything, her prejudice against the rub-doctors would have closed hand and pocketbook against paying them anything now. There was no way out of it. Mince-meat he must be – with maybe all chance of salvation gone too. And the more he thought of it, the more the old dread came back. It was like being buried under a load of hay, with no air to speak of, and no way of getting out.

Old man Rainwater had promised him a ride home, if he waited until he was through trading and all, but he couldn't wait. He couldn't just stand around and think about things all afternoon. Maybe If he could talk to somebody like Andrew Moore, he would feel better. Maybe he could catch old man Rainwater or somebody else afterwards on the corner.

Andrew was reading something out loud, and his voice bellowed above George's scraping and pounding.

> "Why, if the Soul can fling the Dust aside,
> And Naked on the Air of Heaven ride,
> Were't not a Shame – were't not a Shame for him
> In this clay carcass crippled to abide?"

"What?"

"My God! Do I have to go over that whole thing again?"

"No. I heard it all but the last line."

The voice raised three pitches.

"In this clay carcass crippled to abide?"

George swallowed twice, and pounded again, louder.

"Come in!"

He pushed open the door.

"Oh, George, come in! Come in! Anything the matter? You look like you'd just seen a ghost."

The little woman with the pile of black hair smiled and nodded as George gulped.

"Well, in a way, Andrew, I reckon maybe I have."

"What?"

"Oh, Andrew, don't mind me. I'm so nervous and worried, I ain't got good sense."

"Why, George, I thought you got cured down at the hospital, this winter."

"Well, Andrew, I did and I didn't. I got over it, but looks like it's a-coming back."

"Hmmm."

"I was just up town a-talking to some of them doctors, and I thought maybe I'd feel a mite better if I talked to you a while, before I went back, but I ain't right sure that I will. What was that you was a-reading Nance about crippled carcasses?"

"Oh, that's just something from Omar Khayyam. Why?"

George fingered his hat and looked down at his feet.

"Does that mean – the soul cain't resurrect, 'thout the body goes along? That they have to stick together?"

"Not that I know of. As far as I see, there's no hint of resurrection or life after death at all, from this."

"Well, Andrew, what do you think?"

"About what?"

"Resurrection. The Lord's body riz up with his soul – all in one piece. It says so in the Bible. But what about the rest of us? Does the body resurrect too – or just the soul?"

"Oh, George, I'm no authority on such things. Ask your preacher or somebody that knows. Anyhow, what does it matter?"

"Oh, Lord, Andrew, you ain't no idy. Sometimes, I'm might near out of my mind, just a-thinking about things. If the body has to buggy-ride the soul, and the meat's hacked up and the bones kept off to theirselves – how in the name of the Lord air they all a-going to git together to resurrect?"

Andrew's eyes seemed to back back in his head.

"George, maybe you are going a little out of your head again. Maybe it would be better to go back to the hospital a while longer."

"Well, Andrew, I reckon 'twouldn't do no good, now. Nothing would."

"Oh, George, you're not that bad off."

"'Tain't me, Andrew. You ain't no idy. Say, if you'd made some kind of a bargain – you wouldn't break it to save your soul, would you?"

"Well – I never did, that I know of."

"That's what Pa said. Well, I reckon I better be a-going, the way it's a-clouding up."

"Why, you just come."

"I know it, but I got to git home before the rain – that is, before I git any wetter'n what I have to. I just felt like I wanted to talk to you, though I cain't say I feel any better fer it."

The door slammed behind him.

A light mist had set in, which turned to a steady drizzle by the time he reached the highway. Rheumatism again, or maybe pneumonia, like the rub-doctor had said. But he couldn't just wait under a tree. Old man Rainwater had probably gone on by now, and the rain might last all night. Best thing to do was get home and change his clothes as soon as he could. Maybe if he started out, somebody would overtake him and give him a ride, but nobody did. Up and down he tramped, and on each side of the zigzag road, hills rounded up like great sodded graves. A line of lightening ripped across the sky. Oh, Lord, suppose he got hit on the way home? Death, and the rub-doctors, and eternal damnation all in one blow! Maybe he ought to try to see Preacher Ray again. He plodded on, soaked to the skin, in squashing, mud-caked shoes, worrying as he walked. Down there at the hospital he had felt so safe, so secure. And now, things seemed more hopeless than ever, and there was nobody to turn to.

It looked as if spring rains had set in to stay. Mary had set her heart on going to see her folks Sunday. Happy John had been on about a two-weeks' steady binge too, in spite of his sanctification, and with her ma paralyzed like she was, Mary felt she had to go. But, nine chances to ten, it would be pouring rain, and if it was, he just couldn't take her. He must keep shy of rains from now on, no matter what. More than likely Mary would think it was pure contrariness – seemed as if about everybody did, that and laziness, but they'd just have to think. If the Lord let him live through this – he would take no chances again. Anyhow, he couldn't drive the team in the rain, six or eight miles each way, no matter what anybody said or thought. She'd have to go by herself, or somebody else would have to take her. If it had been just ordinary dying, it would have been different. Everybody has to die, sooner or later, but nobody else had his predicament hanging over him.

It was bound to be raining Sunday. It always rained, if there was a drop of wet anywhere. And Lige and Mary would have no patience with him, but his mother would hold out for him. Anyway, he must not go in the rain. No use running your head in the bull's horns. The only thing left to do was wait, and waiting is hard – at least, what he was waiting for.

Chapter 22 : Old Man Jimpson's Accident

Old man Jimspon was on his death-bed, more than likely, though nobody had dreamed it at first. Not till Elvira had heard that knocking, long about four or five in the morning, and when she'd opened the door, nobody was there – nothing but the old black dress Grandma Jimpson had been laid away in. And it had fluttered and faded to nothing in next to no time, so they knew it was some kind of a warning.

Sarah had looked after him most of the time. Came over the very day the hog stepped on his foot, a day or two after that prayer meeting, and kept on coming – even after it got to hurting so bad they'd called in old Doc Ceburn. She'd made onion poultices, and bread and milk, and flax seed, and mustard – one after another, but didn't seem to help none, so *she'd* felt like maybe his time had come, even before Elvira had seen that sign.

Some said he ought to have gone to an uptown doctor right at first, bruised like he was – him barefooted, and the hog's hoof cutting clear to the bone – but he wouldn't. Said he reckoned Sarah and Old Doc Ceburn could do as much as anybody, and the sight of uptowners made him want to vomit. Ben Bragg told him he'd go to that rub-doctor that had cut on Mary. That blood poison might set in, and it might need cutting, and Doc Ceburn didn't have tools to cut with. But old man Jimpson wouldn't hear of it – not for considerable time, that is – and Sarah backed him up. Said if anybody else went to the rub-doctors, the way they were acting already – so out and out anxious to mind everybody's business but their own – the hill people might as well move out.

But when his foot swelled and turned black and got to hurting so much, old man Jimpson gave up and let Ben take him to town, though it didn't do any good. The rub-doctors said he'd have to have his foot taken off to live, and he wouldn't do it. Said he'd just as soon be dead as have one foot in the grave.

But the next day, with it swelled bigger than ever and hurting as bad again, he felt different. Ben took him back to town again, but the rub-doctors said it would have to come off at the knee now – and old man Jimpson wouldn't have it. Said he'd die ten times over first. But that night, he got to hollering every breath, so the rub-doctors came out and took it off – high up as they could cut. Most everybody thought he'd get along all right after that, but he didn't. Sort of went out of his head and kept hollering and taking on that there was dirt between his toes – not the ones he had left, but the ones Bill and J.P. had buried. And, half frozen as the ground was, and hard to get at, and him out of his head anyway, they just wouldn't dig it up again – that is, not until after Elvira had seen that sign and Lawrence had sort of talked them into it.

George had got to going over there, almost as much as Sarah. Not that he ever did anything to help out, or even said much, most of the time. Just sort of sat there and listened to old man Jimpson take on, after he got too bad, that is. Not that it was any pleasure to a body to hear him, but seemed as if there was a kind of great big magnet that pulled him over there – maybe because they were both in the same wagon; both hitched up with the rub-doctors, though not in the same way, of course.

And as he sat there and worried, he could not help thinking how little a body knows – anybody but the Lord, that is – about how long this one and that one was for this world or how soon they'd go to the next. Not a week ago, hardly, or about that, old man Jimpson's voice had been the loudest at prayer meeting and he had been the liveliest of anybody there – even the preacher. And now, one leg was already laid away, and the rest of him liable to go anytime. It just went to show no matter how hearty or stout-acting a body was or wasn't, his time might come any minute.

Before old man Jimpson had let that dirt notion worry him out of his head, he and Sarah had talked considerably about the rub-doctors, and J.P. always listened and grinned. They both blamed the whole thing on them – nobody else. Didn't hardly even give the pig credit for starting it.

"I'd a-been a heap better off if I'd a-stayed away from uptowners for good and all, like I aimed to in the first place," old man Jimpson kept saying, "especially them rub-doctors. But nothin'd do Ben. Said they had away yander the best cutting tools of anybody around, and seemed like I couldn't stand it no longer, hardly, the way things was – and Doc Ceburn didn't have the stuff to cut with. He said so hisself."

Sarah wagged her head.

"Well, it did look like it was for the best at the time, but I reckon it wasn't. There was other doctors a heap closter, and not hitched up with the devil either. Mark my words, them rub-doctors'll keep on now till they buy out half of Hell's Holler. Seems like they're bound and determined to git the mill and dam if they don't git nothing else, so's they can go on with that reservoir deal, I reckon – though what they want it for is more than I could ever make out. They hain't got a bit more use for it than I'd have for one of their rubbing tables. Not as much, for I could use that to iron on."

Old man Jimpson seemed deeply repentant of having gone to them at all.

"I jest wisht I'd a-laid here and died, now. I'd a-been better off, I reckon, dead and buried than stumping around on one leg amongst a hive of rub-doctors. Well, if they do buy the old mill and dam, and try to put up a reservoir down here, I just hope somebody blows 'em to smithereens – all of 'em. It'd serve 'em right."

And he kept saying it over and over, time and again, and J.P. listened and grinned, – a black, broken toothed grin.

But after that, old man Jimpson got to taking on so much about his toes, he hardly ever thought of anything else. Once in a while he'd bring up the rub-doctor and mill and dam question, but most of the time he worried about the dirt between his toes, half in the notion the rub-doctors had put it there somehow, or got it in trying to dig up his leg.

It was Lawrence that finally got them to do it. He'd come over first thing after dinner, the day Elvira'd seen that burying dress, when Sarah'd sent word how bad the old man was – him not long for this world, anyhow.

Old man Jimpson had been taking on worse than common all morning, and begging the boys to dig up his leg and get that dirt out from between his toes – till Bill said he would, and he and J.P. had gone out and stayed long enough to dig up two legs, seemed like. But they hadn't dug any. Just gone out and waited about as long as they'd thought it would take, and come back, seeing as it was all tomfoolery anyhow. But the old man did not stop moaning and taking on when they came into the room, though he looked up as they tiptoed to the bed.

They told him they *had* dug it up and got the dirt out, but old man Jimpson wouldn't have it that way. Said it was still there. That he could feel it plain as ever – right between the big toe and the next. And his old eyes were so watery, and he kept begging them to dig up that leg and get the dirt out so he could rest, till Lawrence got to begging and taking on too. Said if they'd get him a spade or something, he'd dig considerable himself, as much as he could, – that he couldn't bear to hear old man Jimpson hollering and taking on like he was.

And Bill went and J.P. too, when Lawrence did, and they *did* dig up that buried leg, and sure enough wedged in between the big and second toe, like old man Jimpson said, was a piece of dirt, or something or other, about the size of a flattened pea. Bill was still muttering about it when they came back.

"There's no sense to it, any way you look at it. He *couldn't* a-knowed it was there, cause dead things hain't got no feeling, but he must a-knowed or felt something, or *thought* he did, or he wouldn't a-took on so."

The old man was as quiet as a gorged puppy. Bill tiptoed to the bed.

"How is it now, Pap?"

Quietly the watery eyes opened.

"First rate, Son. 'Tain't there no more. Now I can git some sleep and rest, and the Lord knows I need it. Thank you, boys, – Bill and J.P. and Lawrence too. Good boys, all of you. I 'lowed Bill and J.P. had the stuff in 'em, being my boys like they air, and now I know it. You two just keep in the ways of the Lord, and you'll make as good a man as your old pap yet, every whit, both of you. And, Lawrence, you keep in the right way of living, and *you'll* be a good man, more'n likely. You just talk to the Lord every night, and tell him to keep you in the path of righteousness and take care of you, like he done your pa while he was down yander, and He will, I reckon. The Lord takes care of everybody, sinners and all, especially them that's Godly and God-fearing. I knowed he'd look after me soon as he got around to it, though I wisht He hadn't seen fit to let them rub-doctors whack off my leg. I never 'lowed to have nothing to do with 'em. Aimed to keep 'em out of these hills for all time. But Ben Bragg kept at me, and it got to hurting so bad – I couldn't stand it. I reckon 'twas the Lord's will, somehow or other – though I wisht he'd keep 'em out hereafter. Seems like I feel so thankful with that thing out betwixt my toes, I just wisht we could all say a prayer to praise his name, and maybe sing 'When the Roll Is Called up Yander', but I'm so plum tuckered out, I want to go to sleep, now."

He closed his eyes and breathed heavily with a rattle in his throat, and from what Elvira had seen that morning, they knew he was going. George kept looking at him – and seemed to be seeing himself, almost any time now. In some ways they were as like as two peas – him and old man Jimpson. They had both gone to the rub-doctors of their own accord – and this was what happened or was going to happen. In a way, the rub-doctors had had next to nothing to do with it – except to be waiting when their victims came. But, for that matter, what more does a spider do?

Chapter 23 : Mary Wants to See Her Folks

Sunday the sun peak-a-booed with the clouds all morning, but by noon the clouds won out and a light drizzle set in. All during dishwashing, Mary's eyes quarter-wheeled from window to George, who had collapsed on the bed, his head wrapped in both arms, like an egg baked in bacon. When wet dishtowels were stretched to dry, she turned to the bulk on the bed.

"George, I feel like I *have* to go to Pa and Ma's to-day, Ma so poorly all the time, and Pa acting the way he does. I hain't been there since I had my operation, and you a-feeling so well now, I want you to take me, rain or no rain."

He stared at the dripping eaves, and rocked his big body.

"Well, Mary, the Lord knows I don't' want to knock you out of no pleasure, but rainy as it is, and the way I'm a-feeling here lately, I'd just as leave somebody'd beat me into a jell as ask me to go anywhere in the wet. If you had any idy how things air –"

For the second time in ten years, Mary went all to pieces, and sobbed like one of the children.

"I *knowed* I wouldn't git to go. I never git to go no place. Your folks can come every week. They're both well and able, and it's just a little piece over here. But my poor ma, a-laying there day after day, flat on her back, not able to move hardly, a-worrying herself to death about Pa, and me not able to go a-near! All I ever do is work like a dog and never go nowheres!"

George blinked his eyes five or six times.

"Why, Mary, don't take on like that. I cain't stand it. Take Ma's team, or airy one of 'em, and go yourself. You know you're plum welcome to 'em, and Ma and Pa 'll stay here and look after the younguns and me. They said they would – leastways, Ma did."

"I cain't do it. You know I cain't go off and leave little Mark for two or three days and him not weaned yet. I been a-aiming to wean him for I don't know how long, but poorly as he is, and chilly as it stays, I'm afeard to, till it gits a little warmer. And I 'lowed to take Vida too. Ma ain't seen 'em since she had her stroke, and she might go any time. Besides, little as they air, they ort to be with their ma, long as there's no out and out reason for 'em being some'ers else. You never take me nowhere, nor fix no way for me to go!"

His mouth opened twice before words came.

"Well, Mary, I know I ain't been the right kind of a man to you, but I do all I can, that is, what I can stand to do, and if you had any idy how things air, you'd –"

"You've said that a thousand times already. I'm plum wore out a-hearing it! I'm a-going if I have to walk every step of the way and carry the children. I never seed a man do so little for his family!"

Lige blew out a long line of smoke.

"George, why the devil don't you take her? No older'n what you air, and little as it's a-drizzling, it ain't a-going to hurt you none."

He unbuttoned the middle shirt button and scratched under his heavy underwear.

"Now, Pa, you don't know. That doctor said the main thing I had to look out fer, was gitting caught in a downpour and pneumony setting in – that and catching diseases and accidents and the like. And if I do die, you ain't no idy – none of you ain't."

Sarah could keep still no longer. Her mouth tightened and the rocking chair creaks came to a sudden stop.

"Now, Lige, the way George feels, I don't want him to go. I don't want him worried to death, and I don't want to hear no more about it."

Mary raised wet eyes.

"But what about poor old Ma? I writ I was coming, and her flat on her back, she don't have a heap to look forward to. A little rain won't hurt a body no older'n George is."

"Yes, but, Mary, you see how it's a-worrying him. I know how you feel and your Ma does, but I've got to think of George. *You go.* Take the team and wagon, or airy thing you want – but don't ask him."

"I cain't hold two little younguns, and drive a team!"

Lige lowered his pipe and sputtered.

"I'm danged! What do you want to act so much like a durn fool fer, Sary? You never did have good sense about George. A little wet won't hurt him, I tell you. He don't lift a hand other times, hardly. Surely he can take his woman to see her pa and ma onct or twict a year on Sunday. I never seed or heerd of anything so plum foolish."

"Now, Lige, I'm a-doing this. If you're so plum set on somebody taking Mary to see her folks, take her yourself. George ain't a-going to go."

"Durned if I wouldn't if somebody'd hitch up for me."

Sarah's gourd of a face stretched up.

"I'll hitch up fer you, if that's all you want."

But Mary shook her head. "No, Ma Moore. Hit ain't right for Pa Moore to be out, wet as it is, and him feeling so poorly all winter. I'd ruther not go."

But Sarah turned determinedly to Lige.

"If George felt like going, it'd be different. But he don't. He's been through a turrible winter, remember. And 'tain't right for Mary to always stay home and never see her own folks, either, them only six or eight mile away, or such a matter. She cain't drive herself, and hold a umberel over two little younguns. You take her, Lige, like you said."

"Good Lord Almighty, Sary! 'Twouldn't hurt George a particle, no older'n he is, and stout as he claims to be feeling now. I'll go, I reckon, like I said, if he won't, for I aim for Mary to see her folks, but I'm liable to catch my death!"

"Set by the fire and steam out when you git there, and I reckon you'll be all right. You've been wet before and lived through it."

"Yes, but, Sary, a body only dies onct."

"I know it, Lige, but I expect your dying is a long way off yet, if you take care of yourself, anyways near."

"Yes, but going out in a downpour, and driving six or eight mile through mud and rain, ain't a-taking care of yourself, at my age."

"Well, there's things you can do, after you git there, like I said."

Mary bundled up the two youngest children and herself, and Lige slid into a wornout sheepskin, while Sarah hitched up. George did not budge from the bed. In steady drizzle they climbed in, and Lige clucked to the team, as Mary and the children huddled under Sarah's saw-toothed umbrella. Every so often, Mary pushed the thing up to try to cover them all, but it always settled back so that one spoke dripped down Lige's back. If he shifted around, it was only from one stave to another, and the continual trickle and gouge chilled him. Mary did her best, but her efforts only directed the downpour to different spouts of attack.

When they reached Happy John's, Lige's shirt and underwear had soaked up so much drizzle, it took till bed-time to steam out. Happy John did most of the talking, as long as he was able to talk. He started out with his usual apologies.

"Now, Mary, I'm drunk and I know I am, and you ain't no idy how I hate it. I wouldn't a-had it a-happened to-day for nothing in the world, but I was so choked up with cold, looked like I was going to git plum down, so I got me a mite of whusky, down the river a ways, and started in a-taking it, and all of a sudden the cold was gone, seemed like, but I was hog-drunk and been that way ever since. You ain't no idy how I hate it, you being here for the first time in the Lord knows how long."

From the bedroom door came the wavering voice of Mary's mother.

"If some of the children didn't work, and help keep us in victuals, I don't know what'd become of us. Happy John's got so he spends every nickel he gits a-hold of, a tinkering or selling junk and such, for hard liquor." Happy John raised hurt eyes.

"Now, Mathildy, you know I got some sody and salt, tother day."

"Yes, with my egg money, what you didn't swaller."

Happy John looked as if it were all he could do to keep from crying.

"That's jest the way with a woman. No matter what you do for 'em, they want you to do more. I never knowed it to fail. I recollect a feller a-telling something when I was a boy, beat anything ever I heerd. Some'ers in Missouri, as I remember, there was two young women lived four or five mile apart, or such a matter, acrost a woods, and every two or three days, one of 'em 'd go over and stay all night with tother'n. Whoever was going would yell all the way through the woods, so's tother'n hear'd her and come to meet her. Well, one day, one of the two started out a yelling every wagon length or such a matter, and pretty soon, something or somebody answered, and she kept on a yelling, never thinking but what 'twas this other woman, and the thing kept answering, till she got right up on it, might near, and 'twas a panther. Well, she was that scared, she didn't know what she was a-doing. She turned and run like a shying horse, and off went her bonnet, but she let it go. She seed out of the corner of her eye that the thing stopped and nosed it a little, and it come into her head, if she kept on a-dropping things and it kept nosing 'em, maybe she could git back to where somebody lived before the thing et her. Well, she kept on a-dropping petticoat after petticoat – they wore nine or ten them days – and one thing and another, till she came to a cabin, and by that time she was might near stripped – with just a little some thing or other to hide her nakedness. They claimed she jumped plum over the fence without stopping to open the gate, and some man come out and shot the thing. Anyhow, they said this woman bust out a bawling and went all to pieces, mostly, I reckon, cause some man had seed her half naked. And I couldn't help thinking when I first heard it, if that ain't a durn woman fer you!"

Liged hootched a little closer to the heater, and snickered a little. Usually when he was away from home, he managed to do a good part of the talking himself, to make up for other times, but to-night he felt like an empty molasses jug.

"Where'd you ever git all them tales you're always a-telling, Happy

John?"

Happy John pushed back well pleased.

"To tell the truth, Lige, I don't know as I know myself. I didn't make 'em up – leastways, not in the first place, anyhow, though I may have added a little as I keep a-telling 'em. Seems like when I was a boy, somebody was always telling some tale or other, and seems like I recollect 'em all."

He settled back as his face reddened.

"Did I ever tell you about the man that was skinned alive? That was a curious thing. I want to tell it to George or his Ma sometime, or I want you to. I never been able to figure out why they wanted to skin him, or what they done with the hide after he was skun. But I thought, maybe, doc-torish as George and his ma both air, they could ask some of the doctors or somebody, and find out. I know a cow's or horse's hide is worth con-siderable, or even a pig's, but I never heard of human hides being worth anything to speak of, did you?"

Lige wheezed a little and wagged his whiskers.

"No, I cain't say as I did."

Happy John reared back on the hind legs of his chair, and came down with a bang, but he went on.

"Well, about fifty or sixty year ago, or such a matter, there was a party of prospectors went West from Illinois, bound for Californy – twenty wag-ons, near as I recollect. They druv cows, stead of horses or mules or oxen and the like, so's they'd have 'em to milk when they got there. There was one young feller in the party – I forgit his name – claimed the Injuns had done something or other to a relation of his'n – killed or tortured 'em, or something or other, and he swore he's shoot the first one he seed. Well, no-body paid much attention to him, just thought he was a-talking, I reckon, but finally in Nebrasky, or some'ers out West, they come acrost an old Injun woman, a-setting by the road, a-begging. Well, nobody could do a thing with this feller. Nothin'd do him but he had to shoot her, and he did, though they all begged him not to. Well, they went on, and long about the next day a party of Injuns overtook 'em, about three or four times as many again as they was, and they said unless they give up whoever shot that old woman, they'd kill the whole pack of 'em. Well, they give him up – had to, I reckon – and seemed like them Injuns just lit in with their knives and tomyhawks and one thing and another, and sliced his whole skin off, him a-yelling every breath, long as he lived. They made the white folks drive on, but they said they aimed to skin him alive, and I reckon they did, cause somebody's uncle or cousin or something, writ back and said he never would forgit his dying screams. And what I been a-wondering about ever since I first heard it is – is a human hide worth anything to speak of, and if not, what did they want it fer? And I want you to ask George to find out if he can, him or his ma, if when doctors git a-hold of a dead body one way or another – they peel off the skin first thing or not, and if they do, what fer?"

Happy John had just about petered out. He lolled and nodded until Mary helped him to bed where he spraddled out like a gingerbread man, over the whole thing. Supper time came and went, but he lay like a post, except for unusually heavy breathing and occasional sharp snorts. Bedtime came. Mary turned to Lige apologetically.

"Pa Moore, I don't know what to say. I aimed for you to sleep in here with Pa by the fire, Knowing you was used to it, but don't look like you'd have any place to lay, the way he's stretched out, and nobody can wake him or budge him, hardly, heavy as he is, when he's this fur gone. I'll cover him up, but what to do for you, I don't know. I'll make you a pallet on the floor in here if you say so, like I done for me and the younguns in tother room. But that's awful hard on a body, old as you air, when they're used to a bed. Or, if you say so, we'll bring in a featherbed or shuck-tick from the summer kitchen, or, for that matter, the whole bedstead, though it seems like a heap of trouble for a night or two. Or you can sleep in there. Whatever you say. There hain't no fire in there, though, nor no stove. Hain't been all year. The younguns don't seem to need it. Maybe if I'd heat a rock for your feet, or a flat-iron – you'd sleep warm enough. There's plenty of cover, I reckon, now with the children gone. But, whatever you do, I'm afeard you'll take considerable cold."

Lige nodded, lifelessly.

"Well, maybe I will, and maybe I won't, but with a rock or iron het, looks like I ort to keep tolerable warm. Anyhow, I don't want to sleep on the floor. I've tried it time and again, and seems like I never git a wink of sleep. My bones cut right through the hide. I'll be all right in yander, I reckon, after I git the bed warm. We could bring the feather bed in and maybe the shuck tick too, but I'm so wore out, I don't feel like I could go another step, and I know you don't, holding them little younguns eight mile, might near. Just heat a rock and let it go. Anyhow, I've took cold before. Seems like I been a-doing it all winter, might near, and if I take a mite more, I reckon it won't make a heap of difference. Besides, 'tain't your fault. You cain't take the troubles of the whole world on your shoulders. Nobody can. I'll git along, I reckon."

But he had chilled through in the rain. An iron to his feet couldn't warm a whole bed with sheets of ice. His back wouldn't warm up, and if he shifted the iron, his feet numbed. So all night long he lay and shivered, while in the next room Happy John snored.

Chapter 24 : Lige's Illllness and Death

By morning Lige was as chilled and cramped as if he'd sat all night in the cellar, but his face and hands were like lumps of fire. Happy John beamed over Mary's coffee and griddle cakes.

"Lige, you ain't no idy how sorry I am, a-taking up the whole bed like I done. Why didn't you push me over and climb in?"

Lige chattered through bumping teeth.

"Well, for one thing, you ain't so easy to push."

Happy John swooped a saucer of coffee.

"I know it, but looks like you and Mary both could a done it."

He poured molasses on griddle cakes and knifed chunks to his mouth.

"Say, Lige, you ain't teched a thing. You reckon you took cold enough to hurt you last night? I'm that sorry I'd do anything fer you, if I knowed what to do." A light came into his eyes. "Say, what you need, more'n likely, is a swig of whisky. Hit'll knock that cold quicker'n you can say Jack Robinson. I know wheres you can git it too, and I'll just go along with you. I feel like I've took a mite of cold myself."

The griddle turner poked out as if about to strike somebody.

"Now, Pa, you ain't a-going to worry Ma to death again to-day. If you keep on, the way you're a-doing, Ma flat of her back like she is, and nobody to look after her, I'm a going to talk to the police about it, much as I think of you and hate to do it. But I ain't a going to have Ma worried to death. There must be something a body can do."

Happy John's jaw looked as if it had become unhinged.

"Oh, Mary, you wouldn't do the like of that to your poor old Pa –"

She pried under a pancake and flipped it over.

"You'll see. I know where you're a gitting that stuff, and if you keep on I'll tell the police, sure as I'm a standing here. I'll tell 'em you ain't responsible, and they've got to fix it so's you cain't git it – no more'n somebody under age. If you git any more, and I hear about it, and I always do, you can tell that feller for me, he might as well move out, cause he cain't make a go of things, without your trade, and I aim to tell the sheriff."

Happy John's face worked like fomenting yeast.

"Mary, I swear to God, I'll never touch another drop, long as I live, so help me. But Lige, here, ort to have some. Might be the death of him, if he don't. I'll go with him to git it, and walk back."

"You'll stay right here with Ma, till one of the younguns git back, any-way. I aimed to stay till they come myself, or might near, but the way Pa Moore's a-feeling, we'd better go soon as I can hitch up. But don't let me hear of you leaving Ma till there's somebody with her. What if she was to die, and you on one of your sprees, and nobody to take care of her, or maybe even know?"

"I told you I was through, Mary. This is the last time, so help me!"

"You've said that ten thousand times, and not a iotem of difference in you. But just the same, I'm a-telling you, don't leave Ma without some-body's here, and don't let me hear of you drunk again with her all alone. If Pa Moore wants or needs whisky, I know where to go, and more'n likely he does too."

The whiskers wagged vaguely.

"No, I reckon I better not have any. I'll git a-long, onct I git home – leastways, I always have. And if Sary was to smell whisky on me – I reckon I'd be better off dead."

All the way home Lige chilled. The drizzle had turned to a half sleet, and the umbrella kept pecking him like a chicken after corn. The children kept up a continual cry, but Mary seemed hardly to hear. At the first cross road the umbrella made a jab for his right eye.

"Pa Moore, – maybe you *had* better git some whisky. Some say it does help a heap – with colds. I ain't much of a believer in liquor – no time – but you might as well have it as the rest."

He was chilled numb in the rain.

"It ain't for me, Mary. I'd ruther take my chance without it, and it's a pity your pa cain't do the same. Sometimes I wonder if we're better off without prohibition or not – not that it helped a great sight when he had it."

"Prohibition didn't seem to help Pa none, did it?"

"I don't reckon nothing'd help your pa, Mary. He's beyond help."

It was midafternoon by the time they got to George's. Lige shook so he could hardly stand. Sarah made him eat some hot gruel and drink some sassafras tea, though he didn't want it, and then drove on home. There was not a flicker of fire in heater or cookstove, so she had to carry out ashes and build from the start, with paper and shavings and broken-up sticks. When the flatirons were on to heat, and the room warm enough to undress in, she put Lige to bed and unhitched the team. Skunk oil, asafedita, sassafras tea, bone-set, mustard plaster – nothing seemed to help him. She kept flatirons to his feet and back, and piled six quilts over him, but his legs remained like icicles, almost to his knees. It didn't seem as if all the irons in the world would warm them up. His shirt and underwear were wringing wet, but when he pushed back the quilts, he almost shook himself to death. The second day he was half delirious. George, gum-booted and umbrellad, against a threatening rain, clumped up the steps.

"How's Pa?"

Sarah's old eyes watered, as she sniffed a little.

"He's awful bad, George."

"You reckon he'll go, Ma?"

"Well, I don't know."

"Ma, I just *felt* like a-going out in that rain'd kill somebody. That's why I didn't want to go. 'Tain't that I wanted Pa to go, understand – but you ain't no idy!"

"You done right, George. Nobody ort to gone."

"Can I see Pa?"

"Of course you can, but like as not he won't know you. He's out of his head a good part of the time. Keeps a singing old songs he ain't sung for I don't know how long. I'm so worried I ain't got good sense. We'll see if he knows you. Come on in. Lige, George's come to see you."

She bubbled into soft weeping. Lige roused a little and fixed watery eyes on first one and then the other, as his cracked voice rose.

> "As she was a-walking through the fields,
> She spied his cold corpse a-coming;
> Saying, 'Set him down by the side of the road,
> That I may look upon him.'"

Sarah burst into quick swallowing sobs, like a gobbling turkey.

"Lige, *don't* sing sech songs, at sech a time. I'm so worried, I'm might near crazy anyhow. Tell me something I can do fer you. And if you must sing, sing something less mournful."

He focused blank, blue eyes on the gray twist on top her head.

> "Monday morning, I married me a wife,
> Thinking to lead a happy life;
> Fifing and dancing so merrily was played,
> But mark how unhappy I was made.
> "Tuesday morning at the break of day,
> On her pillow she did lay;
> She tuned up her clack and she scolded the more
> Than I ever did hear in my life before.
> "Wednesday morning, I –"

"Lige, don't sing no more. George come all the way over to see you.

Cain't you talk to him?"

A light came into the span above the whiskers.

"Oh, George? George, Happy John wanted me to ask you something, though I forgit what it was now – something about doctors and dead bodies. Oh, yes. He wants to know – do grave-robbers peel off the skin first thing, when they git hold of dead bodies for skeletons and sech, or not, and if they do, what fer?"

George had turned the color of a bullfrog's stomach.

"Oh, Pa, I ain't no idy. Please don't talk like that no more, poorly as you feel, and worried as me and Ma air. I'm already so weak and nervous, I don't know what I'm a doing hardly, and Ma's a taking on like you never seed."

"Lige, don't talk about dying or think about it. If you go, I don't know what in the name of the Lord I'll do."

Lige shifted his attention to the steady drip from two eaves on Sarah's chin, as she kept sobbing like gurgling buttermilk, and his wavering voice went on.

> "The tears from her eyes,
> Like a fountain they did flow;
> Oh, where shall I wander?
> Oh, where shall I go?
> Fol I do, I do, I do, I do, I day."

"Lige, don't, don't –"

"Pap used to sing that song. I wisht – I wisht –"

Sarah blotted mouth and eyes and bent down.

"What do you wish, Lige?"

"I wisht Jim and John Tittle'd come. I want to see 'em."

The fluttering lips fixed in a twisted line.

"What do you want to see 'em fer, Lige? It'd just bring up hard feelings again. Besides I said and I still say neither one of 'em 'll ever step foot inside my door again."

The watery old eyes rolled up, like a small boy's asking for cookies.

"I want to tell 'em I forgive 'em. I forgive Jim for driving cat-a-slaunch-ways through the place, and what-ever else he done, or didn't do, and I want him to forgive me. I never aimed to chop off his ear. Tell him I want to forgive and forgit."

Sarah shook the twist atop her head.

"Now, Lige, I don't want Jim Tittle in my house, or John airy one, after all the meanness they done. I say let 'em stay at home, where they belong."

The plaintive voice mumbled on.

"I want Jim to forgive me, and I want John to, too. I cain't die easy, seems like, without I see 'em before I go. Tell 'em to come, Sary."

For some time she stared from the window, with moving lips and puckered forehead.

"I reckon maybe I'd better. George, do you feel like going after 'em?"

George studied the drab outside and shuddered a little.

"You don't reckon he'd be apt to pitch on to me, for what Pa done to him, do you?"

"No. Tell him your pa's turrible sick – how sick I don't know, and wouldn't say if I did. I wisht Doc Ceburn'd git here, so's a body'd have some idy what was what. But I want you to tell them Tittleses your pa wants to see 'em. You can ride old Spot or Dolly, if you want."

For a time he stared out without saying anything.

"'Tain't a raining out, Ma, so fur, and clost as it is, I reckon I'd better walk."

"Well, whatever you want, but hurry." She lowered her voice. "I don't 'low he'll last long."

A chair scraped across the floor and Sarah sat down where she could watch. Weak, watery eyes turned from the bed.

"Sary, you got any more quilts? And can you heat up this iron? I'm so cold, seems like I'm plum numb, fur up as I can feel."

She changed the iron at his feet and piled old coats over quilts.

"Now, Lige, don't you think you could eat something hot, if I fixed it fer you?"

"I don't feel like I could swaller a bite, Sary."

"Just a little gruel, Lige, to keep up your strength."

The mild, blue eyes only stared. Boiling water bubbled from the teakettle and white corn meal was stirred to a thin paste. Morning's milk was poured in.

"Now, Lige."

But he only stared, and when she raised his head and tried to feed him, most of it spilled on the pillow. She wiped it up with a wet towel and zigzagged her head.

"You cain't git well if you don't eat, Lige. I don't know what to do."

She picked up paper and pencil.

"Lige, just in case something happens, if you *should* take a turn for the worse, – you reckon you ort to put something down in writing, about deeding that property to George? If Tim was a mind to go to law, it'd worry George to death, him ailing like he is all the time, anyhow."

He stared at the bulky blankblock and pencil.

"What's that fer?"

"Don't you want nothing writ, Lige?"

"What? No – o. What'd I write about?"

But the writing reminded him of an old song, and his voice wailed up in a kind of chant:

"She called for a chair for to set her down;
And a pen and ink for to write it down;
At the end of every line she dropped a tear;
At the end of every verse she cried, 'Oh dear!'
At the end of every line she dropped a tear;
At the end of every verse she cried, 'Oh dear!'
"'Go dig my grave both wide and deep,
At the head and foot place a marble stone–'"

"Sary, I'm gitting warmer now. I reckon maybe I'll go to sleep."

"All right, Lige."

Every few minutes she tiptoed in and stared with gimlet eyes, to see if he was gone. For a time there was a soft moaning, with the covers bulging and lowering. When it stopped, she stumbled to the bedside. He had been half dozing and one eye was half closed, but the other had popped wide open.

"Lige! Lige!" she choked, clutching his shoulders.

Tears trickled down gullies on each side of her nose and spattered his face, but the open eye only stared, a gray and blue marble in a yellow bed. She pulled a feather from the pillow tick, and held it close to his mouth, watching, hardly breathing. Where was that little circle of a looking glass she'd had so long? She tumbled and pushed through the bureau drawer, and then doubled down to cover his mouth with it, biting her lips and blotting her eyes. The open eye stared back.

"Oh, Lige, Lige!"

Wherever she went, the eye watched. She was swallowing lumpy sobs, and rubbing his hands when Doc Ceburn pushed in with his little black bag. He stared a minute and then came to the bed.

"Is he gone?"

Her sobs whinnied out till she could hardly talk.

"I ain't right certain, Doc, but I think he is. I tried a feather, and it didn't move fur as I could see, but 'pears to me like this looking glass's got a mite of mist on it."

He stared at it and wagged his head.

"I cain't see nothing, but my eyes ain't none too good, even with specs. I'd better try his heart."

He hooked up heart and ears, listening, and shook his head.

"He's gone. Ben gone quite a little while, near as I can judge. There's nothing I can do fer him now."

As the door pulled open to let him out, Jim and John Tittle stalked in, followed by George. Sarah turned accusing wet eyes on them.

"He's gone," she sobbed," – dead. And he wanted to see you so bad before he went. He wanted you two to forgive him, so's he could die without no hard feelings – and he forgive you. I don't. I don't forgive or forgit. I cain't. But he did. And he'd a rested a heap easier, if you'd a got here before he went."

The two bulks of men stood with bowed heads in a kind of awe. Jim mumbled.

"I do forgive Lige. Fur as that's concerned, I never had nothing agin him. I knowed 'twasn't his fault – that he was just riled to thunderation, with you a stirring him on, like you always done. I never blamed him."

She whiffed out a noseful of air.

"Hit's a pity you couldn't a found that out, before our two best cows went, and all the money we had in the bank. I reckon it's right, though, for you and him to forgive and forgit. 'Tain't right, seems like, to have hard feelings agin the dead."

The two men shuffled their feet and looked down, as Jim went on.

"We hain't got none. And just to show you we ain't, we'd be glad to help dig his grave and carry his box to the graveyard, fer him. And we'll set up to-night, if you don't have nobody else in mind. Or to-morrow night. Whatever you say. Maybe one of us ort to come by after chores and see."

Her gimlet eyes blinked tears.

"Thank you, Jim. Maybe you're mite better'n what I 'lowed. I reckon everybody's got some good in 'em, if you can just find it. I'll let you know.

I don't know myself yit. Ain't give it no thought. Thank you, anyhow, both of you."

When the Tittles had stalked away, she took pennies from the dirty little tobacco sack, safety-pinned to her underwear, and weighted down the staring eyes.

"George, do you think Jim and John Tittle could be trusted to set up?"

He looked up helplessly. All the day the air had been moist and heavy, without a sign of sun. Now the sky was a dull blackboard, continually scribbled and erased with crackling yellow.

"Why, I don't know, Ma. I ain't no idy. I'm so worried about this storm a-coming, I don't know what I'm a doing, hardly. The way things air, there's no hopes fer me if I git caught in the wet. And I won't have time now, to git home before it breaks – and don't look like there'll be no let up to it, once it gits started."

"Don't try to go, George. Stay right here. I don't want to be left alone nohow. Mary'll understand when she knows how things air. If she gits to worrying, maybe she'll come over here."

"Well, Ma, I hate for her to worry, or git caught in the storm, but I cain't go out myself, no matter what happens. If I have to stay all night, maybe you and me could set up with Pa, though both of us ort to try to git some rest, I reckon."

"Oh, relation ain't supposed to set up nohow. I wonder if Ben Bragg and his Ma would, that is, if they knowed? If they won't, maybe Ben'll git somebody. Maybe I ort to let Jim and John Tittle set up one night, stout as they both air, but I never will feel right about airy one of 'em, no matter what they do. And besides, 'twouldn't look right, two big hulks of men, a-staying the night here – Lige just laid out, and me a lone woman – that is, unless you or somebody else is here in the house too."

The door pushed back, and Mary poked her head in.

"It's a going to rain turrible any minute, and I expect I'll git soaking wet, but when George didn't come back, I was afeard Pa Moore was worse. How is he?"

George merely stared, but Sarah mumbled.

"He's gone, Mary."

Mary sucked in a long breath as her eyes filled.

"Oh no, Ma Moore. He ain't. Tell me he ain't."

"If I did it'd be a lie. He's been gone this half hour, I reckon."

Biting her lips, Mary tiptoed to the bed. George cleared his throat.

"Hit's the truth, Mary. We been a-trying to figure out who to git to set up with him. Jim and John Tittle'll do it – was by and said they would – but Ma sort of favors somebody else. Ben Bragg and his ma might come, or M's Jimpson and Bill or somebody, if we ask 'em. What do you think?"

Mary swallowed and wiped her eyes.

"I 'low Ben and his Ma'll come. I'll ask 'em on the way back. I'll be soaking wet anyhow, and a little more rain won't hurt, I reckon. Anyhow, I want to do what I can for Pa Moore. I feel like I'm part to blame for his going."

Sarah's long chin jerked out.

"Well, in a way, you air. But we all make mistakes, Mary. You ortn't to a-gone to your Pa's and Ma's that day, but nothing'd do you. But it's too late to think about that now. All the tears in the world ain't a going to bring him back, and anyhow, I reckon you done the best you knowed. The thing to do now is take care of yourself, after telling them, so's you can help tomorrow. I want Lawrence to come in the morning. He always seemed to think so much of his grandpap, and I want him to understand. I 'low George'd better stay here to-night. Seems like he's worried to death about gitting caught in the wet, and going like his pa. and I don't want to be alone nohow. Lige ort to be laid out, but I reckon somebody'll come before long. If they don't, I'll do it myself, but I cain't hardly bear to think of it."

Chapter 25 : Lige's Burial

While pennies weighted down Lige's lids, and kitchen clicks and watches became pounding threshing machines, outside, wind and rain blustered and bellowed, and dared each other on. Lightening crisscrossed over the sky in great chicken tracks, and thunder rumbled and growled like a dog on the trail of a varmint. About dark, the bottom of the sky seemed to crack open and all the dammed up water came tumbling down. A small boy, dripping as if he'd been washed but not wrung, burst in, toes squshing in water-filled shoes, and eyes holes of wet.

"Grandma, Grandpa ain't dead, is he? They said he was, but I don't believe it!"

Her teeth seemed to pinch her mouth in the middle.

"Yes, Lawrence, your grandpa's gone."

Above twisting lips, his eyes bulged.

"Oh, Grandma, cain't I never see him no more?"

"You can see him if you want, Lawrence. He's in yander, laid out."

They tiptoed into the cellar of a parlor, and the coaloil lamp pointed yellow-pronged fingers at the dead man.

"Why, Grandma, he's all dressed up like he was a-going someplace. Maybe he's just a sleeping sounder'n common. I heard tell of folks being laid away before they was clean dead, and a clawing dirt with their fingers. S'posing Grandpa would!"

Her head jiggled as her mouth-line tightened.

"He won't, Lawrence. Your grandpa's gone. Doc Ceburn said so, three or four hours ago. Put your hand on his head and you'll see. Here."

His hand jerked back from the snake-cold forehead, as if seared by a stove, and his eyes seemed to sink like a turtle's head, as he stumbled after the fluttering lamp, looking backward. In the other room he huddled on the bed, and tried to squeeze back smothered sobs. A bony hand patted his shoulder.

"Don't Lawrence."

"Oh, Grandma, I wisht I hadn't a-touched him. Now I'll always be thinking of him that-a-way, and I'd ruther a-remembered him a-singing or whistling like he always done, when he wasn't in misery. I don't want to never touch no dead people no more. Please don't make me, Grandma. You ain't no idy how awful it is. Poor Grandpa! Maybe if he'd git warm, he'd come back to life. I got to be going, I reckon. Mommy's a-grieving and taking on turrible. Says it's mostly her fault."

"Well, just let her grieve. Maybe she'll be better to George."

"Where's Pappy?'

"He's a-setting in the kitchen a-taking on. He's so worried about his pa a-going and this turrible storm and all, I don't know when he'll get home. Not to-night, I don't reckon."

"Wisht I didn't have to go. It's so pouring wet and dark, I'm sort of scared. 'Tain't that I'm afeard of Grandpa. Hit's that thing I touched."

Swallowing sobs, he pulled open the door, and started out through the pouring rain, at a stumbling gallop.

All night long the sky spouted water that rolled down window panes and seeped in at the edge. In the kitchen, Ben Bragg and his mother seemed to be walking and talking all the time, maybe to keep awake, or maybe to keep coffee hot. George had finally let his mother make a pallet on the floor for him by the heater, and stretched out, his mouth wide open, sucking in and whiffing out great mouthfuls of air. Once he called out, and Sarah, who had not batted an eye all night, roused him, but he only turned over and opened and closed his lips several times, scissors fashion.

Sarah mopped up the floor by the window, and pulled the cover over her.

If it kept on pouring all night, no telling when they could have the burying. A body does hate to put a corpse in a grave full of water, so to speak, and more falling all the time. It seems so cold and heartless-like – like setting them in a drain-clogged cellar to rot right away, and if they scooped the water from the grave – it was an awfully bad sign. Still, he ought to be laid away as soon as they could. He was dead. Doc Ceburn had said so right away, and there was no use letting him lie around until he turned black and began to smell, maybe with preacher Ray already spoke for.

Lige gone. It was hard to believe. They would never work together again after all those years. And now, she would have to go too. After the funeral, she would go to her mother's and Tizzie's at Hell's Holler, more than likely. She couldn't stay on by herself, now, and George's house was not big enough for two families. No house was for that matter.

All next day rain varied from drizzle to downpour, and all night. The third day dawned with a drab lull, that turned to a drizzle. But they couldn't put off burying any longer. Lige was beginning to smell a little, and had started to turn blue at the fingertips.

George was as sluggish as a snake in November. His father's death had clamped down on him like a cider press, and squeezed out what little courage he had left. Hour after hour he lay collapsed on the bed, staring up at the ceiling, as if expecting it to tumble down on him, and mumbling the same thing if his mother tried to rouse him.

"'Twould a-happened to me, if I'd a gone stead of Pa, and if it had, you ain't no idy. In the name of the Lord, Ma, not knowing how things air, don't' ever ask me to go out in the wet. I'm so nervous and worried, a thinking about it, I ain't got good sense."

She kept stroking his shoulder.

"Never mind, George. I never did ask you, and I never aimed to. Only don't take on like that. Folks'll be a-saying you're a-losing your mind again."

"Well, Ma, maybe I am, and maybe I ain't. Half the time I don't know what I'm a-doing, fur as that goes. Anyhow, I don't know as it matters what anybody else says or thinks. You ain't no idy how things air."

Before the grave could be dug, they had to decide where to dig it. There was the family graveyard, where old Tim was buried, new fenced, and away from everybody else, so a body could get to it without walking for miles, but with the eighty acres bound to be sold or divided up within a year, so Tim could have his share, Sarah held out for the Jim Cullop cemetery. She had a right to it. Her own uncle had deeded it to the county. Besides, it was private and free, and well kept up by friends and relatives. A pretty enough place, it was, too, with shells and rocks on the graves, and handy to get to, if she moved to Hell's Holler, though the roads would be mighty bad to get him there now.

Tim made all the arrangements, with Ben Bragg to see that things were done. Had the grave dug during the lull – sixteen men had changed off and done the digging – and the funeral set for two o'clock. But instead of slacking up, so a body could make out what the preacher had to say, it spouted down harder than ever, and turned into hail, for a time, as big as hen eggs. So that nobody but the front pew could hear anything but Sarah's sobs.

Preacher Ray had a way of wringing a body's insides, and squeezing the wet from their eyes, as if they were a week's washing. And when they all sang "Nearer My God to Thee" and "We Shall Meet But We Shall Miss Him", Sarah felt she could stand it no longer. Her sugar sack handkerchief mopped her eyes until it dripped, and her bent body shook as if with a hard chill, as a long chain of hootowl sobs broke out in smothered chunks. And the more Preacher Ray said, the worse it got. It seemed as if he were just trying to bring back to mind all the good things Lige ever did.

Tim had insisted on a hearse, when the time came, and paid for it, as well as the coffin. He wanted to be one of the six to carry the coffin, and George to be another, but as the rains kept on, George broke down in Church and balked solidly, so Jim and John Tittle, Ben Bragg, old man Rainwater and Bill Jimpson finished out. From churchdoor to hearse, the six were as drenched as if they'd just been baptized, and news-papers on top of the coffin were soaked through. Up hill and down the bedraggled little procession followed the black box, but at the end of the first mile, the heavy wheels of the hearse bogged down in Missouri clay, and no amount of prying or pulling would budge it. When everybody gave up, Jim and John Tittle hoisted the black box into their spring wagon, and covered it up with the old horse blanket, they used at times for a laprobe.

On sloshed mule and horse team, with wagon wheels grating and creak-ing through mud half to the hub. Starting up Goose-neck Hill, however, the wagon sank hub deep and stopped. Horses and mules were hitched on to pull it either forward or back, but it was no use. George, huddled in hired car between his mother and Mary, was so worried and worked up, he got out once and wrang his hands, but Ben Bragg tramped back through the drizzling rain for his tractor. If anything would make these roads, it could, he said, but it didn't. Half a mile beyond Tittles' spring wagon, it balked too, and there it stuck, swallowed down in mud, like a spoon at the bottom of a molasses pitcher, with no way of pulling it out until the roads dried. It was almost a quarter of a mile through the woods and fields to the graveyard, but the six got out in the pouring rain, and carried the coffin, followed by a few who were willing to risk rain and storm to see Lige's burial. Mary nudged George, who had made no move to get out.

"George, you'd better go. It's the last thing you can do for your pa, and he's done so much for us, like Preacher Ray said. Please, George, go this time if you never do nothing again. You'll always hate it if you don't, and I will too. Gitting wet once won't kill a body, I reckon."

His eyes fixed on the falling rain. "It did Pa."

"Yes, but, George he was old and rheumatic, and none too stout any-way. Hadn't been all winter. You're a heap younger'n your pa, too."

His face puckered to a crumpled wad.

"It aint' that, Mary. You ain't no idy, and I cain't explain to you, but the way things air, I cain't git out in the wet."

He broke into hoarse sobs, and his mother patted his shoulder.

"Don't take on, George, and don't go if it upsets you. I'll go and Mary'll go, and Lawrence, I reckon, and that's enough to git soaking wet. If it'd do any good, it'd be different, but you nor nobody cain't do nothing for your pa now. Set where you air, and don't take on no more. We'll go."

They struggled through ankle deep mud, after the black box the six carried. At Turkey Run Creek, a little above where it emptied into Crooked Creek, the foot bridge was washed out. Through water knee deep from the swelling rain, the six waded, carrying the coffin. Half way across the creek, Jim Tittle bumped into a snag, and dropped the coffin as he stumbled. Quick as a cat, he plunged in elbow deep and heaved it out. The damage was small, in that coffin and men were already soaked through anyway, but Sarah snorted as she nudged Mary.

"He done it on purpose! I know folks, and I know Jim Tittle. Pretending to be so all-fired good, all of a sudden, just cause Lige wanted to forgive and forgit, when he was out of his head. A-wanting to carry Lige's box, just so's he could drop him in the crick and he'd rot all the sooner. If 'twasn't a burying, I'd give him a piece of my mind. I've a notion to anyhow, but a body hates to, the way things air, and at such a time."

Mary watched the six clamber out of the creek, and waded in.

"He didn't do it on purpose, Ma Moore. Anybody might a-done it in the pouring rain. He couldn't help it. I heard him a telling somebody or other yesterday, he'd always felt mean-like about that fuss last fall. Said he 'lowed it'd half worried Lige to death, and he wanted to sort of square things with him, and this was the only way he knowed."

Sarah tossed her wet head and waded after Mary, her long skirts held high, and her legs looking like broom-sticks.

"Talk's cheap, Mary. If he'd a been so anxious to square things, he wouldn't a dropped Lige in the crick, I reckon. There was five others a-carrying him – one of 'em an old man, and one a boy – but *they* didn't drop him, nary one but *Jim*. I ain't got no patience with him."

She stumbled on another snag, or maybe the same one, and all but went over herself.

The rain slacked a little, while they scooped bucketfuls of water from the open grave, and sobbed "Nearer My God to Thee" again, as they lowered the box. Sarah out-sobbed them all, and could not quiet herself, even after they had shoveled soggy clay over the coffin and all stood bareheaded while Preacher Ray prayed.

"Don't ever say nothing to George about scooping water out of the grave, Mary, nor you, Lawrence. It's him that's meant, of course – nine chances to ten he'll go any time now – but I feel like he's better off not to know."

The drizzle had started in again, harder than ever.

"It has been requested by the bereaved wife that we sing "Let Me in the Life Boat." May I ask that you all join in?"

Sarah sobbed and shook so, she could not utter a word. Lawrence patted her dress.

"Sing, Grandma. Don't cry – though it does look like he needs a boat more'n anything."

As soon as she could control herself, she bit her lip.

"Shhh! 'Twas your grandpa's favorite song – that is, church song."

And there they left him, soaked in water and covered with gummy clay, a little thicker than gruel, and tramped back to the two seated car Tim had hired, and where George, comparatively dry, but with bowed head, shook like a dog that has been thrown in cold water. Sarah touched the block of shoulder.

"Don't you feel no better, George?"

The colorless face had turned to the gray-green of sage tea.

"No, Ma, I cain't say that I do. I been a-setting here a thinking, and I don't reckon I ever will be no better. I feel it in my bones, somehow, that I'm a going like Pa did – any time now, the way the rain keeps up. The doctor good as said so, and when I do go – Oh, Lord, Ma, you ain't no idy!"

Sarah, Mary, and Lawrence got in with George, padding an old coat between them to keep him from the wet, and Tim got in front with the driver, but the car wouldn't budge. While they had gone to bury Lige, the mire had sucked it down beyond prying out. George covered his face with his hands, and started moaning and groaning, but Sarah patted his shoulder.

"Never mind, George, I'll see if you cain't ride back with Ben Bragg, poorly as you're a feeling, and the rest of us'll walk. I reckon he'll git you there all right with them chain things of his'n, and 'twon't make no difference to us, to speak of, wet as we air."

So George rode back with Ben Bragg and his mother, and the rest tramped through mud and clay, in the steady drizzle, to the two-room house. The storm had slackened considerably by the time they got there, but George, in Ben's Ford, had chilled all the way home. When he reached the frame house, he took to his bed, and nobody could persuade him out of it for a week. He seemed half delirious in his fear of storms.

"The next time a turrible storm comes, it'll be a aiming for me, and I ain't going out in it no matter what happens. I tell you it's meant that I go like Pa did, and my only hope in the world is to keep out of the wet. Sometimes I git to thinking, and wonder if the Almighty's got something agin me, and is a striking through these storms. Seems like they're all sort of aimed at me anyhow, and everyone of 'em brings bad luck to me and mine. But I reckon the next one'll wind things up, fur as I'm concerned. I feel it in my bones. Something turrible's a going to happen, and it's a going to happen to me. They didn't dip all that water out of Pa's grave for nothing, I reckon."

Sarah's voice was like thick sorghum. "George, who told you about the water in your pa's open grave? I never aimed for you to find out. 'Lowed it'd just worry you."

"Ben told me, him and his ma. They never knowed 'twas a bad sign till old man Jimpson told 'em. He said he never knowed it to fail."

Sarah's mouth tightened as she talked.

"Well, George, I never neither, but there's always a first time for everything, I reckon. Anyhow, there's other folks in this family, besides you, and some of 'em a heap older. Like as not me and Ma'll go before you do. Being poorly all your life, don't always mean your time'll come any sooner. Sometimes, seems like the sickliest folks last the longest. So don't you worry no more. You're just plum all to pieces now, about your pa. That's what ails you mainly, I reckon."

He stared out over the hills with the look of a new-yoked heifer.

"Well, no, Ma, – I figure it's more than that."

Chapter 26 : The Visit to the Graveyard*

Sarah seemed to take an uncommon interest in graveyard visiting after Lige was laid to rest. Started talking about it a day or two after the burying, but rain and one thing and another kept them away. For one thing, George was ailing more than common – had taken to his bed a good part of the time ever since – and Sarah wouldn't even talk about going without him. He did not *want* to go. Felt as if he'd just as soon be knocked in the head, but with his mother so set on it, there didn't seem any way out. He knew they would have to go sooner or later, but the first Sunday the sun seemed in the notion to even half-way shine, he was as jumpy and nervous as the day he'd married Mary. And the more he mulled things over, the worse he got.

It did look as if Lige's death was the front end of a long string of troubles. With him gone, everything seemed to be headed the wrong way, and no telling how it would all wind up. That deed. He couldn't even hold his place now, or rather the place he'd thought was his. When the year was up, they would have to move, though where on earth they'd go, nobody knew. Not that he'd signed any more uptown papers, but the numbers to the deed were wrong. Tim found it out when he went up to see about dividing things, without having to sell for a little of nothing.

Tim had been out and out good about some things. He'd paid all of Lige's doctor bills, besides his burying – wanted to, he said – but he wouldn't pay George's. said George had no business having doctor bills anyhow, big and stout as he was. And he wouldn't make out a quit-claim deed to George's place like Sarah wanted. Said Lige aimed for him and

George to share and share alike, or he wouldn't have made that deed out like he had. That he was Lige's youngun same as George, and it wouldn't be right for him not to get his part – no matter what he'd got from his grandpa on the other side. Said he'd fight for what he knew his pa wanted him to have, if they had to law the whole thing away.

There was no way of holding it. Mary had gone up to see right away. Gone a horse back. She'd wanted George to go, but ailing like he was, and it looking as if it were fixing for an all day drizzle, he felt he would rather lose the place. Got so nervous and worked up, just thinking about things, he didn't so much as move all the time Mary was gone, hardly – that is, not till Mark just about drowned. That gave him such a turn he didn't know what to do.

Lawrence had come in carrying him like he was dead. Said he'd fallen in the soft water jar head first and drowned himself, but he hadn't. came to on the way over to Ben Bragg's, slung over Lawrence's shoulder by the middle, like he was. Sort of spanked the water out, Doc Ceburn said. Said that was about as good a way as any to pump water out of a body.

But Mary had been as put out as if he hadn't come to, mostly as George. She'd acted as if it were out and out his fault. Said it did look like he could watch the baby with her gone, and in a way it did. Her trying to save the roof over their heads, even though it hadn't done a particle of good.

That deed had been a kind of bug in the blackberry jam. Spoiled everything. It had even brought in the rub-doctors. After George couldn't hold his twenty-five acres, Sarah'd given in. Sort of lost heart. Signed a temporary agreement along with him and Tim to sell everything when the year was out. And after that, it seemed as if everybody got in the notion to sell – Ben Braggs and Webbstringers and three or four others. Hell's Holler was half rub-doctor owned now, and so much mill and dam fixing going on all the time, George was half crazy thinking about it.

Some said they'd got government help like was offered before, or were trying to, anyway. Aimed to dam up the river in a reservoir that would stretch half way to Keatsville. *They* claimed they would fix up the old mill too, and save the paddle wheel and machinery before it all fell in the river. All day long their hammers and sledges kept up a steady pound, and every so often a big boom blasted out dirt and cement. Seemed as if they were trying to blow out the insides of everything.

Mary said the rub-doctors mainly wanted to buy hill property so they could take advantage of that government offer. Said they'd said so all along. But of course she didn't know about the body business. Nobody did but him and them. Nine chances to ten, it was part-way to keep tab on him – that other old man disappearing like he had. Or maybe they aimed to worry him to death all the sooner.

Sunday was the only day a body could call even half-way quiet-like, and with that graveyard visit hanging over them, there didn't seem to be *any* time to out and out enjoy. All day long he had felt this was the day, partly because of a scooped-out inside feeling, and partly from the way Sarah acted. Kept squinting at the sun about every five minutes and eyeing dandelions and timothy in the front yard. Finally she spoke.

"It's turned out to be a right nice day for Sunday, much as it's been a-raining here lately. And I'd like awful well for all of us to go to Lige's grave, and put some flowers on it, if there is any. Nobody's been there since he was put away, I reckon."

George sprawled back on the bed.

"If it's alt he same to you, Ma, ailing like I am, I'd just as leave not go, this time. Seems like, here lately, I'm so nervous and worried, I don't feel like I could stand to look at graves and the like."

Her flint eyes melted to warm taffy.

"I want you to go, George. 'Twon't take a great might of time, and I feel like it's for your good as well as mine. I got my heart set on it, seems like, and besides, what'll the neighbors say, you not going to your own pa's grave, first time we go, and him hardly cold yet. Anyhow, there's something I want to say to you, fur as I see, I cain't say it nowheres else but in your pa's presence, so to speak."

George's mouth gaped like a chicken with the pip.

"Ma, Cain't you tell me some other time, when I feel more able to be out and a going some'ers?"

"No, George, I cain't. No telling what might happen before there's a pretty day again, and it's something that ort to be settled. You can set on the seat if you want, so's you can ride easier, and me or Mary one'll drive, and tother un'll set in the wagon bed with the children. Come on, now, I want you to go."

If she had asked him to jump head-first over the Chariton damn, he could have shown no more reluctance.

"Oh, Ma, if you had any idy –"

"I do, George. That's why I want you to go."

The spring wagon bumped along gullies of ruts, up and donw hornet-nest hills for three and a half miles, and then stopped. Big elm trees at each side of the gate, bowed them into a rickrack of graves, that rounded up like sweet potato beds. About every other wagon length, a great white black of cement, with cut-in letters, and maybe some poetry, reared up, but most of the mounds were marked like young fruit trees, with sticks and little tin oblongs for the name. But all were well taken care of; piled high with mussel shells and rocks, and flowers growing out of the stomachs, so to speak.

Looking for Lige's grave was about like looking for a button in the bureau drawer. Just about had to comb the whole thing to find it. Tim had picked it out, and the only time they had seen it was in pouring rain, with everybody taking on too much to give much thought to what was what. The children edged along each grave, trying to miss the rounded sod. All of a sudden Lawrence yelled out.

"Pappy, come 'ere!"

A few strides and George gaped at the pointing finger.

"Pappy, hain't this a funny one? Looks to me like a great big turtle, don't it you?"

Bullfrog fashion, George squatted to make out the printing.

"Lawrence, you ortn't to talk like that. Don't seem hardly right or respectful-like to the dead."

"Oh, Pappy, I don't 'low they'd care none."

George's finger followed each letter on the tin oblong.

"Why, good Lord, Lawrence! This is your grandpa's grave. Don't say such as you was a saying a while ago before your grandma for the Lord's sake. She'd never git over it, I reckon."

"All right, Pappy, I won't"

George pushed up and pancaked his hands on each side of his mouth.

"Ma! Here 'tis. Here's Pa's grave. Over here on tother side of Grandma Nesbit's second man. Somebody's brung shells fer it, and banked it up with rocks, so's the fresh mud don't show hardly."

They filled up and Sarah's mouth twisted as if she'd just swallowed a dose of bitters.

"I reckon Tim done it, or had somebody do it. Done it for his Pa, but I cain't say as it looks anything extry, myself. Looks to me like a whopping big mud-turtle."

"That's what I thought, Grandma, only Pappy told me not to say it before you."

She circled the grave, arms triangle on her hips, and made mouths at it from all sides.

"'Tain't that I don't like rocks and shells and the like, mind you, but I just don't like to see a body's grave so whooped up, looks like they're about to bust out of it."

George propped himself against an old oak tree.

"Well, Ma, I reckon it's best to have it overpiled than under, fur as that goes."

"Yes. They say it always sags no sooner'n the body rots, and I do hate to see a grave sort of scooped out in the middle, like they'd snatched the body, and the dirt'd caved in. I reckon Tim or whoever done it, knowed what they was a doing in the long run, though it ain't much to look at now. Mary, I noticed there was considerable weeds a growing out of Uncle John's grave, and I feel like they ort to be pulled. I don't know why it is, but ever since them rub-doctors's been a coming down here so regular-like, I've had a feeling we ort to look after our graves uncommon well. I may be wrong, mind you, but I wouldn't put nothing a bit past 'em. I wondered if you and the younguns'd mind weeding graves, whilst I say something to George. I want to say it to him by hisself, first, though I'll tell you later on."

"Of course we will, Ma Moore. Come on, children." V

The little brood stumbled after her sugar sack skirt as it swished over the grass. Every so often they turned to stare back. Sarah turned to George.

"George, I brung you out here for a reason to-day. I want to say all I got to say, whilst I'm alive and in my right mind, cause a body never knows what'll happen or when. More'n likely I'll last considerable time yet, but a body never knows."

George gulped and kicked the bottom bark of the tree.

"Oh, Ma, you'll live a long time yet, more'n likely; a heap longer'n me, I reckon, the shape I'm in."

"Well, George, I may or may not. As I said, a body never knows about such things. I had no idy your pa'd go when he did. After this, I aim to look ahead and have things fixed so's a body'll know what's what no matter what happens, or when. You won't' forgit where your pa's buried now, will you?"

George stared at the bulge of rocks and shells and shook his head.

"Why, no, Ma, I don't reckon I will, and if I do, I figure I could find it with mighty little trouble. This un seems to have a heap more shape than the rest of 'em, like it'd sort of over et."

"Well, Georg, I've already spoke to Jim Cullup's youngest son about more burying ground. If he wants to charge fer it, he's welcome, but he said he wouldn't, and he never has – him relation."

"I don't reckon he will, Ma."

"No, I reckon not, and look George, if I die before you do, and it stands to reason I will, more'n likely, I want you to see that I'm buried next to your pa. I spoke for the two near lots." V

"Who's tother'n fer, Ma?"

"For you, George. I want you put away next to me. If you die before I do, I'll see to it, myself, but I want you buried there whenever you do die. I don't 'low I could rest easy, dead or alive, if you was anywhere else and looks to me like you ort to be a heap easier in your mind, knowing all that's took care of. You hain't no objections have you?"

George had the hunted expression of a rabbit poked from a woodpile, with a pack of dogs ready to pounce on it.

"Well, Ma, – 'Tain't objections exactly, but – I don't what to say. To tell the truth, I don't feel like it's hardly my say so."

"I understand how you feel, George, and I aim to talk to Mary first thing. Don't look like she ort to raise too much fuss over it, though. She's got five children of her own to be buried with."

"It ain't that, Ma –"

"Well, I don't care what it is. I want to plan ahead George. Look at the way your pa went, and airy one of us might go any time the same way. Look, George, I want to be sure you understand what's what right now. Here's where I'll be put away – next to your pa. And, George, here's where you'll be, right here next to me, the second lot this-a-way from your pa, this un by the path here. And no matter when your time comes, and a body never knows, that's where I want you laid to rest – next to your mommy. You won't forgit, will you?"

George was as jiggly as if he had a handful of wooly worms down his back.

"No, Ma, I don't 'low I'll forgit, but the way things air – maybe I won't have no call to be laid away nowhere. I don't want to talk about it no more, Ma, nervous and worried like I am. I'm might near out of my mind. You ain't no idy."

He burst into a gurgle of sobs as Sarah stared up.

"Why, George, what on earth? Don't take on like that. I just wanted to git things settled-like, but if you're too jumpy and nervous now, we'll wait till you *air* able. And, George, you think it over and take airy one of these lots you want. I never thought, but maybe you could rest easier *betwixt* me and your pa. the woman generally *is* put away by her man – but whatever you say. But we won't talk about it no more till you say you're able. I aimed to tell Mary soon as it was settled, but it ain't settled yet, and anyhow, I reckon it'll keep."

*[As a sample of 1940s typing standards, we deliberately left all the indisputable typos in this chapter, not just the bits which demonstrate that generation's more flexible approach to spelling and punctuation.]

Chapter 27 : The Storm

A clump of plates and a subdued scrape of skillets announced dinner.
Chairs slid into place, and a weary eyed little woman with red hair un-
latched the oven door. Sarah tiptoed in from the bedroom.

"Bless their little hearts! A having to stay in bed, when they want up
so bad –"

The red head drooped, lower.

"I know it. I washed out their long underwear last night, 'specially,
so's they'd be nice and clean today, and it got soaked in the rain, and ain't
dry yet. I'm afraid to change 'em, rainy as it's been, so I patched up one
suit apiece, out of the best of their old uns. I thought we could manage."

Sarah nodded at four small suits that dangled behind the cookstove.

"Oh, they'll dry before long. What can I do?"

Mary looked into the oven and clicked the door.

"The chicken's done, and with all you brung, we might as well set
down. I'll fix something for the little uns. No telling when Lawrence'll git
here."

Sarah turned to a bulk of overalls, relaxed on the bed. "Come on,
George."

The overalls unfolded as a low rumble sounded above. "Was that thunder? Seems like it's rained or snowed every Sunday for the last six months.
Leastways when Ma and Pa come."

"Poor Pa Moore," Mary's shoulders sagged, 'twas rain that killed him – it and me, thought I didn't intend it."

Sarah patted the limp shoulder.

"We all make mistakes, Mary. If we'd a knowed how things'd a turned out, you wouldn't a gone, and I wouldn't a made Lige take you. But with all them yaller wooly worms last fall, I knowed there'd be fever, and poorly as George is, I figured it'd be him. And I just couldn't bear fer him to go through the rain, seemed like."

George cleared his throat.

"Well, Ma, like as not considerable more of us'll go yet – no more snow than there was Christmas."

"Yes. 'Twas a black Christmas, and a black Christmas means a full graveyard. No telling how many'll go before spring's over – especially with them rub-doctors down here a pounding all the time, and blowing and dynamiting eternally. Mark my words, no good'll come of it. I reckon Elviry Jimpson ain't been a seeing all them lights for nothing. And if it was to do over again, I don't know as I'd agree to sell when the year's up – no matter what – and I don't 'low M's. Jimpson would. If we hadn't agreed to sell, Webbstringers wouldn't a sold, nor Ben Bragg wouldn't."

"Ben said him and his folks air a aiming to leave to-morrow or next day," put in Mary. "Aim to go to Ioway. Got things all packed up. Said it didn't rain so much up there."

Sarah tossed her head.

"Well, they can go and welcome, fur as I'm concerned. It does seem it's rained a heap here lately, though. Did the rain, last night, damage your crops any, George?"

The butcher knife clattered on the plate, as George slashed off a leg and some white meat.

"Why, – I don't know. I ain't been outside hardly. Doc Ceburn said wet feet might cause pneumony. Did it, Mary?

She looked up from four thick plates of bread and gravy.

"I don't reckon so. The weeds is a taking everything anyhow. That bridge over Turkey Run Crick might near washed out though – the one George's pa was always after him to fix. And we lost a lot of little chickens. I tried to bring 'em to in the oven, but I couldn't. Got less than fifty left, I reckon. How's your'n?"

The twist atop the gray head waggled.

"I didn't lose none. Had 'em shut up last night, but I ain't got nowhere near what I ort to have – taking care of Lige, and all –"

The little woman dabbed at her eyes, as she always did when they talked of Lige.

"Now, now, Mary. You've got George to think of, and the children. Besides, – I cain't help feeling a little hard myself, him a making that mistake in the deed to yours and George's land, here – leastways, if he done it on purpose –."

Mary raised solemn eyes. "I don't know where we'll go or what we'll do – but I reckon Tim *did* have a right to his share."

"Tim's got plenty! Got all his grandpap had, on tother side. He could a signed that place over to George well as not, if he'd a been a mind to."

Two at a time, the younger woman carried out thick, white plates. Lawrence burst in, his hair flying.

"Mommy, it's gitting turrible dark outside! Looks like a regular cloud burst coming. Hadn't we better try to git up the little chickens? Mmmm – roast chicken!"

The butcher knife clashed into the platter. Mary turned to the bulk of overalls.

"George, you go. Put on your gum boots, cain't you, and let the child eat?"

George had the hunted look he always had when anybody mentioned going out in the wet.

"Maybe he better not, Mary," Sarah spoke up. "If he'd git caught in a rain, and this here chronic rheumatism would set in, or he'd go like Lige did – you'd never forgive yourself."

"Well, never mind, George, I'll go. I won't be gone long, Ma Moore."

But Sarah was already on her feet. "I'm a going to git mine in too. The way them clouds look, looks like there might be another cyclone a coming."

Mary nodded. "It does look turrible stormy. George, help your ma hitch up, cain't you?"

The gray twist wagged. "No, George. Set right where you air, and finish your dinner before it's cold. I can hitch up all right. You might git your feet damp anyhow. Goodbye to you all, and George, do take care of yourself. And whatever you do, or whatever happens, keep out of the wet. Remember, 'twas rain that killed your pa!"

The door slammed and Mary turned toward the table, dull eyed.

"I'm sorry, if I hurried her off. Her and Pa Moore's been so good to us. But I couldn't let the chickens drown. They're about all we got now. George, *please* leave something for to-morrow. Don't eat everything up, just cause your ma left. The younguns'll want it – you know they will."

Pleading eyes raised from white meat and dressing.

"Mary, for the *Lord's* sake, don't begrudge me the little pleasure I git out of life. I ain't a well man, and there ain't much I can do – worried like

I am – but I *can* eat."

The woman's shoulders slumped as she banged the door. A clash against the plaster, and the boy run after her. George watched, solemn eyed, and then turned to the chicken. One after another, bones were cleaned and laid on the plate. A spoon ladled gravy over biscuits. On the roof a faint tinkle sounded. George raised eyes and ears questioningly, but his jaws continued to move. Gradually the rain turned to a drizzle, and then a steady downpour. A wooden handled knife hacked out a quarter of pie, and long legs ambled to and from the window. Four little flannelette nightgowns peeped out from behind the door.

"Air they dry yet?"

"Not yet. And you younguns better git back to bed – before you catch your death of cold. I cain't look after you, worried like I am – your ma out in the pouring rain, half drownded for all I know – Go on back to bed, now – "

Softly the crack of the door narrowed to nothing, as bare feet padded bedward. The rain rolled down the window in bucketfuls, and with wind and rain came strange noises. Did he imagine it? Sounded like a scream somewhere – and then a louder scream. His heavy soles tapped nervously. Big fists rammed into overall pockets, as the bulging nose flattened against the pane. Water, washing down the windows, was all he could see. Slowly, his feet shuffled back to the table. The butcher knife hacked out cake. More noises outside.

Like a jointed fish-pole, his long body stretched upward, with the pained look of a tied watchdog. Back and forth from table to window, he tramped – nibbling a little chicken, cutting a corner of pie – hardly realizing what he did. Outside a high voice called.

"Pappy! Pappy!"

His helpless eyes turned from the pouring rain outside to his leaky shoes, as he remembered his mother's last words. No telling where his gum boots were. What could Lawrence want? Slowly, he collapsed in a chair, and his big hand reached toward the platter. Again the voice called, nearer.

"Pappy! Pappy!! Come 'ere!!!"

He jumped up and stalked back and forth, his hands twisting in nervousness and helplessness. Half in a daze, he stumbled to the table and picked at the chicken. Soon only the skeleton of a hen remained. A small boy with streaming red hair burst in.

"Pappy! Pappy! Mommy's gone and drownded herself!"

His mouth opened wider as new teeth clicked.

"Drownded herself? What'd she want to do that fer?"

"She didn't do it on purpose! She busted through that bridge, and she's way down the river – clean dead, or might near it."

He slumped to a chair – staring dully.

"Dead?"

"Pappy! Pappy! Cain't you do something?

"I'm a trying to, Lawrence –"

He pushed himself up – upsetting the chair behind him, and looked about him hopelessly, behind the door, under the chairs. Drowned. They might not even find the body. It might be a way out for him –

"Where's them old gum boots gone to, Lawrence?"

The small red head bobbed up and down, as he turned over chairs, opened doors, and poked under furniture until he finally located them under the cookstove.

"Here, Pappy!"

George pulled them on, one after another, and stared out in helpless despair.

"Lawrence, see if you can find that old coat – the one your ma wears to milk in, when it's cold. I declare I'm that upset – I cain't find nothing."

Four small nightgowns peeped out from behind the bedroom door. Lawrence pushed them aside, and the baby started to whimper, but the search went on until the coat was found.

"Here, Pappy. Hurry! Hurry!"

They started out the back door, but the drenching rain and crashing thunder turned the sick man back. Less than a month ago, Lige had gone out in a storm – not half as bad as this – and pneumonia had nipped him like a canker-worm. If catching his death was all there was to it – he would have died for Mary ten times over – but she was past saving, more than likely, anyhow, now –. And with a houseful of doctors sitting around, waiting, watching every move –

"I've got to git something over my head, Lawrence. It'd kill me to go out like this, and you ain't no idy – the shape I'm in. There's an old umberell, some'ers – but where is it? You better go on, Lawrence. I'll come just as soon as I can."

"All right – but, *hurry*, Pappy! *Please* hurry!"

The door opened and slammed, and the man made up his mind to follow the boy, no matter what. It might be a way out. He might drown and get swept down the river, or wedged under the banks – where they'd never get at him. He couldn't leave Mary out there alone – and little Lawrence. He opened the door, but a dynamite blast of thunder that seemed to come from the earth's insides, and a flood of pouring rain, urged him back for the umbrella. He stumbled around, from chair to chair, from cupboard to cookstove – searching, but seeing nothing. Back and forth, from one rom to the other, in a wide circle like a caged bear, he tramped – but no umbrella. Baby Mark wailed almost steadily now, softly and dismally, something like a dog before death.

The rain outside, the baby's cries, the helplessness of hunting, got the better of George, and he sobbed brokenly, as gum boots kicked hopelessly at objects they had turned over half a dozen times. Round and round, like a tethered colt winding about a stake, he marched in a narrowing circle, until he stumbled over a kitchen chair, and lay collapsed on the bed in smothered weeping. The door blew open, and wind and rain swept underwear from the line, drenched. Outside, through the downpour of rain, voices sounded, as if from another world –

"Thank you, Ben. I'll be all right, now."

"Then I'd best go home. Ma'll be worried turrible."

George raised his head and listened. Nothing more – so he burrowed into the bedclothes again, weeping afresh. For a moment it had sounded like Mary –

They come in like a half drowned hen and chick – dripping water in little puddles over the kitchen floor. The woman quieted the baby and coaxed them all back to bed, but the boy went to his father.

"Don't, Pappy, don't"

The hidden face did not raise.

"I cain't go, Lawrence. I cain't find it nowhere. I cain't do nothing. Reckon 'twouldn't do no good if I could. Cain't swim, nohow. Oh, Lord in Heaven! What on earth'll I do now? Five little younguns on my hands – and no mother! Five poor little younguns, a starving to death, and me not able to lift a hand. My Lord, what'll become of us all?"

The boy patted him softly, but he went on sobbing.

"Oh, Lord, Lord, why *couldn't* you a saved her? What on earth'll I do *without* her? I cain't make a living, the shape I'm in – worried half to death, anyhow – and the place needing fixing, and my tools wore out, and the mules old, and my ailment gitting worse every day! Why, oh why couldn't she a been spared to take care of us all? As a feller says, I don't see what in the name of the Lord'll become of us, now –"

The voice trailed off in a low rumble of weeping. The woman turned to the half drowned boy.

"Git on some dry clothes, Lawrence, before you catch your death. George!"

He stared up at her white face and dripping red hair, as she squeezed water from the wet underwear, and hung it back on the line to dry.

"Mary! I thought you was *drownded!*"

"You *sure* done a lot to help me."

"I was a coming, Mary, or aiming to – fast as I could."

She seemed to be staring at something far away.

"If I'd a waited for you, I'd a had a *long* wait –"

And then he saw it – the black, baggy thing dangling from a nail behind the door.

"There's that old umberell! I looked high and low –"

"Ben Bragg come without no umberell – or I'd a been dead, now. He come right away, through the pouring rain, soon as me and Lawrence yelled – him and that dog of his'n – and fished me out. Reckon the dog done the most of it –"

"He did? I'll give that dog them chicken bones, soon as it clears off."

Outside the storm had sickened to a drizzle. Mary turned from window to table.

"Yes, you et up everything there was. I knowed you would. And the younguns hardly ever git pie or cake – and them down with the colds, much as they air, and having to be in bed all day to-day. There ain't no sense in anybody being so plum hoggish!"

He looked up at her, like a dog with its tail between its legs – half ashamed, yet not knowing why.

"*Scold* me, Mary. Go on, if you want to. I don't care – I'm that glad you ain't dead."

"Well, George, I *am* dead to you."

His puzzled head tilted to one side. "What?"

"I ain't never going to live with you no more."

The red-headed boy paused in snapping suspenders of dry overalls. Outside, rain dripped from the eaves. George's mouth opened, un-understandingly.

"Ain't? Where you going?"

She pushed back her long hair, which hung from the part, like wet towels.

"Ioway. It come to me when I was a laying there, half drownded – with Ben Bragg and his dog standing over me – nobody else come near me – that maybe this was my chance. They'd saved me from the river – maybe they could save me from the hills. I'd been mulling it over in my mind a long time anyhow. I 'lowed I could go with him and his ma and pa and git work some'ers, and send for the younguns, later on – but I wanted to be sure I was a doing right. 'Twasn't right, hardly, to go off and leave you if you *really* cared – cause *'tain't* your fault *altogether*, the way you air – but, you *don't* care. You don't care for nobody nor nothing – nothing but yourself, and filling your stomick, and your ma'll take care of that."

His eyes had the look of a faithful dog, about to be shot in old age.

"You'll never know how much I do love you, Mary. Nobody will."

She curled back dry lips. "Love! You ain't no idy what the word means, George."

She turned toward the bedroom door, but small hands clutched at her bedraggled skirt.

"Mommy! Mommy! Take me with you. Don't go off and leave me!"

She stopped and patted his damp hair.

"I wasn't thinking of leaving you. I wouldn't give you up for nothing on earth, Lawrence, – none of you – though I might have to leave you a little while."

"No, Mommy. Take me now!"

"Well, if Ben ain't got no objections."

In the next room a child whimpered.

"We cain't leave the little uns, can we, Mommy?"

"I don't like to, but I reckon I'll have to, till we can send fer 'em. I cain't take 'em – their underwear all wet, now, – they'd catch their death. Anyhow, I don't know as it'd be fair to Ben and his folks, taking five children, – that is, till I git something to do. I'll have to leave 'em for your grandma to look after, for a while, I reckon. Nobody'd be any better to 'em. She's pretty old fer it, but 'twon't be for long, and she *brung it all* on *herself* anyhow! She *made George* what he is!"

George's jaw dropped until his new false teeth almost slid to the floor. His hasty hand caught at his mouth.

"Mary, you ain't going to leave me – not *really*?"

She stared out toward the haze of the river. The sun came out from behind the clouds, and a wind rose.

"Don't try to keep me, George. I'd go crazy, clean crazy – if I stayed on here, *now*, with you."

He stretched out immense hands, pleading like a child.

"Mary, *don't* leave me! For the love o' God, don't go! Ain't I always been a good man to you, and tried to do the right thing?"

The boy raised solemn eyes.

"We ortn't to leave Pappy, Mommy – both of us – and him sick like he is. Cain't you take him along?"

"No, Lawrence, I cain't. *Never no more*."

The face that lifted now was without hope.

"Mary, – you mean you ain't *never* coming back?"

She nodded.

"You surely ain't a aiming to marry Ben Bragg, – air you?"

"I don't know. I don't reckon so. I don't know what I'll do."

He covered his face with big hands. The woman turned to the boy.

"Lawrence, – maybe you ort to wait – till I can send for all of you. You could help your grandma look after the little uns – and your pa. It ain't his fault, *really*."

"All right, Mommy."

Four little flannelette nightgowns filled the bedroom door, fingers in mouths and eyes staring.

"Mommy, where you going?" One after another she hugged them to her and kissed their small puzzled faces. Then she carried them back to bed, and returned wet eyed with a scanty bundle and worn purse.

"I'm a aiming to stay with Ben Bragg and his folks till the roads is dry enough for us to git out. He 'lowed they might be able to start in a day or two, with the Ford. Anyhow, – 'tain't right for me to stay here – now. Goodbye, George."

He did not seem to hear. She kissed the sad eyed boy. "I'll send fer you – soon as I can, Lawrence, darlin' – all of you. Goodbye."

"Goodbye, Mommy."

He watched until she was out of sight, his small red head pressed against the window. Then he turned to George.

"Pappy, – *don't* take on so. I'm here yet, and maybe I won't ever leave – long as you're sick like you air."

George raised hurt eyes.

"I didn't think she would either. I wonder if I could a *done* something to make her act like that. God knows I always tried to do the right thing. Wonder if it was her education – making her hate the sight of the hills, and all? Lawrence, run over and tell your grandma, – won't you? Tell her your ma's left, the Lord only knows why, and tell her I cain't hardly stand it – me sick and worried like I am, and not able to do a stroke –"

The door slammed. Left alone, George stared in puzzled wonder like a small boy who has been punished for his brother's misdeeds. His eyes wandered to the table, but there was nothing left. In the next room, a child whimpered. Little footsteps padded to the door, and a soft voice whined, "Where's Mommy?" George stared past them – hardly knowing what he was doing. Four little flannelette nightgowns filed out in awed wonder to the world outside, and down the gummy road. A few feet apart, their light gowns whipping in the wind like faded flags, they stood mired down in Missouri mud, wailing, "Mommy!"

But George only sat and stared. Half in a trance, he stumbled to the bed and reached for the thing in the wooden box. His soiled sleeve brushed across his nose and eyes, and then moved up and down.

Chapter 28 : Lawrence's Accident

In this rickity old loft of Sarah's barn, above hickory sapling ladder and tumble down stalls, Lawrence and Bill Jimpson squatted like two blinking toads. They had been trying to outspit each other, with the topmost peak of a jaggily old post as a goal, but had given up without any noticeable success on the part of either. Whatever they did, it seemed they always got back to old man Jimpson and Mary, before long. A straw in Bill's upper teeth wiggled up and down as he talked.

"Hain't it funny like, when you've had a ma and pa both all your life, and then you just got one of 'em?"

The smaller boy's chin bumped his knee, as he stared at the stalls below.

"Yeah, Bill. A grandma ain't like a mommy. Seemed like Mommy could look way down inside a body, and know what was what, without even asking."

Bill shifted his straw. "How's your pa taking it?"

"Turrible. He bawls might near all the time, and just sets there a looking at nothing. Time and again he's said if things wasn't the way they air, he'd hitch up the wagon and mules and go up to Ioway and fetch her back, or leastways have a talk with her, but he always gits to taking on, and says the shape he's in and all, no telling what might happen on the road, and anyhow, seems like Grandmas' agin it, and kind of talks him out of it."

"Don't look like, if he was a mind to go, your grandma could hinder him. Your ma's his woman – not your grandma's."

"'Tain't that, I don't reckon. Seems like that scared look always gits in his eyes, and he starts in a crying and taking on, and just sort of gives up. Says everything's agin him anyhow, and there's nothing he can do."

Bill clucked a little, his eyes on the jaggily post.

"You don't 'low he's a going out of his head again, do you?"

"Shucks, he never was. Just nervous like. Something's a worrying him turrible, but I don't know what it is, nor nobody does, I reckon. My pappy's as smart a feller as ever walked, except Andrew Moore, maybe, and lawyers and doctors and school teachers and the like."

"Do the little uns take on much for their ma?"

"Might near all the time. But Grandma keeps a saying, with Mark weaned now, and all, it could a been worse."

"Do you reckon you ma'll ever come back?"

His eyes filled and dripped over.

"Oh, *surely*, Bill. Seems like I couldn't stand it, hardly, if I never seed Mommy again. But s'posing she'd come back for us younguns, and wouldn't take Pappy? What'd I do, much as he thinks of me – him sick like he is, and nervous and worried, and gitting worse all the time?"

Bill chomped the straw in two, and tossed it downstairs. "Some say your pap ain't sick at all – just plain lazy."

"No, Bill. There's' something turrible a worrying him, like I said. Nobody knows what it is – not even Mommy. Pappy said so hisself."

"Well, I reckon you cain't live with both of 'em, if they don't live together."

"No, but, Bill, I keep a thinking when Mommy comes back for us kids, like she said she would, I'm a going to beg her to stay, and when she sees how Pappy keeps a crying and taking on, I 'low maybe she will."

"Well, Lawrence, maybe she will and maybe she won't. I heard tell of a woman once, went off and left her man and children – anyways her baby

– and never did come back. Went off with a gypsy feller, name o' Gypsy Davy. Hit's a song. Pap used to sing it."

"Seems like I heard Grandpa singing it too. But, Bill, – Mommy wouldn't do the like o' that, surely. If she don't 'low to come back – not ever – then I wisht I was dead, right now."

He kept wiping eyes and nose on patched chambray sleeves, but both continued to drip. Bill picked up another straw.

"Shucks, your Ma'll come back more'n likely. She said she would, didn't she? And a body's ma generally does what she says. Anyhow, let's not talk about it no more. Talk don't help none. Just makes a body think of new things to worry about. Let's do some high dives and swinging and jumping like circuses do. I'll banner you!"

"Whatever you say, Bill. I 'low there's plenty of hay, so we cain't hurt ourselves, hardly. Grandma and grandpa didn't use so much after they sold their two best cows. That's how come we can feed Whitey and Winkey here now. In some ways, Grandma's awful good, but 'tain't like having a mommy. Seems like I cain't bear to think of what's ahead, hardly – unless Mommy comes back to Pappy. A body wants to live with their mommy and pappy both."

Bill crunched his straw to bits. "Yeah, but s'posing you was like me? Then what'd you do?"

"Oh, Lord, Bill, I don't 'low I could stand it, hardly. Must be turrible."

"Yeah – it is. Only I knowed Pap had to go, before a great while, old as he was. Anyhow, we got worse troubles, seems like, now."

"Have?"

"Yeah. I reckon you knowed how much Ma always thought of J.P., him teched like he was. Well – he's gone."

"Gone?"

"Yeah. Been gone ever since that storm tother day – when the dam went, and your ma. We didn't say nothing about it at first to nobody – afeard some of them doctors'd git a hold of him, and ship him back to that hospital place. But they've all cleared out now, seems like, and I've looked all over, and Ma's might near out of her head. Thinks maybe they got him before they left."

"And Elviry's a seeing lights every which-a-ways, all the time now. The night before that storm she seed lights a flickering over our house, and I don't know how many over Hell's Holler way – big again as a bonfire, she said – and she's seed them might near every night since. Her and Ma thinks J.P.'s already done fer – thinks them rub-doctors's mixed up in it somehow – and there's something turrible a hanging over everybody else."

"Oh Lord, Bill! Maybe Pappy's a going to go too."

"Now, I don't reckon you pa'll go – less the whole lot does, anyhow. It's J.P. I'm a thinking about. Where do you reckon he went?"

"I ain't no idy, Bill – less he's off in the woods, some'ers."

"That's what I thought at first, maybe – but I reckon he'd a turned up by now. Maybe Ma and Elviry's right – maybe them rub-doctors's at the bottom of it. They'd been a wanting to rub J.P., for I don't know how long. Said they thought maybe they could help him considerable. But Ma never would let 'em, though she was half a mind to, after Pa went. I reckon they all got plum disgusted after that washout, much work as they'd done – all wasted. Least ways, nobody's seen any of 'em since. Some claim they was disgusted with the rains and roads and all before, and blowed out the dam theirselves – for insurance, or something. There was an awful racket about that time. Recollect?"

"Yeah. I recollect."

"But in a storm like that a body cain't tell whether it's thunder or something else. I wisht J.P.'d come back, and Elviry'd quit seeing that mess of lights and talking about it all the time. Seems like things is worse now, than they was when Pap went."

"Yes, cause you knowed where he was. Then too, you knowed he had to go, like you said. He was old – older than Grandpa Moore, I reckon. Say, Bill, Grandpa Prayter's on the wagon."

"Wagon?"

"Umhum. When he's drinking, he ain't on the wagon, and when he ain't, he is. I reckon Mommy'll be awful glad to hear it, that is, if she does.

She ain't writ yet."

"Shucks, I bet I know why he ain't a drinking."

"Why?"

"That old feller that used to make corn liquor down the river, Long-necker, his name was, died tother day. That is, they found him."

"Did?"

"Yeah. Some claim he pizened hisself with liquor. Done it with a tin can. Said there was a milk can missing down at the depot, one of them five-gallon tin things, for I don't know how long. And tother day, somebody was a-wanting a little liquor, and they went down to that house-boat of his'n, and there he lay, dead as a smashed mosquito, and there was that five-gallon can. And staggering around him, some of 'em clean passed out, was dozens and hundreds of rats. Seemed like it didn't kill none of them. He'd drunk the first, and pizened hisself on tin, and then died and rotted, might near, before they found him. And the rats had et about half of one of his legs, and maybe got drunk that a-way. Anyhow they wasn't no dead uns. His boy had gone off a month or so before, they said, nobody knowed where, so they couldn't let him know even, and nobody'd been for liquor, so he laid there maybe a week."

"What'd they do with him?"

"Boxed him up – that is, what was left of him – and laid him away on his own land, half way up the hill. 'Twas a right fur piece to airy one of the cemeteries, and I reckon they figured he ortn't to be put in no church ground nohow, seeing as he stold. It might be a judgement, for stealing that milk can, and might be, the rub-doctors done the whole things. Carried that tin can down there o' purpose – knowing he'd find it and use it, and pizen hisself – and they could git his body."

Lawrence kicked at the hay. "I'm plum sorry fer him poor old feller – pizened and rotten and et up by rats, and now gone to damnation, or maybe the rub-doctors. But maybe it'll be better for Grandpa Prayter."

"Why?"

"Cause, I don't reckon he'll git drunk no more, now."

"Shucks! He'll be drunk as them rats, next time you see him."

"Now, Bill, you don't know. Time and again I heard him say he 'lowed to stop, but with old man Longnecker's liquor so handy fer him, and him sort of craving it like, I reckon he couldn't hardly. Now with liquor harder to git, it'll be a heap easier for him."

"Shucks! Hit's only ten or twelve mile to Keatsville, from where your grandpa lives – and he goes every so often."

"Yeah, but, Bill, maybe Mommy a leaving and all'll make a difference. It might. I feel so different myself, seems like I'm liable to bust out and bawl any minute, just a thinking about things. Let's do what we said we was a going to. This is a banner and you're in it."

In one corner of the loft, a little nook jutted out by the window, with splintery walls just wide enough for him to span with arms and legs. Bat-like, he stretched himself across and boosted himself upward. Near the top, he turned a flip-flop and landed feet first in the hay. Bill grinned a kind of big brother grin.

"I cain't do that. My leg's too long. But like as not I'll fix you. Let's see. This is a banner. Watch!"

He edged out on an old rafter, and double summersaulted into the hay, half way across the loft, headforemost.

"Let's see you do that."

Lawrence batted his eyes and grinned. "I ain't a saying I can, but I won't be bannered."

He shinnied up to the rickity rafter and crouched and swung his arms. "All ready, boys, I'm a coming some!"

He hesitated a second, and then a sudden spring catapulted him downward. The rafter groaned and crunched as if it were about to collapse after him. Several feet short of Bill's landing place, hidden under loose hay, were broken planks – wide apart. Down went Lawrence, through the hay, through planks, down to the ground floor, but on the way his back banged into the jaggily old post, and for some minutes he lay senseless and still. Bill hung by his hands and dropped beside him, shaking him and yelling.

"Lawrence! Lawrence! Air you hurt bad?"

He started to cry when he opened his eyes.

"Don't tell Grandma, Bill. Please don't tell her. If Mommy was here it'd be different. She understands a feller, but Grandma'll scold till kingdom come."

Bill's solid arm braced his head and back.

"That don't make no difference now. You better tell her and git old Doc Ceburn. Hit's bad business hurting your back, and you've hurt your'n considerable. Might be you've broke it."

"I'll be all right, Bill," he whimpered softy. "Only just don't tell Grandma. You ain't no idy how cross she can be, over nothing. Mommy sort a knowed how a feller felt, that is, when he done things he ortn't to, but I reckon Grandma's too old."

Bill kept trying to boost him to his feet.

"I'll do whatever you say, but I tell you, if you're smart, you'll tell yourself, no matter how much she scolds, and see Doc Ceburn, like I said. I know what I'm a talking about."

Lawrence's whimpers rose to gasping wails.

"No, no, Bill, don't tell her. *Please* don't tell her. You ain't no idy how put out she can be over such things. I'll be all right, I reckon, soon as this hurt gits well, but whether I am or ain't, don't tell Grandma. I'd might near ruther die."

He covered his eyes with his fists, and little ripples of sobs shook his small body. Bill pulled him to his feet.

"Don't cry. Stand up and see if you can walk."

He raised wet eyes as he hobbled to his feet, one hand on his back and the other on Bill's shoulder.

"I can walk all right, I reckon, in a day or two, but Bill, it hurts tur-rible, further up, though the tail end of my spine don't seem to have no feeling. I wish my mommy was here. She'd know what to do. But don't tell Grandma, Bill. *Please* don't. Don't say airy a word to nobody. Grandma'll find out somehow, and holler and scold till I'm half crazy, and like as not give me sage tea and the like. Lord, Bill, I do wisht Mommy was here." Bill watched him like a kindly dog.

"Lawrence, I'm a going to carry you, or leastways help you, till we git might near there. Like as not, if you try to make the whole way home by yourself, you'll strain you back so's you never can walk. And, Lawrence, I'd keep off my feet as much as I could till you find out what's what. And, if 'twas me, I'd tell your pa, anyhow."

"No, Bill. Poor Pappy's got too much to worry about anyhow, the way things air."

"Well, anyhow, play like you're sick or something, and git old Doc Ceburn to look at you. I know what I'm a talking about, I tell you. If you take care of yourself, maybe 'twon't amount to a heap, but a blow on the back's liable to cripple a body for life. I've heard of it time and again. You better lay down, too, much as you can. Tell 'em you ain't feeling none too spry. Or tell 'em you et something that didn't agree with you. Anything."

At the top of the hill, a wagon length or two from the two room house, Bill put him down. He began to cry afresh as he clutched at his back and leg.

"Bill, there ain't no feeling in the end of my back yet, but furder up it hurts turrible, and my leg too. I feel like busting out in a big bawl. It's Mommy I keep a thinking about, Bill. S'posing I was to die or something, and her away off, the Lord only knows where. I wisht she hadn't a left."

"Well, you'll hear from her, more'n likely, any time now, and you or some of 'em can write and tell her. I reckon I ort to be a going now – that is, if you think you can make it by yourself."

"I can, Bill, I have to."

Bill clumped on down the hill and out of sight. Lawrence hobbled to the house, and lay down on the bed. George, doubled up on the other side, looked up, surprised.

"You sick, Lawrence?"

Tears rose to his eyes in spite of himself.

"Oh, Pappy, I keep a thinking of Mommy. I wisht she'd come back, Pappy. I wisht my mommy'd come back!"

Sobs rose in his throat, that no amount of swallowing could choke down, and he kept saying over and over.

"I wisht my mommy'd come back!"

Sarah swished in from the chickens, and pushed back the slat-sunbonnet from her worried eyes.

"Hain't it a shame for a little youngun to take on like that. I reckon if his ma'd a knowed how he'd a been, she'd a done different. I just wisht she was here to hear him, poor little feller."

She tiptoed to the bed and fingered his damp hair.

"Don't take on, that-a-way, Lawrence. I reckon your Ma's a having a good time up in Ioway, and ain't a caring what you do, nohow. A body wouldn't think a woman could be so plum hard hearted."

Four little tow-heads pushed open the outside door, and stared wide eyed, mouthing a finger or two.

"What's Lawrence a crying for?" asked Georgia.

His answer wailed out, and he kept sobbing over and over, "I want my mommy! I want my mommy!"

The children took up the wail, and one after another, and in two's and three's and four's, small faces wrinkled and chorused after him, "I want my mommy! I want my mommy!"

George covered his face with his hands, and a trickle of tears seeped out through big finger cracks.

"Oh, Lord, what on earth'll I do now? Five little younguns a taking on all the time for their ma, might near, and me sick and worried, and not able to lift a hand hardly. As a person says, I don't know what in the name of the Lord'll become of us."

Wet eyed and still sobbing, Lawrence reached out a small hand.

"Don't Pappy. Mommy'll come back to us before long. I'm might near sure of it. I dreamt she was here, last night, and things was like they used to be. Mommy'll come back."

But his voice choked in a sob, as he rubbed his numb back and whimpered softly.

"Mommy! I want my mommy!"

Chapter 29 : George *Starts* to Walk A Hundred Miles

George was on his way back to the insane asylum. No doctors had sent him this time, though, and there'd been no night trial, or sheriffs or constables – nothing, not even a train ride. He'd thought things over and concluded to go himself – afoot, that is, with what rides he could catch. Aimed to get that hospital milking job back, if he could. He'd had considerable trouble getting Sarah to see things his way, but he had. Leastways she'd given in to it, and fixed him a meal of victuals to eat on the road. Even offered to take him in the spring wagon as far as Hell's Holler, seeing as she aimed to move in with her mother and Tizzie anyhow, now with George and the children gone – only he didn't want to wait. Thought it might make a difference about that job, and the job meant doctoring Lawrence.

Sometimes, it just looked as if the rub-doctors had stretched out a great big fish net and had them all flopping inside, so that not even Lawrence could wiggle out. And still, maybe the whole thing was a kind of judgement, of what he'd done. The rub-doctors *couldn't* have sent that flood off a storm, that washed out most of Hell's Holler, the time Mary left, though they *could* have dynamited the dam, and some claim they did. Said no thunder storm could tear out that much rock at once. And, the way they'd acted ever since, it *did* sound reasonable, though nobody knew of any of them being around that day, and they generally wasn't on Sunday.

But they had cured Mary, and talked as if they could cure Lawrence, or anyway help him considerable, and if they could, bad off as he was, with one leg half rotted, smelled like, looked as if they ought to have a right to blow dams, if they wanted to. Sarah claimed every time you went to the rub-doctors, they got a new hold on you, but things couldn't be any worse with *him*, and they wouldn't hardly be after Lawrence's body, little as he was. And the land was already bargained for, now.

Besides, it wasn't him that had wanted the rub-doctors anyhow. It was Mary. Nothing would do her, but the one that had cut on her, had to doctor Lawrence, after she'd smashed that cement thing off, that is, and saw how bad off he was. And in a way it was her say-so now.

And for that matter that rub-doctor had acted out and out human, that morning, same as anybody else, though he never had before. Said they'd do all they could for him. Said he'd look over him, himself, and find out what was what, and student doctors would rub him as long as he needed it and not charge a cent, though if he had to have electricity – and more than likely he would – that would *cost*.

Maybe Sarah and old man Jimpson had been wrong. Maybe these doctors *weren't* hitched up with the devil – leastways, not all of them. Like as not there were good and bad rub-doctors, same as other folks. This one came from somewhere way off, so he *couldn't* be mixed up with any skeleton deals yet, hardly – that is, none but his. Of course he aimed to keep an eye on him, paid for and all, like he was, and for that matter, he had a right to look after his undivided interest, so to speak, though, come judgement day, no telling what that might include.

And maybe they did want to raise cattle and have a reservoir, and help the government save the old mill and dam like they said, though what either outfit wanted a mill for, nobody knew. Worn out, like it was, with the floor about to cave in any time, it would have taken considerable to fix it up, even if the storm hadn't washed it all in the river. And, it wasn't much account when it was fixed, for that matter – that is, not for outsiders. Sometimes, when the water was too high or too low, or a big fish got caught in the paddle wheel, a body had to wait half a day or such a matter to get his corn ground, unless they had meal ahead, that is. And no outsider would wait five or six hours for the mill to get in a corn grinding notion, when he could drive to Keatsville and back for it in half an hour. Besides, nine chances to ten, uptown doctors and government people didn't like cornbread anyhow, so what did they want a mill for?

And then too, if they *had* blown all the machinery – old steel wool carder, and heavy stone burs for corn grinding, and all – to the bottom of the river, so that it would take a derrick and no end of time and money to get it out, didn't look as if they wanted to save the old mill so bad.

Of course, the storm *could* have done all this, that is, it *might* – but there was an awful racket about that time, and the rub-doctors *hadn't* been back since. So it looked as if they'd done all the damage they aimed to, and then skipped out. Of course, with the damn blown to smithereens, and water standing everywhere knee to waist deep, there wasn't much they could do if they did come. And anyhow, if they doctored Lawrence so he could walk, who cared whether they'd blown the damn, or the storm had?

It did look though, unless the rub-doctors did have Hell's Holler in a kind of devil's clutch, that is, as if the Almighty had considerable against them all, though like as not, it was aimed at him, – Lawrence crippling himself like he had, nobody knew how, and then that county doctor plastering it up and never coming back, on top of all their other troubles. Sarah wouldn't allow a rub-doctor, or one that had been mixed up in that hospital business, to step foot in the house, hardly, so they had to get somebody they didn't know anything about, when old Doc Ceburn didn't have any putty. And Lawrence had lain there all there time, two or three months or such a matter, taking on with his leg and saying it was a rottening inside the thing, but the doctor wouldn't come or didn't, and nobody knew what to do, until Mary'd slashed it off with a borrowed sledge hammer that morning. And, like that rub-doctor said, she *might* have smashed his whole leg off, but she didn't.

About Mary. It didn't look as if things would ever be any different now. When she'd come for the children, after she'd written and they even had a lawyer write – he'd took on and begged her to stay with him, but she wouldn't, though she'd wiped her eyes considerable. Said it'd be all she could do to raise the children and take care of herself, poorly as she was since that operation, and George'd have to look after himself, or his ma would. Said anyhow, when he didn't lift a hand to save her in that storm, seemed as if all the soft feeling she had for him inside, had sort of turned to gristle, and she'd made a vow and said she aimed to keep it.

When she left, she'd took all the children with her, even Lawrence. Packed them in the Ford with her brother and Ben Bragg, and piled in a few bundles – children's clothes and the like, a few dishes this one and that one had given her, and a house plant or two – to take up town, where she aimed to live and do washings and clean houses for people. It just seemed to George as if he couldn't stand to see them go, but with him ailing all the time like he was, and Lawrence flat of his back, Sarah said it was the thing to do, and Mary did. But if Lawrence was to take sick and die up there, bad off as he was, or even have to have his leg taken off like old man Jimpson, George felt he would just about go out of his mind. That was why he had to have that job, just about, or some job.

Beyond Hell's Holler, the road zigzagged up and down like saw teeth, and the noon sun beat down and sucked out what little strength a body had, squeezing out sweat like water from a dishrag. Nobody asked him to ride, though he waited first under one tree and then another, and slowed down considerable when cars passed. Nobody knew him, of course, and maybe they were a bit leary of picking up strangers, like Sarah said, stout looking as he was and all. Or maybe they thought their long cars were too fine for him. Anyhow, they didn't. Up and down his knees doubled and straightened until the oil seemed dry in his joints, but he kept on.

Four or five miles the other side of Hell's Holler, he stopped for a drink from the creek and a bite from the meal sack, and things tasted so good, he sat longer than he intended. When he started on, it seemed as if both legs had stiffened to the crotch, maybe from rheumatism. If it was rheumatism, more than likely it was fixing to faint, though it didn't look it. Whatever happened he didn't want to get wet, so it would hardly do to get too far and no rides, with a storm coming up. Maybe if he sat down and waited long enough, and watched each car, somebody would see how worried he was, and ask him to ride – maybe all the way in. He doubled up under a big elm tree, and, as he waited, he munched at the meal sack.

All the time, back in his mind, he kept mulling over his troubles. Suppose one of those Missouri downpours, like the time Mary left, came up all of a sudden and caught him between farmhouses? What in the world would he do? He couldn't go on hardly without rides, but if he didn't get that job, what would Lawrence do? The way that leg looked, he'd need *everything* to save it – spindly, shrunken thing, with no more flesh than a dead chicken's foot, and about the color of water-soaked pie dough. That smell, too, like spoiled hog's flesh – only worse. Suppose it *had* rotted, and they'd have to take it off clear to the crotch, high up as that plaster thing had gone, and he'd have to cripple around the rest of his life, with one pants leg flapping – on the hickory crutches George had made and brought in that morning? Or, with that leg like it was, he might even die. If it *was* a judgement, it didn't seem fair, or right, any way you looked at it. It must be the works of the devil.

And still the rub-doctors didn't seem all bad either. If that doctor *would* oversee the whole thing, and maybe save Lawrence – he wouldn't hardly begrudge him anything. He *almost* wished he had another body to sell, if he could only save that leg, somehow, and pay for electricity. And still, if he could get that job at the hospital, maybe he could save Lawrence, and buy his body back *too*. The only thing was, Lawrence might die while he was down yonder.

It might be Tizzie and her mother would let him have that empty shed at Hell's Holler, to take a try at blacksmithing, like Sarah'd said something about. Tim always had blacksmithed, and he'd helped considerable, before he'd married Mary, though he never would shoe horses, with his back like it was. But he'd do anything else, all he could get to do, that is, what he could stand to do, and send the money to Lawrence, though like as not that wouldn't be a drop in the bucket to that hospital job. That job would have saved everything.

The only thing was, suppose he couldn't get down there. It didn't look as if he were going to get any rides, and hot as the sun was, he couldn't walk a hundred miles, hardly. He'd walked ten or fifteen or twenty miles already, and his legs were stiff now. Still, he *must* go on. It was his only hope – his and Lawrence's too. Surely somebody would ask him to ride before long. He blotted his face with shirt sleeve. Did the sun over out and out kill a body, or just drive them out of their heads? His brain felt half addled already. Still squatting, he backed against the tree trunk and nibbled some home baked bread and chicken. He was so tired, so stiff and sleepy, so worn out and no account. Still eating, he stretched back under the elm's shade and closed his eyes. Half way down the hill he could hear the trickle of water.

When he awoke, the sun was almost down and the air had cooled off considerably, but his throat seemed dry all the way down, and his tongue a thick slab of bread. His legs felt like cane stalks, but he made his way down to the water – a branch of the Chariton that curled back around the hills.

Squatting on all fours, he was about to suck up a long swallow of water, when he smelled something dead. He backed back and his hand jabbed into something cold and soft, like fat meat. The stench became stronger. He turned around to examine the thing he had touched, and backed back two or three wagon lengths, shaking till he could hardly stand. It was *somebody*. Somebody dead and half rotted, like he'd always figured might happen to him. It was several minutes before he could make himself go close enough to try to see who it was, and all the time he was getting sicker and sicker at his stomach. It was a wonder the rub-doctors hadn't found it and made away with it – and they would, like as not, if they'd been down there. He edged a little closer. It was a man or boy, drowned no telling how long ago, and now washed up on the shore, water-soaked and unrecognizable, with his mouth half open, like a gasping fish. His shirt and overalls were still good, seemed like, though some of the pockets were turned almost inside out.

As he bent over the thing, George shuddered in a nervous chill. What if it had been him? Evidently, it was the work of the devil, one way or another. Like as not the rub-doctors had something to do with it, one way or another, though of course, it *might* be one of the rub-doctor crew. The side pockets were stuffed with soaked dynamite, looked like, and the watch pocket with washed off matches. Maybe this was the one that had blown out the dam and reservoir, if it *was* blown out. Maybe he deserved to be dead. Maybe he'd made away with J.P. Jimpson. Nobody'd ever seen or heard of J.P. since the storm. Maybe he could trade himself out with this body, even – this dam-dynamiter and destroyer of J.P. – and then he noticed the front tooth – short and broken off and black, like J.P.'s. Maybe it *was* J.P. Maybe he'd better tell Jimpsons.

There was a rain coming up, and his toes and heels seemed blistered to raw beefsteak. He had to tell Jimpsons, and besides there was no chance of a ride now until morning anyhow. If he slept out a rattler might crawl up and bite him, or a mad dog, and if he walked all night, his blisters might turn into quick cancer, and his rheumatism to paralysis. Such things did happen, and then he couldn't get a job if there was one, and would go in no time. Anyhow, it stood to reason there was no chance at that job now. He'd been gone two months or such a matter, and with that Roberts boy in such a fidge to quit, and the hospital something like six miles from a whole city chuck full of men out of work, what chance would he have after all this time? Besides, if that was J.P. – it seemed like a warning to him – that there was no hope nohow.

He rubbed his legs. They were stove-poker stiff, and his feet were raw. It was ninety-five miles on to the hospital and not over five to Hell's Holler. Surely Tizzie and Grandma Nesbit wouldn't object to his staying one night. They *might* even let him get a few tools and do a little blacksmithing on the side, for the sake of Lawrence. Tim had always made a good living at it, but then Tim was stout – always was. Or surely he could get some easy work in Hell's Holler. If anything *should* happen to Lawrence, he wouldn't want to be anywhere else. Anyhow, he had to go back now. The meal sack was empty. He had eaten all. And if he went down there with no money to speak of and nothing to eat, and didn't get that job, what on earth would he do? He couldn't walk a hundred and ninety-five miles on an empty stomach, and it didn't look as if he could depend on rides at all. Maybe he could write to the hospital, or get somebody to. He wadded the empty meal sack to a ball and threw it over the fence and down the hill. Then he pushed himself up, empty handed, and tramped down the hill toward Hell's Holler. His stiff legs limbered as he walked and he seemed to forget his blisters.

He reached Hell's Holler in less than an hour. Sarah and Tizzie, in long muslin nightgowns and tatting trimmed caps, met him at the door with a coaloil lamp. Tizzie was muttering something, when Sarah broke in.

"Why, George, is anything the matter? I knowed that job'd be took, might near, but I never dreamt you'd git a ride all that way and back so soon."

He looked from one lined face to the other.

"I didn't go, Ma. I got a right smart piece, but I couldn't catch no rides, seemed like, and my legs got uncommon stiff, and my heels and toes blistered, and I'd et my grub, so I didn't think I ort to tackle it, with no money to speak of, and that job took more'n likely, anyhow– so I come back."

Sarah's mouth softened. "You done right, George. I'm glad you come. Nothing'd do you but start out, though I knowed 'twas all tomfoolery, and I wouldn't a rested easy, you away off down yonder with them crazy people, nohow. Supposing somebody'd a killed you and drug you off and cut you to giblets, like I've heard tell about in the papers – and we'd never knowed a thing about it, maybe?"

George collapsed on the porch, squeezing his head with both hands.

"Oh, Ma, – don't talk about such things now. I found somebody dead, down the river a ways, drownded I don't know how long ago, and washed up on the bank, and I'm so nervous, I ain't got good sense. That's the main reason I give up going."

"Why, George, – you reckon it's some of them rub-doctors, caught in their own trap?"

"Why, no, Ma. Looked like that Jimpson boy from his teeth – the one that was sent off to the crazy house. J.P., they called him."

"J.P. Jimpson! Elviry's said all along the rub-doctors got him. Seems like they git everybody sooner or later."

"Well, Ma, maybe they did and maybe they didn't. You recollect old man Jimpson a saying if the rub-doctors took over the mill and dam, he hoped somebody'd blow 'em both out? I've heard him say that time and again. 'Twas might near his dying words, near as I recollect."

"Well, George, you may be right, but I believe and I always will believe that the rub-doctors air at the bottom of it somehow."

"Maybe they air, Ma, but J.P. was always a great hand to do whatever a body said. I shouldn't be surprised but what he burnt down the dance hall too. Anyhow, I aim to tell Jimpsons in the morning, and they can figure things out theirselves. Couldn't do nothing to-night nohow, I don't reckon. Couldn't even find him now. And I'm so dead tired and stiff as a board, with my feet blistered till there's no feeling in 'em hardly, I want to git to bed, some'ers."

"That's all right, George. I done spoke for a room here fer you, till things is settled more anyhow, and it's all right. Ma and Tizzie's still got another extry room besides your'n if anything happens so's they need it."

"Did you ask about blacksmithing, Ma?"

"Yes, I asked 'em. They don't put no stock in it, but seeing as it's for Lawrence, they said if I'd pay for the tools, somehow, you can take a try at it. Anyways, they'll furnish the shed."

All this time, Tizzie had said nothing, but now her lips curled.

"'Twon't work out, like me and Ma said. When a body cain't make a go of things in thirty-eight years, looks like a plum waste of money, a trying something else."

Sarah's mouth tightened as she jiggled her head.

"Now, Tizzie, you don't know. Tim always made a good living at it."

"Yes, but Tim's Tim, and George's George."

"Yes, Tim's a heap stouter'n George – always was."

Chapter 30 : The Epidemic. Sarah's Death

The storm that washed out mill and dam – and Mary, so to speak – seemed to have done damage all down the river. Turkey Run Creek puffed out like a snake that has swallowed a chicken, and bottom-land farmers had to turn fishermen for the summer or find new land. Every so often, like sparrows rained out of an eaves trough, a family drifted through Hells' Hollow, looking for land to tend.

The sorriest of these was a little man and a woman named Blanketship, whose heads drooped like fishing poles, and whose eyes stared and disappeared like blinking frogs. How they intended to get land was a question. Didn't look as if they could buy one good meal for the mules – or ever had – wall-eyed, bony things, with backs caved in like hills upside down. The woman didn't look as if she had spunk enough to say "scat" to a fishworm – on the cobweb order, like a good whiff of wind would blow her away. Sure enough, all of a sudden, over she went, limp as a gunny sack, and about the same color. Somebody went for the doctor, but her man, propped against the wagon in a kind of mutual support, only stared with the helpless look of a grasshopper with one leg gone. George, who had come to spend most of his time, nowadays, slumped open-mouthed on the main store steps, like an open bag of potatoes, squinted one eye.

"Say, – air you the Blanketship lived down Turkey Run Crick, four or five mile toward town?"

The man's eyes seemed to be looking backwards.

"Yeah. I'm him."

"I thought I heard some'ers, your woman left you, long while back. Did she?"

The man kept staring – as if words would come if he waited.

"Yeah. She done it."

"How'd you git her back?"

"Told her I didn't 'low to whup her no more. That is, no more'n she ort to have."

"I never touched my woman – and she left –"

For a time the man seemed to come to life.

"Maybe that's where you done wrong. A 'oman's got a right smart of mule in her. A lick every now and then does a heap of good. Shows 'em who's boss."

All this was new to George. He stared out over the hills.

"Where's your children?"

For a time it seemed as if the man had made up his mind he'd answered enough.

"Dead. Bot' of 'em – and every last, living thing we had."

"What ailed 'em?"

Twice the mouth started and stopped.

"We ain't no idy. We lost a bruid sar fu'st. Jest afore that bad storm, and the 'oman took it awful hard."

For a moment George's neck craned toward the open store door. Then he settled back as if the effort was too much.

"I wouldn't let that worry me none. I b'lieve you can git 'em in here, for about ten cents a piece. I know you can in town."

"No, no – *bruid* sar, to raise lil' pigs! We couldn't bury her for I don't know how long – water standing knee deep all over, might near, and what wasn't under water, caked mud like a dried up pond. And there she was to look at, day after day. 'Twas jest like losing one of the family, and I reckon the critters took it the same way. Anyhow, they curled up and died, one after another – shoats, cow, chickens, chilern and all. Lil' boy about the age of that oldest un o' your'n – could read, purty as anybody, what he knowed – and lil' tow-headed girl. The 'oman wouldn't stay there after that. Said the Almighty was agin us, so we up and pulled out."

Doc Ceburn got the woman up and on her feet, but she was as wabbly as a new born calf. He gave her some pills and told her to go to bed and stay there. Said it wasn't anything but old fashioned grippe, but to get well, she had to have a bed and medicine. The man turned in a voice like the tall-end of a cow's moo.

"Doc, we're that poor – we hain't no better off than a couple of tumble-bugs. I want her to have medicine and all – but I cain't pay fer it. We had so much trouble I hain't got another shirt to my name, hardly. I cain't jest set here and let her die – but what kin I do?"

The doctor turned to the big man on the steps.

"George, your grandma Nesbit's got a extry bedroom, hain't she? Grippe ain't catching. I wouldn't send anybody to 'em, if there was any danger of them taking something. But all this poor woman needs is rest and a little medicine, and somebody to look after her. And, nobody'd be better'n your ma fer it. Wonder if they'd be willing to give that room to this sick woman and her man?"

"I'll stay with the mules," the man put in, as if to make the load as light as possible. "They're all I got left anyhow – but I wisht she could go."

George pushed himself up and stretched long arms.

"Well, I'll ask 'em, and put in a word fer her myself. I know what it is to have your woman about to die."

Sarah did everything she knew on her own account. Greased the thin neck with skunk oil, and wrapped it with one of George's yarn socks; fixed a mustard plaster for her chest, and tied a bag of asafetida around her neck; mixed sulphur and sorghum and fed her a little for bad blood; made bone-set tea and stewed pieplant for constipation – but in spite of everything, the woman got no better. By midnight, she was completely resigned to die.

"Don't work no more, M's. Moore. You'll jest wear yourself out, and t'won't do no good. I feel like my time's come."

Sarah pried her from the pillow and steadied a glass of water."

"Well – a body never knows that – till they're clean dead. Anyhow, a little medicine won't hurt nobody, I reckon. Here, take these pills."

The sick woman gurgled and swallowed.

"Well, – I feel like, if it's meant for you to go, you'll go, spite of everything, and – if it ain't, you won't. Medicine's a heap like kid gloves – nice to have if you kin – but something you can do without."

"Pears to me like a body can do without kid gloves a heap easier than medicine. I wouldn't have no more use for kid gloves than one of the pigs would."

"No. But they're so soft and purty to look at. They're a somethin' I always wanted, though I never had any – and don't expect I ever will. Reckon it don't matter none now – with my time come."

Sarah wagged her head briskly.

"I don't 'low it's as nigh as you think. Don't look like you'd be a-talking about kid gloves – and you a-dying."

The woman's eyes fluttered like bugs around a lantern.

"Why? I always wanted 'em so bad – though I knowed I couldn't have 'em. What ort a body talk about – when time comes to die?"

"Looks to me like – what they want done with their property – and how they want to be buried, and such."

The woman closed her eyes for a moment or two like a sleepy bird.

"Well – I cain't have what I want nohow – and I 'low it don't make no difference, now – but I always wanted a big crowd at my funeral. Somehow, seems less lonesome like, rumbling along on your last ride – if you know there'll be a crowd a-follering – "

"There'll be a plenty," Sarah soothed, "that is, if you do die. 'Pears to me like you'd be a heap better off to git that out of your head and try to git some sleep."

She shook her head. "M's. Moore, my time's come."

In the next room, George was as uncomfortable as a snagged bullfrog. Suppose this woman was right – that they were all marked out ahead, in spite of medicine and all – like rows in a garden, according to who went first – and he was among the radishes and green onions, so to speak? His hands were tied – and the rub-doctors all waiting to pounce on him!

Before morning, the woman was dead. Sarah and George relayed her last words about burial, and most of the small town and near farmers turned out. They were in town anyway, Saturday afternoon – and they wanted to show respect for the dead. The man who mended wagonbeds, and carpentered a little on the side, nailed up a box for her out of odds and ends, and Jim Tittle and his brother hauled her to the cemetery – back of the church, a quarter of a mile down the road. There were a few mule teams in the procession, but most of them straggled along afoot – like chickens following a plow. All through the sermon and "Nearer My God To Thee", the man said not a word, but when clods of clay started thumping on her coffin, he hugged his head, and long whinnying wails, something like a hoot-owl, rocked his shoulders. An hour or two later, they found him dead on his wagon – maybe from a broken heart.

That night Grandma Nesbit, well and hearty as a girl before, died in her bed, and Sarah who had hardly been sick a day in her life, was bleary-eyed by morning. When she tried to get up to get George's breakfast, everything went black and she sprawled on the floor. George helped her back to bed, and went for Doc Ceburn. When he came, she was half delirious.

"I don't know what ails me, Doc, – but I 'low I ain't long for this world. I was afeard I might not last till you got here. I been a chilling all night, and at the same time plum wet with sweat. And, Doc, I wanted to tell you – if they possibly can – won't you have 'em bury me by the side of Lige? He ain't in Hell's Holler's cemetry, but hit's mighty little furder – Jim Cullop cemetery. Hit's private – and free – and now with Lige there, I want me and George laid away with him. And I reckon Ma'd better be put there too. Her second man is."

The doctor coughed and wheezed a little.

"Well, M's. Moore, I'll do what I can fer you, and George too – that is, if he gits this thing, and goes."

"Oh, I reckon he will. If we took it from the woman, he was the first to talk to 'em, and if it's something we et – I reckon he et the same thing. Besides, bad luck always comes in three's, and now with his pa gone, and me a going, I reckon he'll be the next. Anyhow, whenever he *does* go – hit's my dying wish to have him laid near me. Seems like I couldn't rest easy – him put away some'ers else, without me and his pa to look after him, so to speak. You're willing, ain't you, George?"

George, standing at her bedside, was as wiggly as a half baited worm.

"Well, Ma, – God knows *I'm* willing, but – "

The soft look in her eyes hardened.

"George, – I don't feel like Mary's got no claim on you – now. You'll do what you can, Doc, won't you? Seems like, somehow, George cain't look ahead and see what's good fer him and what ain't. Promise, so's I can die easy."

The doctor's kindly eyes turned from the hollow-eyed man to the dying woman.

"I'll do all I can, M's. Moore. Is there anybody you'd like to talk to – Tizzie maybe, or Preacher Ray?"

The dull eyes lighted a little.

"Yes, Doc," her breath came in little gasps, "airy one of 'em – or both, if I could – a little while."

She motioned to the other part of the house. The door eased to after him. George clasped bulks of hand and squatted by the bed.

"Where do you hurt, Ma?"

Her eyes filled as she turned toward him.

"I hurt all over, George. But it's you I'm a thinking of. If you do die, and I reckon you will, I killed you, same as if I'd hit you with a sledge hammer. I brung death into the house and killed my own boy – and Ma too, fur as that goes, though I reckon she was old enough to die anyhow."

Soft sobs wracked her body and the covers bobbed up and down like a spring wagon seat. George watched with blurs of eyes and choked in a monotone.

"Don't take on, Ma. You aimed for the best."

"I know it, George. I aimed to do all a mother could fer you, but look what I *done!*"

"Why, Ma, 'twas Doc Ceburn sent that woman here in the first place."

"Yes, George, but I told him to. Told him to send anybody that needed home-doctoring, when I first come. I always done for other folks – and seemed like that woman needed help uncommon bad. I never dreamt it was catching. You won't hold no hard feelings agin me, will you, George – after I'm gone?"

"Oh, Lord no, Ma, I couldn't, good as you've been –"

A coughing spell left her heaving and gasping like a tired dog, and jiggled the tatting trimmed nightcap over one eye. George kept tucking it up, but it wouldn't stay till Tizzie's competent hand straightened it with one turn.

"Sary, – is there something you want me to do fer you?"

She swallowed twice and looked up.

"Yes, Tizzie, there is. I been a thinking all night long, and I've concluded this ailment and all's a judgment of the Lord, sent on for selling out to the rub-doctors, and saying we was a going to."

"Maybe it is, Sary. Leastways some of the rest seem to think so."

"Even if that Jimpson boy did blow up the dam and reservoir, I reckon the Lord put him up to it. He was teched, and I reckon a little closter to the Almighty than the rest of us."

"Yes."

"And, Tizzie, you're so uncommonly stout-willed, I want you to talk to the rest of 'em – them that's sold, and them that said they was a going to – and try to git this land back for the hill folks. And if you cain't git a hold of Ben Bragg – he's some'ers up at Keatsville, Mary says – couldn't you buy his'n for a while anyhow? You got a plenty, Uncle John a leaving you all he had, and I feel like, them rub-doctors hitched up with the devil, like as not, the whole place'll be wiped out – hills, hollers, folks and all – if we don't git it back like it was."

"I'll do what I can, Sary."

She coughed and gasped a little and then went on.

"Maybe with the dam and reservoir blowed out now, them doctors won't be so anxious to buy or keep what they got. But whether they air or ain't – don't let 'em have it. I feel like this is the Lord's property down here, same as our'n, and it ort to be kept like he made it. He made it for corn and oats and meader and woods, like it's always been, and like He aimed it to stay. He didn't want His hills and trees and such all under water – and Lige wouldn't – and I don't. If I'd a had airy notion how much water there'd a been, I wouldn't a let 'em touched a spade to it, no matter what. But, – you'll do all you can to git it back, won't you, Tizzie – that that's sold, and that that's a going to be? Promise?"

"Yes, Sary. I promise."

She had talked herself out. Everybody knew she couldn't last a great while longer. Tizzie took up her hand and her dripping eyes sort of washed around the blue veins till they stood out like wire. George doubled down and blotted his eyes and nose with a corner of the blanket. He kept trying to think of something he could do or say, but it seemed he could do nothing but swallow. Finally he had to leave to spit. When he got back, the bedclothes shook with Sarah's coughs. After that, coughing and vomiting spells came every few minutes, and in half an hour she was dead.

George went out on the porch and hugged the post, his eyes swimming. He kept thinking of all she'd done for him all his life and wondered how in the world he could get along without her.

"Oh, Mommy, Mommy," he kept sobbing, "what did you have to go fer?"

His throat felt like a dried-out pan of cornbread. He pumped a dipper of water and had it about half way down, when he had to spit it out. It just seemed like it wouldn't go down. Anyhow, did a body have a right to drink water – when she couldn't?

Preacher Ray was coming up the back road. It looked as if the worry and doctoring of the past few days had made him thinner and longer legged than ever.

"How is she?" he asked.

George bit his lip to steady his voice. "She's dead."

Preacher Ray seemed uncommonly sorry that he hadn't got there before she was gone, and made up his mind to read a verse or two of scripture for her anyhow. Figured it would be considerable comfort to them that was left. He got out his bible and spectacled his nose.

"Verily, verily, I say unto you, The hour is coming, and now is, when the dead shall hear the voice of the Son of God; and they that hear shall live.

"Marvel not at this; for the hour is coming, in the which *all* that *are in the graves* shall hear his voice.

"And shall come forth; they that have done good, unto the resurrection of damnation."

He closed the bible. Old Doc Ceburn fingered his beard, and Tizzie dabbed at her eyes. Spouting gullies of tears, George edged over to him and steadied his voice.

"And them that *ain't* in their graves, Preacher Ray, – hain't they got no chance of resurrection?"

Preacher Ray stared over his spectacles.

"Well, I reckon not – though –"

"It don't make no difference – no matter how sanctified a life they've led – them that ain't put away proper?"

Preacher Ray scratched one ear.

"Well, look like it."

"No, it don't. it sure don't – not according to the Scriptures, though to tell the truth I ain't never give it much thought –"

"You don't reckon there'd ever be any exceptions?"

"Well, I reckon not. It says plain out – 'all *that air in their graves*' – don't it now?"

George wet his lips. "It sounds like it."

"But, George, you ain't got no call to worry. Your ma'll be in her grave soon as we can git her there."

George had turned a katy-did-wing green, and then faded to the color of dead grass. He burst into sobs.

"Oh, Preacher Ray, Preacher Ray! You ain't no idy."

Chapter 31 : George's Death

It was time for alarm. Half the town and surrounding community were sick in bed, and every few hours, somebody died. Jim and John Tittle, stout as mules always before, were snapped off like green beans, and all Hell's Holler seemed doomed, sooner or later. The rub-doctors had come down and offered to help out, as soon as word spread to Keatsville, but who wanted to trust rub-doctoring at a time like this?

Old Doc Ceburn had his hands full, old as he was, with everybody sick at once, and only his legs and a horse and buggy to get around in. but hands full or not, he objected to uptown doctors of all descriptions – rub or otherwise. He felt he had been put in the hills for a purpose, and that purpose was to look after the sick. And he aimed to do it without outside help. For thirty-five years he had mixed their tonics and prescribed their pills, not to mention carrying out doses of this and that for years while he was learning the trade – and it was hard for him to turn them over to anybody else. But this had him stumped. All day long he hobbled from house to house, or buggy rode, and sometimes all night – but one after another his patients died and new cases developed. Each time a new victim was stricken, he rubbed his rabbit tail of a beard, and his eyes sank deeper.

"'Tain't nothing but grippe," he kept saying, "though grippe medicine don't seem to help none. Leastways, don't keep 'em from dying."

After six deaths, he called in the man who fixed wagon beds, and car-pentered a little.

"Hit's something ketching," he said, "and I don't know what. I'm a going to call in all the doctors from up town – soon as they'll come – and try to figure out what's what, and what's best to do. We may have a heap of dead, so we'd best send for all the lumber we can git, and start in making coffins ahead. They keep a dying – and they ort to be laid away quick as they do, so's not to spread whatever it is."

The doctors from up town were about as much help as a pack of dogs on the wrong trail, at first, but they kept at it, taking no end of blood and serum for investigation. The only thing was, everybody might be dead by the time they figured out what was what, for they kept going like victuals in harvest time – didn't seem so sick at first, and then vomited themselves to death. The main thing, the doctors said, was to keep it from spreading – above all things. They advised and urged that victims be buried at the soonest possible moment after death was determined.

Everybody who could drive a nail, and was able to be up, kept building burial boxes – big, little and medium, as long as the lumber lasted. Then they sent out for more.

George took to his bed soon after his mother's death, and gave up all hopes at once, like a chicken with the croup. All who took the disease, died like bugs in coaloil – and they all took it sooner or later. He huddled under cover till a sweat broke out all over him, and pushing cover aside, shook like a dog. All night long this succession of chills and fever kept up. He knew now what the woman meant. His time had come – and the time for the rub-doctors too. It was only a matter of hours, now – till they would be cutting, hacking, slicing –

His eyes seemed to be pried open, and he turned and twisted almost all night. If he dozed off, devils with pitchforks took after him, a long line of them – or was it the rub-doctors? Some of them seemed to have hatchets or knives. They were both coming. That paper had signed away salvation, burial and all.

And all through this nightmare of devils and rub-doctors, he kept think-ing of the six who had died, and the ones that would. If it *was* a judgment, brought on by the body business, what a terrible thing he had done, and he had meant to be so good! No telling how many would be taken yet – the whole town and community might be completely wiped out – all because of him. And not only that, but some of them might be dug up and cut to pieces to find out what ailed them, and try to save the rest –

with maybe all chances of salvation hacked away too, and them not having done a thing. It might be selling the land or agreeing to sell, like Sarah said, had brought on the epidemic – but it wasn't likely. And besides, if it was, it looked as if the thing should stop now, with Sarah sort of fixing things up like she did, before she went. But, more than likely it was the body business, and nothing else, though it didn't seem fair to the others – anyway you looked at it. Maybe though, when they found out about him, *he* would be enough to cut and haggle on, and the rest could rest in peace, and go to their eternal reward altogether.

Sometimes he had a flickering hope of resurrection for himself, in spite of things, but when he thought of the cut up chunks and spare rib skeleton that would answer to his name and maybe grope for his robe and halo, he gave up. Besides, it was down in black and white, *"All that are in the graves"*. That settled it. There would be no grave for him – nothing. Even if he didn't tell and they buried him, the rub-doctors would come down and dig him up, and they had a right to. But he *would* tell, when the time came. He had signed away body and probably soul, but he would keep his bargain.

He was so wet you could wring water out of his shirt, but if he so much as pushed back one cover, he almost shook himself to death. The quilts weighted him down and made him sick at his stomach. He kept getting sicker and sicker.

By morning he was almost to the vomiting stage, and the doctor, sensing the cold sweat on his arms and legs, realized he had not long to live. George had given up hope long ago.

"Doc," he said, "there ain't no hope fer me, is there?"

The doctor tried to be kindly, yet truthful too.

"Well – I reckon not, but I wouldn't worry none, till the time comes. Anyhow, you ma's done planned your burying. 'Twas might near her dying words."

George choked a little and batted his eyes.

"Yeah, – but, Doc, I reckon *living* words'll have more effect."

"What do you mean?"

"Well, Doc, – I better tell you ahead of time. You cain't bury me at *all*!"

"Cain't?"

"No. You see, – well – you know about them rub-doctors up town – especially the one with the black goat beard? Well – I *belong* to *him*."

"Why, George –" his mouth kept opening wider and wider, "I'd a *swore* you was Lige's boy."

George's jaws opened and closed, like scissors.

"Oh, I *am*! *Surely*, you didn't think – why, good Lord, – Ma'd turn over in her grave! It's this-a-way, Doc. When Mary had to have her operation, I had to raise some money somehow – cause Ma's twenty-five dollars wasn't a drop in the bucket – so I sold my body to the rub-doctors for fifty dollars, and took it out in trade."

"Why, George, – I wouldn't a dreamt it –"

"Well, that's how it is, anyhow. Ma nor nobody knows, but me and them. So, I thought I'd better tell you, before it's too late. Save lumber and burying, and digging me up again, too – only, you better tell 'em right away, So's they can come and git me, soon as I'm gone."

The doctor's eyes bulged out like a frog's.

"Lord, George, – you're a better man than what I thought. Sold your dead body – for Mary – . I don't reckon many men'd a done it. I'll send word to 'em, first person goes to town – but, Lord, George."

"And, Doc, – I was a thinking – now, understand, when I'm gone, my body's his'n; that is, all of 'em, and they can do whatever they want – but I don't think they know or care about nothing but bones and rubbing and a little cutting. And I 'lowed, maybe – after they'd hacked the meat off – they could sort of dish it up, and passel it out to the pill doctors. And, maybe they could find out what ailed me, and all of 'em, and maybe save the rest of Hell's Holler, before the whole town goes. The Lord knows I'm none too anxious to be whittled to giblets, but seeing as it's going to be anyhow – looks like – might as well kill two birds with one bullet, that is, if the *rub-doctors* is willing."

"Why, George, – and all this time –"

But George was vomiting beyond talking or listening. A kind of coma had come upon him. Sleep settled on his mind and eyes and pushed everything else away off, or made it a part of the pounding of his blood. The hacking and the cutting he had dreaded so long, maybe even the sawing and breaking of bones, seemed to vibrate with a drowsy rhythm – to mark off in a kind of tick-tock regularity the running down of the last lapse of life, and lull his body to a dreamless void –

Before noon the doctor pronounced George dead. Word spread like wild fire of George selling his body, and his last words; and all the little town, that is, the ones not sick or dying, buzzed of his unusual deed. Seven people had been swept away in a few days, but none of the others had sold their bodies to save somebody's life, or offered their flesh to save the rest. All the world loves a hero – especially after he is dead. People tiptoed past his mother's house, hoping to get a glimpse of him without endangering themselves; lamenting that they had never realized how good George really was, while he was alive. Boys climbed trees to gaze down at the house where he had lived.

Doctor Ceburn was in a quandry. According to all rules and regulations, George should have been buried as soon as he was dead, but George seemed to be beyond rules. With the shortage of lumber, and the horrible fear of the whole community of getting near enough to the dead to bury them, there was nothing to do but wrap him in a blanket, and wait. So there he lay and would lie until word came from the rub-doctors, and no word would come till the wagon mender's man came back. And with twelve miles each way, even by the short cut, and ruts ankle deep, a span of mules and spring wagon couldn't make it in less than six or seven hours at the soonest. It was a long, tedious wait for the three who were brave enough to watch the body, but felt they should be with the sick.

A clump of hoofs, a creak of wheels, and there he was. Outside, he removed one shoe and delivered from the sole a much folded paper, keeping his eyes on the thing in the blanket, and backing away, crawfish fashion, as soon as possible.

Twice the doctor studied the worn message, and then read it aloud to the eager ears of the preacher and the boy.

"Under the circumstances, we think it best to release all claim to George Moore's body, feeling it our duty to do all in our power to curb this epidemic, and wishing to avoid any publicity his story may have aroused.

In regard to his suggestion that we turn over the flesh to the M.D.'s for experimentation, we feel this to be entirely unnecessary, inasmuch as the blood and serum already taken should be sufficient for months of testing, and the danger of hauling his body fifteen miles might start a new wave of infection, before this one is checked. In the interest and welfare of the community, we urge burial as soon as possible. We enclose the contract he signed, hoping he will rest more peacefully, if it is buried with him."

For a time Doc Ceburn stared at the thing, and then tucked it into the blanket.

"I reckon we'd best git him under ground, right away," he muttered. "I wouldn't want 'em to change their minds."

Chapter 32 : George's Burial

There were plenty of people to dig graves, so they were dug ahead, but only
two people brave enough to bury the dead – young Bill Jimpson, calloused
against fear or feeling since his father's death, and Preacher Ray. Even the
few mourners huddled in the rear of the cemetery during burial. When
word came that George could be buried, these two pushed the two-wheel
cart around for the body. The doctor, torn between duty to the sick and
desire to get George under ground, was waiting.

"You reckon that box is big enough?" he asked.

"It's the biggest one they got," Bill said, "but the lid's come loose like,
and don't fit like it ort, nohow."

The doctor's eyes tetered from box to blanket.

"That's something we didn't figure on, hardly – burying him. Well, –
we've got to do something – him a laying here all this time. We better
git him boxed and over there soon as we can. Remember, he goes to Jim
Cullop Cemetry. The grave's done dug – right next to his ma's. I sent word,
soon as I heard. And, there's a lantern already over there, so's you can see
what you're a doing."

They picked him up and jammed him into the box. It was a little short,
but dead men can't be choosers – though whether it's an actual gain to
escape rub-doctors to rest eternally with a cramped neck, might be open
to question. The carts wheels shrieked as if they too were being backed
for burial, or maybe what came after it, and sometimes came to a dead

halt, as the wooden box bumped over ruts to the graveyard.

Everybody, who could leave the sick, followed – five or six wagon lengths behind. When they reached the cemetery, new difficulties arose. A screw was lost from the coffin lid – and the grave was too short. When they set one end of the box in, the other hootched up like a beehive.

"I'll dig it longer," Bill volunteered. "I want to. I'm a doing it for Lawrence. He done for my pap, and now, that he ain't able, I aim to do for his'n. You reckon you ort to say a prayer fer him, Preacher Ray? Not that he needs it, after all he done – but looks like he's earned it, and then too, I 'low Lawrence'd like it. After that – maybe you could git a screw or something, whilst I dig."

Preacher Ray stared at corpse and box.

"Well, yesterday – I 'low I could a said all the good I knowed about George in might near no time. But since I heard about him selling his body for Mary and all – I don't know who I'd ruther say more fer."

"Well, don't say too much. I got a heap of digging to do, and I cain't dig with my eyes shut."

The preacher bowed his head and began.

"Father in Heaven, We ask you to look down on this here poor, misjudged man. Lord God, how misjudged the critter's been. Selling his dead body to save his wife's life – the noblest thing a feller could do – and saying nothing about it, till he was on his deathbed. No wonder he was afeard to die, and scared of everything! Who wouldn't be? And us poor, ignorant humans – doctors too – thought he was crazy, and had him shipped off to the insane asylum to be cured, and him a heap smarter and better'n the whole lot. And everybody a thinking him plain lazy – and I reckon he was too, a mite, just like You and me. But look what he done, nobody a-knowing it – and at the last, a offering up his flesh to save the rest of us, a mite like what you done yourself, Lord. Oh, Lord, Lord, the suffering he must a-gone through – thinking about 'em cutting him up, after he was dead, and a worrying about the resurrection of his soul. Just put Yourself in his place, Lord. Think of the awful dread that must a hung over him eternally, and Lord, think over what I said, and see if you cain't make it up to him – up there."

From among the women came a series of muffled sobs. Preacher Ray turned to the stocky boy with the spade.

"I'm a going to git that screw now. I reckon enough's been said fer him."

"Yes, if that won't send his soul to salvation – nothing will."

The lanterns swung on a stick at the head of the grave. Every time Bill pitched out a shovelful of dirt, he could look into George's face. The more he looked, the sorrier the whole thing seemed. Didn't look like there was room enough for a man *half* George's size. When Preacher Ray came back, Bill threw down the spade.

"Say, they got plenty of lumber now, and I'm a going to see that George gits a box big enough fer him, if I have to fight to do it. He cain't rest eternally, cramped up like he is. Nobody else from these parts ever done what he done, and he's got it coming to be comfortable."

He clumped off, pushing a screaking wheelbarrow ahead of him. All this time, the moon had moped behind a cloud, peeping out every few minutes and then disappearing again. Now, on a sudden whim, it pushed out in plain view, a shimmering pie of light, that glowed down on the whole cemetery.

The mourners huddled together like timid cattle, and whispered of the dead.

"I always said George'd make 'em all take notice one of these days. Whenever you see a feller a setting around a thinking, you can be mighty sure there's more to him than he lets on."

"And Lord, was he strong! I reckon he could a lifted a house if he'd a been a mind to. Bill Jimpson said onct him and his pa seed him lift a hog weighed four or five hundred pounds, all by hisself, easy as nothing. No telling what all he'd a done, if them rub-doctors hadn't a got a hold of him."

"I reckon we ort to have more respect for dumb critters – the Lord born in a manger, and George marked by a sick cow. Looks like they're kind of holy-like."

"Well, I always knowed George was plum out of the ordinary, but I had no idy we had an out and out *saint* a-living right amongst us."

"You recollect the way he took on at his pa's burying? I always said whenever you see a man cry, like as not he's got something to cry fer. We ort to knowed as much then."

"And if you ever notice, when some turrible ailment breaks out anywhere, it always spreads like a prairie fire till it gits the cream of the crop, somebody too good to live, and then it stops. Like as not, now that George is gone and it's too late to save him, they'll find a cure for this thing right away."

When Bill came back, he wheeled a brand new box, a foot longer and half a foot wider, braced all around with blacksmith's iron at the corners. Six men, farmers, wagonmenders, blacksmiths, that pitched in and nailed the thing together, stumbled along beside the wheelbarrow and box, and steadied it over ruts. The moon burned up like a coaloil lamp, new filled, and threw out a wagon width of light on the procession behind the wheelbarrow. All the rest of the town and community, that could get out of bed, had left their sick, and followed the faded flag old Doc Ceburn insisted on carrying. Besides the ones on foot, there were two horsemen or rather mulemen, and at the end, a Ford roadster. Ben Bragg shut off the chugging and popping, and climbed out, hanging his head as if in apology for noise at such a time. Somebody recognized him and yelled out.

"Didn't his *wife* come, after *all* he done for her?"

Ben's voice was hollow.

"Mary wanted to come, uncommon bad. When she heard what George'd done, she like to went all to pieces. But her brother told her and I did, she might be killing her own children, to come to the burying, catching as this thing is, so she stayed."

"How'd she find out?" somebody mumbled, "she ain't been a-near."

Ben swallowed and looked at the ground.

"One of them rub-doctors told her to-night, when he was a doctoring Lawrence. He said too, they think they got this thing headed off, now, so's no more'll die, to speak of. Said 'twas a kind of new fangled cholera morbus, only it starts with grippe. That's what got 'em off the track. Mary was a taking on turrible when she told me, and the younguns too. They all wanted to come, especially Lawrence, but we felt like 'twasn't no ways near safe."

It was several swallows before he could go on.

"I wouldn't a come myself, more'n likely, but I'm a batching anyhow, and Lawrence kept a taking on so about his pa, a wanting somebody to come, we was afeard he was a going to make hisself sick, and the doctor said if he takes care of hisself, he'll be a walking again in a month or such a matter. Seemed like we all felt *somebody* ort to come, fur as that goes, the way we'd misjudged George all his life – and him so out and out ahead of the rest of us, all the time –"

Ben stopped and swallowed and Bill Jimpson stuck out his lip.

"Ben's right. Nobody ever seed or ever will see another feller like George around these parts. He was head and shoulders above the whole pack. Too plum good for this world, so the Lord took him to be with him."

Bill and Preacher Ray hoisted the blanketed body from the old box to the new, carefully replacing the folded paper that fell to the ground, and one could almost see a look of peace come into the dead face. More digging and the box was lowered.

"Now, let's all bow our heads in a silent prayer for his good life," suggested Preacher Ray.

"Yes," urged Bill. "After we pitch the dirt on him, we cain't never be so close to him again."

When the last clods were piled on the grave, the mourners turned red eyes to one another. Big drops of rain began splattering down, but nobody moved. Bill eased his spade to the ground.

"Looks to me like, George ort to have some kind of a tombstone, and it ort to say something. I 'low we could git one of the blacksmiths to make it right cheap, so's it wouldn't cost much."

But old Doc Ceburn wagged his scraggly beard.

"Yes, only, Bill, let's git him a good un, whilst we're at it – one that'll last always. We can all chip in, and do without things, and have something that'll be here long as Hell's Holler is. So that people a coming through here, two or three hundred year from now, 'll know what we had, and what we lost. I doctored George nigh on to thirty-five year, I reckon, and I thank the Lord that maybe my doctoring had something to do with keeping him with us this long, but I had no idy he was what he was, till this thing come up. As unselfish and out and out good as he was, it's a wonder to me he ever lived at all. I feel like he's got it coming to have the biggest and best tombstone we can git."

Everybody seemed to feel the same way, and Bill Jimpson added, "Looks to me like the *saying* is turrible important too. Looks like a tombstone for George ort to say something plum out of the ordinary – something worth saying."

All heads wheeled to the stocky boy, and whispers chorused, "What do you think it ort to say?"

Bill eyed the new piled earth in thoughtful awe.

"Well, looks to me like, seeing as George is the only hero Hell's Holler ever had, or ever will more'n likely, it ort to say so, in the best-writ saying we can git together – and maybe tell what he done."

All heads nodded, their eyes on the over sized mound.

"Better not say too much," suggested old Doc Ceburn, "rock's turrible hard to cut on."

"Yes," said Bill, blurry eyed, "but look what *George* done."

They all dabbed at their eyes, and agreed to do all they could. Then, solemnly, the little procession filed out from the swinging gates, and down the hill toward the little town.

Epilogue

Highways stretch out as time goes on, so that fingers of roads reach even the most out of the way places. Fishermen to-day, from here and there, squat on the patched up dam at Hell's Holler, by an old shanty of a tumbledown mill, whose entrails rust at the bottom of the river, and wonder how things would have been if storm and dynamite had not washed and blown out the immense reservoir that prominent uptown doctors had hoped to make a government project. And as they sit and wait, the whole story comes back to them.

Not far away, overlooking the river from a hill, is a private cemetery, well kept up with blue grass sod, and graves rounded with rocks and mussel shells. On the highway, a rusted double iron gate, covered with creeping vines, swings always half open, and many armed trees on both sides seem to bow a welcome to all who pass. At the highest peak of the cemetery is an oversized grave, completely covered with what appears to be barrels of rocks and shells, and headed by a giant slab of cement, that towers over every other stone in the graveyard. The crudecut letters can be made out from the highway, and almost every passer-by, no matter where he is from or in how big a hurry, slows down long enough to make out the words: "HERE LIES HELL'S HOLLER'S HERO."

Afterword to *Hell's Holler*: Ruth Ann Musick and the Angels of the Underdog by Judy Prozzillo Byers

I am elated that the good folks at *Missouri Folklore Society Journal* are publishing Ruth Ann Musick's creative dissertation, *Hell's Holler: A Novel Based on the Folklore of the Missouri Chariton Hill Country*. Since her Ph.D. defense at the University of Iowa in 1943, this 400 page novel has laid dormant like an enchanted creature waiting to be awakened from a deep sleep.

Dr. Musick never forgot the lessons she learned in writing *Hell's Holler*, or her desire to see it published. Shortly after I began to study with her, she told me that she dreamed of stealing time from her heavy teaching and researching schedule to edit the novel for publication. Dr. Musick, as I always addressed her, went so far as to use an hourglass to measure out precious hours to accommodate her projects, new and old. As she accumulated new enterprises, I believe that the novel became an old friend who had already served her well by completing her formal education and launching her into her career.

Hell's Holler also afforded Dr. Musick a gift that all dissertations should give to their authors: confidence. Through the creative writing process, she had tried her hand at unfolding plot and developing character in a local setting that revealed cultural beliefs and superstitions through description, details, and dialect. The novel was most successful in portraying the struggles and hopes of characters caught in the ups and downs of the human condition. Since the best writing comes from the personal perspective, Dr. Musick hinted at aspects of her own life and circumstances.

Having the opportunity to become her biographer, I observed in her own life the sympathy and concern towards the underdog, the disenfranchised, and the forgotten people shown in the novel. Dr. Musick became a vegetarian at a tender age because she couldn't bear the hog butchering on her family farm outside Kirksville, Missouri. After moving to West Virginia, she became a vocal activist for animal rights through her leadership in local and state humane societies. Equally, she rallied for the protection of nature against the strip mining and mountain top removal that butchered the hills and laid waste the valleys.

In the unfolding of George, the protagonist in *Hell's Holler*, one can sense her struggle to advocate for the unsettled. On one hand, she had created one of the most downtrodden losers in regional literature, a lazy man filled with self-pity. Yet, just when the reader is resigned to George's fatalistic demise, Dr. Musick redeems her character by turning him into a folk hero in the community. His single good deed—saving Mary's life by selling his future corpse to the medical school and thus securing funds for her operation—becomes the stuff of legend. Not only did the "rub-doctors" not use his body as a cadaver in the end, but his critics honored his memory by building a huge rock monument at his burial site inscribed with the words, HERE LIES HELL'S HOLLER'S HERO. Obviously, the power of the writer can be used to celebrate virtue in unexpected sources, as Dr. Musick learned in creating this story. Later, she began to find other avenues in which to advocate for the underdog that would direct her life's work.

In 1946, two years after completing *Hell's Holler*, Dr. Musick came to West Virginia, a newly-minted folklorist anxious to establish herself professionally. When she accepted a teaching position at Fairmont State College, the world of regional folklore scholarship was open to her. She took seriously the encouragement of her former teacher and advisor, Dr. Edwin Piper, and, especially, that of her friend and mentor, Vance Randolph, to collect a rich sampling of the regional folklore and folklife of rural America before the traditional cultures were lost to industrialization and modernism. Professors Piper and Randolph were leaders in preserving American folklore through its ancestral roots, Piper collecting 828 American folksongs, according to the University of Iowa, and Randolph publishing *Ozark Folk Songs*, as well as five volumes of Ozark folktales. Randolph's correspondence with Dr. Musick is housed in the Ruth Ann Musick Estate

Archives in the Frank and Jane Gabor West Virginia Folklife Center at Fairmont State University.

As the the postwar boom increased the student population at Fairmont State, it seemed that every student wanted to take classes taught by the perky new professor who stood on her desk to recite the ghostly monologues from *Hamlet*, encouraged students to collect their family stories, and created a new course, English 371, Folk Literature, that is still popular. The boundless energy expressed in her infectious laugh made Dr. Musick a legend across campus and community.

Long before I joined those students, I knew her as the lively lady sharing Sunday afternoon spaghetti dinner with my family. My Uncle Tony would pick her up from Colonial Apartments on the edge of campus and carry her big mahogany reel-to-reel tape recorder, placing it atop the china hutch in my mother's big kitchen. Dr. Musick would be seated next to Nonna Julia, the keeper of wisdom and lore in the family; there she would fit into the loud, joyous atmosphere as we ate and talked. From my grandmother, mother, and aunt, she collected over four hundred tales, mostly supernatural stories from our Calabrian background.

Expanding on the example of Vance Randolph, who collected many folksongs through his column in the *Pineville Missouri Democrat*, Dr. Musick established not just one, but three newspaper columns throughout West Virginia, soliciting readers to share their family and community lore. "Sassafras Tea" and "The Old Folks Say" became so popular that she added "Sassafras Tea Two" for more state papers. She reached out to fellow folklorists and cultural enthusiasts to revive the West Virginia Folklore Society under the leadership of Dr. Patrick Gainer, a respected folk music collector teaching at West Virginia University. He had been mentored by Dr. John Herrington Cox, author of *Folk Songs of the South* and one of the founders of the original West Virginia Folklore Society in 1915.

In 1950, the Society selected Dr. Musick to establish the *West Virginia Folklore Journal* as its official publication. As editor and principal archivist, she used the little quarterly journal as another avenue to collect folklore. She became a speaker and active participant at the Society's local and statewide meetings and programs held at schools, 4-H extension clubs, county fairs, and churches.

Through all of these collecting endeavors, Dr. Musick saw a common pattern developing. Most of the oral literature emerging from the heart of Appalachia fell into the supernatural category, predominately the ghost tale. She devoted the rest of her academic life to analyzing these ghost tales of West Virginia. She had carried a fascination with the ghostly narrative from her own childhood when she heard spook tales from her father, Levi Prince Musick, to whom she dedicated her first major published collection, *The Telltale Lilac Bush and Other West Virginia Ghost Tales* (University Press of Kentucky, 1965). More significantly, she had what may be described as a "ghostly epiphany" on traveling from the Midwest to her new life in West Virginia:

> I shall never forget my entrance into West Virginia, by way of Wheeling and Route 250. To those who don't know that particular section of Highway 250, it is a roller coaster route from Mount Olympus to a bottomless pit. But, oh, the splendor and beauty of the Garden of Eden that rises up from the velvet green valleys to become mountains again are indeed a glimpse of heaven. I can never forget this sight as long as I live, and hopefully, even longer, if I am lucky enough to become a ghost after death.
>
> I was a passenger in a fellow teacher's car, and to most drivers I'm afraid this road seems to be a kind of descent into or an ascent from hell, depending on whether one is going up hill or down. To me the experience was so spectacular that I kept going into outbursts of sheer delight about the unspoiled beauty of the place until the driver, whose brakes were smoking along with his nerves, told me, jokingly, perhaps, that I would have to walk the rest of the way if I didn't curb my enthusiasm! I did remain silent for the remainder of the journey, lost in my own hope that there might be ghosts or at least ghost tales amid the labyrinth of those green hills and dark valley.[1]

What had started as girlish naivety about the spiritual world of the supernatural as seen in Halloween antics and storytelling around campfires on brisk autumn evenings would evolve into a serious crusade, supporting a new understanding of the ghostly in the three major collections of supernatural tales she published through the University Press of Kentucky: *Telltale Lilac Bush and Other West Virginia Ghost Tales*, 1965; *Green Hills of Magic: West Virginia Folktales from Europe*, 1970, reprinted in paperback

---

[1] "Notes on Coming to Fairmont," Ruth Ann Musick Archives, Frank and Jane Gabor West Virginia Folklife Center, Fairmont State University.

by McClain Printing, 1989; and *Coffin Hollow and Other Ghost Tales*, 1977. Dr. Musick organized the layout for each of these collections according to the events and circumstances surrounding the location of tales. And she commissioned her brother, Archie Musick, to illustrate eah collection.

Historically, West Virginia, born from slavery into statehood during wartime, has had a tradition of violent deaths, typically murders at the hands of renegade native wanderers, cruel slave owners, and brothers against brothers in Civil War feuds. Bloody accidents caused by the early Industrial Revolution took lives in deep coal veins under the hills, along railroad lines, or on the vast timber tracts rising into the sky. The dramatic topography that thrilled Dr. Musick depressed others with the loneliness of the high country that seemed to encourage the murders of wandering peddlers, traders, and tinkers, as well as the patchy fog and deep shadows along valleys. It was as if the environment wore contrasting faces by day and by night. The majestic vistas and lush green terrain seen under sunlight turned foreboding and hellish with darkness, and the ghost was born.

In the complex environment of the tales she studied, Dr. Musick identified the ghostly characterization emerging through the "basic elements" identified in Stith Thompson's *Motif-Index of Folk Literature*. She was grateful to further researchers, such as Ernest Baughman, whose Ph.D. dissertation, *A Comparative Study of the Folktales of England and North America*, devoted 128 pages to the concept of "motif" and to adding other motifs to Volume E of the *Index, Motifs of the Dead*. Her analysis of these motifs in many of the ghost tales she collected led her to a deeper appreciation of the importance of the ghostly stories of the people as a mirror to reflect their inner lives—their beliefs, fears, and hopes. In short, she was inspired to become a passionate advocate for the ghost, as well as for the tales, as expressions of the plight of the underdog in rural cultures, such as Appalachia.

Traces of the thinking that supported her conclusions can be found in the personal journals and other papers among the unpublished folklore articles in the Musick Archives here at Fairmont. Many became the bases for essays, articles, talks, and forums she later shared before civic, historical, and cultural organizations at local, state, regional, and national venues, such as the American Folklore Society.

Spirits returning in ghost tales can be classified into two basic categories. In analyzing the patterns of ghostly encounters in her tales, Dr.

Musick concluded from the behavior of the apparitions to the protagonists in her tales that most came back as benevolent spirits for the purpose of saving the lives or fortunes of living people, usually relatives or friends. Though these kindly spirits returning to help loved ones in distress are usually adults, like the coal miner returning to save a comrade from a mine fall in "Big John's Ghost," they could be animals or children, like the little girl who appeared to help her sick mother in "Help" (both tales from *The Telltale Lilac Bush*).

Though less common, she found a second category of ghosts who return to earth seeking justice for mistreatment or death at the hands of the living, by revealing the oppressor. As in real life, it was often social underdogs, such as the young, old, sick, or lonely, who were preyed on by the corrupt and cruel. The ghost does not usually seek revenge, but desires the closure resulting from revealing the truth about the crime. One famous story in this category is "The Shue Mystery" in *Coffin Hollow* in which the young wife, killed by her husband, returns for justice. Often called "The Greenbrier Ghost," it is the only recorded West Virginia tale in which testimony from a ghost helped convict a murderer, an account of which is studied in the West Virginia University Law School.

Both of these categories shed light on the ghost as a powerful protective force against oppressors who victimize the underdogs of society. Like a guardian angel, the ghost is a spiritual force for good. Dr. Musick did not want to confuse the revenant with the traditional understanding of angels as heavenly heralds. Instead, she made a figurative comparison by which the benevolent qualities of returning ghosts made them seem angelic and, in many cases, heroic. Ghosts ultimately became models for the golden rule of doing unto others what we want to have done to ourselves.

Shed of their earthly existence, ghosts, she noted, are free to do what their earthbound state would not allow. As guardians and messengers, ghosts are the ultimate protectors of the living. This theme—that help is available—has been expressed over and over in the tales of the people. A universal hope for benevolence and aid dwells eternally in the hearts of the folk, especially in the backwaters of society, reinforced through storytelling.

Unfortunately, despite all of their good deeds, ghosts have often been misunderstood. People have an innate fear of dead spirits, equating ghosts to the loss of warmth, light, and vitality, qualities that give meaning to life. This negative attitude about ghosts has shrouded them from receiving the accolades that they deserve. Dr. Musick was determined to not only dispel such negative attitudes about ghosts, but to broaden the appreciation of their benevolent nature, insuring their rightful place as protectors of the underdog.

Traces of the thinking that led to her crusade to correct the negative view of ghosts can be found in passages of her journals and in the loose notes that became the genesis of talks and lectures she delivered to local gatherings and scholarly councils. Her respect for ghosts and, indeed, her admiration, were apparent in personal observations:

> I seem to be inordinately fond of ghosts. Sometimes it seems to me that many returning spirits put ordinary living folk to shame, just by their natural gentleness and genuine well-wishing. I have seen no ghosts myself, but I have collected over 2,000 tales, and judging by them, not too many living people can measure up to the standards of some 90 percent of returning dead. And according to the tales, regardless of the bad reputation the living have given them, most ghosts seem to be reasonably gentle, and some of them positively saint-like in their zeal to help others.[2]

Typically of Dr. Musick's behavior in her own life, these views were not mere speculation. She was naturally an activist for the issues she identified around her whether animal rights, environmental issues, or civil rights. As she spoke out, wrote to editors, and marched in protests, she considered herself applying the lessons she drew from ghostly tales to everyday life.

> Naturally, I am not suggesting that everyone should become a ghost as soon as possible. On the contrary, I feel rather strongly that everyone should do something to justify his existence before he passes on. But, the living could profit by following some of the splendid examples of good deeds on the part of the dead.... I am particularly partial to the spirits that come back to help some living creature, especially in life-saving, often aiding the person to avoid the same fate that ended their own lives.[3]

---

[2]"Notes on Non-Malignant Ghosts," Ruth Ann Musick Archives, Frank and Jane Gabor West Virginia Folklife Center, Fairmont State University.

[3]"Notes on Defending Ghosts," Ruth Ann Musick Archives, Frank and Jane Gabor West Virginia Folklife Center, Fairmont State University.

Dr. Musick's call for an outpouring of support to honor ghosts became a standard opening for many of her informal talks, speeches, and even radio talk shows:

> Because [ghosts] have given so much pleasure to me, in both my collecting and publishing as well as my tale-telling, I should like to do something for them in return . . . . There is no doubt in my mind that ghosts have not only been greatly maligned, but [are] also deeply deserving of a great deal of praise. Actually, those spirits who save lives should receive some kind of recognition or award.[4]

In the novel, George is still in the world of the living when he makes his early and painful decision to sell his corpse to the Medical School for fifty dollars to support Mary's treatment. His predicament is the morbidly-comic reverse of the ghost who suspends Resurrection in some sense to return to earth on its helpful mission. Preacher Ray's reading of the Bible convinces George that Heaven is available only to those "that air in their graves." In other words, George has sacrificed his afterlife—and Resurrection—to aid Mary and little Lawrence.

In the final chapters, despite his terror and despair at being turned over to the Satanic rub-doctors, George goes still further to suggest that his flesh be studied by "pill-doctors," after the rub-doctors have "whittled" him down to "giblets," so they can identify the nature of the epidemic that killed his mother and six others in the community. At that point, he is recognized as a heroic spirit so great that he can be compared to only One. As Preacher Ray prays at George's funeral: "But look what he done, nobody a-knowing it—and at the last, a offering up his flesh to save the rest of us, a mite what you done yourself, Lord."

As for Dr. Musick's advocacy for the ghost, her campaign to unspook the undead had equivocal success. Forty-six years after her own death, it is apparent that the public still loves to shiver over "Ghoulies and Ghoosties, long-leggety Beasties, and Things that go Bump in the Night" as much as they did in 1909 when Alfred Noyes collected an earlier prayer in *The Magic Casement*.

However, for Dr. Musick's greater campaign, her ceaseless promotion to heighten awareness of the power of oral literature, especially regional

---

[4]*ibid.*

ghost tales as a channel for appreciating the underdogs in our society, her success can be seen in the regional popularity of her folktale collections, all of which remain in print. Moreover, folklore and museum studies minors became part of the academic fabric of Fairmont State. In 2013, the Center published Dr. Musick's fourth major folklore collection, *Mountain Mother Goose: Childlore of West Virginia*, collected by Ruth Ann Musick and Walter Barnes, with new illustrations by her niece, Pat Musick (Fairmont State Press).

It was largely due to her continuing influence that in 2010 the Frank and Jane Gabor West Virginia Folklife Center was established at the College, now University. The Center continues her efforts at identifying, preserving, and perpetuating the cultural heritage of central Appalachia—a heritage which had branched into Missouri before Ruth Ann Musick was born and continues to enlighten both states. Dr. Musick's personal papers and folklore archives are housed in the Gabor Center for analysis, interpretation, and publication. Other important parts of the Folklife Center have been established: The Fidura Special Collections Library; the Phyllis and Jim Moore Archives of West Virginia Writers; and the Patty Looman Old Time Music Archives. The West Virginia Storytelling Guild and The Kennedy Barn String Band offer concerts at the Center. As a member of the Appalachian Regional Commission, the Center is now actively involved in the Appalachian Studies Association to sustain rural communities through history and heritage.

Presently the Center is partnered with AmeriCorp in sponsoring a preservation project—part of its West Virginia Preserve—to organize and prepare for publication the rest of the unpublished Ruth Ann Musick folklore estate. Moreover, the Center still publishes *Traditions: A Journal of West Virginia Folk Culture*, a renamed continuation of *The West Virginia Folklore Journal* which Dr Musick began in 1950.

But now, the Gabor West Virginia Folklife Center is excited to welcome *Hell's Holler* as the latest publication bearing Ruth Ann Musick's name. It stands as her first foray into exposing the suffering of the underdog in rural society. Later, in her extensive collecting of regional ghost tales, she found the same elements of struggle and suffering among the poor, downtrodden, and vulnerable in the recesses of those oral tales; yet in the end she found that the ghost is generally given credit for advocacy. In both novel and stories, most storytellers agree that ghostly encounters are mainly benevolent. The angels of the underdog abide.

Considering Dr. Musick's long-suffering protagonist George, I believe that he would feel at home in the West Virginia Folklife Center since Dr. Musick, during her years in Fairmont,lived in the Colonial Apartments Building which now houses the center. That is where she died in 1974. The building had originally been built in 1902 as Michael Kennedy's milking barn for his dairy farm. Years later, Fairmont State purchased it as part of its campus expansion from college to university status, and refurbished it back to its Dutch Colonial Revival style. Campus folklore has it that students have seen or heard Dr. Musick walking the halls of the building after evening classes. One fall evening, I was teaching the section of Introduction to Folklore which deals with the universal qualities of the tale in the classroom where her old apartment had been located. The side door opened quietly and closed. The students looked at each other, whispering, "What was that?" I said, "It's time to take a break."

About the Author

Judy Prozzillo Byers is Abelina Suarez Senior Professor of English and Folklore, Emerita, at Fairmont State University; Founding Director of the Frank and Jane Gabor West Virginia Folklife Center; and Executrix and Archivist of the Ruth Ann Musick Unpublished Folklore Estate.